Searchers After Horror

Searchers After Horror:

New Tales of the Weird and Fantastic

Edited by S. T. Joshi

FEDOGAN
&BREMER

Nampa, Idaho
2014

"Searchers after horror haunt strange, far places. For them are the catacombs of Ptolemais, and the carven mausolea of the nightmare countries. They climb to the moonlit towers of ruined Rhine castles, and falter down black cobwebbed steps beneath the scattered stones of forgotten cities in Asia. The haunted wood and the desolate mountain are their shrines, and they linger around the sinister monoliths on uninhabited islands. But the true epicure in the terrible, to whom a new thrill of unutterable ghastliness is the chief end and justification of existence, esteems most of all the ancient, lonely farmhouses of backwoods New England; for there the dark elements of strength, solitude, grotesqueness, and ignorance combine to form the perfection of the hideous."

—H. P. LOVECRAFT, "The Picture in the House"

Introduction

The motif of the "weird place" is as old as the genre of supernatural literature itself. The early Gothic novelists were fond of portraying the untamed forests of the Apennines or the Rhine valley as a suitably grim backdrop for their tales of supernatural or psychological horror. Mary Shelley's *Frankenstein* opens and closes with vivid vistas of the Antarctic. Edgar Allan Poe found weird landscapes chiefly out of his own imagination, as the imperishable first paragraph of "The Fall of the House of Usher" testifies. J. Sheridan Le Fanu's tales of the remote Irish countryside; Ambrose Bierce's chilling depictions of the loneliness of deserted mining towns in the American West; Arthur Machen's unforgettable images of the "wild, domed hills" of his native Wales—all these are permanently fixed upon our memories.

Algernon Blackwood may be the master of weird landscape. Whether it be the remoteness of eon-freighted Egypt, or the lofty heights of the Swiss Alps, or the seemingly placid but throbbingly vital vistas of his native England, each one of his landscapes embodies to the full the mystic pantheism at the core of his thought. H. P. Lovecraft, as the opening lines of "The Picture in the House" suggest, may have felt that New England was a uniquely suitable backdrop for literary weirdness, but he was far from being the first to vivify that ancient corner of America: Nathaniel Hawthorne, Mary E. Wilkins Freeman, Sarah Orne Jewett, and others had done so before him.

The trend continues to the present day. The increasing urbanization of our society may be reflected in the nightmarish New York of T. E. D. Klein's best work or the seedy Liverpool of Ramsey Campbell's; but today's weird writers find an unrestricted fund of weirdness in landscapes from around the world, augmented by the fervor of their own imaginations.

In this book you will find an updated but still haunted New England in Nick Mamatas's "Exit Through the Gift Shop"; a spectral Midwest drawing upon the work of both August Derleth and Clark Ashton Smith in John D. Haefele's "The Sculptures in the House"; the horror both in the landscape and in the denizens of rural Virginia in Steve Rasnic Tem's "Crawldaddies"; the remoteness of a Pennsylvania highway in Darrell Schweitzer's "Going to Ground"; the strangeness of the Pacific Northwest in W. H. Pugmire's "An Element of Nightmare"; and the remoteness of a barren Colorado in Ann K. Schwader's "Dark Equinox." British writers Ramsey Campbell and Gary Fry draw upon the ancient heritage of their native land in "At Lorn Hall" and "The Reeds," and Canadians Donald Tyson ("Ice Fishing"), Richard Gavin ("The Patter of Tiny Feet"), and Simon Strantzas ("The Beautiful Fog Ascending") do likewise.

Less precise topographies are at the focus of Michael Aronovitz's complex, nested narrative "The Girl Between the Slats" and Melanie Tem's "Iced In," but they are no less vivid for all that. Hannes Bok's "Miranda's Tree" evokes the pantheism of Blackwood in a tale probably written in the mid-1950s but first published here. The ancient catacombs of Italy serve as the eerie setting for Nancy Kilpatrick's pensive reflection on death and dying, "Flesh and Bones," while Jonathan Thomas's "Three Dreams of Ys" takes Brittany as the backdrop for a tale deftly fusing fantasy and weirdness. Brian Stableford ("Et in Arcadia Ego") reaches back to ancient Greece, with its nymphs and satyrs, for a tale whose classical setting gives way insidiously to Lovecraftian horrors.

Weirdness of landscape can be utilized in all genres of imaginative fiction, and John Shirley ("At Home with Azathoth") and Lois H. Gresh ("Willie the Protector") draw upon it in vivid tales that fuse horror with science fiction. The paleogean horrors in Caitlín R. Kiernan's "Blind Fish" and Jason V Brock's "The Shadow of Heaven" are rendered more pungent by crisply realized settings.

Weirdness of landscape is only one component in all these tales, which simultaneously succeed in the careful etching of the complexities of human character as well as in the evocation of terror in a multiplicity of themes, motifs, and images. Each one of these authors is searching after horror out of the depths of their own imaginations, and their readers will find themselves inexorably becoming the denizens of bizarre realms of fantasy and terror beyond anything they could have envisioned.

—S. T. JOSHI

Iced In

Melanie Tem

There was no snow. Things looked bare, and no more dangerous than usual, until daylight or moonlight made them glimmer. Everybody called it black ice, but that was misleading. Kelly was used to being misled, but it wasn't fair.

In truth, the ice was transparent, at least translucent, with little or no color of its own, black only where it turned roads treacherous, tree limbs heavy and fragile, roofs into mirrors reflecting the sky's slate light. You could see everything on that mouse she'd found frozen in it when she was little—open puppet-like eyes, tiny tail. Stupid mouse.

Absence of snow made all this feel like her fault, as if the problem resulted from a character flaw—incompetence, ignorance, tendency to dramatize. Feeling guilty about everything all the time was solipsistic and self-indulgent and egocentric and dumb, and it wore her down, but she couldn't seem to stop it. Maybe something bad being her fault was better than it being random, and bad things happened all the time. Maybe culpability was better than helplessness—not much better, and she couldn't have said why, but better.

Kelly had lived all her life in this house in this town out here on the Kansas plains. This wasn't her first ice storm. So pretty to a child taken care of, so smooth and so quiet. Man-sized tree branches frozen to the driveway like dead soldiers, but because you knew they weren't dead soldiers you could play that they were. Binding the star-pattern quilt with Mom, which didn't make the long iced-in days go any faster but did give them edges and design; she still used the quilt, in tatters now because she hadn't kept up with the mending. "Sorry, Mom."

The icicles growing from her house as she watched, or when she wasn't watching, reminded her of teeth, swords, needles. Just what they were should have been plenty: giant icicles among all those that hung from power lines, fences, trees, buildings, nearly every other surface and edge in the snowless countryside. Eyelashes, hair. Bones. Growing the way they did—by melting and dripping in cold sunshine as if they were done, as if they would disappear now, and then at the next first light visibly longer and thicker—was enough to deal with. Too much. She shouldn't have to deal with so much.

As night came on again now, the wind was picking up, snaps and crashes all night long that might be things falling on the house or parts of the house falling off or icy sinkholes opening underneath. She wouldn't know till daylight, if then.

Denny used to say this house would kill her someday. Of course, she took that personally; who wouldn't? It had started as one of his jokes that weren't really jokes but sneaky ways to criticize her and then accuse her of having no sense of humor and taking things personally when she got mad or just didn't laugh. Later he'd insisted his sneer was a smile—"maybe a worried smile because I love you, maybe a little put out because you make things worse for yourself"—when her foot had gone through the back porch floor, cutting her ankle. The hole was still there, bigger now in the rotted wood, and her blood was probably still there, too.

He'd said it when she'd fallen down the stairs trying to maneuver around all the stuff she kept meaning to move off them; that time the faux joke had been a faux cover for how mad he was at her. Since then the stairs had gotten even more

obstructed, and the particular clothes, newspapers, shoes he'd been complaining about were now near the bottom. Kelly just didn't go up to the second floor very often anymore.

He'd said it again when he left. "You're going to catch some disease in here, Kelly! You've got to clean it up. I'll help. We'll get somebody to help." Then: "Clean it up or I'm outta here. *Do* something!"

She hadn't told him to leave. It had been his choice. He hadn't needed to go out in that weather. But the thought of getting iced-in together, maybe without power for days, had sent her out onto the frigid and gusty back porch looking for things she could break up into kindling in case she had to build a fire in the middle of the living room, since the fireplace hadn't worked in years, and him out into the grey frozen noon pointlessly proclaiming, as people always did, "It doesn't look that bad." Days later, when the roads were passable again, they'd found him along the ditch bank a little closer to his house than to hers, his truck a few yards behind him by then in danger of getting stuck in grey mud instead of sliding on black ice.

For a long time, especially when the forecast called for winter rain and sleet, Kelly had imagined how twilight must have accentuated the flatness of the plains, the horizon line over which you could not see and so had to take on some kind of faith wasn't the end of the world. He'd made a choice: take the risk of walking home rather than the risk of waiting in his immobilized truck when nobody was likely to pass by any time soon.

"You must choose," some philosopher had decreed. "We are condemned to freedom of choice, and that is what makes us truly human," or something like that. Turned to ice on the side of an empty road in the middle of nowhere: that's where making decisions got you. Being fully human was overrated.

Now, wind sliced through thumb-wide cracks in the bedroom walls and swooped from under the door. That room had been impossible to get into for years anyway, bed and dresser and lamp and desk and computer and who knew what else heaped over with stuff she couldn't decide what to do with, couldn't decide what to call, junk or keepsake, useful or trash, so she'd just kept the door shut and tried to avoid the strip of cold that seeped into the rest of the house.

Just today she'd noticed a crack growing down the north living room wall, icicle-shaped, and she wondered what would work its way in, from inside the wall or from outside. The foundation had been crumbling for a long time; you could see it plainly, so she'd just quit looking at it. Snow might sift in, but not now, because there was no snow.

The poor old house was cold. It creaked and groaned around her in the thick absence of electrical sound. The power company made a big deal about how civic-minded they were to turn service back on during the coldest spells for people who couldn't pay their bills, but that didn't do much good when *nobody* had heat or lights. How civic-minded was it not to have equipment that could handle something as basic around here as ice storms?

Being so cold made her feel sorry for herself, and with good reason. She seemed to have used up all the heat that was going to be produced by her father's two stocking caps, a pair of lined wool earmuffs, three coats from various phases of her life including Denny's brown one, layers of sweats, as many pairs of gloves and mittens as she could wear and still use her hands, as many pairs of socks as she could stuff into her boots. Even when she tried to be responsible and resourceful and prepared, she wasn't very good at it. Mom and Dad had always been prepared, but they hadn't passed that along to her. It wasn't fair.

She could crawl back into the mound of blankets, towels, clothes, curtains, pillows in the space she'd managed to clear to sleep in between the collapsed bookcase and the unopened boxes from the Shopping Channel from back when she'd been able to afford such things. But it couldn't be good to spend so much time under there, ice storm or not, and her sleep was fitful anyway no matter what time of day or night, no matter the season or weather.

Outside there was a boom, close by. Kelly took a few startled steps backward, stumbled over piles of books and slippery stacks of magazines, made herself edge along the narrow path she tried to keep open to the front door. Maybe the noise had just been a knock, stylized by the ice. Maybe it was somebody come to help her, or just to check on her and then leave again, or somebody come back to try again to love her even though she'd let them drift away when she hadn't known if she loved them enough. Abe, Chet, Stefan, even Bradley in junior high, with all their possibilities that hadn't quite held Kelly's interest. Carole and Pam and, in a way, Robin, until the friendship had started to make Kelly feel trapped. Denny.

It wouldn't be any of them because Denny was dead and the rest of them had left her alone when she couldn't make up her mind. Maybe it was somebody come to do her harm. But why would any of those people bother, and in an ice storm?

The inside door stuck when she pulled at it but finally moved inward, letting in a wall of cold through the screens always up because she had nobody to switch them out for the storm-door inserts she hadn't seen around here in years anyway. It seemed to her that a miniature icicle clung to every hole in the screen—the tiny, neat, rusted ones that were supposed to be there because that's what made it a screen, the fist-sized jagged ones that showed how old it was and how badly maintained. She did the best she could.

It seemed to her that a face was pressed against the screen, bracketed by splayed hands. Someone was out in the cold. She'd have to decide whether to shelter them.

She was thinking about demanding, "Who are you?" when she realized it was debris—maybe a piece of black plastic, a soaked and then frozen cardboard box, a man's empty coat or a woman's or child's—blown up against the screen and stuck there with ice. After the ice melted, it would be on the porch floor, and it wouldn't look like a person anymore.

Finally managing to get the inside door shut tight and locked again, she made her way back along the living room path. Crisscross patterns of ice came into the house with her, sliding off but staying solid, not turning into water right away. Things fell ahead of her and behind her; she stepped away from and over them. The house was noticeably colder than it had been before she'd foolishly opened it to the outside.

She was hungry and thirsty, as if in anticipation of being famished and parched. The grocery store should be open, if they cared about their neighbors, but without mail delivery, meaning no food stamps or disability check, there was no money. She shouldn't have wasted $5.87 on that ice cream and chips last week.

Although stuff piled and hanging and collapsed would prevent her from feeling her way, she'd expected the familiar stench to lead her to the kitchen. But the standing water in the sink, clotted with garbage, must be frozen. At least it didn't stink now, she heard no scratching in the walls, the dribbles and piles of droppings would be like dust and pebbles, and the many-legged lines and blobs on the counters and floor would have stopped moving.

Making her way in the general direction of the kitchen, she tried to remember what food she still had. About half a loaf of bread, she thought, maybe not completely moldy. A couple of cans of tomato soup she could manage to eat cold, a mushy and browning banana or two, part of a cucumber, food-bank rice she had no way of cooking but maybe the hard grain would provide some emergency nutrition if she could get it down. Some very old snack packs of cheese and crackers somewhere around here.

That wasn't much. Somebody needed to help her. Why didn't anybody want to help her? So much for Midwestern neighborliness.

The banana had turned to slush. She dropped it back onto the counter. In the silent, dark refrigerator that smelled warm but was still somewhat cooler than the current room temperature. The cucumber was soft to the core and adhered to the shelf with a long accumulation of other mystery substances. She shut the door. She just wouldn't look in there anymore.

There might be a can or two still left in the "just in case" basement room. Kelly could almost hear her mother tsking over her not having kept it stocked the way everybody did around here, in case of tornado or nuclear attack or ice storm or some other disaster they didn't have a name for yet but knew was coming because that's how life is.

Disoriented in the dark, icicled, wind-noisy house, she must have taken a wrong turn, or the configuration of the house she'd lived in all her life had changed—which, of course, it had, with all the things that had accumulated around her on its floors, walls, steps, sills, ceilings. Such as black ice. She fell. Her right ankle twisted inside its boot and icy-hot pain flared as she skidded down the crooked basement steps whose railing had come loose a long time ago because she had nobody to fix it for her.

Leaning against a wall that crumbled like pie crust, she fumbled for her cell phone, then remembered it was on the floor somewhere near where she'd been sleeping, then realized reception would be even less reliable than normal out here because of the ice. Anyway, the phone company had probably cut off her service again because she'd missed just a couple of the payments she'd agreed to in order to get them to turn it back on. It had been a while since she'd needed to call anyone, but now she did, and this was exactly the kind of situation she'd been doing her best to prepare for. And the phone company just wouldn't let her.

From down here the wind was a muted throaty roar. Something big crashed, likely a branch or an entire tree like the giant cottonwood in the front yard, just on the other side of this wall. Where her car had been parked since the transmission had finally gone out months ago and she didn't have money to get it fixed or friends who would do her a favor, but she'd been holding onto vague hope of driving it again someday.

She was worried about her face. Her nose and cheeks burned from the cold. Her tear-wet lashes might freeze the eyes shut. Somewhere around here were scarves and at least one ski mask; she should have thought of that.

Maybe she should get back upstairs, on the chance that the main part of the house would be a few degrees warmer. Or maybe that was wrong, maybe it was actually warmer underground. Maybe the best plan was just to wait for somebody to find her down here in the basement when the ice storm was over.

But who would miss her? Who would bother to come looking for her?

When she tried to stand up, her ankle buckled. Her padded and cold-stiffened hands couldn't find a grip on the unstable walls. The steps splintered, dropping her into the dark cold dirty space against the foundation that was probably deteriorating around her in the frozen ground though she couldn't see or hear or feel it.

Shivering violently, she had a memory flash of Mom putting quilts in the emergency stash, geometric and curvaceous designs and soft-edged plastic-covered bundles anchoring bright boxes and wavy water bottles and the cylinders of canned goods and toilet paper. Where was the "just in case" room from here? She'd always been directionally challenged, especially inside, and now any cues had been obscured, in one way or another, by ice.

A sudden rumble above her head set off a spurt of panic until she could identify it. First she imagined it as the refrigerator motor trying to keep going, but without power that was implausible. She settled on ice inside the freezer compartment finally giving up.

A fuzzy blueprint came into her head, along with the conviction, probably fleeting, that if she could just get to the quilts and food—warmth, sustenance, the comfort of somebody else's forethought—she might outlast this storm. If she was under the kitchen, the emergency supplies were in the far left corner of the basement.

No. Far right.

Pick one.

What if it's wrong?

Do something.

Why wasn't anybody here to help her?

In the tight space under and among the broken steps, Kelly feinted left and then made her move to the right, as if tricking something. More than her ankle had been hurt in the fall—the small of her back, something internal. Hands and knees wouldn't support her weight. So she squirmed on her belly, much more work than walking or crawling, but what choice did she have? The bulk of her clothing impeded her progress and made her colder as the damp dirt from the basement floor soaked in. When her mittened and gloved hands trailed a wall to keep herself oriented, they stuck and came away stiff, and she realized the walls were coated with ice, here inside. Those were icicles, then, pressing into her belly and face, spreading under and, now, over her. The ice was coming in.

She struggled to pull herself along in what might turn out to be the wrong direction and all this pitiable effort wasted. Would snakes be around in an ice storm? Serial killers? Or would she just freeze, starve, bleed, worry to death alone?

The basement was more or less rectangular, and its walls abutted each other. If she could keep going long enough, wouldn't she reach her destination no matter what direction she'd started in? But there was so much stuff piled along the walls, and she was discovering so many pocks and protrusions, and ice was getting in, had probably been getting in and freezing and melting and re-freezing for a long time. It would be easy to get disoriented and keep missing the "just in case" room, maybe by fractions of an inch, maybe by the shifting width of the house.

Something above her broke with a bang and a whoosh. The refrigerator, maybe; Kelly's understanding of the working parts of anything was hazy. Water torrented over her, glazing every surface it found, warm at first in comparison to the invading ice but turned frigid within split-seconds as it wormed its way through her clothes. She kept moving her limbs, but she didn't think she was making any progress, and she'd lost focus, couldn't quite grasp anymore where the emergency provisions were or why she had wanted to get there. Something large and sleek moved a little farther down the outside of the wall she was trying to follow.

Suddenly the wall vanished and she lurched sideways into a stack of slabs that collapsed on top of her without, it seemed, actually doing harm. Some were slick under her mittens as she struggled to push them away, others tufted and ridged. Quilts, she realized. Wet and then iced over. Unusable.

Everything else in the "just in case" room was ruined, too. Cardboard containers had frozen in mid-disintegration, tears and flaps jagged. Cans were like cylinders of concrete. Light bulbs had shattered; slivers stuck in her mittens. Rolls of toilet paper had settled into semi-solidity. Bottles of water had burst to add their contents to the ice mass.

It was only to escape the "just in case" room that Kelly pushed herself backward and over to the right, not out of any actual plan. But the motion brought her up against what she recognized as a door to the outside. She could see a sliver of different darkness, touch a bowed gap. The door was very slightly ajar, whether from the weak impact of her body or the freezing and thawing ice or just the failing of old wood she hadn't noticed till now.

She didn't know what to do. Outside was black ice. Inside was ice, also black, also spreading. What difference would it make?

Not making a decision was making a decision, and easier.

The gap at the doorway glistened. There was motion. Kelly lay down in the path of the transparent encroaching ice. There was no snow.

At Home with Azathoth

John Shirley

When **Frederic DuSang** saw the eye text from Filrod, he knew the bait had been taken. He knew it before he even read the eye-t. He had that tingle, as when code was about to become a program; that particular shiver of closure.

But it wasn't over yet. He still had to reel him in . . .

Walking down the Santa Cruz Beach boardwalk to the VR ride, on a wet September morning, Frederic tapped the tiny stud, under the skin beneath his right eye, the contact cursor in his fingernail telling the device to transcribe a subvocalization—he had learned to subvocalize his voice-recogs for security. And he subvocalized, "Text, 'Come over at seven tonight if you want it, FilRod. FdS.'"

The head chip heard and obeyed, sending the text to Filrod's palmer.

The guy's name was Rodney Filbern, but everyone called him by his screen name, and Filrod replied almost immediately, *Not a good time 4 me. Just tranz it?*

Frederic responded, "Tough, sorry, leaving town. Not offering it any other way. Wouldn't work. Need you there in person."

Filrod bit down harder on the hook. "OK, Fred U dick, will be there."

Frederic snorted. He hated being called Fred.

He reached the perpetual carnival on the boardwalk, waved to his manager, a bruise-eyed, rasta-haired old surfer, and went to work at the VR ride, putting pallid teenagers through full-body virtual experiences and cleaning up the stalls afterward. . . . As always, as he mopped, thinking, *I need a new goddamn job. Vraiment, yo.*

Frederic's thoughts were sometimes in French because his parents were French and they'd tried to make him bilingual. Never quite got there, but they left their mark.

His mom had left them four years earlier, after Jackie killed himself. Jackie was . . . had been . . . Frederic's younger brother . . .

Frederic's *père* was a thin man with shoulder-length white hair and an eaglebeak nose. When Frederic came home that evening, he looked at Frederic over his glass of Bordeaux—with that familiar dull wince, that "depression nerveuse" expression he got when he thought about his son.

Okay, Frederic thought, *so I'm almost twenty-six and still living with you, so what. I know what you don't know, you old fils de pute.*

He nodded to his dad, in honor of the free rent, and started for the basement door.

"Frederic," Dad said muzzily, "a moment, eef you please. We should talk about . . . Oh, I don't know, somezing . . ."

Frederic paused and looked back at his dad. There was a little extra slurriness, a particular mush in his father's voice, and more French accent than usual, too much for a bottle of wine. Probably he was back on the oxycontin. Supposedly he took it for a work-related injury. Right, Dad. Frederic's father had been a computer programmer in Silicon Valley. Made good money, too, till Jackie died and Mom left, and then Dad started sinking, slowly sinking, and now they were living mostly on his disability, since Frederic spent most of his money on AI and chip augs.

"Dad, I thought you weaned off that shit."

Dad opened his mouth to deny he was on it, but Frederic looked at him evenly—and his *père* gave him the ol' Gallic shrug. He licked his lips and articulated more carefully, "Oh, well, you know, zuh scan . . . the scan, it said the crack in the vertebrae was open again, so . . ."

"Whatever. Come on. You're just . . . it's about Mom and Jackie. So if you gotta self-medicate, whatever. You do that, go ahead. I've got my own thing. Okay?"

Frederic turned and went down into the basement, thinking he should probably get his old man to go to a therapist, but Dad hated shrinks and Frederic just couldn't carry the weight of dealing with Dad's stuff. He did, in fact, have his own thing.

He veered between storage boxes and went to his basement room.

Once his father's den, the room was now Frederic's own little soundproofed warren of linked-up used hard drives, monitors, transervers, low-grade floating AI, a desk he used for extra shelf space and, in a corner, almost an afterthought, an old futon with yellowed sheets reeking of mildew. *The skuzz den,* Frederic's mom had called it. Laughing, though, as she said it. That was something he loved about her, that she laughed at you in a way that meant she didn't care if you had failings, it was all good, no one's perfect. Now he hardly ever saw her.

Frederic sat on the futon, bunched up pillows behind his back, and reached over to the hardware to activate the tranz box. The virtual screen appeared in front of him—something only he could see, at the moment, thanks to his implants—and Frederic muttered the keywords that would activate the floating AI ovoid bobbing near his bed. The AI chirped and Frederic muttered the first password, got his menu, flicked a finger at the air to open *SpaceHole,* got the prompt screen, and . . .

And hesitated. It always made him nervous, kind of sick and giddy, to open this program. Buster Shecht was still missing. But Buster was a crazy fuck, could be missing for lots of reasons. The reason didn't have to be the Azathoth place.

Anyway, Buster Schecht wasn't half the programmer Frederic was; couldn't hack his way out of a paper bag. Could be he'd screwed something up and got some kind of brainfry—maybe the yellowflash feedback effect in an implant? It wasn't unheard of. Frederic was not going to screw up.

He licked his lips and spoke the three entry words—words that Buster had found online, in the Necronomicon file.

The "screen" flickered in his mind's eye, shashed, pixel bits spinning like water going down a drain in the center . . . and then in the very center of the virtual screen they interacted, as cellular automata do, and they formed a spreading organization—something ugly, jagged, but hinting darkly at life.

The whirling finished, and the image sucked away into the SpaceHole—and the Realm of Azathoth unfurled to fill the screen . . .

That's what Buster had called it . . . *Azathoth*. Claimed the thing living in Azathoth itself taught him the name. If it had, that must mean it was, in fact, the result of a program some brilliant game design engineer had worked up, the gamer having put that in somewhere, and not—as Frederic theorized—the result of a series of meta-program worms linking up in cyberspace, almost like the way the early forms of life had linked up to make more complex organisms, in that giant bowl of hot primordial soup the sea had been.

Of course, there was Buster's explanation—or what he claimed to believe, the last time he'd been here in the skuzz den. Probably just playing Frederic for lulz:

"Dude, I'm going to tell you this and you're gonna think I'm snagging, but man, this is for real: the fractal set I worked up outta the Rucker formula, it opened a door into a real place, man. Check with Jacques Vallee: information is a form of energy. In fact, everything's a form of information. And, deep down, information is the form of everything. So we can create real objective stuff with pure information long as it's the right information . . . And I'm telling you, Azathoth is a for-real place. But see, it's a place and an entity, both at once. That's what people don't get—every person is a place. They're a world to themselves. And some big nasty messed-up entities are big, nasty messed up worlds . . ."

"You do know I stopped smoking dope, right?" Frederic had said. "You think you're gonna get me all freaked and shit, but it's flat not happening, man . . ."

Frederic shook his head, remembering. What he was seeing couldn't be a real place. This place couldn't *really* exist . . . except in the mind of some lunatic. It was just a cellular automata model, tessellation automata, iterative arrays.

Automata cellulare, his dad would say.

They were fractal patterns generating templates of life forms in a three-dimensionally modeled artificial environment, purely digital, and he knew from looking at great special effects all his life how animation could seem crazy-real.

And of course he was seeing it in a virtual screen, the floating AI's work projected to his chip, his chip projecting to his mind, his mind projecting to his mind's eye, so that he saw a three-dimensional place, and the things in it, hanging in space just up above . . .

There was no clear-cut edge, unlike other virtual projections. It was squamous, wrigglingly ragged along the edges of the "tank" of image that floated over him. It just plain seemed *alive.* Amazing animation work, really, given the source of it—a couple of deep-web eccentrics, Buster figured, had worked it up, made it out of some bits and pieces of online gaming environments, movie clips copied and altered, someone's personal animation program, all mixed together.

That was the only acceptable explanation for what he was seeing: a *place* that was an *entity;* an entity that was a *place.* It was as if he were looking with X-ray eyes into something's body, but he was also looking into a world, an entire landscape. Those numerous writhing protracted pyramids of ichorous green were organs of perception, maybe; but at the same time they were a kind of forest and somehow he knew that if he were to go there (horrible thought), the growths would tower menacingly over him; yet for sure that thicket was some kind of living cilia; that jade and purulent sky was a high enclosure of living tissue—at the same time he was certain that if he were to reach it, himself, to ascend to it, he would penetrate *into* it, and it would go on and on and on, unending. And surely that iridescent, spiky compound tetrahedron in the foreground, slowly whirling, fulminating with bloody fury, was an angry thought crystallizing in a trapped mind.

He could almost . . . *almost* . . . hear it thinking. It thought in minatory buzzing sounds; its words became its form . . . its mind defined its world . . .

Frederic shivered. *C'est fou.* He was having some kind of weird psychological reaction to the program. And this was only the first mode; overdrive mode was faster, captivatingly visual, something you had to use big willpower to look away from . . .

He stared into the mêlée of brutal abstract shapes, the slow-motion maelstrom of Azathoth, wondering about Buster . . .

And *Buster appeared* there, at that exactly moment, within Azathoth. Buster's chunky, acne-spackled bearded face materialized in the center of the translucent compound tetrahedron. Buster's mouth moved; after a moment Frederic heard the words, materializing in his mind.

"Frederic, bro, I'm stuck, digesting in Azathoth, no hope for me, doesn't matter, ready to disintegrate, only way out, but your brother, nearby . . ."

Frederic's stomach lurched. "Shut up about Jackie, Buster!" he blurted.

Then he snorted at himself. Buster wasn't really there. His mind had probably superimposed the image, made up some story about Buster, put it in the program. Supposedly the AI wasn't supposed to take anything from your mind but a literal interpretation of your words, subvocalized, and occasional motional directions, and certain very defined projections . . . but for a while ecog chippers had suspected that there was an unpredictable involuntary telepathic level to the connectivity.

Here it was—this *fantôme,* this digital ghost, was proof of espering chips. He'd have to tell DG and the torrent skaters about it.

The iridescent crystal entrapping "Buster" mutated into a solid icosahedron—and went opaque.

Buster vanished.

Had Buster been—digested?

Cut it out, you're getting sucked into the fantasy. This program is some kinda lulz hoax and somewhere some programmer's laughing his fucking ass off right now.

Didn't matter. It'd do for what he had in mind—it'd do for Filrod.

He had planned to insert Jackie into the images; to toss in the candid footage he had of Filrod jerking off over tranny porn, which he'd gotten when he'd hacked Filrod's webcam system, whirl it all together in this sick place, let it iterate, copy and paste it into every variant of youtube there was. Make Filrod pay for what he'd done.

The plan was to get Filrod stuck in this place, long enough to really make him feel it—because when you went into overdrive mode on this program, that's what happened. It was hypnotic, was Azathoth, inexplicably hard to look away from, and you could mix in any image you projected so it looked as if you were in Hell surrounded by . . . whatever the programmer inserted. If he wanted to put images of the new Republican president's inauguration into it, you'd see the Prez and his backers splashed all over the Azathoth landscape. And you could feel weirdly trapped there . . . Images of Filrod's shame, Filrod's guilt, could be wrapped around him in overdrive mode . . .

But now—he might have a more direct mode of attack on Filrod.

Filrod himself. He had an ecog chip, after all . . .

He glanced at his watch—and right then, as if on cue, the doorbell rang upstairs.

Filrod was a broad-shouldered college student, with widely spaced front teeth, a dull, blunt face and faux-hawked brown hair. Frederic had heard that Filrod was barely passing his classes; the jock was not exactly stupid but never far enough from his interchatter channels to focus on anything. He was a wide receiver on the football team and wore the school jersey with his number, 8 on it.

Behind the eightball, you asshole, Frederic thought, as Filrod hunkered on the futon beside him.

"You wanna hit some syntha?" Filrod said, when he came in, waving the e-pipe.

"Nah, I gave it up, you go ahead," Frederic said, distractedly, as he tinkered with the hardware by the futon, trying to get the best signal.

Filrod sucked on the e-pipe, blinking at the floating AIs, and asked as he blew out a stream of chemical-laden water vapor. His eyes glazed as the drug hit him. "Don't those things use up a lotta power, floating around?"

"They're made of super-light materials, man, and they tend to get less interference from the drives if I keep 'em floating . . . do have to change batteries pretty often." Frederic finished tinkering and waved smoke out of his face. "Enough with that shit, I don't want your secondhand smoke, dude."

"Whatever." Filrod switched the pipe off, tucked it away in a pants pocket. "So can you get me the stuff I need to see or not?"

"Yeah, *if* you transfer the money to my account." The money he never actually expected to get. This wasn't about money.

"You show me the stuff, I transfer, right here."

Frederic shrugged. "'Kay, fair enough." He prepared the virtual screen and gave Filrod the frequency, so he could see it too. Then he decided to prep Filrod himself a bit more. Set him up good. "Okay, you sent me the password, the ISP, all that— file names. You sure you sent me *everything?*"

"Everything! My mom's will's in there, man. I need to see it, I gotta know. She's pretty sick. But the mean ol' cow lingers on and on." He shook his head sadly. "I think I'm gonna get kicked outta school—won't have my school money, nothin' to live on. I need to know if money's coming."

Frederic looked at him. Something in Filrod's voice, a certain tightness, said *cover story.*

Christ. Was Filrod thinking of killing his mom, easing her off into the ether, since she was sick anyway? Was he going to if he had enough inheritance coming to justify the risk of a murder?

Wouldn't be surprising . . .

"Okay, Filrod, so . . . this isn't going to look like a conventional penetration program. This'll look—different. It's three-dimensional, it's cyberspace stuff, it's very . . . hard info-animation." He'd made up that last term to keep Filrod confused.

It worked. "Hard info . . . whatever. I just need to see her will and testament stuff and I know this fucking attorney has it on e-file."

"Sure, we'll get there. But see, this technique is more . . . stealth. You know? Don't want 'em to know we did this, right?"

"Right, that's for fucking-A sure. Don't want nobody to know."

"Then—lock in. Stare right into that circle you see forming there. It's called SpaceHole. Look right into it, keep your eyes on it, and we'll see what we find."

"That thing? It doesn't look like any kind of . . ."

"Trust me, dude, this is what you need to see."

Filrod blinked and stared into the SpaceHole, and Frederic sent a message to the AI, moving into Mode One of Azathoth.

"What the *fuck!*" Filrod blurted, staring into the change-world, the shifting landscape that was a mind—that was an entity, Azathoth; that was a program, really—and what would be Filrod's Hell, if Frederic had anything to say about it.

Frederic sent the second signal, to overdrive Azathoth into full manifestation—and looked away from the floating three-dimensional screen as he did so . . .

Filrod gasped.

Frederic smiled grimly—then uploaded the first vid, of Filrod pleasuring himself as he gaped at some serious porn.

Filrod made a choking sound.

"Turn that shit off!" he managed, his voice hoarse, almost inaudible.

"Why, man?" Frederic asked calmly, looking at him. "It was you who found that video of my brother posing all sexy for an under-twenty gay dating service. My brother wasn't ready to come out to my folks yet—we got some old-fashioned grandparents he was worried about—and he was going to a private school because Dad was trying to get churchy. My *père* was raised Roman Catholic . . . and there's been big pushback from the religious types about gay marriage last few years and the school is like brainwashing these kids against gays and . . . well, my brother Jacques, little Jackie, he was full-on *gay*. I knew it, but we didn't really talk about it much, and he didn't tell anybody else, he wanted to do it all private until he could face the bullshit as an adult living on his own. But then you hacked him, Filrod, because he was talking to your girlfriend and *man* did you misread that shit, until you found out he wasn't hitting on your girl, you saw the dating service video he'd made for Gay Youth Meet-Up. And you told everyone, showed the jocks at his school, and they beat him up and he lost feeling in some nerves in his arm, and his left hand wasn't working, and then the priest saw the dating video, when you guys put it up online, and brought him into his office and gave him the hellfire talk and made him *thoroughly* miserable . . ."

"I didn't know that was going to—"

Frederic shook his head and pressed on. "And *then* you posted some lies about him stalking some teenager, that Danny Zoski, which was *totally* not true, and so then people said Jackie was a pedophile—he was all about real adult men, not *kids*—and then people stopped talking to him and he took some drugs over it that left him depressed and then they were going to kick him outta the school and . . . lemme see, I leave anything out? Oh yeah. He killed himself. *He fucking hung himself.*"

"I . . ." Filrod made an *uck* sound.

Frederic could see Filrod was trying to look away from the hypnotic drain of Azathoth . . . and Frederic was careful not to look into it himself. "Yes, 'Filrod'?"

"I . . . I . . ."

"Spit it out, dude!"

". . . didn't know he was your brother."

"Jackie didn't like the surname DuSang, 'cause it means 'of blood' and Jackie had hemophilia, and my folks said he could go by grandma's name, once he turned eighteen. So he

changed it. Then you met him. Then he killed himself. Cause
and effect: sensitive person runs afoul of an emotional cretin
and dies."

". . . sorry."

"Oh, because he was my brother? But it's okay to hound a
gay kid into suicide? Long as they're not related to someone
you know?"

"Um . . . no."

"Yeah, well, *fuck* you—and you're *sorry.* You *boasted* about
what you did after he killed himself, I got the e-mails . . . see
'em there? They're going up around you too. Read 'em, asshole. You're in that world, in your mind now, and it's not easy
to get out. *All* that stuff is there. Now I'm going to upload
some—"

Then Frederic heard Jackie's voice. And for a moment he
was struck dumb.

"Sorry to see you hurting dumb animals, Frederic," Jackie
said, gently chiding.

"What?"

The voice had come from the floating screen. And Frederic
had to look.

He saw his brother's face, in a wobbling globe of translucent
emerald and gold, a *fantôme* floating over the Azathothian landscape.

His brother was looking right at him.

And Jackie said, "The idiot Filrod here is just a dumb animal.
It's like poisoning a dog that bit you 'cause it went crazy being
locked to a short chain all day. Not really the dog's fault it bit
you. But I do hate Filrod, that's true. Even now. And it's hard
to hate anyone where I am now."

"Where you are . . . ?"

"I'm in a kind of limbo sorta place kinda oblique to Azathoth.
Where Azathoth is, that's where lotta people get stuck. Poke
their noses in the wrong place. Me, I'm in another world, and
it's not bad. It's pretty awfin' awesome. I'll be here a thousand
years or so, the guardians tell me, and I don't mind. But see,
it's like it's a through-the-looking-glass inside-out upside-down

mirror place in relation to Azathoth; they're opposites, you know? Symmetrical opposites. It ain't Heaven, where I am, and Azathoth ain't Hell—but close enough."

Frederic gawked at the apparition of his dead brother. It sounded exactly like him; sure *looked* like him, even down to that typical humorously rueful expression.

Frederic wondered if he were being *pwned* somehow. Was this some hoax? Had Filrod outsmarted him?

But he could see Filrod himself, a replicant of his mind inhabiting Azathoth—trapped in a crystalline world of self-loathing. The miniature Filrod in the floating screen image was a kind of Filrod avatar, matching the physical one who gasped and moaned and whimpered beside Frederic.

Frederic shook his head slowly. "Jackie . . . is it really . . . ?"

"Yes. It is. I'm not in Azathoth—but I heard you messing around in it, I heard your mind . . . and I'm able to talk to you *through* it, because I'm in its opposite, and they're *connected,* in a weird way. Like, you know, those old Yin Yang symbols, the white and black going around and around in one circle together. You know?"

"I guess . . ."

"So I'm able to talk to you from my world. See, dude, Azathoth is *real.* It's not a program. Azathoth is a real world. And a real creature—all at once. But you've got a kinda digital device for looking into it. You're not seeing into a program— you're seeing it *through* a program."

Frederic felt sick, hearing that. Somehow, it all came together in his mind with a click. *This is real.* "I'm going to get sucked into it!"

"I don't know if you are or not. I hope not, bro. Once you're there, I probably can't help you. Your body'll die and . . . well, let's see if I can head it off."

"Jackie . . . listen . . . I'm sorry I didn't help you . . . I should've *helped* you when you were so depressed. I was caught up in my own stuff . . ."

"I know. It's okay. I just . . . wanted to say . . . don't worry about me. I'm in pretty good shape now. It's not Heaven, where I am— I'm stuck in this place for awhile, but it's not a bad place. It's just somewhere you go if you kill yourself. Then you get held up there, for a long, long time. So that part's not good. Killing yourself, you get *stuck* in the next world, and you have to work that off. So don't ever do that, Frederic. But it's not bad here, and one day I'll move on. And that's something I got an ache to do, to move on . . ." Jackie smiled. "To move on in the right way."

Frederic couldn't smile back. He felt a mounting terror, seeing the hideous, encroaching reality of Azathoth widening, stretched out from the floating screen, like a beast widening its jaws to swallow him . . .

Then Jackie's image seemed to expand—and seemed to rush at him, getting between him and Azathoth, Jackie's face coming like the grill of an onrushing car bearing down on him, Jackie grinning mischievously—

And then Frederic felt the shove. He heard Jackie shout, *"Go, bro!"*

And there was a tremendous pressure, physically throwing Frederic backwards, so that he crashed into some of his hardware. That was going to hurt, later.

But now all he felt was dazed, as he lay on the angular pile of electronic odds and ends, sparking smoke around him, staring at the ceiling.

Frederic was distantly aware that he'd been about to fall into Azathoth . . . and now he was free, staring at the AI bobbing near the ceiling, the light on it like a green eye glaring down at him . . .

Jackie had saved him—his brother had pushed him out of the jaws of Azathoth.

But what about Filrod?

It's like poisoning a dog that bit you 'cause it went crazy being locked to a short chain all day.

Filrod howled pitifully.

Wincing from his bruises, Frederic sat up—just in time to see Filrod's soul sucking out of his body; his naked form, translucent, turning in midair to try to claw its away back, struggling against the hungry vortex, face contorted with horror. Mouthing *Please help me!*

Then there was a nasty sucking sound . . . and Filrod's soul was gone, into the whirling SpaceHole.

In Frederic's room, Filrod's body slumped—lifeless.

Frederic looked at the Azathoth image, now in Mode One . . . saw Filrod's soul in there, mangled but recognizable, as jaws of crystal closed and crushed and chewed and chewed . . . and chewed harder.

Frederic looked away.

He called to the AI, floating overhead, to come to manual station—meaning into his hands.

It floated down to him, he grabbed it, switched off its flight power—and then threw it, hard as he could, at the wall.

And the AI smashed into crackling pieces.

The floating 3-D screen vanished—Frederic thought he heard a cry of despair from Filrod as it went . . .

Frederic sat for a while, trembling. The trembling seemed to metamorphose into sobbing. And once, loudly, he shouted, "Jackie!"

He glanced over at Filrod's body. He didn't want to touch it. But he had to.

He got up, grimacing, and knelt by the ungainly body, felt the still-warm wrists for a pulse.

No. Nothing. The guy was stone dead.

That wasn't something Frederic had planned for. But it was hard to feel bad about it. What was he going to tell the police?

The truth. *Hey, the guy was smoking that synth dope, just a lot of it, then he keeled over. Bad ticker, I guess.*

Frederic turned away, stood up, looking for a cell phone. Sooner he called the cops, the better.

He heard the door open—turned to see his father looking at him, puzzled, concerned. The old dude had heard his yell about Jackie.

Frederic felt as if he'd never seen his father's face clearly before . . .

The look on his father's face was so deep—had so many levels of pain. Like someone trapped in Hell.

Frederic wiped his eyes and got up. He wended his way through all his gear, went to his dad, and put his arms around him, and together they wept—though Frederic knew his dad didn't understand any of it.

It didn't seem to matter.

The Girl Between the Slats

Michael Aronovitz

Madeline Murdock crept to the edge and leaned over it with her hands clamped up at her chin. The snowflakes looked like little angels falling into the darkness of the pit, replaced by their sisters the moment they vanished.

"Walk the plank, idiot!"

Madeline's mouth turned down to the hideous frown Mommy was trying to help her manage. Her palms wiped the air before her chest as if she'd just eaten something hot, and they were all laughing now as they had in the classroom, the gym, the beginning of recess. But it wasn't fair! She just liked to touch things and taste them, that's all. It wasn't her fault that the cobwebs under the radiator in the choir room felt like the soft mane of some baby unicorn. She wasn't the one who made the kickballs look like big cherry jawbreakers, and it wasn't her idea for the puddle under the slide to have rainbows in it just like the Giant Swirl lollipops Daddy brought home from the store when she was good.

"Stop calling me names," she said, turning back toward the group of third-grade girls gathered on the other side of the caution tape. "At my old school they were nicer!"

Brenda McGilicutty pushed her black glasses up the bridge of her nose.

"Your old school had you in a resource room! My mother told me. And you went there every day on the dummy bus, with extra padding on the walls and the seats."

"That's not true!"

Rhonda Schlessinger sucked up her snot with a rattly honk. She'd been swallowing it all day, but here she hawked it forward and pushed it through her teeth all lady-like and slow. The slick package was a hanger for a moment, then flew off left from her lips to smack the Porta Potty over by a padlocked tool chest and pile of timber. A few of the girls paused to "ooohhh," in appreciation, and for the millionth time Madeline wondered why things like spit-bombs were cooler than puddle rainbows, or pee bubbles, or elbow scabs shaped like half-moons and clover, or those orange traffic cones that looked so much like candy corn *everyone* had to lick them just once!

"I believe you, Madeline," Rhonda said, making everything slow down, like a movie, like a snowglobe. "Go ahead and walk across. I'll be your best friend, I swear. Then you can be a part of our boy-hater's club." She batted her lashes. "But you have to hurry so we don't get in trouble."

"Yeah, don't be chicken," someone piped in.

"Don't you like us?"

"We'll tell you secrets about everyone, even the Principal!"

Madeline couldn't see anything behind them through the wooden slat fence, but down below she could hear the teacher's aides roaming the playground, starting to break up the game circles in order to collect footballs, Frisbees, and hula hoops. It was almost time for the bell, and if she didn't move soon they were going to get caught up here off school property amongst all the *dangerous equipment:* the bulldozers, trash drums, sawhorses, and border posts with little yellow warning flags.

And of course, there was the humongous hole surrounded by caution tape, the one with the plank going across it. The one that was so deep the little angels got lost in it.

Madeline looked down at her shoes, both mud-spattered now, especially the right one with the skinny black buckle-strap that was worn to threads where the prong went through. She'd gone pigeon-toed because she was afraid, and her stockings itched. She wanted to rub her legs together, but she was terrified the girls would think she had to wee, that she was the weird girl who licked things plus the stupid retard who still did a first grader's Indian dance when she had to make water.

So what was it going to be: dimwit or daredevil? Porta Potty or snowglobe?

She stepped forward with a squeal and made a run for it, clicking her shoes along the grained and splintered board almost tippie-toe, all the way to the middle where it bowed down with her weight and went wobbly, where the wide black hole yawned on either side of her and flakes of sediment filtered from the bottom of the wood into the blackness that was still swallowing snowflakes. Madeline froze there, terrified, lost, and then she focused on a knot in the plank before her that seemed just like one of those almonds her mother saved for her in the cabinet above the sink, alongside the flour, brown sugar, and extract.

"So pretty," she thought, and the voices of her new friends drifted off to the background. Madeline Murdock wanted just one taste, just to see. She made to go down to her knees, and her foot slipped off the edge. The board came up fast and angry, whacking her in the mouth and driving a tooth straight through her nasal cavity. She loved that moment before pain, that sliver of an instant that felt royal and tasted like Red Hots and pennies.

This was a good one.

The sky did somersaults.

When she hit bottom, they all heard the snap.

Mike Summers reviewed what he'd just scrawled into his notebook, cursed, and ripped out the pages. He was no fiction writer and it showed. First, he was unsure of the rule concerning "voice" and "point of view." He was in Madeline Murdock's

head, but was he supposed to stick solely with a third grader's lingo? The description of her running tiptoed across the plank was well executed, but he seriously doubted a nine-year-old girl would use the words "sediment" and "filtered." He ran his thumb along the steering wheel and gnawed at his lower lip. He liked the movement of the piece, but the background characters were disappointing, especially Rhonda Schlessinger, the spitter. He had pictured her in a light blue winter coat with an Eskimo hood, big nose, and spot-freckles, one above an eyebrow and two below the left ear, the bottom one raised like a mole. She had pale skin, imploring eyes, and a practiced sort of sincerity woven into her speech based upon a soft, well-developed interpersonal intelligence her parents praised and nurtured to the point of absurdity. She would wind up being the one who was always elected to speak for the friendship group when they got into hot water, the one who sang with gusto and danced poorly, destined to be the star of the fifth-grade choir extravaganza, yet merely a high school under-study when looks and talent started to mean more than heart.

But he'd gotten none of this across whatsoever. Rhonda Schlessinger was a stick figure, and while Hemingway prom-ised the audience would fill in the balance, it was easy to mis-trust the process when you were in it knee-deep.

Mike got out his cell for a time check and then looked across the parking lot. He still had ten minutes or so before he was due inside for this multi-school in-service training, and he cringed thinking about Knickman choosing St. Mary's Elementary as the central location, in fact he cringed just thinking about her in general. Even before she was named department head at Kennedy High she was the type to *volun-teer* for those God-awful curriculum committees, where they pored over mission statements best delivered in their bulleted trend words, the idea that English was a beautiful and neces-sary universal human discipline, merging the triad of cognitive development, historical interpretation, and cultural meta-diver-sity or some such lame horseshit. Blah. Her students hated her, and the rest of the English staff wasn't too far behind, a roll-your-eyes/look-at-your-watch kind of thing.

And Knickman had most certainly chosen this old relic of an elementary school for the sake of contrast, to show all the other department representatives in the Central League how superior she was in terms of didactic technology and state-of-the-art formative learning platforms as compared with this antiquated facility run by a dying archdiocese where they still kept the girls in plaid skirts and rows, chanting their parts of speech and copying notes off the board.

Of course, Mike had misread the instruction section of the e-mail, making him arrive here a half hour early; hence the note-book and the story attempt here in the lot. Pure boredom. It was either that or chance doubling back up Dutton Mills Road to the McDonald's for a sausage McMuffin with egg. But there was the possibility of getting caught in a line, and Mike Summers was more for relishing his guilty pleasures than rushing them.

It was the perfect setting for a horror story, though, wasn't it? The building before him was made of old church fieldstone with dark bay windows and doors with high arches. There were outdoor floodlights in the upper corners covered by wire-mesh baskets, and basketball hoops without nets. The playground had a jungle gym, a slide that leaned a tad left, and an ancient carousel that revolved ever so slightly when the wind picked up.

To the left up the hill was a construction site barred off by wooden slat fencing most probably erected by property owners more than two decades ago, all dark grey and weather-spotted, rambling along the rise in an alternating rail pattern that let slivers of daylight squeeze through. It was difficult to make out anything on the other side of it really. Mike knew it was a jobsite from the crane. They were building a new facility up on the rise: it was meant to replace the dinosaur down here, at least that's how it seemed. And with a half hour to kill, Mike Summers had made his first attempt at writing a short piece of fiction. So called. He crumpled up the three sheets of notebook paper and jammed them into the compartment below the radio where he discarded his dry trash. He'd stick to discussing the classics with a boyish enthusiasm, going easy on the grammar and making the kids laugh once in awhile. Stick to what he was good at.

He shut down the engine and opened the door. It gave its usual little metallic yowl, but the way it transitioned from the friendly and bumpy sound of the motor to the whisper of winter wind coming over the hood was creepy. If only he'd been talented enough to truly capture this setting with words. He stepped out, checked his zipper with practiced mechanical surety, and moved those long Hollywood bangs off his forehead. He was a bit skinny and slump-shouldered, but never forgot to mousse the top and dangle the front, doll it up a little. No, he wasn't advertising. He hadn't sauntered over to Home

Ec. and asked Brandi Cohen out for drinks, even though she smiled at him shyly over her cup of herbal tea every time they sat across from each other in the teachers' lounge. He hadn't offered to help Jennifer Dooley set up her biannual CPR session on her prep, even though everyone and their mother knew it was a chance to be alone with her in the weight room when she'd typically wear those stunning pink shorts. He hadn't even clicked the box on his Facebook that offered photos and profiles of "Mature Single Women in [His] Area," nothing since Stephanie died. He just had nice hair. And wouldn't it be a piss-poor example for his little Georgie to start bringing strange women into the house? Granted, it had come awfully close to falling apart for awhile, too close, but Mike was a fighter, a role model, and his three-and-a-half-year-old son brought him far more joy than any patch of fur ever could.

He opened the back door to reach in for his bookbag, and there was sound from behind, so faint he wasn't even sure if he really heard it floating down through the pattern of the wind. It was a suckling sound, coming from up on the hill. He turned, stepped a bit wrong, and wrenched his ankle in a way he was sure he would feel more tomorrow. Up on the hill there was something moving, there in the fence between the slats. Something . . .

"Well?" Professor Mike Summers said. "Comments?" It was a small fiction-writing class, yet one with surprising gusto. Trudy Bell had short butchy hair, wire frames, a nervous laugh, and a scarf, always. She was quick as a whip, though, really good with timelines and structural stuff. She was the typical literature major, well used to ruling the roost in these electives where you earned your "fun and easy" credits, and she was sort of at war with Mackenzie Dantoni, with her tight yoga pants, waist-lengthed blonde hair, big eyes (heavy on the mascara), and a startling ability to unpack characters and follow them down to the bitter ends of their neurotic little life journeys. The other three were lowerclassmen and bench talent: Nicholas Donahue, a thick kid who wore shorts even in the middle of winter, and the Stellabott twins, Donald and Daniel, both in dress shirts and ties, both rather shy, both experiencing the mild discomfort of landing in a course where grammar and expertise in the MLA discipline didn't matter anymore.

Professor Summers gently crossed one leg over the other while his students gathered their thoughts, and he looked rather blankly at the pages before him. There were some unwritten rules in university life. When tutoring in the Writing Center, you never told the students that their papers were "good," because anything their professors assigned below an "A" would be your fault. You didn't change rules on the syllabus unless it was in the student's favor, and you didn't bring in your own work for classroom review. It smacked of juvenile conceit and most often shook out to a clear lose-lose scenario. If it was dazzling, the students felt they could never live up. If it was a "work-in-progress," they wouldn't respect you. But here, Summers hadn't really a choice. He had expected at least a roster of twelve and had built the course around the idea that they would review student drafts. The first two weeks had been magnificent, but he'd already exhausted their two pieces of flash. He'd gotten critical responses for five stories from the 30/30 anthology, and they were in the dead zone between that initial rush and the ten- to twelve-pager. He'd needed something for filler.

"I liked it," Nicholas said, putting his ankle up on his knee and playing absently with the Converse All Star decal that had started to peel. "I mean, I think you were good as a high school teacher, Professor Summers, even though it got a little clunky and boring with the technical stuff the department head lady was into."

"Knickman," Trudy said dryly. He looked at her sideways for a second.

"Whatever. I got lost in the jargon."

"It built the character."

"Seemed forced."

"I thought it worked," Mackenzie said. "He countered all the theoretical language with words like 'God-awful,' 'horseshit,' and 'blah,' letting us know his expertise with it all and at the

same time his . . ." She fought for the right terminology, and
then smiled rather triumphantly. ". . . disdain and dismissal."

Trudy stared at her fingers clamped white across the front of
the knee, clearly uncomfortable that she was in basic agreement with her rival.

"I liked his hair," she finally offered in a rare moment of sardonic remittance, and Nicholas chuckled.

Playing it, Professor Summers "casually" moved those random (yet perfectly) placed strands off his forehead and then
looked off, thoughtfully stroking his salt-and-pepper goatee to
complete the cliché. That got a laugh from the whole group,
and Daniel, the more rigid of the two brothers, cleared his
throat.

"I . . . uh . . . know this sounds silly, but that little girl scares
me."

"You haven't even really seen her yet," his brother argued.
"Not as a ghost, anyway."

"That's the point," Mackenzie said. "You have to hide the
monster."

Trudy folded her arms coldly and spoke without looking at
anyone.

"There's more than that here. The narratorial echo makes it
so the author can build her in levels. In a way it's a cheap move,
allowing him to add material from his brainstorming lists
through his inner monologue about the writing process. But
notice, he pays more attention to Rhonda than Madeline
Murdock. He plays a trick with the trick, and that makes it
interesting."

"And the fence is a perfect barrier," Mackenzie added,
"because there's a chance we'll only see her in flashes and
flickers. If she walks or floats behind it, she'll just be this dark
form moving between the slats."

"Yes," Donald said, "and things could pop out from behind
the fence." Everyone turned and gave him a glance when his
voice cracked on the word "behind," but he pressed on brave-
ly. "I could imagine the teacher inside the school for his staff
development, and out of the corner of his eye he sees move-

ment out the window. Then, from up on the hill, there's something coming over the fence, bouncing in slow-motion toward the parking lot with the snow fluttering down all around it. A red kickball."

"Wouldn't be slow-motion," Trudy said. "It'd have to be in real time or it would give the implication that the Mike Summers character has lost his mind. If that's the author's intent, it's too soon."

"A tongue!" Nicholas said, so loud it made Mackenzie jump in her chair and put her hand to her chest. "Sorry," he muttered. "Anyway, the slats of the fence make it so she can stick her tongue through, darkening the wood, maybe picking up splinters like a pincushion and leaving a trail of blood and saliva."

Silence.

"That was a little too good, Nicholas, but thank you for sharing," Professor Summers said, and everyone smiled. "In what other ways could we utilize the fence as a masking element?"

Another silence, but a good one. Summers hadn't expected that they would necessarily add to his fragment of a tale, but if this was the way it was meant to go, it was the way that you let it. Teachable moment, right?

Daniel loosened his tie and folded his hands, then doing the thumb-twiddling thing: "You could have the Mike Summers character march up the grassy incline and grab two of the slats in order to pull close and put his eye right up to one of the voids."

"Right!" his brother chimed in. "And just when you think something will poke him in the pupil, another set of hands, dirty with the mud of the hole, grab his knuckles from the other side!"

"I'd save that for the climax," Trudy said. "The real question we should ask is what the suckling sound is."

"Her tongue," Nicholas said. "Licking the fence 'cause it looks like an elongated Kit Kat or something."

"I don't think the sound can be licking," Mackenzie said. "The teacher is down in the parking lot and the fence is up on a hill, far enough away for the girls to convince Madeline

Murdock to walk the plank without being heard by the aids on the playground."

"Playground's further than where Summers parked."

"But still . . ."

"Maybe it's her head," Trudy said. "When she hit there was a 'snap,' right? Of course we could assume it was a leg or an arm, but consider the alternative. Maybe she broke her neck clean off the spine and when she moves now, her head sloshes around. That would be louder than licking if she's really rolling it across her shoulders."

"Maybe it's a sexual sound," Nicholas tried. "Like a symbolic echo of the intimacy Mike Summers struggles to recall from his dead wife."

Silence yet again, but the thick kind now. Professor Summers's wife Stephanie had actually died three and a half years ago almost to the day while giving birth to their son George. Nicholas clearly hadn't gotten the memo. Professor Summers felt his eyes dampen, but he kept his voice smooth and professional.

"My apologies, Nick. I should have at least changed the names. We write what we know, often bringing up personal issues in dichotomous contexts, maybe for a bit of self-misdirection." He smiled. "No cry for help intended; I just needed to build a character. I'm fine with it at this point, but I must insist that it goes in the hopper."

"In the hopper," the rest of the class echoed. It was their code for a piece of writing that was too close to the vest to be scrutinized. Nick nodded and rubbed his nose.

"Well, I like the 'monster' here regardless. She has good backstory and she's scary."

"Definitely," Mackenzie said. "Way scarier than the girl in 'The Ring.'"

"I don't know about that," Trudy said.

"Really?" Mackenzie returned, head cocked so that mane of blonde hair hung down behind her like some velvety curtain. "Girlfriend was totally tame and utterly dependant on the effect that made her jump camera frames."

"The hair in the face was disconcerting."

"Please. She needed a brush, a hug, and some foot cream."

"Ha!" Donald said. "For her rotted, waterlogged toes. Ha!"

"So insightful," Daniel said, rolling his eyes.

"Yes," Professor Summers interjected. "I was aware of the possible similarities between the two characters, but I had more reservations about the idea that Madeline Murdock had severe special needs."

"Since when are we so worried about political correctness, especially in horror fiction?" Trudy said.

Summers pursed his lips and shook his head gently.

"You misunderstand. I had most of the fellow instructor-characters from Kennedy High worked out in my head, and none of them were meant to play moral compass, including Mike Summers. There was an intellectual snob who would insist it was not in her contract to teach a research paper, an old biddy who was afraid of the move toward holistic grading techniques, since she had gotten by with focus corrections and minimal output for years, and a bald grammar Nazi named Matthew who drilled subject-predicate and dangling participles even to seniors." He paused. "The point is that Knickman's big announcement was to be that they were on the verge of adopting the trend of dumping all the special ed. kids in the same classes, thirty at a time, and excusing it by throwing in a special-needs instructor to co-teach. Mike Summers was going to be furious . . . seeing it as a transparent short-cut that bypassed inclusion and turned him into a zoo keeper. That was his connection with Madeline. He only saw those with disabilities as roadblocks, annoyances, strains of a virus that would do nothing but tarnish the paradigm of 'cool teacher' he'd so carefully constructed throughout his tenure."

"Sounds good," Donald said, his brother nodding in agreement.

"But does it not sound like something else that's familiar?"

"Like what?"

"Like Jason."

"Who?"

"Voorhees!" Nicholas said. "Yeah. A kid with special needs that the campers tease and the counselors ignore."

"Too similar in plot and theme?" Professor Summers posed.

"Definitely not," Trudy said, pulling her feet up onto her chair and drawing her knees in. "The whole *Friday the 13th* thing was never even scary, except for a few select moments in the first."

"I agree," Daniel said. "You never actually have a feeling of trepidation watching those. You just cheer his kills." He looked around uncertainly. "If that's your thing, anyway."

"It's true," Mackenzie said. "*The Girl Between the Slats* doesn't spell killfest, at least not now as it stands. It's creepier. More mystery, depth, and suspense. More a focus on people and their intricate struggles, at least if it goes the way Professor Summers seems to intend." She looked at him shyly. "Sorry for the third-person reference. Not trying to be weird or anything."

"No," he said. "Not at all, Mackenzie. I truly enjoyed this class and I look forward to seeing you all back here on Monday. And since there isn't anyone else here in the alcove with an office hour during our class time, I think it's better to reconvene here in the lounge. It's cozier with the six of us, don't you think?"

They mumbled agreement. Usually, Trudy stayed behind to discuss some elevated principle, but today she left with the rest of them. Professor Summers pushed up and made his way across the lounge to his office with the limp he'd recently inherited. In the elevator this morning he'd stopped the door from sliding shut with his ankle because he had his bookbag in one hand and a latté in the other. The coed who had called out, "Oh, please hold that!" was grateful, and the awkward moment was rather humorous he'd thought, more her embarrassment than his, and a chivalrous deed well done in the end. But now, he'd developed a bit too much of a hitch in his giddyap, and he hoped he wouldn't have to put a call in to his primary over it.

He made it to his door and had just gotten out his key when he heard something bump in his office. He stepped back instinctively, winced, then shuffled off left past the corner to look down the carpeted foyer. Professors tended to leave their doors open when they were using the space, yet Pat's door was closed, as were Tara's, Robert's, and Dianna's. Besides, they were too far away. His office was at the entrance to the alcove, and the sound hadn't come from fifteen feet down the hall. It had come from just inside of his door, there was no mistaking it.

He repositioned himself back in front of his office and paused. Was it Yvette? They hadn't shared the space for two years, ever since he'd attained full-time status, so he didn't think it was her that was poking around in there. Besides, they had held class right here in the lounge for the last two and a half hours, and he'd been in the office right before it to throw his coat over the chair. He would have seen her go in.

He brought up his key, inserted, turned, and gave the door a push.

There was something on his chair.

-It was a mud-stained kickball that had moist spots with strange etchings around them. They were bite marks, and the only inconsistency in all the whitened impressions was the missing front right incisor.

Dr. Michael Summers shut his laptop, leaned back, and ran his palm over his smooth, bald crown. He hadn't taken a classroom assignment in years, and he missed it. He hadn't tried to write anything creative for just as long and that had been worse somehow, as if some fundamental connection to his current position of Dean of the College of Arts and Sciences had been corroded and severed . . . the inspiration for it all lost in the scatter of time. He had started on this path as the young tenth-grade English teacher with the moussed-up top and Hollywood bangs, all bright-eyed, bushy-tailed, and pure piss and vinegar. He'd understood kids, their clumsy passion, their insight and anger. But as a result of all the silly and destructive boardroom politics he'd moved on, earned a second master's in order to become the lowly adjunct professor slumming between universities until a full-time position opened at Widener where he moved all his books to the third floor of the Kapelski building, first office on the right in the alcove where he set up camp for a good while, where his hair went partially grey, where he grew a matching goatee as if it was his plan all along, where he taught lower-level rhetoric and the occasional fiction class out in the lounge.

After the doctorate, there was a chance to move up the ladder, and he took it. The decision wasn't an easy one and he'd called his father about it, actually. A retired professor himself, he'd claimed that these kinds of opportunities only came around once in awhile, and even though it was clear that his "rebel son" didn't like meetings and mission statements, it was better to dictate policy than to become no more than the hired help architecting someone else's vision of the landscape.

In the end Dr. Summers didn't despise it as much as he'd anticipated, but it wasn't the classroom with its teachable moments and glorious student epiphanies. In fact, the most contact he had with underclassmen of late was as mediator in a string of plagiarism cases, and for the first time in his career he wasn't in their corner. There were grade grievances and lawyers, policy meetings and enrollment projections.

And this was his cherished Christmas break, his time to relax. He'd made a personal vow not to check his e-mail and go putting out fires, and he'd gotten out his laptop to unwrap an old guilty pleasure, that Big Mac at the drive-thru, that *Friday the 13th* sequel you'd never admit you got off of Netflix.

Writing fiction was like getting back on a bicycle, right?

It had gone well in more ways than he had anticipated. He liked the falling snow as background motif just as much as that weather-worn slat fencing that leaned and rambled across the hillside. He hadn't had to stretch all too far to "see" it either; the window in the third-floor den overlooked his sprawling back yard where the Feinbergs' ancient alternating rail barrier divided their properties. It was an ugly, outdated piece of construction, but had become a part of his collective subconscious, his background mural, and he found it comforting somehow. The flurries just made it that much easier to write about.

In terms of problems and logic errors, he felt that he'd come out of this rough draft with a "pass-plus" or so. He agreed with his "Nicholas" character that the curricular phraseology in the first Mike Summers section in the parking lot was too rich, ringing of "Momma, look how good I'm writing here, huh?" and that it would have to be trimmed. The physicality of the office lounge in the fiction class scene was rather incomplete, yielding a muddy sort of impression of the logistics, and the biggest disappointment was Mackenzie Dantoni, the blonde bombshell with a brain whose type he knew all too well but somehow couldn't draw with any sort of credibility. First off, he'd initially sold her as an expert in character dissection, yet merely delivered a detail hound, sort of borrowing from the "Trudy" character's skillset. The blonde hair hanging like a curtain was a clumsy metaphor, difficult to visualize, and she was more a cliché than the girl who sat across the aisle and took your breath away.

He'd vaguely wanted to make her akin to a young Stephanie, and had wound up painting this poor dear in a startlingly unflattering manner when compared to her better. But his deceased wife was a tough act to follow, her memory still haunting him in life and in fiction. All his "Mike Summers" characters had lost a "Stephanie," but that was as inaccurate as all those mirrors of his own persona being portrayed in a modern timeline. In reality, he had married Stephanie Walker in 1984 straight out of college, and they'd put off having kids while they built their careers. He taught at Kennedy High for the rest of the decade, worked his adjuncting shuffle through most of the 'nineties, his full-time stint up until the Phils won the series in '08, and that's when they'd thrown away the diaphragm.

Stephanie was forty-seven when she died giving birth to his Georgie. All the charts and graphs warned that it was too late to try, but she'd still seemed so young and so strong. She was tall with daring eyes and beautiful knees. *God,* she looked good in a skirt! She was a senior lecturer at Temple for seventeenth-century poetry and she'd still hushed a room when she entered it. She was the type who could wear stiletto heels to a department function and get away with it, drinking white wine with the vice president of the college and saying things to her like, *"What an exquisite elder faerie you'd be."* She sang rock and roll opera style in the shower, she was one of those nutcases who wore face paint at Philadelphia Eagles home games, and she made sitting under a tree and reading a book seem like art.

Dr. Summers carefully used his index fingers to wipe under the rims of his eyes, then made a loose fist and bumped it against his lips. To say that he missed her made the feeling sound trite. It was horrifically empty now in the hollows of his heart, in the corridors of this house with its grand banisters and elevated ceilings.

All empty except for his Georgie, his love.

"Daddy!" the boy called, as if on cue. "Come look, come now! Please, Daddy, come see back yard, come see, come now!" Dr. Summers pushed away from his desk and made for the hall. Georgie wasn't supposed to be downstairs by himself, especially at night. He was probably looking out through the sliding glass doors, watching the snow. In fact, considering the muffled nature of his son's plea, it was probable that his nose was pressed right up against the glass, his breath-clouds advancing and receding like misted little spirits.

Dr. Summers rose and pulled firm his robe-tie, marveling (and not for the first time) over the odd acoustics of the place. Georgie could pad down the hall to the bathroom up here and Michael wouldn't know he was there until the flush. On the other hand, the boy could be building a Lego castle in the living room or playing "Teletubby hockey" (Tinky Winky was the puck) out in the back den, and you could hear him puttering around as if he were next to you.

The stairs had a long sweeping curve to them, and tonight Dr. Summers wished he'd had one of those silly rail riders they advertised on the same channel that plugged the walk-in tubs, hearing aids, and call-button necklaces you used when you'd fallen and couldn't get up. In his hurry to leave the house four days ago, he'd cracked his ankle at the base of the coffee table, and the 600 mg. ibuprofen wasn't helping that much. He limped down the stairs, and his son's voice carried to him:

"Hurry, Daddy, or you're gonna miss it!"

God, what a gem. If Stephanie only could have seen what she gave to this world before leaving it. True enough, Dr. Summers coddled him, but how could he help it? Georgie was the model boy, soft blond hair curling at the top, crystal-blue eyes, heart-shaped smile welcoming the world. He had a smidgen of chubby-cheek syndrome, but it was the last of the baby fat he was shedding. He was gorgeous, and it wasn't just "Dad" saying it with the equivalent of a loving parent's "beer goggles." Georgie was just that boy you wanted to put your arms around and squeeze. Everyone said so.

Dr. Summers almost tripped over the lip at the edge of the kitchen. He'd initially been against having a rise there going from carpet to hardwood, but the installer had said this was the type of tongue and groove that warranted a step. It was the way royalty did it in one of those Middle Eastern countries Dr. Summers couldn't remember at the moment, and when he was tardy lifting his knee his toe grazed the edge, almost sending him sprawling. There was that moment before pain that felt plush and high, and then the shooter through his ankle made him bite back a shout. Blasted contractors. They'd been a nuisance, and he'd succumbed to suggestions he'd been against simply because guys with tool belts, suspenders, and leather kneepads always seemed so damned sure of themselves.

He limped across the floor, past the island with the pots and pans hanging on the square rack above it, and when he got to the back den he froze in the archway.

There was his Georgie, pressed up to the glass. The lights were off, but the auto-floods in the back yard were shining, doubling the snowflakes with their shadows and casting a pale wash over the figure on the other side of the transparent door, twinning him. It was Madeline Murdock in Catholic school clothes, broken neck, head leaning so far to the left that her ear was pinned to her shoulder. They were playing mirror, hands splayed out to the sides, but she was taller, making the image of the cross gain two levels. Georgie was stretching his neck, trying to pull his head down to the side, but couldn't manage to get it quite parallel.

"This is my special friend, Daddy," he said, "and this is my special hug so I can be just like her."

She started to lift her head off her shoulder, and it lolled around like a zoo balloon on a stick. Shadows slanting down from the roof overhang moved up and down her face, and her smile came up in flashes and glare. It was a circus creature's grin with lips bloodied and swollen, broken nose pushed to the side with a tooth rammed straight through the nostril. Georgie was doing his best to mimic her, but the way her head dangled and flopped on its stalk was impossible to duplicate. Frustrated, hands still pinned to the glass beneath hers, Georgie started shaking his skull back and forth, so violently it seemed he was going to hurt himself. Dr. Summers burst through the room in shuffles and hitches. He reached out and screamed, but was too late.

Georgie slid open the door. It took everything he had, but the little guy was just tall enough to flip the lock, reach the handle, and pull the apparatus across.

Madeline Murdock had vanished.

The haunt of her frost and her snow swept through the archway, enveloping Georgie Summers and making whirlwinds around him. Dr. Summers grabbed his son by the shoulders, trying not to scream when he turned him and the head bobbed unnaturally, the boy's eyes rolling in dim recognition, lips bruised and bloody, front right incisor rammed straight though his nostril.

The man paged through it all one last time in helplessness or disgust, it was difficult to tell which. There were pieces of copy paper filled with slanted scribble and scratchings, a stack of sheets written on in haste and then ripped from a spiral-bound notebook, leaving the confetti-frills on the side, Post-It notes both yellow and rainbow colored, a few napkins, a piece of toilet paper.

"Mr. Summers," he said.

"Mike, please."

"As you wish." He gave a half-hearted attempt at rearranging the strange medley and removed his reading glasses.

"I just don't know what you expect me to do with all this."

"I want you to help him, father."

"I'm not a priest. I'm a therapist."

"And you can do nothing for my boy?"

The man made his way over from the desk, sat in the chair, and carefully rested the points of his elbows on the cushy arm-rests. Slowly, he sat back, simultaneously crossing his legs and linking his smooth fingers in a little bridge before his chest.

"I'm not his therapist, Michael, I'm yours, and I believe this is to be our last session."

"But . . ."

"Michael. You're tired. You're sleep-deprived. You have not eaten a square meal in three and a half years, and if you think it is at all positive that I play into this delusion it just represents a setback too extreme for the tools I have available here."

"He's possessed, can't you see?"

"Michael . . ."

"No," he said. "My Georgie is a beautiful boy."

"Of course he is, Michael, but you must affix that to the way he is, not some fantasy about who he could have been under other circumstances."

"He's intelligent! He's a gem! He's going to play lacrosse, get straight A's, and go to the prom with the Homecoming Queen! And when he graduates summa cum laude from Cornell, Harvard, or Duke, I'm going to buy him a Ferrari!"

"You won't, Michael, and it's actually time to talk about the business end of things since you've opened that door."

"You're talking finances? You're kidding. I'm the Dean of the College of Arts and Sciences at Widener University for Chrissake!"

"You're not, Michael. Not anymore. You lost that position three years ago. You never recovered from Stephanie's death, you refused to get Georgie professional help, and you wore yourself down to a thread. You lost the house, and Margaret informed me that Blue Cross Keystone hasn't received a premium from you in six months. You can't even afford to drop him off at the center at this point."

"It's a lie! I just got a late start today and—"

"Regardless, I believe we should discuss aid from the state and possible institutionalization."

"I'd never *ever* put my Georgie in a nut house!"

"I meant both of you, Michael. Separately. For your safety and his."

"That's ridiculous."

The man sat forward, hands folding atop the knee ever so softly.

"Michael," he said, "your son George has severe obsessive compulsion, sociopathic tendencies, and a highly impressive sensory disorder."

"How dare you!"

"You have spent the last three and a half years trying to reason with a damaged human being whose special needs warrant professional attention."

"No."

"If you don't take action he could fatally harm you."

"It was an accident. I banged my ankle on the edge of the coffee table."

"You didn't, Michael, and I won't support your denial. Your three-and-a-half-year-old son got out of the crib you still keep him tied down in, found the toolbox, brought in the ball peen hammer, and smashed your ankle as you slept in one of those fitful twenty-minute naps you try your best to sneak when you can. He wanted to hear the sound of crunching Kit Kats, he'd said."

"It's not true!"

"It is," Dr. Kalman insisted. "And you're going to have to face up to—"

The door burst open and Georgie Summers darted into the room, screaming at the top of his lungs, hands flailing before his chest as if he'd just scorched himself. He was wearing a neck brace and halo because he'd so liked the dizzying feeling that accompanied a constant violent shaking of his head, the doctors had feared he would suffer from brain-bruise and whiplash. He had a mouth guard that was fastened all the way around his skull, because he'd lacerated his tongue licking the splintered back yard fencing and had torn his lips to ribbons from the constant biting and sucking that he claimed tasted like Red Hots and pennies. Inside his mouth he was missing his right front incisor, surgically removed from his nasal cavity after he'd purposefully run straight into the edge of a sawhorse the landlord had set up in the kitchen to cut a board while he was fixing a leak under the sink. Georgie had claimed that when he bit down hard it tasted like the almond extract he'd stolen from the cupboard a week ago, and if Daddy wouldn't give him another bottle, he was going to make his own juice. Mike had told the emergency room doctor that his son had tripped over a kickball and hit the corner of a playground slide.

Margaret hurried in after the boy, her hair loose on one side.

"I'm so sorry, Doctor, but it's not in my job description . . ."

They were all on their feet now, Dr. Kalman frowning, hands in his blazer pockets. Mike Summers limped after his son, walking cast making clumping sounds on the floor. His eyes were reddened at the rims and his face sagged with grief. Georgie had gone flat on his stomach and was banging his mouth guard against the crown floor molding, screeching incoherently. Margaret's hands fluttered up to her face like frightened birds.

"Dear God, make him stop. He's trying to lick the outlets."

Mike Summers was on the floor now wrestling with his son from behind, looking up at his doctor, trying his best to avoid the meaty little fists flailing back at his face.

"There's got to be a reason," he said. "There's got to be." Georgie started banging his forehead against the wall. Mike assumed the restraining position they'd taught him at the Children's Hospital, arms over arms, the body beneath him writhing in spasm, and he pressed his lips to the side of the headgear, as near as was possible to his son's sweaty temple.

"Buttercups," he whispered tenderly in his son's ear. "Buttercups Georgie, I know . . . Daddy knows. You think the outlets are white chocolate buttercups."

The Patter of Tiny Feet

Richard Gavin

Against his better judgment Sam stopped the car and allowed his smartphone to connect with Andrea's. The earpiece purled enough times to allow him to envision Andrea sitting smugly cross-armed, eyeing her vibrating phone, ignoring his extension of the olive branch. Choking back the indignation he still believed was truly righteous, Sam obeyed the recorded instructions and waited for the tone.

"Hi, it's me," he began, trying not to be distracted by the escarpment's belittling sprawl of glacial rock and ancient forests. "Look, I'm sorry I stormed out like that. It was child-ish of me, I admit. I'm happy about your promotion, I truly am, it's just . . . well . . . I suppose I was a little shocked by how much your new position alters our plans." He was lecturing again. Andrea had accused him of it often enough. Was he also being high-handed, as she liked to claim? "Anyhow, I really do have some scouting to do, that wasn't a lie. But I wanted to call you before I got too far out and lost the signal. I've got my equipment in the car with me. I'm going to snap a few locations just to get Dennis off my back. I should be home in a few hours, so hopefully we can talk more then. Don't worry, I'm not going to try and get you to change your mind about anything. I . . . I guess I just need to know that a family's not completely off the table for us. It doesn't have to be tomorrow, but at some point in the not too distant future I'd . . ."

He could feel himself babbling. Already his first few statements had grown hazy; he winced at their possible fawning stupidity.

"I'll see you when I get home. Love you lots."

The jeep that was scaling the mountain behind him gave Sam an unpleasant start when he spotted its swelling reflection in his rearview mirror. The deafening beat of its stereo, no doubt worth more than the vehicle itself, caused the poorly folded maps on Sam's dashboard to hum and vibrate as though they were maimed birds attempting to flap their crumpled wings. The jeep rumbled past and the girl in its passenger seat was whooping and laughing a shrill musical laugh that Sam half believed was directed at him. He started his engine and cautiously veered back onto Appleby Line to resume his half-hearted search for a paragon of terror.

He'd not been lying about the mounting pressure from Dennis, a director who possessed the eccentricities and ego of many legendary cineastes, but completely lacked their genius. After helming two disastrous made-for-television teen comedies Dennis broke off to form his own miniscule film production company, Startling Image. Freak luck had furnished his operation with a grant from the Ontario Film Board, which Dennis said he planned to stretch as far as it could go. His scheme was to produce shoestring-budget horror films that would be released directly to DVD. Dennis believed this plot was not only foolproof but in fact an expressway to wealth and industry prestige.

Although Sam's experience in moviemaking allowed him to see the idiocy of Dennis's delusions, being a freelancer required Sam to accept any jobs that came his way during leaner times. Location Manager was an impressive title on paper, but with anorexic productions such as *Gnawers,* Startling Image's inaugural zombie infestation film, Sam found himself working twice as hard for a third of his usual compensation. He

was contracted for a major Hollywood studio film that was going into production in Toronto next spring and had only accepted Dennis's offer in order to bring in some extra money. The draconian hours, the director's tantrums, and the risible script for *Gnawers* would have all been worth it had Andrea kept her word.

But now it seemed there would be no need to furnish their guest bedroom with a crib and rocking chair and a chiming mobile on the ceiling. Instead, there would only be Andrea's customary seven-day workweeks, her quarterly bonuses spent on ever-sleeker gadgets and more luxurious clothing. Sam's wants were simple: to know the pleasures of progeny, fatherhood, to watch someone born of love and blessed with love growing up and sequentially awakening to all the wonders of life. His grandfather had advised Sam years ago that there comes a time in every man's life when all he wants is to hear the patter of tiny feet.

At thirty-eight Sam had come to appreciate the wisdom of the cliché, and also the cold sorrow of realizing that this natural desire might shrivel up unfulfilled. What then? Sunday afternoon cocktails with Andrea's fellow brokers, with him chasing an endless string of movie gigs until, perhaps, he could found a company of his own?

Only when the car began to chug and lurch in an attempt to scale the road's sudden incline did Sam realize he'd allowed his foot to ease off the gas pedal. He stomped down on it, and the asthmatic sounds the engine released made him wince. This far up the escarpment, well past the Rattlesnake Point Conservation Area, the road hosted surprise hairpin turns that required a driver's full alertness. Sam shook the cobwebs from his head and willed his focus on the narrow road before him.

Had he not been so determined to exceed Dennis's expectations, Sam might have let the sight pass by. But his determination to prove his worth, now not only to Dennis but also to Andrea, maybe even to himself as well, inspired Sam to edge the car onto the nearest thing the narrow lane had to a shoul-

der and exit his vehicle. He gathered his hip bag and, eyes fix-
ated on the quirk in the landscape, began to climb the rocky
wall that fed off the laneway.

The stiff pitch of a shingled roof was what had silently commanded his attention after a rather long and uneventful drive
around the escarpment. It jutted up, all tar shingles and snug-
ly carpentered beams, amidst the leafless knotty tree-line. As
he climbed upward and then began to wriggle across the
inhospitable terrain, Sam questioned the housetop's reality.
Had his anxious state conspired with his imagination to
impress a structure where one should not be?

A few more cautious footsteps were all that was required to
confirm the substance of his glimpse.

It was a wooden frame-house whose two stories might have
sprouted stiffly from the overgrown rockery that ringed its
base. Blatantly abandoned, Sam couldn't help but note how the
house's battered walls, punctured roof, and boarded windows
did not convey the usual faint melancholy or eeriness that most
neglected homes do. Instead, there was an air of what might be
called power. Sam wondered if the house had drawn strength
from its solitude, become self-perpetuating, self-sufficient, like
the mythical serpent that sustains itself by devouring its own
tail.

The site was so tailored to his wishes that for a moment Sam
almost believed in Providence. Lugging the film crew's equipment up and along this incline would be arduous, but he was
confident that it would be worth the extra effort. Given the
anorexic budget for *Gnawers,* even Dennis could not balk at
the richness of this location.

The place was almost fiendishly apt. They would have to
bring generators here to power the equipment, and a survey of
the house would be required to gauge its safety hazards, but it
could work. More than work; it could shine.

As he entered the clearing where the farmhouse stood, Sam
lifted his hands to frame his view in a crude approximation of
a camera lens. Yet this simple gesture was enough to trans-
form his roaming of the derelict grounds into a long and elab-

orate establishing shot. One by one he took in the set-pieces that may well have been left there just for him: the crumbling stone steps that led up to the empty doorframe, the rust-mangled shell of a tractor that slumped uselessly at the head of the gravel clearing, the wind-plucked barn whose arches resembled the fossilized wings of a prehistoric bird of prey. It was glorious, perfect.

Sam wished he had someone there to share it with. But surely Andrea would not draw as much pleasure from this as he did. Her interest in movies extended only as far as attending the local premieres of any productions Sam had worked on. Beyond that, Andrea's world revolved around crunching numbers for her clients.

For a cold moment Sam imagined one day teaching his son or daughter the thrill of seeking out the special nooks of the world. For Sam, movies were secondary. Their presentation invariably paled against the sparkling wonder of discovering the richly atmospheric settings that often hide out from the rambling parade of progress: art deco bars, grand old theatres, rural churches, and countless other places like this very farm.

He fought back the wring of depression by freeing the camera from his hip-bag and beginning to snap photos of the potential set. Moving around to the rear of the house chilled Sam, even though the April sun was still pouring modest warmth on the terrain. Perhaps the sight of the high shuttered room unnerved him. Regardless, it would make an excellent shot in *Gnawers*. With this many possibilities Sam's mind began to thrum with startling revisions that could be made to the script.

A wooden well sat at the edge of the property, mere inches from the untamed forest. Sam approached it, struck by just how crude it was. The surface of the well had not even been sanded. It still bore the mossy flaking bark of the tree from which it had been hewn. Sam might have mistaken it for the stump of a great evergreen had the mouth of the stout barrel not been secured with a large granite slab that was held in place by ancient-looking ropes. Or were they vines?

Regardless, the well or cistern could have been part of the topography, for it did not look fashioned in any way, merely capped. It was as if a massive log had been shoved down into the mud. Its base was overgrown with weeds so sun-bleached they resembled nerves.

Sam frowned at the thought of how its water might taste.

The house had no back door, so Sam hastened his way to the open doorframe that faced the incline, excited by the prospect of the house's interior.

The forest had shared its debris with the main hall. The oiled floorboards were carpeted with broken boughs and leaves and dirt. Sam clicked several shots of the living room with its lone furnishing of a broken armchair, of the pantry that was lined with dusty preserves, of the kitchen with its dented woodstove.

To his mind he'd already collected more than ample proof that this location would suit the film, but just to cross every T: a few quick shots of the second story. After that he would go back home. He had a strange and sudden need to snuggle up to Andrea, in a well-lit room, with the world held at bay beyond locked doors.

Something in the way the main stairs creaked underfoot gave Sam pause. He came to question whether the house was truly abandoned after all. It must have been the echo of the groaning wood, but the sound managed to plant the idea that the upper floor was occupied.

"Hello?" he called, only scarcely aware of the fact that his hand had begun fishing one of the contracts for location use out of his hip-bag. Drawing some absurd sense of security from the legal papers in his fist, Sam scaled the steps, listening all the while for noises that never overpowered his own.

An investigation of the first two rooms revealed precious little beyond more dust, greater decay. Sam's discovery of a dismantled crib in the front bedroom did summon a lump in his throat. Why should he be so moved by so banal an image— slatted wood stacked in a corner? No doubt because he and Andrea would likely never have to do the same in their home.

His emotions were running unbridled, a delayed response to his argument with Andrea. One last room and then home to see if his own desire for a family could be rescued or merely erode until his heart became as rotted and hollow as this house.

The final room sat behind a door that was either locked or merely stuck in a moisture-warped jamb. Amidst the gouges on its surface was a carving of a humanoid figure dancing upon what Sam assumed was intended to be a tomb. In place of a head the figure bore an insect with thin legs represented by jagged slashes in the door wood. Beneath this glyph the word SEPA had been scratched.

Sam wriggled the iron doorknob until frustration and mounting curiosity impelled him to wrench it, slamming his weight against the door itself.

If the owner had secured the door with a lock, it had snapped under Sam's moderate force. Still, Sam allowed a quick pang of guilt to pass through and punish him for the damage he'd wrought. But really, who would ever discover it?

The window in the room was half-covered by planks, but poor workmanship did not allow the wood to block out the light or protect the grimy glass. A cursory glance led Sam to believe that this room has been used for storage, for there were more items here than in all the other rooms combined: a long table, a wall-mounted shelf upon which books and what looked to be little wooden toys or figurines had been set, even a thin cot mattress carpeting the far corner. Bulging black trash bags were heaped along the wall. Sam daringly peeked into one of the open hems, discovering a bundle of old clothing, men's and women's both, wadded up in a gender-bending tangle.

All the items in the room suddenly quilted themselves together in Sam's mind, forming a larger picture that suggested the house was someone's home. He felt his bones go as cold and stiff as pipes in midwinter. Fear had bolted him to the spot. He listened, cursing himself for lumbering through the house so brazenly, so noisily.

Ribbons of sunlight poured in between the askew planks. Sam's gaze followed them as they seemed to spotlight the coating of dust that covered the mattress, the rodent droppings that littered the brownish pillow. The table reposed under streamers of cobweb and the titles on the book spines were occulted by dirt. A bedroom or squatter's den it might have been, but no longer. Sam exhaled loudly with relief.

After three or four shots of the room he indulged himself by stealing a few pictures of the neglected items: first the grubby bed, then the desk, and finally the items that lined the bowing shelf.

He regretted blowing on the row of books once the dust mushroomed up, flinging grit into his eyes and choking him. When the cloud settled Sam squinted his runny eyes at the spines: *The Egyptian Book of the Dead, De Vermis Mysteriis, The Trail of the Many-Footed One.* Leaning against these cloth-bound books was what looked to be a photo album or scrapbook. Sam carefully shifted this volume to face him and pulled back its plain brown leather cover.

Photographs that appeared to have been torn from entomology textbooks were sloppily pasted next to Egyptian papyri that, if the ugly handwritten footnotes were to be trusted, all dealt with an Egyptian funerary god named Sepa. There were also sepia-toned photographs of tiny churchyards. Some of the graves appeared upset. Repeated misspelled notes praised the Guardian of the Larvae of the Dead. Upon one of the pages was a poem in faded pencil scrawling:

Arise O Lord of the Larvae of the Dead!
Burrow! Race! Appear!
Your tendrils drip with dew from the caverns of Hades,
the jewelled filth from Catacombs of Ptolemais,
& the great silent dark that holds fast between the worlds.
Glut on the meat of the temporal realm so that I may gain yet
*   one more day of life above the tombs!*

Sam closed the cover and wiped his fingers on his jacket. His attempt to return the scrapbook to its perch was made sloppy by his unsteady hand. Something fell from the shelf and landed on the table with a clunk. Not wanting to touch anything else in the room, Sam tugged his jacket sleeve down to protect his hand while he lifted the Mason jar from the tabletop. Whatever the brownish substance was inside, it certainly had heft. Sam rotated the jar slowly, trying to discern its contents without truly wanting the answer. He took a step toward the window. Through the boards he could see the capped well, looking much like an ugly coin lying within the weedy lawn.

Holding the jar up to the light, Sam saw enough to suggest that what it held was indeed a wad of centipedes preserved in some sludgy liquid. His stomach turned, and he quickly returned the jar to the shelf. Next to it Sam noticed the wooden phallus. But this sexual aid was spiked with a number of toothpick-like legs. He did not bother to count them.

Shock was the only force that retarded Sam. Had his brain not registered the sight of the closet door opening, had his eyes not caught the suggestion of the shape in the darkened alcove, he would have run wildly, been out of this house, been racing through the sunlit woods, his car keys in his fist.

But the image of the seated cadaver was strange enough, *stunning* enough, to momentarily stifle Sam's instinct to flee. Its flesh was the color of fresh concrete, causing it to glow like greying embers within the lightless closet. The legs were spindle-thin and the chest was sunken. Its head was obscured by a cowl of some kind.

What an awful way to be interred, Sam thought. He marveled at how the mind almost short-circuits when its limitations are exposed.

When the figure suddenly rose and bounded into the room it was clear it had not been left to rot in some locked farmhouse room. It had been waiting in the closet, like an ascetic in a confessional. Its face was shaded by what resembled a flowing habit of fringed brown leather that crackled as the figure advanced, sounding like something dry, something moulted.

Sam wondered if he had stumbled into one of the improved scenes he'd been imagining.

But in the movies the dead do not move this quickly.

In a swift and seamless motion the monkish figure reached into one of the piled trash bags, causing it to tip. The bones it held clattered out onto the dusty floor like queerly shaped dice. The skulls stared with grinning indifference as the figure clutched Sam with one hand, while the other raised the chunky femur and brought it down like a primitive club. Sam never even had time to scream.

The pain in the back of his skull woke Sam and also played havoc with his perceptions. What else could explain the presence of the moon or the fact that everything else around him had been swallowed by darkness? He pressed his hands down on the cushiony surface beneath him and slowly, achingly, pushed himself upright before slumping right back down again. The air was frigid and damp. He could see his breath forming ghosts on the blackness. Confusion over where he was gave way to a sharp panic as memories of the farmhouse shuffled their way back into Sam's consciousness like cards being dealt: the tomes and the symbols and the grey attacker . . .

With an unsteady hand Sam prodded his trouser pockets, pleading silently that his smartphone was still there. It was, though its screen was cracked. He mashed at it with bloodless fingers, trying to connect with the world by any means possible. But the device's only use was as a source of weak glowing light. Its graphics were but a smear of color.

Sam waved the phone about like a torch. What it illuminated was an upright tunnel of textured wood. Grubs and clumped soil dangled here and there. The atmosphere was uncomfortably moist.

The well . . .

Craning his aching head, Sam watched as clouds scuttled across the moon's face and he wondered how long he had been down here. The light on his smartphone began to flicker like a guttering candle. Another shadow suddenly blocked the moon. This one did not pass but instead stretched across the crude mouth of the well.

The figure that was bent over the rim then made a gesture.

Only after Sam had screamed out "Help me! Please!" did he conclude that this shadowy visitor must be the man who'd attacked him.

Words came down the chute, ricocheting off the wooden walls. They were indecipherable, guttural, almost inhuman. Whether there was meaning to them or whether it was merely the vibration of the alien voice, the ground began to shift in response to the stimuli. And soon Sam felt himself being flung as the cushioned base upon which he'd been lying began to rise and scale the side of its den.

It was immense. Sam foolishly wondered how long it must have taken his attacker to find a log large enough to shelter such a creature. By the moon's pallor-glow Sam could just see the man raising his arms to imitate the flailing mandibles of the great scuttling thing that bucked its head in mirror-perfect mimicry of these gestures. The barbarous words were now being bellowed in a near-euphoric tone. Their rhythm matched the clacking of the thick stingers that parted and shut on the insect's rump.

Horror and irony besieged Sam in a great steely wave. He could only listen to the sound he'd so longed to hear: the patter of tiny feet. Only this time they were multiplied a hundredfold. Sam almost laughed, and a second later his light went out.

At Lorn Hall

Ramsey Campbell

Randolph hadn't expected the map to misrepresent the route to the motorway quite so much. The roads were considerably straighter on the page. At least it was preferable to being a directed by a machine on the dashboard, which would have reminded him of being told by Harriet that he'd gone wrong yet again, even when he knew where he was going. Although it oughtn't to be dark for hours, the April sky beyond a line of lurid hills had begun to resemble a charcoal slab. He was braking as the road meandered between sullen fields of rape when he had to switch the headlights on. The high beams roused swarms of shadows in the hedges and glinted on elongated warnings of bends ahead, and then the light found a signpost. It pointed down a lane to somewhere called Lorn Hall.

He stopped the Volvo and turned on the hazard lights. The sign looked neglected except by birds, which had left traces of their visits, but Lorn Hall sounded like the kind of place he liked to wander around. The children never did, complaining to Harriet if he even tried to take them anywhere like that on the days he had them. They loved being driven in the rain—the stormier the better, however nearly blind it made him feel—and so he couldn't help feeling relieved that they weren't with him to insist. He could shelter in the mansion until the storm passed over. He quelled the twitching of the lights and drove along the lane.

Five minutes' worth of bends enclosed by hulking spiky hedges brought him to a wider stretch of road. As it grew straight he glimpsed railings embedded in the left-hand hedge, rusting the leaves. Over the thorns and metal spikes surrounded by barbs he saw sections of an irregular roof patrolled by crows. Another minute brought him to the gateway of Lorn Hall.

He couldn't have given a name to the style of the high broad house. Perhaps the stone was darkened by the approaching storm, but he thought it would have looked leaden even in sunlight. At the right-hand end of the building a three-storey barrel put him in mind of a clenched fist with bricks for grey knuckles. Far less than halfway from it on the unadorned frontage, a door twice as tall as a man stood beneath a pointed arch reminiscent of a mausoleum. Five sets of windows each grew smaller as they mounted to the roofs, where chimneys towered among an assortment of slate peaks. Even the largest of the ground-floor windows were enmeshed with lattices, and every window was draped with curtains that the gloom lent the look of dusty cobwebs. Apart from an unmarked whitish van parked near the front door there was no sign of life.

The signpost had surely been addressed to sightseers, and the formidable iron gates were bolted open, staining the weedy gravel of the drive. One of the gateposts in the clutch of the hedge had lost its stone globe, which poked its dome bewigged with lichen out of the untended lawn. Ivy overgrew sections of the lawn and spilled onto the drive. The shapes the topiary bushes had been meant to keep were beyond guessing; they looked fattened and deformed by age. If Harriet had been with him she would have insisted on leaving by now, not to mention protesting that the detour was a waste of time. This was another reason he drove up to the house.

Did the curtains stir as he drew up beside the van? He must have seen shadows cast by the headlamps, because the movements at all three windows to the left of the front door had been identical. Nobody had ducked out of sight in the van either. Randolph turned off the lights and the engine, pocketing his keys as he turned to face the mansion. The sky had grown so stuffed with darkness that he didn't immediately see the front door was ajar.

To its left, where he might have looked for a doorbell, a tarnished blotchy plaque said **LORN HALL**. The door displayed no bell or knocker, just a greenish plaque that bore the legend **RESIDENCE OF CROWCROSS**. "Lord Crowcross," Randolph murmured as though it might gain some significance for him if not summon its owner to the door. As he tried to recall ever having previously heard the name he felt a chill touch as thin as a fingernail on the back of his neck. It was a raindrop, which sent him to push the heavy door wide.

The door had lumbered just a few inches across the stone flags when it met an obstruction. Randolph might have fancied that somebody determined but enfeebled was bent on shutting him out, perhaps having dropped to all fours. The hindrance proved to be a greyish walking boot that had toppled over from its place against the wall. Several pairs grey with a mixture of dried mud and dust stood in the gloomy porch. "Don't go any further," Harriet would have been saying by now, "you don't know if you're invited," but Randolph struggled around the door and kicked the boot against the wall. As he made for the archway on the far side of the porch, light greeted him.

Little else did. His approach had triggered a single yellowish bulb that strove to illuminate a large room. Opposite the arch an empty chair upholstered in a pattern so faded it wasn't worth distinguishing stood behind a bulky desk. Apart from a blotter like a plot of moss and earth, the desk was occupied by a pair of cardboard boxes and scattered with a few crumpled pamphlets for local attractions. The box that was inscribed **HONESTY** in an extravagantly cursive script contained three coins adding up to five pounds and so thoroughly stuck to the bottom that they were framed by glue. The carton marked **TOUR** in the same handwriting was cluttered with half a dozen sets of headphones. As Randolph dug in his pockets for change, his host watched him.

The man was in a portrait, which hung on the grey stone wall behind the desk it dwarfed. He stood in tweed and jodhpurs on a hill. With one hand flattened on his hip he seemed less to be surveying the landscape in the foreground of the picture than to be making his claim on it clear. The wide fields scattered with trees led to Lorn Hall. Although his fleshy face looked satisfied in every way, the full almost pouting lips apparently found it redundant to smile. His eyes were as blue as the summer sky above him, and included the viewer in their gaze. Was he less of an artist than he thought, or was he meant to tower over the foreshortened perspective? Randolph had guessed who he was, since the C that signed the lower left-hand corner of the canvas was in the familiar handwriting. "My lord," Randolph murmured as he dropped coins in the box.

The clink of metal didn't bring anyone to explain the state of the headphones. They weren't just dusty; as he rummaged through them, a leggy denizen scrabbled out of the box and fell off the desk to scuttle into the shadows. "That's very much more than enough," Harriet would have said to him in the way she did not much more often to their children. If you weren't adventurous you weren't much at all, and the gust of wind that slammed the front door helped Randolph stick to his decision. Having wiped the least dusty set of headphones with a pamphlet for a penal museum, he turned them over in his hands but couldn't find a switch. As he fitted them gingerly over his ears a voice said "You'll excuse my greeting you in person."

Nobody was visible beyond the open door beside the painting, only darkness. The voice seemed close yet oddly distant, pronouncing every consonant but so modulated it implied the speaker hardly cared if he was heard. "Do move on once you've taken in my portrait," he said. "There may be others awaiting their turn."

"There's only me," Randolph pointed out and stared with some defiance at the portrait. If Lord Crowcross had taught himself to paint, he wasn't the ideal choice of teacher. The landscape was a not especially able sketch that might have been copied from a photograph, and the figure was unjustifiably large. The artist appeared to have spent most time on the face, and Randolph was returning its gaze when Crowcross said "Do move on once you've taken in my portrait. There may be others awaiting their turn."

"I already told you I'm on my own," Randolph protested. The headphones must be geared to the listener's position in the house, but the technology seemed incongruous, as out of place as Randolph was determined not to let the commentary make him feel. "I'm on my way," he said and headed for the next room.

He'd barely stepped over the stone threshold when the light went out behind him. "Saving on the bills, are we?" he muttered as he was left in the dark. In another second his arrival roused more lights—one in each corner of an extensive high-ceilinged room. "This is where the family would gather of an evening," Crowcross said in both his ears. "We might entertain our peers here, such as were left. I am afraid our way of life lost favour in my lifetime, and the country is much poorer."

The room was furnished with senile obese sofas and equally faded overweight armchairs, all patterned with swarms of letters like the initial on the portrait. A tapestry depicting a hunt occupied most of the wall opposite the windows, which Randolph might have thought were curtained so as to hide the dilapidation from the world. Several decanters close to opaque with dust stood on a sideboard near a massive fireplace, where cobwebbed lumps of coal were piled in the iron cage of the hearth. Had the place been left in this state to remind visitors it had fallen on hard times? Everyone Randolph knew would be ashamed to go in for that trick, whatever their circumstances. Quite a few were desperate to sell their homes, but all his efforts as an estate agent were in vain just now. He turned to find his way out of the room and saw Lord Crowcross watching him.

This time his host was in a painting of the room, though this was clearer from the positions of the furniture than from any care in the depiction. Sketchy figures sat in chairs or sprawled languidly on the couches. Just enough detail had been added to their faces—numerous wrinkles, grey hair—to signify that every one was older than the figure in the middle of the room. He was standing taller than he should in proportion to the others, and his obsessively rendered face appeared to be ignoring them. "Do make your way onwards whenever you're ready," he said without moving his petulant lips. "I fear there are no servants to show you around."

"No wonder the place is in such a state"—or rather the absence of servants was the excuse, and Randolph was tempted to say so. By now Harriet would have been accusing him of risking the children's health. He loitered to make the voice repeat its message, but this wasn't as amusing as he'd expected; he could almost have fancied it was hiding impatience if not contempt. "Let's see what else you've got to show me," he said and tramped out of the room.

All the lights were extinguished at once. He was just able to see that he'd emerged into a broad hallway leading to a staircase wider than his arms could stretch. He smelled damp on stone or wood. By the dim choked glow through doorways on three sides of the hall he made out that the posts at the foot of the steep banisters were carved with cherubs. In the gloom the eyes resembled ebony jewels, but the expressions on the chubby wooden faces were unreadable. "Do continue to the next exhibit," Crowcross prompted him.

Presumably this meant the nearest room. Randolph paced to the left-hand doorway and planted a foot on the threshold, but had to take several steps forward before the light acknowledged him. Fewer than half the bulbs in the elaborate chandelier above the long table lit up. "This is where the family would dine in style," Crowcross said, "apart from the youngest member."

The table was set for ten people. Dusty plates and silver utensils stained with age lay on the extravagantly lacy yellowed tablecloth. Like the upholstery of all the chairs, every plate was marked with **C** . Doilies to which spiders had lent extra patterns were spread on a sideboard, opposite which a painting took most of the place of a tapestry that had left its outline on the stone wall. Although the painting might have depicted a typical dinner at Lorn Hall, Randolph thought it portrayed something else. Of the figures seated at the table, only the one at the head of the table possessed much substance. The familiar face was turned away from his sketchy fellow diners to watch whoever was in the actual room, while a servant with a salver waited on either side of him. "Subsequently the situation was reversed," Crowcross said, "and I made the place my own."

Was the painting meant to remind him of the family he'd lost—to provide companionship in his old age? Randolph was trying to see it in those terms when the pinched voice said "By all means make your way onwards." He could do without a repetition, and he made for the hall. As the chandelier went dark he glimpsed somebody turning the bend of the staircase.

"Excuse me," Randolph called, moving the earpiece away from his right ear, but the other didn't respond. If they were wearing headphones too they might not have heard him. He'd only wanted to ask whether they knew what time the house closed to the public. At least he wasn't alone in it, and he picked his way along the hall to the kitchen, where part of the darkness seemed to remain solid as the weary light woke up.

It was a massive black iron range that dominated the grey room. A dormant fragment of the blackness came to life, waving its feelers as it darted into one of the round holes in the top of the range. How long had the kitchen been out of use? Surely nobody would put up with such conditions now. Chipped blotchy marble surfaces and a pair of freezers—one a head taller than Randolph, its twin lying horizontal—might be responsible for some of the chill that met him. A solitary cleaver lay on a ponderous table, which looked not just scored by centuries of knife strokes but in places hacked to splinters. Randolph looked around for a portrait, but perhaps Crowcross felt the kitchen was undeserving of his presence. "My father

enjoyed watching the maids at their work," he said. "Red-hand-
ed skivvies, he called them. I did myself. Since then the world
has changed so radically that their like have been among the
visitors. Perhaps you are of their kind."

"Not at all," Randolph objected and felt absurd, not least
because he suspected that Crowcross might have disagreed
with him. He was searching for some trace of the people who'd
worked here—initials carved on the table, for instance—when
Crowcross said "There is no more to see here. Let us move
on."

He sounded like a parody of a policeman—an officious one
used to being obeyed. Randolph couldn't resist lingering to
force him to say it again, and might easily have thought a hint
of petulance had crept into the repetition. The light failed
before Randolph was entirely out of the kitchen, but he
glimpsed a door he'd overlooked in the underside of the staircase. As he reached for the heavy doorknob Crowcross said
"Nothing of interest is kept down there. I never understood its
appeal for my father."

Perhaps Randolph did, assuming the servants' quarters were
below. He wondered how his guide's mother had felt about the
arrangement. The scalloped doorknob wouldn't turn even
when he applied both hands to it. As he looked for a key in the
thick dust along the lintel Crowcross spoke. "I have told you
nothing has remained. Let us see where I was a child."

His petulance was unmistakable. No doubt the basement
rooms would be unlit in any case. Randolph was making his
way past the stairs when he heard whoever else was in the
house shuffling along an upper corridor. He wondered if there
was more light up there, since the footfalls were surer than his
own. They receded out of earshot as he pushed open the door
of the turret room.

The room was lit, though nothing like immediately, by a single bare bulb on a cobwebbed flex. The round aloof ceiling
caught much of the light, and Randolph suspected that even
with the curtains open the room might have seemed like a cell
to a child. It was furnished with a desk and a table in propor-

tion, each attended by a starkly straight chair. While the table was set for a solitary meal, it had space for a pile of books: an infant's primer on top, a children's encyclopaedia many decades old at the bottom. Even when Randolph made the children read instead of playing, Harriet rarely agreed with his choice of books. The stone floor was scattered with building blocks, a large wooden jigsaw depicting a pastoral scene, an abacus, a picture book with pages thick as rashers, open to show a string like a scrawny umbilical cord dangling from the belly of a pig spotted with mould. The desk was strewn with exercise books that displayed the evolution of the omnipresent handwriting; one double page swarmed with a C well on its way to resembling the letter that seemed almost to infest the mansion. "This is where I spent the years in growing worthy of my name," said Crowcross. "In our day parents hired their delegates and kept them on the premises. Now the care of children is another industry, one more product of the revolution that has overtaken the country by stealth."

Above the desk a painting showed the room much as it was now, if somewhat brighter and more insubstantial. Crowcross stood between rudimentary impressions of the table and the desk. His arms were folded, and he might have been playing a teacher, except that nobody else was in the room—at least, not in the picture of it. "If you have learned everything you feel entitled to know," he said, "let us go up."

Did Randolph want to bother going on, given the condition of the house? Harriet certainly wouldn't have, even if the children weren't with them. He'd had nothing like his money's worth yet, unless he retrieved the payment on his way out. Perhaps the person upstairs might know more about the history of Lorn Hall, and Randolph didn't mind admitting to a guilty fascination, not least with the companion at his ear. "If you have learned everything you feel," Crowcross said and fell silent as Randolph left the room.

He was on the lowest stair when he noticed that the cherub on the banister had no wings. Somebody had chopped them off, leaving unequal stumps, and he couldn't help suspecting that the vandal had been Crowcross, perhaps since he'd found himself alone in Lorn Hall, the last of his line. He had the uneasy notion that Crowcross was about to refer to if not justify the damage. "If you have learned," the voice said before he could let go of the shaky banister.

From the bend in the stairs he saw the upper corridor, just about illuminated by the dimness beyond several doorways. Whoever he'd glimpsed on the stairs wasn't to be seen, and no light suggested they were in a room. Presumably they were at the top of the house by now. Barely glancing at a second mutilated cherub, Randolph made for the nearest room along the corridor.

Its principal item was an enormous four-poster bed. Burdened by plaster sloughed by the ceiling, the canopy sagged like an ancient cobweb. More plaster glistened on an immense dressing-table and an upholstered chair that must once have looked muscular. Most of the light from the few live bulbs in the chandelier fell short of a side room, where Randolph was just able to distinguish a marble bath with blackened taps and a pallid hand gripping the side to haul its owner into view, but that was a crumpled cloth. "You are in the master bedroom," Crowcross said tonelessly enough to be addressing an intruder. "Would you expect the master to have left more of a mark?"

His portrait showed him gripping the left-hand bedpost. As well as declaring ownership he gave the impression of awaiting a companion—watching with feigned patience for someone to appear in the doorway at Randolph's back. His imperiousness was somewhat undermined by crumbs of plaster adorning the top of the picture frame. "Will you know what robs a man of mastery?" he said. "Pray accompany me along the corridor."

Randolph couldn't help feeling relieved not to be given the tour by his host in the flesh. He suspected the commentary had been recorded late in the man's life—when he was turning senile, perhaps. The chandelier in the next room contained even fewer bulbs, which faltered alight to outline another bed. Its posts were slimmer than its neighbour's, and the canopy was more delicate, which meant it looked close to collapsing under the weight of debris. Had a fall of plaster smashed the dressing-table mirror? Randolph could see only shards of glass among the dusty cosmetic items. "Here you see the private suite of the last Lady Crowcross," the voice said. "I fear that the ways of our family were not to her taste."

He held a bedpost in his left fist, but it was unclear which bedroom he was in. His depiction of himself was virtually identical with the one next door. A figure identifiable as a woman by the long hair draped over the pillow lay in the sketch of a bed. Randolph couldn't judge if Crowcross had given her a face, because where one should be was a dark stain, possibly the result of the age and state of the painting. "Please don't exert yourself to look for any signs of children," Crowcross said. "They were taken long ago. My lady disagreed with the Crowcross methods and found another of our fairer counterparts to plead her case."

"I know the feeling," Randolph said, immediately regretting the response. There was no point in being bitter; he told himself so every time he had the children and whenever he had to give them up. As he caught sight of the bathroom shower, which was so antiquated that the iron cage put him in mind of some medieval punishment, Crowcross said "You'll have none of the little dears about you, I suppose. They must conduct themselves appropriately in this house."

While Randolph thought his and Harriet's children might have passed the test, at least if they'd been with him, he was glad not to have to offer proof. As he made for the corridor he glimpsed a trickle of moisture or some livelier object running down a bar of the shower cage. "That's the style," said Crowcross. "There's nothing worthy of attention here if you've taken in my work."

It almost sounded as though the guide was aware of Randolph's movements. To an extent this was how the commentary operated, but could it really be so specific? He was tempted to learn how it would react if he stayed in the room, but when the lit bulbs flickered in unison as though to urge him onwards he retreated into the corridor.

The adjacent room was the last on this side. Shadows swarmed and fluttered among the dead bulbs as the chandelier struggled to find life. All the furniture was stout and dark, the bedposts included. One corner of the laden canopy had almost torn loose. The room smelled dank, so that Randolph wouldn't have been surprised to see moisture on the stone walls. "This was the sanctum of the eldest Crowcross," the voice said. "His wife's quarters were across the corridor."

Presumably the portrait was meant to demonstrate how the room had become his. He was at the window, holding back the curtain to exhibit or lay claim to a version of the landscape in summer. His eyes were still on his audience; Randolph was beginning to feel as if the gaze never left him. He was meeting it and waiting for the next words when he heard a vehicle start up outside the house.

The bedposts shook like dislocated bones as he dashed across the room, and debris shifted with a stony whisper. The gap between the curtains was scarcely a finger's width. They felt capable of leaving handfuls of sodden heavy fabric in his grasp, and he knew where at least some of the smell came from. As he dragged them apart the rings twitched rustily along the metal rail. He craned forward, keeping well clear of the windowsill, which was scattered with dead flies like seeds of some unwelcome growth. The grid of cramped panes was coated with grime and crawling with raindrops, so that he was only just able to make out the grounds. Then, beyond the misshapen bloated topiary, he saw movement—the van near which he'd parked. Its outline wavered as it sped along the drive and picked up speed on the road.

Was Randolph alone in the house now? In that case, how had the driver sneaked past him? As the van disappeared into the rainswept gloom Crowcross said "Will you see the woman's quarters now? Everything is open to you, no matter what your pedigree."

How distasteful was this meant to sound? Randolph might have had enough by now except for the weather. He felt as if he was ensuring he outran the voice by hurrying across the corridor. A few bulbs sputtered alight in their cobwebbed crystal nest to show him yet another dilapidated bed. A hole had rotted in the canopy, dumping plaster on the stained bedclothes. Crowcross was holding a bedpost again, and a careless scribble behind him suggested that someone had just left the sketched bed. "Any little treasures would be barred from all these rooms," he said. "Have any found their way in now? Do keep an eye on their behaviour. We don't want any damage."

"I think you're having a bit of a joke," Randolph said. How senile had the speaker been by the time he'd recorded the commentary? Had he been seeing his home as it used to be? The light stuttered, rousing shadows in the bathroom and enlivening a muddy trickle on the initialled tiles above the marble trough. "If you have had your pleasure," Crowcross said, "the eldest breathed their last next door."

"My pleasure," Randolph retorted, and it was a question too.

The chandelier in the adjacent room lacked several bulbs. In the pensioned light a pair of four-posters occupied much of the cheerless space. Although the canopies were intact, the supports showed their age, some of the thinner ones bowing inwards. "They came here to grow as old as they could," Crowcross said. "Tell any little cherubs that, and how they had to stay together while they did."

Randolph thought the commentary had turned childish in the wrong way, if indeed there was a right one. He'd begun to feel it was no longer addressed to him or any listener, especially once Crowcross muttered "And then older."

The beds were flanked by massive wardrobes almost as dark outside as in. Both were open just enough to let Randolph distinguish shapes within. The figure with a dwarfish puffy head and dangling arms that were longer than its legs was a suit on a padded hanger. Its opposite number resembled a life-size cut-out of a woman drained of colour— just a long white dress, not a shroud. Nobody was about to poke a face around either of the doors, however much Randolph was reminded of a game of hide and seek. He'd never prevented the children from playing that, even if he might have in Lorn Hall. As he did his best to finish peering at the wardrobes Crowcross said "Are you still hoping for diversions? They await your judgement."

Randolph was starting to feel like the butt of a joke he wasn't expected to appreciate, since Crowcross didn't seem to think much of his visitors, let alone their views. When a pair of the lamps in the next room jittered alight, a ball on the billiard table shot into the nearest pocket. Of course only its legs had made it look as large as a billiard ball. Packs of battered cards were strewn across a table patched with baize, and cobwebs had overtaken a game of chess, where chipped marble chessmen lay in the dust beside the board. "This is where games were played," Crowcross said, "by those who had the privilege. Mine was waiting, and in the end I won."

He might have been talking to himself again, and resentfully at that. "We haven't seen your room yet," Randolph said and wondered if all of them had been. "You aren't ashamed of it, are you? It's a bit late to be ashamed."

He was heading for the turret room when Crowcross said "Eager to see where I was visited by dreams? Since then they have had the run of the house."

After a pause the room was illuminated by a stark grubby bulb. A bed with no posts and less than half the size of any of the others stood in the middle of the stone floor. The only other furniture was a wardrobe and a comparably sombre dressing-table with a mirror so low it cut Randolph off above the waist. Perhaps the soft toys huddled on the pillow had at some stage been intended to make the room more welcoming, but that wasn't their effect now. The pair of teddy bears and the lamb with boneless legs had all acquired red clownish mouths that contradicted their expressions. So much paint had been applied that it still resembled fresh blood.

They were in the portrait, where their sketched faces looked disconcertingly human. Perhaps the alterations to the actual toys had been a kind of preliminary study. Crowcross stood at the sunlit window, beyond which a distant figure stooped, hands outstretched. "I used to love watching the keepers trap their prey," Crowcross said. "They are put here for our pleasure and our use."

As Randolph turned away he saw what the painting didn't show. The toys on the pillow almost hid the clasped pair of hands protruding from beneath the quilt, which was blotched with mould. No, they were wings, none too expertly severed from the body—a pair of wooden wings. "This could have been a child's room," Crowcross mused. "We always raised our children to be men."

"Don't we talk about girls? I thought I was supposed to be unreasonable but my dear lord, my wife ought to listen to you," Randolph said and seemed to hear a confused violent noise in response. The window was shuddering under an onslaught of rain. He turned his back to all the eyes watching him—the portrait's and those of the disfigured toys, which were exactly as blank—and heard soft rapid footfalls on the stairs above him.

They were shuffling along the top corridor by the time he reached the staircase. "Excuse me, could you wait?" he shouted, raising the other headphone from his ear as he dashed upstairs so fast that he couldn't have said whether one cherub's face was splintered beyond recognition. Whenever he grabbed the banister, it wobbled with a bony clatter of its uprights. In a few seconds he saw that the top corridor was deserted.

None of the rooms showed a light. Perhaps whoever was about was trying to fix one, since otherwise their presence would have triggered it. Perhaps they were too busy to answer Randolph. Had the driver of the van been in the house at all? Presumably the person Randolph had glimpsed earlier was up here now. They couldn't have gone far, and he made for the turret room in the hope of finding them.

He saw he was alone once the meagre light recognised him. A lectern stood beside an imposing telescope that was pointed at the window. Astronomical charts—some crumpled, others chewed or torn to shreds—lay on the floor. "I never saw the appeal of the stars," Crowcross said, more distantly now. "I've no wish to be reminded of the dead. They say that's how old their light is. I preferred to watch the parade of the world. The glass brought it close enough for my taste."

He could have used the telescope to spy on the grounds and the road. Beyond the blurred fields Randolph saw an endless chain of watery lights being drawn at speed along the horizon. It was the motorway, where he promised himself he'd be soon, but he could finish exploring while he waited for the rain to stop, particularly since the family wasn't with him. He left the turret room with barely a glance at the portrait in which Crowcross appeared to be stroking the barrel of the telescope as if it were a pet animal.

The next room was a library. Shelves of bound sets of fat volumes covered every wall up to the roof. Each volume was embossed with a C like a brand at the base of its spine. More than one high shelf had tipped over with the weight of books or the carelessness with which they'd been placed, so that dozens of books were sprawled about the floor in a jumble of dislocated pages. A ladder with rusty wheels towered over several stocky leather armchairs mottled with decay. "This might be tidier," said Crowcross. "Perhaps that could be your job."

What kind of joke was this meant to be? Randolph wondered if the last lord of Lorn Hall could have pulled the books down in a fury at having nowhere to hang his portrait. He couldn't have done much if any reading in here unless there had been more light than the one remaining bulb provided. It was enough to show that Randolph was still alone, and he dodged across the corridor.

An unshaded bulb on a cobwebbed flex took its time over revealing a bedroom. All four bedposts leaned so far inwards that they could have been trying to grasp the light or fend it off. The canopy lay in a heap on the bed. Although Randolph thought he'd glimpsed clothes hanging in the tall black wardrobe as the light came on, once he blinked at the glare he could see nothing except gloom beyond the scrawny gap—no pale garment for somebody bigger than he was, no wads of tis-

sue paper stuffed into the cuffs and collar. "This could be made
fit for guests again," Crowcross said. "Would you consider it to
be your place?"

He sounded as furtively amused as he looked in his portrait,
which showed him standing in the doorway of the room, gazing at whoever was within. It made Randolph glance behind
him, even though he knew the corridor was empty. "I wouldn't
be a guest of yours," he blurted, only to realise that in a sense
he was. Almost too irritated to think, he tramped out of the
room.

Next door was a bedroom very reminiscent of its neighbour.
The fallen canopy of the four-poster was so rotten it appeared
to have begun merging with the quilt. The portrait beyond the
bed was virtually identical with the last one, and the light could
have been competing at reluctance with its peers. Nothing was
visible in the half-open wardrobe except padded hangers like
bones fattened by dust. Randolph was about to move on when
Crowcross said "This could be made fit for guests again. Would
you consider it to be your place?"

The repetition sounded senile, and it seemed to cling to
Randolph's brain. As he lurched towards the corridor
Crowcross added "Will you make yourself at home?"

It had none of the tone of an invitation, and Randolph wasn't
about to linger. Whoever else was upstairs had to be in the last
room. "Have you seen all you choose?" Crowcross said while
Randolph crossed the corridor. "See the rest, then."

The last room stayed dark until Randolph shoved the door
wider, and then the lights began to respond—more of them
than he thought he'd seen during the rest of the tour. The
room was larger than both its neighbours combined, and
graced with several chandeliers that he suspected had been
replaced by solitary bulbs elsewhere in the house. They were
wired low on the walls and lay on the floor, casting more shadow than illumination as he peered about the room.

It was cluttered with retired items. Rolled-up tapestries
drooped against the walls, and so did numerous carpets and
rugs, suggesting that someone had chosen to rob Lorn Hall of

warmth. Several battered grandfather clocks stood like sentries over wooden crates and trunks that must have taken two servants apiece to carry them, even when they were empty of luggage. Smaller clocks perched on rickety pieces of furniture or lurked on the floorboards, and Randolph couldn't help fancying that somebody had tried to leave time up here to die. Crouching shadows outnumbered the objects he could see, but he appeared to be alone. As he narrowed his eyes Crowcross said "Here is where I liked to hide. Perhaps I still do."

"I would if I were you," Randolph said without having a precise retort in mind. He'd noticed a number of paintings stacked against the wall at the far end of the room. Were they pictures Crowcross had replaced with his own, or examples of his work he didn't want visitors to see? Randolph picked his way across the floor, almost treading on more than one photograph in the dimness—they'd slipped from unsteady heaps of framed pictures which, as far as he could make out, all showed members of the Crowcross family. Even the glass on the topmost pictures in the heaps was shattered. He'd decided to postpone understanding the damage until he was out of the room when he reached the paintings against the wall.

Though the light from the nearest chandelier was obstructed by the clutter, the image on the foremost canvas was plain enough. It portrayed Crowcross in a field, his arms folded, one foot on a prone man's neck. He looked not so much triumphant as complacent. The victim's face was either turned away submissively or buried in the earth, and his only distinguishing feature was the C embossed on his naked back. It wasn't a painting from life, Randolph told himself; it was just a symbol or a fantasy, either of which was bad enough. He was about to tilt the canvas forward to expose the next when Crowcross spoke. "The last," he said.

Did he mean a painting or the room, or did the phrase have another significance? Randolph wasn't going to be daunted until he saw what Crowcross had tried to conceal, but as he took hold of a corner of the frame the portrait was invaded by darkness. A light had been extinguished at his back—no, more than one—and too late he realised something else. Because the headphones weren't over his ears any more he'd mistaken the direction of the voice. It was behind him.

The room seemed to swivel giddily as he did. The figure that almost filled the doorway was disconcertingly familiar, and not just from the versions in the paintings; he'd glimpsed it skulking in the wardrobe. It wore a baggy nightshirt no less pallid and discoloured than its skin. Its face was as stiff as it appeared in any of the portraits, and the unblinking eyes were blank as lumps of greyish paint. The face had lolled in every direction it could find, much like the contents of the rest of the visible skin—the bare arms, the legs above the clawed feet. When the puffy white lips parted Randolph thought the mouth was in danger of losing more than its shape. As the figure shuffled forward he heard some of the substance of the unshod feet slopping against the floor. Just as its progress extinguished the rest of the lights it spoke with more enthusiasm than he'd heard from it anywhere else in the house. "Game," it said.

Blind Fish

Caitlín R. Kiernan

The backward look behind the assurance
Of recorded history, the backward half-look
Over the shoulder, towards the primitive terror.
— T. S. Eliot

May 14, 2031 (Tuesday)

Since Istria, Jeremiah's life seems portioned, divided into a monotonous triad: the dread presaging sleep, his nightmares, and the hours of disorientation after waking. He is dreamsick. A psychiatrist might prefer to label it PTSD, but to him *dreamsick* seems a far more appropriate term. The triad is monotonous, despite the terror, the cold sweats, the claustrophobia. He imagines that soldiers must often fall into an emotional routine not so very different, long periods of boredom between the sudden violence of battle. Having spoken to women and men who served in Pakistan, Korea, and Somalia, yes, what his life has become since Istria seems very much the same, as though he exists now in a continuous cycle of mental plateaus and spikes. But he picks and chooses from among the cheap buffet of black market pharmaceuticals he buys off the Cambodian and Laotian street vendors crowding O'Farrell and Jones streets. Rice-paper envelopes that once held the pills litter his nightstand, because he only rarely bothers gathering them up and throwing them away. Those who are dreamsick have deplorable housekeeping skills.

Their gods are not our own.

Jeremiah opens his eyes on a rainy morning in June, and Aden is still sleeping, coiled into the sheets beside him. So, she wasn't only a part of the nightmare, and that brings both relief and the daily realization that he has survived actual events existing beyond the labyrinth of his subconscious. He sits up and wipes at his face, the stubble on his face and head, his aching eyes. The room is all shadows and the gloom of the day leaking in through the apartment window. The room is the same shades as the dream that clings to him as sure as the sheen of sweat. He wants a cigarette, but there's no smoking when Aden is around. She has enough trouble breathing as it is; he settles for a Tic-Tac and a yellow pill. He leans against the headboard and tries not to remember the dream, the way it was not so very different than what actually happened off Kolone Isle.

He reminds himself to breathe.

He reminds himself to take slow, measured breaths.

It's always bad enough without hyperventilating.

He alternates between watching the rain streaking the window and watching the clock on the nightstand, a refugee among all the dope and rice-paper envelopes, until Aden wakes up half an hour later. She opens her eyes, which he still finds unnerving, even after seven years and in spite of his feelings for her. They are the black eyes of certain sorts of sharks, which makes them more like the eyes of humans than the eyes of bony fish, possessing retinas, corneas, and pupils that dilate and contract. Her night vision is amazing, adapted to the depths at which the Monsanto germliners designed her to function, but she's not so great at diurnal. She blinks, and smiles, and the respiratory assist vest hums to life, giving her sleep taxed lungs a rest, pumping salt water across the pairs of

gill slits on either side of her sternum, just above her tiny breasts. In truth, Jeremiah only vaguely understands the mechanics of the RAVs provided to marine hybrids.

Their gods . . .

"You don't look so good," she says, and the chip implanted in her larynx does its halfway decent job of making her voice sound human.

"What else is new?" he says.

"The hole again?" she asks, and he replies "The hole again."

She puts an arm around his legs, and hugs his knees. Her smooth, hairless skin is almost the same color as the light in the room, smudgy greys and blues and blacks.

"You ought not keep going back there," she says, as though he has a choice.

"I know."

The yellow pill is starting to lift the pall in his head just enough that *these* moments seem somewhat more real than *those* moments, the ones he has presumably awakened from. Jeremiah has spent many hours entertaining the notion that he's still more than five hundred and fifty meters below the surface of the Adriatic, trapped in the submersible lit by the sickly red emergency lights while his days and nights in San Francisco are the *dreams*. Or a delirium he's slipping into as his oxygen levels are rapidly depleted and hypoxic hypoxia sets in.

"I dreamt of swimming," Aden says sleepily, which is what she almost always dreams of; if he were a deep splice, like her, Jeremiah supposes he would also mostly dream of swimming. If he, like her, had been fashioned to be a creature of the sea, but found it necessary to spend the lion's share of her life on land.

But it was a conscious choice, he reminds himself. *It was a choice she made. I never asked her to do it.*

"I should take a shower," he says and considers a second yellow pill.

"I wish I could show you the way the sea is for me. Then maybe you would not be so afraid, even after what happened in the hole."

With alien eyes, they did fashion their gods.

Eyes far more alien than Aden's. Inscrutable windows into inscrutable, ancient souls.

"Are you hungry?" he asks, and she nods and tells him she'll make breakfast while he showers. Jeremiah isn't ever hungry anymore, but it's easier to go through the motions than let people think he's trying to starve himself.

"Ramen and eggs?" she asks, and he nods.

He's lucky, and this is one of the days there's hot water. He stands beneath the spray, letting it beat down on the back of his neck and against his shoulders while he stares at water swirling down the drain set into the pink ceramic tiles. The steam smells like soap and shampoo. He could easily stay here until the water turned cold. If he were lucky all over again, that might not be for another half hour. But Aden is making breakfast, and the only thing less appetizing than the thought of breakfast is the thought of breakfast cold.

He shuts off the water, stands dripping a moment, then dries himself with a towel that should have seen the inside of a laundry two weeks ago. He shaves quickly and nicks himself twice. He dabs at the tiny cuts with tissue. All these simple, mundane acts, somehow they only serve to underscore the detached fog of his days, the dreamsickness, the inability to detach himself from the nightmares that are, in the main, only endlessly regurgitated memories.

Breakfast. An egg. Sriracha. Noodles. Two pieces of toast with the last of a jar of marmalade. Strong black coffee. A red pill from its rice-paper envelope, just to balance the effects of the yellow wake-up pill, which is making him jittery.

Aden makes a joke about going back to bed and fucking the day away, and Jeremiah laughs, though his libido has seen better days. *Everything about me has seen better days,* he thinks, wondering how long it will be before Aden tires of his shit and finds another lover. She says she would never do such a thing, but he's never been a romantic. All relationships can be reduced to acts of selfishness, and when the self ceases to be satisfied—on whatever level—they dissolve. If you're fortunate, relationships dissolve amicably.

They dress, he in jeans and a rumpled T-shirt almost as in need of washing as the bath towel, and she in one of the skin-tight bodysuits that help marine hybrids regulate primary electrolytes, and also avoid dehydration and overheating. She kisses him, her lips and tongue only faintly salty, only faintly tasting of fish. Then she takes the mag-lev to Oakland, and he crosses the bay to Berkeley. He'll spend the day supervising work on the fossils recovered from the seafloor off Kolone.

Which, of course, is where the nightmares began.

Perhaps a man with more resolve would seek some other position at some other institution, instead of facing daily reminders of the *mater* and *pater* of his dreamsickness. But Jeremiah doesn't. The Kolone fauna is his, and, likely, he will never have the opportunity to work with anything so important ever again in his life. Here is the sort of discovery that not only makes a career, but divides successful academic from scientific celebrity. Here is a life's work laid out before him. He hasn't the courage to give that up, regardless of its daily toll on his psyche.

"You could take the Caltech offer," Aden might say, whenever the subject comes up (and she's usually the one who broaches it). "Or Harvard. It's not as if you don't have good options available to you."

She never mentions the Atlanta offer. Or Denver. But he understands her phobia of being landlocked, as much as he understands his own fears. Or so he likes to think.

There's an accident on the bridge, just past Yerba Buena, which makes him late enough that both Galton and Loeuff have gone to lunch by the time he reaches the campus and the lab. He'll have at least an hour to himself. It means being alone with the fossils, yes. But it also means not having to wear the mask he wears for his colleagues and everyone else but Aden.

Their gods, their faces.

Jeremiah picks up part of a fragile jawbone, then sets it down again.

He dislikes handling the bones, no matter how often he's done just that.

. . . their faces.

The path leading to this moment, this day, to the dreamsickness, to his sharing a bed with a hybrid—*all* of it—began with an eight-year-old Croat boy stumbling across the battered fragments of a sauropod vertebra while beachcombing not far from Bale. The fragments were eventually brought to the attention of the Hrvatski geološki institut in Zagreb. That was almost fifteen years ago, and for a time the fossils had sat ignored in a cabinet drawer, as those who'd been charged with their keeping happened to have very little interest in anything beyond microfossils and local mineral resources. But then the boy's find had been noticed by a visitor from the Museo Paelontologico Cittadino di Monfalcone, and she'd been the one to discover that the broken pieces of dinosaur bone had come from beds of late Early Cretaceous—age limestone exposed on the seafloor, half a mile from shore and all those fathoms down. She'd also been the one who contacted Jeremiah, aware of his pioneering work in underwater collecting techniques.

A Croat boy goes beach combing.

An Italian woman pulls open a dusty drawer.

A phone rings at Berkeley.

One hundred and thirty million years ago—give or take—the beds of limestone had been deposited in a lake, at a time when a vast carbonate shelf supported an archipelago that had spanned the proto-Mediterranean, the *Tethys* Ocean between *Gondwana* to the south and *Laurasia* to the north. Fanciful names spun with great solemnity by geographers to label hypothetical landmasses that would seem, to most, as mythic as Atlantis and Lemuria. Names for a vanished geography that Jeremiah has taught Aden in their time together, she so eager to learn and, he thinks, hoping that the more he talks about what took place that day off Kolone and the Istrian Peninsula, the better will be his chances of recovery. Never mind that he talks about it all day. That talking about it is his job. That he spends five or six days a week, every week—never one for vacations—describing, measuring, preserving the fossils the joint Italian-US-Croatian expedition had managed to gather before "the event" that had almost destroyed the Woods Hole submersible *Sunfish*. That had almost cost Jeremiah his life.

Most days, it seems that would have been a mercy.

Wishing one were no longer alive, he has said to Aden, is not the same as being suicidal. Jeremiah isn't suicidal. So, there's another mercy he's been denied.

The seafloor was littered with the bones of dinosaurs that had been exposed by the slow process of marine erosion. On his first dive, he'd been amazed at this graveyard, not yet consumed with the problem of how the fossils would be disinterred and brought to the surface. That day, he could only gawk. Scorpion fish and black seabream had dashed by the porthole, scales flashing in the glare of the *Sunfish's* forward lighting array. Jeremiah had hardly noticed them. He'd only had eyes for the petrified remains of those dragons that had lived and died and turned to stone. The jigsaw puzzle of an ecosystem he would have the chance to put together.

He had not yet realized that his curiosity is a curse.

That the curiosity of *all* humanity is, and forevermore will be, a curse.

"If you would see someone, then maybe—" Aden said, days before this day. An attempt at beginning a conversation they've had more times than he can recall, and that always ends the same way. So, this time, he goes directly to the end, interrupting her.

"—nothing would change. I wouldn't forget."

She's watched him with her shark eyes, and sometimes he's surprised how much emotion those blank, empty orbs are capable of conveying. *I want to help,* they say. *I desperately want to help. You can't see that. You won't. But I do.*

He forces himself to pick up the jawbone again, squinting at it beneath the lab's fluorescent lights. This left mandible is no longer than his hand, the delicate marriage of dentary, splenial, surangular, angular, a few serrate teeth still in their sockets, and so forth. No matter how many times he examines this bone—or any of the dinosaur bones from that limestone at the bottom of the sea—he is amazed at their diminutive size. Here in his palm is the left side of a jaw from an allosaur, but the jaw is hardly twelve centimeters from end to end. Still, it is almost identical to that of an adult *Allosaurus,* a theropod with a skull averaging over *eighty* centimeters. This tiny jaw was the result of insular dwarfism, a population of dinosaurs that had adapted to life on one of the archipelago's islands, to its limited resources. The same was true of the sauropods, brachiosaurs and diplodocids whose mainland counterparts included the largest land animals ever. The limestone had piled up over hundreds of thousands of years, entombing an unprecedented assortment of miniature dinosaur species, as well as mammals uncharacteristically *large* for the Mesozoic, some— both carnivores and herbivores—as big as full-grown Great Danes. And there had been enormous crocodiles, too. So, here was a lost world entirely turned on its head. It had not been an environment where the "ruling reptiles" ruled.

"If you would only try harder," Aden said.

"I need to you back off," he told her. "I know you *mean* well, but I really don't need to hear this shit all over again."

"I don't know how much longer I can live this way."

"You didn't see—"

"I've seen photographs. I've seen some of the specimens."

You weren't down there that day. You didn't see what I saw. You cannot imagine. You're a foolish, naïve bitch if you think you can. But he knew better to say any of this aloud, and he still has enough self control not to do so.

Their gods are not our own.

Their idols . . .

Aden turned her head toward the windows, winding a strand of her long bluish hair about an index finger. Jeremiah had to tap the invisible Dazzler hanging above the bed three times before it had flickered to life and called up the weather. Nothing there to lift his spirits. The rain wouldn't last much longer, and then the scorching May heat would go back to baking the city again. The local report gave way to a thread on the Canadian drought, and he tapped the Dazzler three times before it whirred and shut off.

"Not a goddamn thing in this place works," he muttered, and Aden only laughed.

"I have to run depth trials today," she said. "Out past the Farallons, off Mussel Flat. Sometimes, I think I'll just keep swimming. Sometimes, it's hard to turn back. You know. Sometimes."

But she always does. And he knows she always will. Because that's how the germliners put her together. Aden is a creature straddling two worlds, belonging truly to neither. She needed the companionship of other people, fully *human* people as surely as she needed her precious hours in the sea.

But, still, "Sometimes, I know I'd be better off," she says quietly.

The jaw in his palm is a gem, priceless, the end product of natural selection working its magic down countless generations to make giants into midgets. The bone was almost the same color as Aden's eyes. This one piece had taken two weeks to free from its rocky prison. It would be years before all the material collected off the coast of Kolone Island was prepared, and maybe decades before it was all described. He'd published three papers so far, one based on this very mandible: *Microsaurophaganx inexpectatus,* the "unexpected tiny lizard-eater." That the allosaurid had fed mainly on lizards was only conjecture, but Jeremiah had liked the name.

After that abbreviated conversation, days before this day, he and Aden had fucked. Despite his sluggish libido, it was always easier than talking, easier than facing the truth that whatever there had been between them was fading away, evaporating, and soon she'd be gone, and it would only be him in the shitty Tenderloin apartment. She straddled him, and as soon as he slipped inside her, the stubby rudimentary pelvic fins on either side of her labia has closed tightly around the shaft of his cock. It's a sensation he's never grown accustomed to, and one that has never ceased to elicit a moment of panic. But, also, which has never ceased to make him harder. Like her eyes and her teeth, it made a primal act much more so. It made the act almost savage. There was an undeniable thrill, knowing that she could rip his throat out as easy as he might bite through a stalk of celery; he's seen video of sharks mating. He placed his hands on either side of her ass, careful because the vagaries of her genome meant randomly distributed patches of minute, sandpaper-rough denticles along her spine, buttocks, and thighs. Shagreen. She's drawn his blood more times than he can recall.

When she reached orgasm, her black eyes rolled back to the whites, and she dug her fingertips—entirely devoid of nails—into his shoulders.

You'll come back, he thought. *Not to me, no. But you'll always come back.*

She'd been late to the docks, and had almost missed the big blue SWATH ferrying the research team to the Farallons.

He'd spent the rest of the day tangled in the sheets, listening to the rain.

Today, Jeremiah sets the *Microsaurophaganx* jaw back into it foam cradle and rubs his eyes. In five or ten minutes, Galton and Loeuff will be back from lunch, and he'll no longer have the lab to himself, the luxury of being alone with his demons. He'll have to at least make an effort to appear as though he's working. He's gotten fairly good at the pantomime. Good at participating in conversations that only seem to hold his attention. Good at going through a plethora of quantitative motions. If anyone's noticed, they've not said so. Jeremiah has even learned to navigate departmental administrative meetings with a minimum of actual participation. It's an inevitable consequence of existing ever more in dreams, the prevailing symptom of his dreamsickness.

He looks away from the jaw, at the pages of paper stacked up neatly next to the fossil's container. He's always preferred writing in cursive on actual paper, with actual ink, a habit as expensive as it is impractical. To his knowledge, he's the only person with whom he is acquainted who even knows cursive. As a child, he taught himself from an old textbook.

His neat handwriting, sepia on white, the beginnings of a monograph on one of the Istrian fauna's two dwarf sauropods:
. . . prominent deltoid crest extends down the lateral margin of the bone from near the proximal end . . .

"What the hell did you see down there?"

And he'd replied, "Look at the fucking tapes, okay. The fucking cameras saw more than I did."

Then he'd vomited on the deck.

He and an Italian grad student from Monfalcone had been finishing up with the mapping of Quadrant 18 when the hole—The Hole—had come into view. The submersible's pilot radioed topside and been advised to proceed with caution, as the sensors were reading unpredictable currents in the area. The hole had been about fifty yards in diameter, a freakishly perfect circle punched through the layers of fossiliferous limestone.

"What the hell is that?"

"Fuck all if I know," the pilot had said. "Some sort of sinkhole, maybe?"

"Not with a perimeter *that* regular."

Whatever else it was, Jeremiah recognized it as a chance to view a perfect stratigraphic cross-section of the bone bed. He'd consulted the pilot, who'd reluctantly consulted the mother vessel far above them, which had very reluctantly given them permission to enter the hole. "Exercise extreme caution. We're getting some weird turbidity readings along the rim." That's exactly the word the relay had used. *Weird.* The crew's three hybrid escorts—which included Aden—had been ordered not to accompany the *Sunfish*. It was just too risky, and the hole might exceed their depth limits. He hadn't yet known Aden back then. Back then, he'd still harbored the revulsion at hybrids that most people felt.

When we venture in that unfamiliar sea, we trust blindly in those who guide us, believing that they know more than we do.

Do we? Do we *do* that?

The submersible had moved forward, then slipped over the edge. The hole had obligingly swallowed them in a single gulp. How long had it been waiting, indescribably patient and hungry. Insatiable.

"How deep is this thing?" he'd asked the pilot.

"Give me a moment. I think the fathometer is acting up."

"Is it the transducer?" the graduate student had asked.

"No idea," the pilot had replied.

But Jeremiah had been too occupied with the procession of horizontal strata beyond the porthole as the submersible sank deeper into the hole, and so, effectively, deeper into *time*. Alternating limestone, sandstone, thin lenses of what looked like greywacke. The Horizon-D4 camera jacks hummed, tracking his most subtle eye movements. He felt hardly any dread at all, in those first few minutes, despite the worried tone of the grad student and the pilot's consternation at what seemed to be malfunctioning sonar. But for Jeremiah, this was a windfall. The expedition had budgeted thousands of dollars to extract core samples, and here he was getting all that data free of charge and without the costly days spent drilling.

He'd only half heard the pilot when she'd said, "It's almost like this drop doesn't *have* a bottom." Jeremiah had only half heard her nervous laughter. It had taken the *Sunfish's* first collision with the wall of the hole to get his attention.

"Fuck, fuck, fuck. Were getting some sort of vertical pulse . . ." and then the pilot had braced herself and told them all to double check their harnesses.

Fuck, fuck, fuck.

The bottom had fallen out beneath them, and the submersible fell as though there were only air were beneath it.

Loeuff comes in, but not Galton. "He's got that meeting with the exhibit team," the anatomist had reminded Jeremiah. "Probably won't get out until three or so. You know, the board still wants to use this as an opportunity for a press conference, to get the herpetosapients into the public eye, the artifacts, all of it."

Herpetosapients. Jeremiah had been the one to coin that term, just as he'd invented *Microsaurophaganx inexpectatus* and would be christening the macronarian sauropod described in his handwritten notes *Istriasauros petricola*. Sometimes, it seemed all this nomenclature was no more than latter-day sorcery, struggling to keep the monsters at bay. Talismans to bind the night pressing in at him.

It was a time of dark dreams. They washed in like flotsam on the night . . .

So, take this night, and wrap it around me like a sheet.

"I'll be out until Sunday," Aden said before leaving the apartment. "Four days of playing keep-your-distance with Great Whites."

A regular family reunion, he thought. It was a vicious thought. The ugly sort of shit he kept buried deep down to gnaw at no one but himself.

They built temples to their gods.

We build temples, and so did they.

The *Sunfish* had tilted violently to port, and the pilot had cursed and wrestled with the controls as the vessel plunged into the abyss.

"We're going to die down here," the grad student had squeaked. He had. He had actually fucking *squeaked.* Like a goddamn mouse. Jeremiah had wanted to slap the sorry son of a bitch.

"No one's going to *die,*" Jeremiah had said, instead. "Now shut up and try not to piss yourself. Unless you already have."

The poly-titanium/cobalt hull had begun to groan, then, and the graduate student was babbling in Italian about blowing the ballast tanks. Never mind they had almost four-days of life support for a three-man crew. The pilot growled that she wasn't fucking dropping ballast. Several seconds later, the aft hydraulic propulsor had gone offline. The voice interface with the *Sunfish's* AI crackled, popped, and both the screens crashed. The submersible took another hard blow as it slammed a second time against the wall of the hole. The way the craft had shuddered, Jeremiah felt it in his bones and teeth and behind his eyes. The pilot had frantically switched over to manual ops, her fingers dancing a tarantella across the pad of old-fashioned toggles.

. . . if you ride these monsters deeper down, if you drop with them farther over the world's rim . . .

Jeremiah had turned back to the blur of strata beyond the eighteen-centimeter thick forward-facing port. There had been nothing else reasonable he *could* do, and it was better than giving in to panic. It would be better, if these were his last moments, to see that which he would die to have seen.

"He knows," says Loeuff, "how strongly you feel about releasing any information on that shit before all the dating is finished. But he says no one's listening. They want to put the goddamn skull on display. The skull *and* the hull shards."

Jeremiah laughed, making a great show of examining his notes for the sauropod paper. "You *know* they're never going to get military clearance to display that shit. I'm still surprised the specimens haven't been spirited away to some secret goddamn NSA bunker somewhere. And there's our non-disclosure—"

"I think they mean to ignore that."

"Well, I'm not ignoring it. I'm not that keen to vanish into the fucking detention camps. Anyway, before the day's over, I expect they'll get a polite reminder from D.C. of the arrangement."

Loeuff shrugs, takes a seat at one of the prep stations, and goes back to work on one of the mammalian skulls. In life, it would have looked something like a small hyena, that animal. It would have *preyed* on dinosaurs.

Only four minutes and forty seconds after the *Sunfish* had entered the hole, the submersible settled on the rocky seafloor. All things considered, touchdown had been surprisingly forgiving. A jolt, but definitely not the jolt that Jeremiah had expected. By then, the motors had powered down, the cabin was bathed in the scarlet wash of the emergency lights, and the pilot had managed the release of a beeper buoy. Two of the 5k-watt spots were still running, as was video. If the fathometer was to be trusted (and many of the vessel's instruments were on the fritz), the submersible had come to rest more than one hundred and five meters below the opening of the hole. But they hadn't landed on stone.

"Guys," said the grad student, pointing, "someone please tell me that isn't what it looks like . . . please."

At the bottom, the hole had widened from fifty yards to almost seventy-five. Below and all around the *Sunfish,* the spots reflected off a dull battleship-grey metallic surface. It was perfectly flat, that plane interrupted only by a smattering of rubble that had fallen from above, possibly dislodged by their descent.

Why isn't it buried under silt from slumping and mass wasting?

That had actually been Jeremiah's first thought. Not, *What the fuck is that thing.* Not even wonder or momentary disbelief.

Why isn't it buried?

While they'd waited on the retrieval detail, while the pilot worried over her machine, he and the student had done all they could do. They'd used the two manipulator arms to gather as many samples as there was space remaining in the containers to hold them. These had included the fragments of a basicranium, frontal, right zygomatic arch, and several teeth that would be the first hint of Jeremiah's "herpetosapiens." There was enough spare energy in the cells to run the drill for just two minutes, and so they'd also recovered shavings and chips of the metallic substrate.

Almost an hour had passed before either of them had noticed the pattern in the metal. Or, rather, before the loops and swirls and angles had begun to add up to an image.

Their gods are not our own.

A Sistine Chapel crafted by minds that were not the minds of human beings.

A GPR scan would eventually reveal a hollow icosahedron embedded in rocks that had been deposited on a delta adjacent to the Cretaceous lake that had preserved the bones of the tiny dinosaurs and the unusually large mammals and giant crocodilians. The polyhedron had proved to have a volume of 2,427,613.6 cubic meters, roughly that of the Great Pyramid of Giza. There could be no doubt it was an artificial structure, that it had been constructed.

By whom, and by what?

After that initial survey, the government had stepped in, with its own scientists and its own methods. No one had asked Berkeley to hand over the specimens already in their care, but the Department of Homeland Security had threatened all parties involved with immediate legal action, including suspension of civil liberties, should any data from the "herpetosapient" specimens or the icosahedron be published or released to the media until further notice.

Which, of course, made this talk of a press conference inexplicably insane.

He'd only spoken with the Italian graduate student once after the expedition.

"What do you believe we saw down there?"

"I don't see any point in speculating."

"But you do speculate. You can't stop speculating."

"Maybe I don't. Maybe I never think about it."

"Sei un bugiardo . . ."

"Perché gli sarai testimone davanti a tutti gli uomini delle cose che hai visto e udito. Si?"

Jeremiah has told Aden about the finds; it only seemed fair, the way she has to bear the consequences of his nightmares and the dreamsickness that follows. Afterwards, she told him that she wished he *hadn't* told her. Not because the knowledge frightened her, but because of all the scary shit with the DHS. So, he'd apologized.

"You people," she'd said, shaking her head, "you have no idea what's down there, in the deep places."

"Probably, it's better that way," he replied, thereby declaring himself a scientific apostate.

Three weeks after Jeremiah had returned to San Francisco, he'd gotten word that the graduate student from Monfalcone had hung himself.

Probably, it's better that way, Aden.

The UC Berkeley team had been allowed to analyze what they'd taken from the object—less than six grams, all told. But the tests had been carried out by another department, and Jeremiah has never asked after the results. They've never been volunteered. The twelve pieces of permineralized bone he'd used to reconstruct the "herpetosapient" skull had been enough. It was kept in a specially-designed vault, cushioned by a nitrogen-cooled HTS, and he's only entered the vault twice since his preliminary investigations.

So, Aden . . . once upon a time, there was a string of islands in the middle of the Tethys Ocean, back about one hundred and thirty million years ago. And the animals that had migrated to these islands, or that had been stranded there when the sea went to highstand, some, the dinosaur species, experienced what biologists call insular dwarfism, but others, mostly mammals, went through island gigantism. Either way, these were adaptations to the demands of a new environment. But there was something else on that island. Likely, there was something else over the whole world, but we had no idea until that day I almost died at a hole in the bottom of the sea.

There was a civilization.

There were people . . . people whose ancestors hadn't been primates.

"But isn't that marvelous, Jeremiah?" she'd asked. "What could you have ever discovered, in all your life, that could have been half so marvelous?"

As though he didn't understand the paradox, the counterintuitive foundation of his dreamsickness and the Italian's suicide.

Maybe, Aden, maybe what we saw was a warning.

She'd only sighed and shaken her head dismissively.

They'll open it. The government, I mean. If it can be opened, they'll open it.

Two hours pass, Jeremiah scribbling half-heartedly at his notes on *Istriasauros,* Loeuff genuinely engrossed in the task of removing the hard limestone matrix from the skull and jaws of the eutherian carnivore.

"I'm going to call it a day," Jeremiah says, rubbing at his eyes after glancing at the clock. "Maybe I can beat the worst of the traffic."

"Yeah, right. Good fucking luck with that."

"Tomorrow, then."

"You're all so arrogant," Aden had said, "having gone this long believing you were the first technologically advanced race to have come and gone on this old planet."

"There was never any evidence."

"Absence of evidence is not evidence of absence," she'd said. "I don't need axioms, Aden."

That day, below the Adriatic waves, he'd stared into the faces of gods as alien as if they'd come from the stars. And it had seemed that they'd stared back. What *does* a man *need* after that?

The offer from Caltech is good, like she'd said. He could walk away from Kolone, from the scraps he'd brought to California, and he could never look back. He could *try,* at least, never to look back. He could divorce himself from the project.

Fuck celebrity.

He can make up just-so stories that the move would be enough.

Halfway across the bridge, the rain finally stops, and the sunset over the bay turns all the sky into a cascade of fire and smoke. It might be the ending of a world, that sunset. It might be the beginning.

An Element of Nightmare

W. H. Pugmire

And in this muted heart of mine
Something awakens ever after—
From lips half-drunken with her wine
An echo of her pagan laughter.
                                    —SAMUEL LOVEMAN

You came to us with storm clouds, rushing into our demesne on your frail bicycle. Because we love the sound of rain, we paid no attention as you flew into our inn and dripped upon its floorboards. You approached the bar and asked Selma if a room was available, and it was then that I turned to look at your pathetic form in its disheveled state. The long gabardine that encased you shone wetly in the inn's pale light; and when you removed its hood your damp hair hung like sodden weeds over your large ears.

"The Amber Room is available," Selma informed you as she offered you a cup of coffee. You leaned against the bar and held the hot cup with both hands.

"I can show you the way, sirrah," I uttered. You turned to regard me, and I noticed the momentary look of surprise and vague unease in your eyes. It was almost as if you had recognized me, although I knew that we had never met. Thus I, too, experienced a sense of disquiet as, rising from my chair, I reached for my hat and placed it on my dome. Clutching tightly to your red leather briefcase, you followed me out of the dining area, into the dusky hallway and up one flight of carpeted stairs, to the second landing. Entering the Amber Room, I went to the small table and turned on the lamp, which filled the room with soft golden light.

You looked around the room and nodded, and then you studied me again with your peculiar gaze. "This is Sesqua Valley, isn't it? I wasn't certain, I thought there was a huge mountain."

"She has been draped by storm clouds and thus hidden from view. Is it the mountain that has drawn you to our land?"

"No, it was poetry. My name is Ezra Klum, from Tacoma. My grandmother lived here for a few years when she was a girl in the 1940s. Hilda Young, the poet?" I pretended that the name meant nothing to me. "Long before your time, no doubt." You removed your raincoat and draped it over the room's one wooden chair.

"Have you no dry clothing?"

"In my duffle bag, tied to my bike. I parked in-between this building and the next, beneath the eaves and out of the rain. I'll fetch the bag in a moment. I wanted to ask you—" You paused and looked at me beseechingly.

"Simon Gregory Williams, your servant."

"Mr. Williams, are you familiar with a local poet, Davis somebody? You see, my grandmother used to read to me when I was a kid, and one of my favorite books was this slim purple volume of poems by this Davis guy. It was a long time ago, and I can't remember the author's full name; but Davis stuck in my memory for some reason. My mother has recently been admitted to a nursing facility, and I've been in charge of going through her things. I was hoping to find my grandmother's books, but apparently they've been given away or misplaced. You see, and this will sound weird, but I often dream of my grandmother reading me those poems, and of the tone in her voice at those few times she spoke of Sesqua Valley. Kids are impressionable,

and it really affected me, the way her voice would alter, the
peculiar light that brightened her eyes when she read those
poems. Sometimes, when she reminisced about this place, she
would hold a photo in her hand and stroke its image." You set
your briefcase on the bed and unclasped it, and when you
turned to me again I saw what you held. "I was able to find
this," you said as you handed me the small framed snap.
"That's my grandmother—isn't she young!—and that fellow is
the poet, Davis. The image is kind of faded, and some of his
face is in shadow. Are you related to him, Mr. Williams? You
resemble him."

"We are kindred. His name was William Davis Manly."

"And is that his house they're standing in front of? God, I'd
love to see it. I've become a bit obsessed with finding a copy of
his poems, and I figured the best way to do that would be try
and find this town."

"And find us you did, how clever. I doubt you'll discover anyone willing to part with their edition of Manly's poems. It's a
rare book."

"Wasn't there a pirated second edition, published in Boston
in the 1960s? I'd settle for one of those."

"You are very well informed," I answered, trying to keep mis-
chief from my voice. "The majority of those were destroyed in
a warehouse fire—or so the story goes. They're probably rarer
than the original edition." You bit your lip and nodded sadly,
and then you stepped to the small window and pushed aside its
lace curtain. We listened to the rain.

"I hope this storm is temporary. I wasn't planning on staying
long, but I did want to find that cabin and have my photo taken
in front of it, holding my grandmother's photo. Do you know
the place?"

I sighed. "It's sequestered within the woodland and is little
visited. Yes, I can show it to you. But for now you'll want to
fetch your bag and get into dry clothing. There is kindling and
wood in the stove there. You'll be quite cozy."

"Damn, that thing's ornate! Must be an antique." You walked
to the wood stove and placed your hand upon its cool metal.

"You must be exhausted after your long ride, despite your youth. Your limbs are full of aches. You'll find the bed extremely comfortable. This is a good room to dream in." I spoke in my lowest tone, and you began to yawn as you listened to my words. We walked together out of the room, and I laughed as you hopped down the stairs and rushed out into the storm.

The others studied me as I re-entered the inn and strolled behind the bar, and they remained silent as I took up a glass and began to pour certain liquids into it. I then examined a series of small bottles that were filled with powders of different hues, and choosing one I pulled off its stopper and sprinkled some of its contents into the liquid. Turning to Selma, I smiled.

"He'll return to ask you questions, and you will offer him this. It will make him dream."

I exited at a side door and stepped into the rainfall, raised my face, and let the water slip into my mouth so that I could taste the sky. With smooth language, I spoke to the storm and listened to it melt away. Laughter came from inside the inn as I turned my face to the small window of your room, which was lit with lamplight. Welcoming the purple shadows of evening, I scanned the skies, where cosmic wind pushed clouds away so that I could feel cold starlight on my eyes. Time passed, and then the light in your window went out. Reaching into my jacket's inner pocket, I produced a lean black flute and played a melody that would coax the cosmic wind. As I performed, that upper gust descended and deteriorated the clouds that had clothed Mount Selta. The white mountain stretched her twin peaks as something that lurked among them howled to heaven. I could almost see, with my wizard eyes, the particles of mutated windstorm that shook the building before me and crept through crevices at the window of your little room, where it would dream-toss your mortal mind.

The morning broke in brilliant light. Feeling reckless and restless, I entered the Hungry Place, a spacious burying ground where the first white people who came to Sesqua Town buried their dead. The ground in certain places of the valley is unwholesome, tainted by unearthly subterranean forces that rise and clutch at psyches. To dwell too long on such ground is to be despoiled by rich dementia. Being rather fond of temporary lunacy, I sometimes visit these spots of infected soil. I strolled to where the statue stood on its rough-hewn stone dais, studied its countenance, and remembered days of yore; and then I felt your shadow on the ground beside me and heard your quiet voice.

"He visited me last night." I moved so that my eyes pierced yours, and thus you beheld my bestial visage clearly for the first time. You could not conceal your shocked confusion. To your kind I look monstrously grotesque, and some human instinct within you seems to understand that I am not of your nature, but outside it. "The poet," you continued. "He recited one of his poems, one that I sort of remembered from when I was a kid. It was weird, because sometimes his voice was his own as he recited, and sometimes it sounded like grandmother's; and then sometimes it didn't sound like a human voice at all, but like a wind that mocked human speech. Dreams are crazy." You turned to study the statue of William Davis Manly that had been erected in the Hungry Place after the poet's disappearance. "He looks so much like you, although more refined." You smiled crookedly. "No offense meant, of course."

"Of course," I answered; and then I took your arm and guided you from the place. "Do you remember the poem?"

"No, I don't have any memory for words. The poem expresses a kind of yearning for far-off travel, I think; something about visiting moonlit towers of the North, and sunken secret catacombs in the East. But I remember the effect it had on me when I was young, because I've always suffered from an intense sense of loneliness. Maybe that comes from being raised by a single parent, I don't know. I've had a difficult time fitting in. What was it Oscar Wilde said, that other people are a mistake and that the best 'society' is oneself? I've always felt that, and hearing Davis speak the poem in my dream reminded me of how emotionally I feel those sentiments; for I could sense the poet's outsider nature, his feeling of being an alien among humanity." You stopped moving and stood staring at the sparkling white stone of our majestic mountain. "Funny, I feel differently since my arrival here. Something in me feels—found."

I grinned and led you into the woodland, and I knew beyond doubt that your coming to us was no accident. The seed had been sown long ago, when in childhood you had listened to the poetic lore of Sesqua Valley, from a woman who had once lingered here and whose memories colored your dreaming. To dream of Sesqua Valley is to trigger her interest and her appetite; and thus she lures you to her, in time.

You could not help but notice the uncanny nature of our woodland, the way the trees are bent, the shape of low branches that rake the pathways, the phosphorescent patches of moss that compel to be kissed.

"This place is rather creepy," you muttered.

"It owns a fantastic aura," I agreed. "Why do you smile?"

"I'm just remembering the times when my grandmother's voice would take on a mysterious tone when she was reading me poems from the Davis book. There was an odd light that sometimes darkened her eyes—it spooked me. I loved it because it confused me. I mean, it's nonsense—how can light be dark? I remember the creepy sensations of those times when I visit strange haunts like the old Granary Burying Ground in Boston. Oh, the first sight of that place gave me a thrill! I'd never seen anything like it, the slates so black with age. Standing among those antique slabs reminded me of the queer sensations I experienced as I listened to my grandmother read the bizarre poems of that purple book."

"I understand the charm of such realms," I told you, "and have searched for them in far places. There are hidden pockets on this globe, sinister and uninhabited. How one thrills to find them, to listen to their sinister secrets whispered to one's imagination. Ah—here is one before us, which few mortal eyes have beheld."

It had squatted there for two hundred years and more, protected from the elements by the wizardry that occupied it. The unpainted timber with which the cottage had been constructed was beautifully aged, and its exterior cast a spell on all who looked on it. Dappled sunlight fell through thickly tangled branches, feebly illuminating some few of the patches of moss that covered the building's slanted roof. You stared in amazement at the structure, and at the two huge leafless elms on either side of the bungalow.

"Damn, I should have brought my camera." I looked at you as you motioned to the cabin. "It's his home, where he stood with my grandmother when they posed for that photograph. God, look at it! It's like something out of a spooky fairy tale, so old and—odd. It looks like it rose out of the earth, doesn't it? Isn't it strange, the way some houses can affect your sense of fear? Ha, my imagination's working overtime! The very air seems bewitched."

I walked to the cottage and pushed open its door. "You must cross the threshold of your own volition," I informed you, as your eyes revealed that you were becoming more and more aware of the spectral elements that wove into your psyche. I have often mocked the inadequacy of the human brain; and yet, it has the power to mold one's personal actuality, potently. It was, after all, this mortal energy that awakened us children of shadow and mist, in our realm outside your reality, and helped us to locate a pathway to your sphere. It was now our turn to show you another path—to the Outside, that place that has so touched your imagination through the mystic poetry read to you as a child.

Stealthily, you advanced toward the cottage and stepped onto the rough, mossy rock that served as doorstep. You looked, for one moment, as if you would not enter in; but then the perfume of the inner air wafted to you, caught you, entranced you. You crossed into the low-ceiled chamber that was illuminated by numerous candles, the scented wax of which helped to perfume the place. Your sense of wonder ignited and succumbed to the sovereign influence of Sesqua Valley. You then noticed the figure who sat, unmoving, in one dusky corner of the room, like some figure from a book of fairy tales. The shadows of the place at which she sat seemed almost to weave into the texture of her black skin, and when she began at last to move and work her spinning wheel you saw that she was unclothed from the waist upward. You listened to the faint sound of her moving wheel and tried to comprehend the garment on which she worked. I could almost hear your heartbeat quicken when she rose off her stool and floated to where you stood.

"Will you help me into this?" she asked, as one breast brushed against your arm. You clasped the thing she held to you with fingertips, and marveled that a woven garment could feel so light as to seem almost nonexistent, as though it were spun of web and shadow. Something in its quality made you feel so wonderful that you wanted to press it against your face and wash it into you flesh; instead, you watched as the black woman, her back pressed against you, wound her hands into sleeves and then used those hands to lift her length of red hair, into which you buried your face. Wasn't it fantastic, when you closed your eyes, that an optical illusion whirled before you, bright particles that might have been stars dancing in some heaving heaven? We could not help but chuckle at how you whimpered when Marceline moved out of your embrace. She turned to smile at you, and you admired the perfection of the breasts that remained uncovered. Rank human lust polluted the atmosphere as your teeth began to grind.

I raised my hand so that a glimmer of light flickered momentarily at one place, and your noise transmuted as your eyes fell upon an item that was on a nearby table. Moving like a dreamer, you approached the table and took up the purple volume. When you brought the book to your nostrils and drank its old aroma you almost purred. Your eyes had adjusted to the dim lighting of the room, and thus you were able to read when you opened the volume to a middle page.

> You wheel above me in some haunted space
> And plot to pull my eyes into your dance.
> I feel your cosmic cyclone on my face.
> I lose myself within some phantom trance
> That would disintegrate my firm foothold

With which I am cemented to this sod,
And transport me unto that region told
Of in the tomes that speak of Elder God.
I see the Elder God within my mind,
That Beast that dances in-between the stars.
I'm drawn to secret path on which I find
The Revelation that mutates and mars.
It is a ruin into which I ride
In celebration of the bleak Outside.

A feminine voice quietly joined your speech as you breathed the poem, and you raised your eyes to glance at Marceline as you quoted the final lines. It perplexed you to see her mouth unmoving while still some lovely voice accompanied your own, and it came to you that this voice was more like memory than actual articulation.

I said, "You seem quite familiar with that sonnet."

"Yes," you answered, "my grandmother read it to me often. I asked her once about this thing, 'the bleak Outside,' and she would tell me the most outlandish things, in a voice that trembled as fever burned her eyes. I think that was when I knew I wanted to write poetry myself, although I've never had the nerve to show my stuff to anyone. I love poetry—it's transporting." You stopped and thought. "Transporting—that was a word I learned from grandmother, when she whispered of the Outside. You'd think the description of it would arouse a sense of horror or fear, but I found it alluring, far more enticing than dull reality." You then removed your jacket and hung it over a wooden chair. "Not much circulation in here, is there?" you said, smiling as you strolled to one small window, at which you frowned. Instead of windowpane you found what appeared to be a surface of highly polished obsidian. We watched as you raised one hand at the black surface, as you shuddered at the chilliness that your hand encountered there. Marceline moved to you and placed her hand over your own. She guided your hand to the window, and through it, and laughed at your yelps as you touched the bleak Outside. She reached through the

window with her other hand and then pulled out, in your con-
joined hold, an ebony substance that simulated the texture of
Marceline's skin of jet.

"Let me take that, Ezra, and place it in my lap as I ready my
wheel. Yes, the instrument is antique. We like olden things
here, and drink their aura of past eras. You are a soul who cher-
ishes the olden realms, we know. Let us clothe you, now, so as
to enter the eldest of all realms."

"You have been nourished," I spoke, "by the spell of wonder-
ment that spills from the spoken poetry of a child of Sesqua
Valley. That magick has rooted in your soul, and thus you
sought and found us. We understand how delicious it is to be
kissed by the Outside, and how provocatively that passion
plays within mortal blood and pumps audacity into the human
heart. Oh, the longing—the dark elements that bloom in solitude and form a perfect approval of what to those who lack
imagination is hideous." I moved to you as I spoke and wound
my talons in your hair. I breathed upon your eyes as I began to
undress you. Nude, you watched the witch rise from her wheel
and hold to you the newly fashioned robe as I backed into a
shadowed place and brought forth my flute. You seemed to
understand Marceline's twinship with the cosmic void and with
them that howl within it, and you tilted back your head to wail
as she draped her fabric around you. As you bayed, you
reached with one trembling hand for the book of Manly's poetry, which you pressed to your heaving chest. Bringing the reed
to my mouth, I filled the room with enchantment. Bending to
you, Marceline kissed your mouth, and then she guided your
lips to her perfect breasts, which you worshipped with your
tongue. And as your mouth tasted her sorcerous essence, your
ears reverberated with the woman's impious laughter. Your
eyes became lost in the black texture of her necromantic hide,
that husk of darkness in which she kneaded you, until you felt
like some lunatic god, passing through an element of nightmare wherein you stalked among the stars, the book of unholy
poesy in your eternal hand.

The Reeds

Gary Fry

I'm going to take a walk around the area, to see if there's anything I fancy painting." David paused, swallowed awkwardly, and then asked, "Do you fancy coming with me, Helen?"

His wife didn't look up from her work on the kitchen table. "I've got this page to finish," she replied, her voice no less strained than it had been back in the city.

"But your deadline isn't for a few days, is it? I thought a bit of fresh air might do you . . . well, I mean, might do us both good."

"I'm *fine*," Helen added, the emphasis on the second word implying anything but.

David sighed inwardly, examining his wife stooped over yet another translation project. He'd hoped moving to the country-side might result in a reduction in her freelance workload, but here she was, two weeks on, still pulling in commissions. She was in demand, of course—fluent in three foreign languages—but that wasn't the point. After his early retirement package, they no longer needed the money. But Helen definitely needed to relax.

It was still early days, of course. Their dream move to this cottage would surely serve them well in the future. David retreated from the kitchen and headed for the front door. He let himself out and then breathed in crisp autumn air. He looked around, listening. There were no yobs in the streets, no surveillance helicopters buzzing overhead, no distance sounds of police cars or ambulances rushing to scenes of human distress . . . There was just blissful silence.

Well, that wasn't quite true, David thought as he commenced walking down the garden path, into the quiet lane, and then along a fringe of woodland. Listening carefully, he heard many sounds: birds twittering at a distance; the gentle whistle of a breeze; animals at furtive work in the undergrowth. The smell here, too, was very different from what he was used to. No longer the stench of burned petrol or frying fat from convenience diners. Now he could detect only a lively scent of moist tree bark as well as the heady aroma of rich vegetation. The sky when he looked up was a clear fragile blue, with not a hint of city smog or dissipating exhaust fumes. After reaching a farmer's gate, he clambered over its stile and then found himself within audible range of gurgling water. He headed that way at once, swinging his arms with unfettered joy.

He'd earned all this, of course, and shouldn't feel guilty, despite still carrying a working-class chip on his shoulder. Three decades in teaching, trying to persuade unruly youths of the virtues of social science, surely granted anyone pardon from whatever cosmic forces ruled the universe. Smiling, David glanced up at a mist-ensnared sun. Despite his wife's recent breakdown and resignation from her own teaching post, life wasn't too bad. And Helen would soon get over it; this place had power to heal, he was convinced of it.

He'd reached a narrow stream whose banks were muddy slopes boasting no plant life. Indeed, the whole area—extremely flat and shielded from prying eyes by the surrounding woodland—was characterised by an uneven ratio of mud to vegetation . . . with the notable exception of a circular patch of head-high reeds, to which David started walking. He guessed that he was now about five hundred yards from his new home and that he'd be able to reach this area more quickly from his back garden. But he'd figure all that out later. Right now, he was too intrigued by the patch of reeds.

It was about twenty yards in diameter, to judge from this perspective. The many thousand strands of grass were taller than he was, at a modest five foot nine. They waved back and forth with stately indifference, caught in a soundless breeze. Insects too small to identify busily flitted the stalks, as if relying on their seeds for sustenance. After David paced forward, hesitating several yards from the reeds, he stooped to examine shadows clustered among their lower halves. He thought he could see about three yards inside the mass, where darkness grew legion and concealed the place's secrets. But what secrets could such a humdrum place have? Then he spotted several dead shrews curled up on the earth, but that was far from unusual. The soil around them appeared muddy and moist, perhaps residual seepage from the nearby stream. There was a sharp scent of sulphurous soil. But again, there was nothing strange about this. The whole thing was simply a patch of untended grass growing out in the wild.

But why did David feel uncomfortable in its presence?

Pacing backwards to get a better look, he recalled a concept from a school lecture, about the way humans attempted to get "maximum perceptual grip" on the world. They adjusted their bodies until sights, sounds, and smells around them could be satisfactorily assimilated. This had always worked for David, even when his wife had been driven to desperation by thugs in her classes. He'd recently taken to standing apart from Helen, not threatening her with familiar intimacy. Thirty years of marriage had resulted in a number of habits, and physical contact was one, particularly after discovering, in their early twenties, that they were unable to have children. But when Helen had suffered a nervous collapse, she hadn't wanted him near her. He'd sensed this rather than having to be told it. Intuition had left him mindful of her difficulties. He'd been unable to recognise her lately, but surely that was only until she pulled herself together, adjusting to shattered beliefs she'd held for most of her life.

The reeds swayed back and forth, continuing to resist David's anxious gaze.

Then a cloud covered the sun and the world grew dark.

The problem was that Helen was physically incapable of bearing children.

They'd discovered this early in marriage, after a few years spent trying to conceive. Medical tests had proved conclusive, and although Helen had taken it badly—she came from a close family and loved children—unbreakable youth had sustained her career as a schoolteacher.

Later in life, they'd considered adoption and even fostering, but mutual commitment to their jobs had preoccupied them, and the years had passed quickly. Working daily with children had served as an acceptable alternative, offering enough inti-mate contact to satisfy their parental needs.

But then school life had grown far worse.

After starting work in the 1970s, David and Helen could recall days when youngsters had had respect for authority and had been eager to learn. Working in inner-city schools had eliminated any idealistic expectations concerning pupils—most had come from poor backgrounds and struggled to study—but at least they'd tried and had been grateful to people who'd helped them. But more recently, children had developed a disdain for education and a genuine dislike for teachers. The profession simply hadn't been the same.

David, more robust than his wife following a less than cosy upbringing, had tolerated daily classroom battles. But Helen, barren in middle age, had been pushed too far. A girl in her German class had slapped her across the face, and despite claiming to have coped after this episode, a few weeks later David had found his wife crying at home, sitting on the floor in the corner of their kitchen.

With no offspring to support, there'd always been plenty of money to invest and when David, at fifty-five, had decided last year to take early retirement, Helen—three years his junior—had reluctantly agreed to do the same. Their move, from urban sprawl to rural splendour, had occurred soon after, and surely now only pleasure would follow. The nearby village apparently

had a number of children-based voluntary groups to get involved with, and David had attracted his wife to the area by alluding to these. What on earth could go wrong?

That night, after David's curious experience near the reeds, Helen nearly forgot to take her sleeping pill. She'd been pre-scribed medication several months ago, but this made her so woozy that David had to ensure she took it when she was sup-posed to.

He stepped into the bedroom with a glass of water and found his wife half-asleep with a lamp on beside her. She looked strained under the shade's arc, her face lined with turmoil. This wasn't just a recent phenomenon, David realised; it had been building over years, a culmination of the devastating news they'd failed to address as callow youngsters, little more than children themselves.

David roused his wife, trying not to let her hands touch her breasts under the thick material of her nightwear. When she grumbled an incoherent response—for a mistress of so many languages, these phrases were surprising gibberish: "Fhtagn . . . Yog . . . Sothoth . . ."—he pushed the pill between her lips and then made her to wash it down with water.

Reassured that she'd now sleep—she'd lately developed a habit of sleepwalking, a revival of a childhood tendency—David crept across the room to shut the curtains against a preternaturally quiet evening.

He could see the patch of reeds from here, bathed in silvery moonlight. *Well, how about that,* he thought in a not entirely comfortable way.

The following day, while Helen finished her latest translation project, David gathered together his painting gear and returned to the stream he'd located yesterday.

He'd always had a creative streak but had had little time to develop this while teaching psychology, sociology, and philos-ophy. He was nonetheless keenly aware of debates about the limitations of science and how art could illuminate things empirical investigation struggled to quantify. He was a great reader of novels and listened to much classical music—Bruckner, Mahler, Strauss: the cosmic masters—but he'd chosen to pursue painting. He was very much an amateur, but eager to practice now that he had time to do so.

After reaching the stream—no, he should be honest and admit that it was the patch of reeds he'd come to paint—he set his gear on a muddy plateau: stool, easel, and flask. Then he sat and mixed a palette of paint—greens, browns, and blues—and started sketching the phenomenon ahead.

He'd arrived today a different way, cutting through his back garden and across a field to this one. It was milder this morning than yesterday, with less damp in the cool air. Nevertheless, a breeze continued to sweep across the area, causing the reeds to writhe with ruffling haste. Shadows stirred among the multiple stalks, like too-thin creatures, eyeless and vague. Once David got down the outline of the thing, he started filling in with broad brushstrokes, attempting to capture its solidity without losing its *aliveness*.

Meanwhile, he reflected on his wife back at home. The truth was that her failure to engage in these early dalliances in their new community troubled him. They hadn't made love in months, either, mainly because she'd been heavily sedated or irritably standoffish. At such times, he felt unable to do anything right, and she certainly held few reservations about reminding him of that. The present distance between them was saddening.

He glanced up at the reeds, comparing what he'd captured on canvas with the real image. It was a bad fit, the *thereness* of the thing evading his repeated attempts to elucidate it. The way the breeze rifled through its shimmering strands made David feel almost queasy and hardly lent him confidence about his burgeoning artistic abilities. The more he looked at the reeds, the less he felt able to paint anything at all. The grass appeared to dance beyond the grasp of his bewildered mind. He thought of a phrase he'd recalled yesterday—"maximum perceptual grip"—and realised that, with the possible exception of Helen's recent behaviour, he'd rarely felt less in control of anything.

David had had a similar experience with Magic Eye books back in the 1990s. These had served as a useful way of teaching children how the brain made sense of the world. But he'd never been good at seeing the images hidden amid so many dots; he was too reflexively aware, and understood that people like him struggled to free up their psyches for such tasks. Whenever he'd managed the trick, however, he'd been conscious of how a chaotic realm could snap into focus, revealing meaning where previously there'd been nonsense . . . and a troubling nonsense at that.

The patch of reeds put him in mind of this. Nevertheless, despite observing the thing for more than an hour now, he'd still failed to achieve the coherence that accompanied success with a Magic Eye illustration. This was how a short-sighted person must feel when they put on spectacles, a sudden resolution of tension-evoking fragmentation . . . But it simply wasn't happening for David right now.

He got up from his stool and moved closer to the reeds, pushing aside in his mind further thoughts about Helen. The grass swayed back and forth, as if mocking him with its aloof indifference. At the foot of several stalks, David noticed that the dead shrews he'd spotted yesterday were gone, replaced by scattered bones so tiny they could only belong to such ineffectual rodents. *Someone's inadequate lunch,* he thought, imagining tiny hands with nothing like fingers snatching at the mud in which their dwelling was rooted. That would surely account for so many small grooves in the ground, where a darkness as hungry as the place's tenants shifted uneasily, like glutinous liquid on the move . . . But then David glanced away. It must be an after-image of staring too long at the canvas that made him see red dots—nothing at all like avaricious eyes—lurking amid the writhing reeds.

He had to leave. He'd begun to feel physically ill. Retreating to his painting instruments and drawing in mouthfuls of autumn air did little to alleviate his sense of having been violated by the patch of grass behind him. After packing up, he turned away involuntarily and offered one final look at the thing . . . but the noise he heard from deep inside—a hideous creaking and rasping—sounded nothing like children sniggering.

Or at least, that was what he told himself.

An ex-colleague called that afternoon to ask if David would like to meet up in the city the next day for a few beers. David, watching Helen preparing dinner, reluctantly agreed, and after hanging up he went across to his wife to help cook the chicken and its accompaniments.

"I'm not an invalid," she replied, her eyes averted while adding stock to the bird's juices.

"I know that. I was . . . just being courteous."

"Then bugger off and leave me to it."

She hadn't sworn much before her breakdown. The more David witnessed of the new Helen, the less he liked the old truism about their former profession: *Teachers learn more from pupils than pupils ever learn from teachers.* He shuddered to think what damage that abusive child had done to his wife. And even though Helen had probably just been joking with her sharp rebuke, he still felt slightly affronted.

"Well, I won't be a burden to you tomorrow, anyway," he said, a tad stiffly.

"Why's that?"

As she hadn't appeared troubled by his comment, David quickly added, "Off out for a few with Kenny. Back on our old stomping ground."

"How will you get there and back?"

"Bus there, taxi back." He was touched by her concern—at least she still felt something for him—even though she'd spoken as if he were a child. "It's not as if we can't afford it."

"Yes, we're rich indeed," she finished, and then, with a stiffness of the shoulders he was unable to decode, she continued making their meal.

Later, while eating the meat and boiled vegetables, David showed his wife his painting. Now that it was dry, he thought it looked even less like what he'd attempted to elucidate, but surely that was more a consequence of his limited skills than anything else. He could ascribe his curious thoughts earlier, while standing beside the writhing reeds, to stress and strain.

Helen sat looking at the picture for a long minute, captivated in a way that exceeded its merits. Then she glanced up at David, her eyes bright and eager.

He grew hopeful; he hadn't seen her look like this in months.

"Where *is* this?" she asked in a voice full of borderline awe.

Keen to encourage any renewed interest in the world on her part, he talked about the patch of reeds and how it could be found by taking a shortcut through their back garden. But he held off mentioning all his unsettling impressions. It would be unwise to project his own pathologies onto those of his wife; life was hard enough at the moment.

After another few minutes, while neglecting the meal she'd spent hours preparing, Helen ran one hand across the painting, as if its manic frenzy of country colours were still wet and could be conveyed to the face she then fingered with a mother's delicate touch.

"Their eyes," she said, looking fixedly at the picture. "Their burning red *eyes*."

David was confused. *Red,* he wondered? He hadn't prepared any paint of that colour and certainly couldn't remember cutting himself or developing a nosebleed. Nevertheless, after getting up to examine his work over his wife's rigid shoulders, he noticed what she clearly had: tiny specks of red lurking amid the deep shadows of the reed, each doubled up with only millimetres between them, like onlooking demons.

Tiny demons, he meant. The reeds were as tall as an adult, after all. And the faces—if that was what they were, rather than just accidents arising during haphazard composition—were placed at half that height.

They were no taller than children.

The truth was that he couldn't remember much about painting the reeds, nor about pacing home across mud. If he'd suffered a nosebleed—and he had been prone to them in the past—that would account for the specks of red on the painting.

He went upstairs that night without considering Helen and her condition. He now had his own worries and felt needful of a good night's sleep. Tomorrow he'd experience some merciful normality, talking over beer with an old friend about cars, sport, and investments—all the usual stuff for men of their age.

You forgot about children, a tiny voice said in his mind. *Kenny has kids—hell, the whole world has kids. But his are grown up and at university—a genuine source of pleasure to him and his wife. Sure, he's still heavily mortgaged and has no way of retiring early, but is that such a large cost to escape a world that can do . . . do . . .*

David silenced these thoughts and then closed the bedroom curtains against that distant patch of reeds. It looked as if a mist had settled in the area, most obviously above the swaying grass. A stream of moonlight dramatised the whole scene, and small shadows clawed at its fringes, like little hands reaching out in desperate hope of more to eat.

After waking far too early, he felt alone . . . and soon realised why.

Helen was gone from the bed.

David got up quickly and switched on his bedside lamp. The first thing he saw was his wife's sleeping pill; she'd forgotten to take it, and in unsettled confusion the previous evening he'd failed to remind her.

After strapping on his dressing gown, he rushed into the rest of the cottage, calling his wife's name like that of some wayward child. After realising that she wasn't in any of the other upstairs rooms, he descended to search the ground floor.

But there was nothing. Just his muddy boots in the hallway and . . . the front door key hanging in the lock.

David stepped forward and tried turning the handle. The door opened freely. He was unable to recall locking up the previous evening, but his mind was so unsettled that this was hardly surprising. Nevertheless, the implication was clear: Helen had gone outside and David would now have to go and find her.

Back in the bedroom, he dressed within minutes and then descended again to strap on his muddy boots. His wife would be horrified if he'd trampled muck in the house—this was another symptom of her depression: obsessive cleanliness—and so he went quickly outside, leaving the door unlocked behind him. He didn't want Helen to find the house inviolable if she returned before he did, and he was certainly unconcerned about intrusion from others in the area. After all, nobody lived within at least a mile.

Red dots in his mind—just residue from sleep, of course—sent him around the back of the property and then to the foot of the garden, where a shortcut would deliver him to the field leading to the reeds. That was surely the place to which Helen had ventured. David recalled the brightness of her eyes when he'd shown her his inept painting yesterday. She'd looked rapturous and had asked about something she'd appeared to see in the picture . . . something with burning red eyes . . .

But he was being foolish. His wife's condition was getting to him. He was susceptible because, as his thoughts the previous night had suggested, he held the same regrets about their childless lives and might even still be repressing what Helen had been unable to.

Rushing through undergrowth and across damp grass, he finally reached the reeds, whose writhing bulk was illuminated by clear moonlight. The dark made the place no more easy to get a satisfactory perceptual grip upon. The breeze was stronger now, pushing through countless stalks like a parent's hand ruffling a beloved child's hair. There was a whisper like ineffectual gratitude, the sound an infant makes following a healthy feed. It pained David to continue observing, his gaze flinching away after a long minute, during which the hissing movement of the thing clawed inside his skull.

But then this sound was broken. Something moved among the reeds, tramping David's way. The swaying back-and-forth noise was replaced by crunching footfalls as whatever occupied it paced through. The grass parted, shadows squirmed, and then a figure emerged, carrying a large metal object that glittered in the moonlight.

It was Helen.

Standing just outside the circle of reeds, she held a pan from their kitchen, which David noticed, after approaching her, was full of stripped chicken bones, leftovers from their meal the previous evening. The carcass had been picked clean, and if other food—vegetables, stuffing, gravy—had also been in this receptacle, the ravenous diners had made even shorter work of that. Its silver gleamed, as if licked clean by hundred impish tongues.

David glanced up at Helen and for a moment was unable to distinguish her from the churning background. She looked vague, insubstantial, elusive to observation . . . but then he achieved perceptual grasp and saw her as she was: disturbed and vulnerable; fodder for entities with few compunctions about exploitation.

From his eye corners, he thought he saw movement—a flash of reds, like distant brake lights moving. He looked around, among the deep shadows of the reeds, but saw nothing of any import. Then he glanced up, at mist coiling way above the grass, which resembled a nebulous ladder leading to or from the stars, its rungs little more than ragged wisps, with a stream of moonlight forming the uprights . . .

He quickly returned his gaze to his wife and asked, "Helen, what are you *doing?* Why are you out here?"

"Je m'assure que les petits aient à manger," she replied, her eyes staring beyond him, at a patch of sky above their home where darkness gestated like a foetus in a womb.

David sighed with unnerved exasperation. When they'd first met at university, Helen had often spoken to him in foreign languages. In those days, this had been a form of affection, and he'd found it sexy. Ever since then, whenever they grew intimate together, she'd sometimes express herself in this way. It was only recently, after she'd begun to do this more to conceal than reveal her feelings, that he'd wondered if she'd always hidden emotions behind the linguistic device.

Je m'assure que les petits aient à manger, she'd said. And what had this meant? He knew it was French, but had only a basic, get-by-in-cafés grasp of the language. He guessed that "je m'assure" meant "I'm making sure." And would "petits aient" translate to "little ones"? The last word—"manger"—was obvious: "fed."

I'm making sure the little ones are fed.

Now disturbed, David asked, "You're not making sense, Helen. Come on, let's get you home."

But as he reached to take her arm, she squirmed again in his peripheral vision, as if writhing like reeds. Then she added, "Sie haben anderen so viel beizubringen."

That was German, and David's command of this language was a little better. He was sure his wife had just said: *They have so much to teach.*

"Possiamo adottare e imparare da loro," Helen went on, but David's Italian was hopeless and he had no idea what this unsettling statement meant. But he no longer cared. He was now shocked to notice that Helen was dressed only in her body-length nightdress. Her feet were bare and squelched in mud as he tugged her away from the swaying reeds, back towards their secure new home.

The footprints he saw among hers on the ground were surely nothing of the sort; they lacked the usual structure, bearing too many toes. They were also smaller than any youngster's had any right to be, however hungry they'd become and keen to draw into their lair anyone offering sustenance.

"I don't know what to do, Kenny."

"Show me your picture again."

David handed over the painting, feeling self-conscious about others in the pub observing it. He'd brought it along on a whim, not knowing what his friend would make of it. Kenny was an art tutor at the city college and always had much to say about a variety of issues. David guessed that he'd hoped the man could help.

Looking up from the incomplete sketch, his friend said, "I can see how Helen might have interpreted the red specks in the way she did. They *do* look like eyes lurking in there."

"I know. But nothing could have been further from my mind. I didn't even mix a red, let alone . . . well, see anything looking out at me."

"Okay, so they're just random blotches, which your wife has interpreted in an idiosyncratic way. It's like a Rorschach test, isn't it?"

David was familiar with the psychoanalytic technique used to elicit material from patients' subconscious minds. And what did Helen seeing small people in his painting of the reeds imply?

At that moment, Kenny anticipated his thoughts. "Are you worried about having no children and how this might be affecting your wife? I know you're both ambivalent about that."

"We *used* to be ambivalent, mate," David replied, the beer freeing him up for voluntary exposure. "But I'm not so sure these days. I think that now we're too old even to adopt, the cold truth is hitting home. Helen was desperate for children; her own family was very close. Me, I grew up in a pretty cold household, so I've never had the same desire for offspring. But I wonder whether I'm just fooling myself. I mean, isn't that what the purpose of life is—to procreate? To keep the species going?"

Moonlight tumbled in through the uncurtained pub window, the same moon that had brought such mysterious life to the circular patch of reeds close to his new home. But then David suppressed these treacherous impressions and listened carefully to his friend's response.

"I don't know, mate," Kenny replied, raising one self-conscious hand to his face and stroking his beard; the ring of gold around his third finger shone like a curious eyeball. Still committed to paid employment, the man looked jaded and beaten. "Having children has its charms, but it's one hell of an expense and responsibility."

"Oh, I don't romanticise it," said David, but secretly wondered whether this was what he'd always done. However rationally one regarded the inevitable pressures involved in being a parent, didn't a private part of all childless people remain hungry for its inconsistent joys? And wouldn't many exchange their relative wealth and security just to sample what it was like?

"Hey, that's odd," Kenny said, snapping David out of his impromptu speculative reverie.

"What is?" he replied, glancing up to observe his friend looking closely at his painting again. Kenny had his face almost pressed up against it, as if it were a Magic Eye illustration he was trying to solve.

"If you stare really hard at the areas behind those red dots, you can see . . ." The man hesitated, pulled away, took a needful slurp of his pint, and then went on: ". . . yes, you can see small figures, dark and bony."

"Bugger off, Kenny!"

"It's true! It must be a trick of perspective or something . . . Oh, but no, it can't be." Kenny hesitated, took another gulp of beer. Then he finished, "I mean, what on earth could remain alive while remaining *that* thin?"

David was unable to see the figures his friend had alluded to in his picture, but as a taxi took him home, he had more important things on his mind.

His academic training in social science had offered him many hints about life, if few certainties. In psychology, indisputable facts were rare, but even so, he'd always suspected—his perspective informed as much by experience as by book learning—that his wife had been overprotected as a child, and that this had led her to think that families were havens in such a world of woes.

Helen was egocentric, slightly manipulative, and not always in touch with reality. David had first observed this after they'd married, especially when he'd expected to have a say in their long-term plans and had been frequently overruled. He'd always acquiesced to her sulky character—passive-aggressive, he guessed it would be called in these jargonised days—and had loved her enough to accept the paths she wished them to take. She was sexy and charming, quite a catch in comparison to his bespectacled, studious persona. He'd felt lucky to be with her, especially given his affectionless upbringing. And when Helen had learned that she was physically incapable of bearing children, he'd become bonded to her forever.

As the taxi stole along country lanes, David glanced out through one window, at stars scattered across heaven like fierce beacons. He guessed that in the grand scheme of the universe, one childless couple meant nothing important. But he'd never bought into the idea that human beings were cosmically insignificant. It surely depended on perspective. To whatever sentient beings lurked beyond the stars and regarded the earth with outrageous indifference, he and Helen would mean very little. But to the two of them, and to their friends and what remained of their families, they meant a great deal. Even jaded, acerbic Kenny had expressed regret at their woeful lack of offspring.

Wouldn't they exchange their relative wealth and security just to sample what it was like? David thought again, and after looking through the taxi's window, he saw that writhing patch of reeds, bathed in strange, new light.

He thought he'd just seen something moving inside the grass. After telling the taxi driver to stop short of his home and then paying the fare, David recalled his wife sleepwalking the previous night and wondered whether she was suffering a similar episode. Once the vehicle had departed, he mounted the stile alongside the lane and then dropped into the field, his smart shoes sinking into mud. But he wasn't concerned about that. It was nearly midnight and chilly with incipient winter. If Helen was out again in the dark, he'd have to get her back inside, where it was warm and secure.

And childless, added another treacherous voice in his mind, but he ignored that and cut across the rain-sodden field to the reeds. Although the powerful moon shone down like some cosmic revelation, he saw nothing in the area but churned-up mud. He examined the ground in front of the reeds and noticed tiny scrapings, as if someone had taken a small object to the ground and carved these innumerable grooves. But who in their right mind would do that? And if they had, what instrument had they used? The markings looked deep yet narrow, each terminated by multiple spikes like untrimmed toenails. They led all the way back to his silent home.

David had reached his back garden before he noticed the things that couldn't be footprints die away. But that might be because his lawn was green and full, and not because whatever cosmic intruders had emerged from the reeds had turned back to their temporary habitat. He quickly crossed the garden to the rear door and tried its handle. It was locked. But on the path running around to the front of the house, he spotted more erratic shapes, countless scrapings of mud.

If the things had come so far to enter the building, had they been beckoned to the main entrance by its only dweller?

As well as prints on the path, there were moist, hip-high markings on the walls, as if whatever had shambled so erratically this way had used the cottage's sides for support. Maybe malnutrition and hunger had rendered them all unsteady; perhaps they'd moved in such haste to receive more of the sustenance with which their newfound nurturer had tempted them here . . . But David shouldn't dwell on such crazy ideas. It was his wife who'd had a breakdown, and he must be strong for her.

The front door was unlocked. He entered immediately, seeing more muddy footprints and handprints—little more than blobs from narrow bones, surrounded by the delicate flecks of too many febrile toes and fingers—all over the hallway. Some ran towards the kitchen, and he quickly followed these. After switching on the light to overrule the property's darkness, he noticed nothing untoward . . . except for several new paintings he could only assume Helen had executed while he'd been out with Kenny . . . and before the *things* she'd tried to elucidate had quietly come visiting.

She'd used dark colours—blacks and greys and a vibrant red for their eyes. David wondered whether his wife, bereft of children and crushed by this truth, had attempted to lend them a human aspect: although their bodies were merely streaks of emaciated flesh and angular bone, their faces resembled those of people, with toothy mouths for devouring and oval slits for nostrils. But it was their eyes that captured most of David's attention. He simply stood there, silent and transfixed, observing the pictures. The eyes were bright red and as large as fruit, like hellish beacons from another world.

He dropped the paintings and rushed back into the hallway. In his peripheral vision, he saw kitchen cupboards open, each with little or no food inside. Perhaps the *things* had been allowed to eat, before receiving more intimate ministrations upstairs. The rest of the muddy prints—so sickeningly unnatural that none endorsed the human quality in Helen's pictures—covered each riser and zigzagged below the banister. David advanced up the staircase, his heart hammering hard. After reaching the light-less landing, he listened carefully, thinking how cruel it was for the universe to deny him and his wife the ego-enhancing gift of children, while being happy to use them as surrogates for crea-tures who treated their kindness as a trigger in some nefarious campaign. He stepped up close to his and Helen's closed bed-room door . . . and then heard noises coming from inside.

"Let's repeat again, everybody," Helen said in a singsong voice usually reserved for communicating only with children. "La terra orbita intorno al sole."

Despite being spoken in Italian, this was easy enough for David: *The earth orbits the sun.*

Then Helen added, "Nous descendons tous des singes."

He was able to make short work of this, too; his mind was now sharp and focused. In French, the comment had meant: *We're all descended from apes.*

And finally his wife said, "Unsere Köpfe sind durch das Unterbewusstsein regiert."

German this time, but he'd come across most of these words during his psychological studies: *Our minds are governed by the subconscious.*

Christ, she was teaching the creatures about the three great scientific blows to human egocentrism. And what did that say about her state of mind? Had she now given up the desire for offspring of her own? David recalled thinking how self-absorbed his wife had always been. And was this turn against humanity and the need to tell the Others about it the darkest symptom of her illness?

David was unable to speculate further because another noise had just emerged from the room. It sounded like a whisper of breeze-strewn reeds, all hisses and rasps and creaks. He heard other noises in there—harder sounds that resembled words: *"Fhtagn . . . Yog . . . Sothoth . . ."*—that failed to prevent a final notion from entering his faltering psyche: *Teachers learn more from pupils than pupils ever learn from teachers.*

Red light spilled from the gap under the door. There was a sound of febrile limbs scuttling around the mistress of language. Then, as that whispering grew stronger and began speaking weird truths in an alien tongue, David leaned forward and opened the door.

And stepping inside the writhing room, he didn't know which role he was about to play: teacher, therapist, or father.

Crawldaddies

Steve Rasnic Tem

Thirty years after his mother had taken him out of Rayburn Twist, Josh discovered that getting back in hadn't gotten any easier. If anything it was more difficult now that the new highway bypassed that forgotten little appendage of the state boundaries. With but a small population to answer to and no businesses to speak of, the state of Virginia had apparently decided to stop maintaining the two remaining access roads. One was taken out by a slide impossible to repair—half a mountain collapsed into a dying lake and no place to adequately support a bridge. The other was mostly gravel and clay with occasional craquelure patches of ancient asphalt.

You might be able to travel it on horseback, but, not having a horse, Josh was making the journey up from the highway on foot carrying a loaded backpack. Arlene had dropped him off at a wide spot in the road.

"What if you get hurt? Do you really think they'll have doctors up there?"

"I've got first aid supplies, and I'll be careful. People are always getting hurt; I imagine the locals have ways to take care of them. Even if it's just a mountain witch-woman with some nursing skills. At least I've had all my shots." He tried to grin, but it didn't help. Arlene was mad, and scared. Josh had made sure his affairs were in order, his life insurance substantial and paid up. But that was not the sort of thing to bring up now.

"You think the locals would lift a finger to help you? A stranger? An outsider?"

"I was born there, honey."

"You left when you were five."

"Well, I'll make sure they know I'm family right away. It'll help."

She gave him that familiar look that said *I love you, but right now it's more like I'm saddled with you.* He kissed her and said, "Tell Trace I love him, every day I'm gone."

He knew it wouldn't help things to say more, so he opened the door of the old station wagon and stepped out onto the gravel curb. The whole car rattled when he slammed it shut. When she got home she'd find money in an envelope and a note telling her to get the car fixed up, or buy a new one if she preferred. A woman by herself with a toddler needed a reliable car.

Josh knew she might take the cash and the note as some kind of goodbye, a confirmation of her fear that he had no intention of returning. He did intend to return, after finding out all he needed to know—he just wanted to make sure they were taken care of just in case. But nothing he could do or say would ever reassure her. That had always been one of the truths of their marriage.

Another truth was that whatever it was in him that repelled other women—some untraceable scent, some hormone vaguely sensed, some hidden anatomy or geometry or psychology—somehow attracted her. He'd never been entirely sure if that was a good thing for either of them.

Descending the embankment from the highway to the traces of old road below was made easier by a well-used series of makeshift steps dug out of the ground and lined with flat stones. Clearly some of the locals had jobs or family somewhere off the mountain.

Trees shielded much of the way from whomever might happen to gaze down from the road. Josh soon found himself by a small creek that ran alongside the old broken road as it wound its way higher up into the hollow between two steep ridges. Compulsively he kept looking down into the water, but had no idea what he might be searching for.

Small creatures scuttled along the bottom of the stream where it curved slightly, partly sheltered by the bank. "Crawldaddies," he whispered.

Nothing he had seen until that moment had triggered any memories. He'd only been five, after all, his world restricted to patches of bright color, lines of dramatic movement, the occasional mostly forgotten game or song, the stronger flavors of food, the scents of the adults who carried him. But "crawldaddies," the word evoking both a strange delight and a stranger terror, echoed clearly through the years.

Until her death the previous year his mother had still talked about how that had been his "baby word" for crawdads, the name these mountain people used for crayfish, those smaller relatives of the lobster who lived in the fresh running waters that didn't freeze to the bottom. His mother thought they were disgusting because they didn't care whether the plants and small animals they ate were alive or dead. Now he thought of them as dark and ugly but good with lemon juice.

Before she died they'd talked about his need to come here, to know what he'd come *from*. Her own memories were failing her, and she'd never been much help filling in the details of his distant past, "we all best just move on" being her standard answer. But even through the fuzziness it was obvious the idea made her anxious; she thought the whole notion was bad business. "Why'd you want to go there?" she asked from her bed, pushing her head up to look directly at him, even though it was an obvious strain. "Nothing to see there, 'specially now. We left all that to find something *worth* seeing."

"It's where Dad grew up, and I hardly know a thing about him. Even looking at his picture I can't really remember him. And frankly, Mom, you haven't been much help over the years."

"Not much to tell," she rasped. "He grew up there, and he stayed there. That place is pretty much all he was. I wanted better for you." She started crying.

"I'm sorry, Mom. I know you did the right thing for us. I have a life—I'm not sure what I would have had there."

"If you go." She lay back down with a deep sigh. "It's your daddy's hometown, but you won't be seeing him there. You'll want to feel some—disappointment—over that, but don't allow yourself to give in to it. He'd only make a mess of things. Believe me."

"You mean he's still alive?"

She blinked, shrugged. It was the last time they talked.

So Josh knew next to nothing else about the place. What research he'd done in books and on the Internet told him nothing about the people, but a little of the local geology. As in much of the region, beneath a few feet of rich earth was a recurring sequence of beds including coal, sandstone, shale and clay, and marine limestone. In many spots the limestone directly underlay the coal. The deep-shaft coal mine, Clyburn, just on the other side of the ridge, had given out early when the difficult landscape had made it too expensive to mine further. The remains of a couple of the old coke ovens were apparently still there, the tipple, the ruins of the company store with advertising still hanging on part of a free-standing wall. Some hiker had posted photos on the Internet.

Then there was some information about the uniqueness of "the twist" itself. A diagram showed how several lines of strata had been pushed up and turned into something resembling the warped corner of a tissue, the folds turning and growing tighter as they entered the twist. Reference was made to the huge volcanic forces required to create such a phenomenon, and its inherent instability. Mountain streams had percolated through the porous limestone layer, creating a random series of caverns and tunnels. Even though the whole thing was encased in millennia of dirt and rock debris, the nature of the twist was still evident in aerial photographs.

In the midst of all that lay Rayburn Twist where Josh was born and his father had lived, and perhaps still did.

As Josh got farther up the old mountain road he found fragments of old houses deserted and torn down, pieces of wall left standing or blown apart by growing trees.

So far he'd seen no attempts to preserve anything. Halfway up the mountain he stopped to rest at an abandoned house by what had become no more than a path with occasional asphalt flagstones. He sat in the doorless doorway for benefit of the shade, but not trusting the roof enough to venture in farther. He ate an orange and a protein bar, washing it down with a bottle of water. He liked oranges and wondered if he'd be able to buy any in the Twist. Probably no bottled water, but he'd keep the empty bottle and borrow someone's tap, and pray that he didn't poison himself. More protein bars were unlikely—he'd try to stretch the supply he had.

Before he left he did a quick check inside. One large room and a small bathroom—that was it. He watched his step. He could see the bare dirt cellar through gaping holes in the floor, and he kept looking up to make sure insects, snakes, or roof beams weren't about to fall on him. The little house had been stripped—no cabinets or fixtures, no doors, no pipes, and all the copper wiring yanked out. There was a small rusted child's wagon twisted up in the middle of the floor. It looked as if it had been run over a few dozen times.

At first the long dark streaks looked like tire marks, as if a motorcycle had driven around the walls as in a circus act. But by the time he'd left he'd decided they were some combination of scraping and rubbing, almost as if something large had been trapped here, or a group of such things, and had struggled to get out again.

Now and again the creek wandered back into view. Dark came early to these shadowed ridges, and he had no desire to travel the path at night. But there was something so compelling about the proximity of the stream that he just couldn't keep himself away, and he wandered off the path again.

The stream here ran narrow, constricted by the large rocks on either side, but it ran deep. Moss and plants and layers of dead specimens of each caked the banks. Beneath all that was leaf mold several inches thick. He looked down into the clear waters. But not completely clear. Here and there a trail of fog, or light smoke, marbled the stream. Still, he could see most of the bottom, and the scuttling creatures there, so like rough bark or broken rock suddenly given legs. He went down on his knees and then to his side to get a better view. The crawdads ignored him, going about their business.

The water smelled vaguely of metal, or maybe some chemical. But deeper than that—and it surprised him that he could actually perceive layers of smell—was something old and long dead, bathed in the waters. So much for trusting the water supply. But Josh didn't think it was dangerous. Just different, perhaps, from what he was used to.

His eyes kept straying back to the crawdads. They were certainly ugly brutes, festooned with an unsortable battery of legs, and pincers, and miscellaneous appendages whose purposes he could not begin to fathom. He used to draw them when he was a kid, using crayon and pencil stubs or whatever he could get his chubby little hands on. It disturbed his mom, who didn't understand how he could have remembered them so clearly, and who thought they were horrendous looking (which is what he liked most about them—they were bold, they had presence, they were *scary*).

But what seemed to disturb his mother most was how he drew the crawdads. Instead of segmented legs and pincers he gave them a forearm, biceps, elbow, and shoulder. Human arms, big, inflated arms for the pincers, little ones for the antennae. He'd bend the arms in ways human arms weren't normally bent. Sometimes he would add little tattoos to the arms: an anchor, a boat with sails. He would paint the crawdads different colors: forest green, pale yellow, blood red. And when his researches taught him all about swimmerets, those small appendages along the edges of the thorax, he drew those like long, wiggling fingers.

Crawdads liked it dark, cool, and isolated during the day. Josh had understood that very well. Sometimes he'd lie under his bed all afternoon and wouldn't come out even when his mother called him. Sometimes he would sneak out of his room during the middle of the night and steal a piece of cake out of the fridge or a banana off the counter. Sometimes he'd even take something that tasted bad, like a piece of raw fish or a spoiled dish of vegetables he discovered at the back of the fridge, because crawdads couldn't always be picky—they ate what they found. He'd tear the food into tiny little pieces with his fingers and stuff it into his mouth.

During the long summer afternoons he would hide under the covers and try to sleep, imagine that his skin was molting. He would grow to many times his size in his dreams and he would destroy his room.

He passed no one else on the trail; no one was out working, or even lazing about, no voices echoing down the valley. No more houses, either, not even abandoned ones. Now and then something would rustle through the brush alongside the trail, animals of some kind, although whatever wildlife was native to the place was staying out of his way. Maybe because he was a stranger.

He reached Rayburn Twist, near the top of the mountain, around sunset. If there used to be a paved road through the town there wasn't one now. A wider passage of compressed clay and traces of wheel ruts with weeds growing out of them. He didn't see any cars, or signs of their recent passage. No one said hello, but he saw several women perched up on the weathered grey porches, staring down at him with somber, broken faces. He waved, but they didn't wave back.

Josh thought maybe it would be better to find some place more official than a private residence. If not a mayor's office (he couldn't imagine there was one), at least a store. At a store they might talk to him—even here a store owner might want to encourage business.

A couple more houses with women on the porches. One old lady waved and he waved back. He was beginning to wonder if this was a town of all women when he saw an old man in a rocker sitting on the ground outside his house, a shotgun across his lap. The man looked stuffed, except for the rocking, and Josh didn't try for his attention, turned his head and kept walking.

A little girl peered at him from beside a tree. Her face was as pale as something out of a cave, her eyes grey in her dirty face. "Is there a store?" he asked, smiling broadly. She didn't smile back but she pointed.

The battered old building looked like all the others except for "Store" painted in faded black letters beside the front door. Three men standing at the counter turned to look at him. On the wall behind them a lot of shelves displayed very few goods—a few cans, some boxes, a few bags. Most of it looked aged and out of date. On the counter itself, however, were some fairly fresh-looking bags of meal and beans.

"My name's Josh Morgan. I lived here a long time ago, with my mother—"

"Emmett Morgan's boy." One of them stepped forward and studied Josh. His face was a series of flaps of skin, as if it no longer fit his skull. He raised an arm that looked too long and too thin for his body. "You look like him, or the way he was before."

One of the other men chuckled. "He means before he got old. I'm Andrew, Josh. We're cousins."

The third man laughed then. "Hell, Andrew. We're *all* cousins up here." And then all three of them laughed.

"My father, so he's alive? He's living here somewhere?"

They stopped laughing then. "Don't live here, but he checks in from time to time," Andrew said. "He checks in."

Josh was taken into one of the houses where he met dozens of people, all introducing themselves as cousin this-or-that, or aunt this-or-that. Most of them were elderly, his mother's age and older. The women looked sad even when they smiled. All the men seemed to have that same skin condition—which was too much of it, finally, as if they'd lost a large amount of weight very fast.

"So, I reckon you'll be seeing your daddy while you're here?" one of the women asked, which caused the rest of them to quiet their talking for a time.

"If he's around," Josh replied. "If not, maybe some of you could tell me something about him, and about the rest of the family too, if you would. My mother never told me much."

"Your *ma* never should have taken you out of the Twist in the first place, especially with you being a son in the family." The others tried to shush the woman. "'Specially when you ain't reached your majority yet."

"Majority? I'm thirty-five years old."

"Think you're an old codger, do ye?" one of the old men chuckled. "Well, maybe out there. But up here, you're just a *naup*." A little girl giggled, and Josh realized then that some younger people were in the room. He looked around and saw them hiding behind the older women and back against the walls, little kids and teenagers with sullen, red, and pock-marked faces. He saw, too, the pale young girl who had first pointed the store out to him. They nodded at each other.

There was a meal at some point, and another round of introductions, and a sweet drink home-brewed from roots and berries that made him sleepy. But he was already tired, having hiked most of the day to get up there. He didn't even remember going to bed.

When Josh got up the next morning there was no sign of anyone else in the house. He searched the rooms that were open and knocked on those doors that were locked, but there was no answer. He figured they'd all gone out to jobs and chores. A couple of the women in the house were quite old, but he supposed up here everybody was expected to work. They had a lot of mouths to feed.

He stepped outside. The air was warm, but there was a taste of fall. Smoke hung over the trees up the rise ahead of him, at the top of the Twist.

The pale young girl from the day before suddenly appeared at the edge of those trees and waved.

"Hey there!" he cried. "You must be Cousin Something-or-other." The girl just smiled and waved some more. "Is that smoke I see?"

She looked back up the hill in the direction of the smoke. Then she turned around and motioned him to follow her. She kept her distance, but she stopped periodically to make sure she didn't get too far ahead of him. Finally they cleared the trees, and the hill continued a few more feet, ending in two great lips of stone poised as if speaking to the sky from the top of the mountain. The creek bubbled out of there, and steam floated above it.

"So this is where the creek starts?" But she had run ahead again, and was pointing at something at the top, mounds of smooth clay by the stone lips.

He walked up to her, and she backed away. He looked down.

They were the ends of enormous clay tubes, or maybe smokestacks, maybe chimneys, that went down into the water as far as he could see. Water filled them, but if he looked closely, and God knows he didn't want to, he could see that dark shapes swam just beneath the surface in each one. Around the edges were large pellets of mud, like bricks, that had been worked and smoothed. And several bits of shattered armored plate, like thin flat sections of bone, worn and scratched and frayed along the edges.

Something seemed to move inside him, as if a rib or a muscle had slipped free. It wasn't painful, but it felt dreadful just the same.

That night there was another huge supper. And more of that sweet root drink, which he was beginning to see as some blend of dessert and liquor. It left him soft and sleepy and barely able to move.

He didn't even notice the old people leave. Suddenly it was just him with the younger ones—the sullen teenagers; the anxious-looking twenty-somethings; that shy, pale girl whom he'd come to think of as his only friend in this strange homeland. There were even a few babies in the mix, squalling and fussing in the arms of the older children.

Andrew appeared in front of him. "You're oldest of these, I reckon, so you're in charge of these youngins, but not for very long, I 'spect. Visiting day, you see. Won't be long now."

When Andrew left, the pale girl looked over at Josh, but not smiling. Josh tried to get to his feet but couldn't quite manage it. "Visiting day? Did he say visiting day?"

He heard the rumble. The whole house shook. Some of the smaller kids fell onto the vibrating floor. Josh thought of how much he missed Arlene.

A dozen or so came in, but they more than filled the room. Some of the little kids were crying "Crawldaddies! Crawldaddies!" and squealing with delight.

He kept thinking how scared his own son Trace would have been, and how much he missed him.

And they did have human arms, or what might have once been human arms, too many of them, and they walked on them, and some of the arms did have faded tattoos. They moved as if they had broken backs, their heads hanging down as they crawled over the furniture and gathered their children up in their enormous daddy arms. "Crawldaddies! Crawldaddies!" the children cried, and even Josh found himself whispering it as he felt the changes beginning inside, as his own father held him up in his powerful backwards Daddy arms.

Three Dreams of Ys

Jonathan Thomas

Survivor's guilt is ridiculous, for crissakes. Mom was ninety, smoked a pack of clove cigarettes every other day, fried breakfast, lunch, and supper, and took pride in spending $10 tops on a weekly liter of vodka. Miraculous that she held out so long.

Too bad ornery spirit didn't inhabit self-reliant flesh. Till she died my life was on pause, and the transparency of this to us both couldn't have enhanced her sunset years. It must be my view of death as positive outcome that eats at me sometimes, like now, as I roam Breton tidal flats instead of sizing up the hotel where I contemplate sinking my inheritance.

The tidewater in this plaza-sized basin has dwindled to a silty channel. Skiffs, dories, and shallops lie tilted on glutinous sand till incoming sea refloats them. They describe an unruly horseshoe within the hoofprint outline of the basin. Sure, the collective tonnage of small craft rests stably atop the slime, but that's no guarantee one wrong step wouldn't mire me knee-deep.

Besides which, the pickings are slim for any self-respecting beachcomber. Maybe motorboat traffic discourages shells and other marine oddments from accumulating. On this blank slate of a beach, the merest suggestion of a half-buried nub, casting a thimble's worth of shadow, looms conspicuous. It lures me out between the semicircle of boats and the shallow cleft of the channel. Water oozes up around my loafers as they indent potential quicksand.

I'm already queasy at prospects of engulfment before I bend low and start digging, and churn up the dizzying ferment of seafloor muck. I gag haplessly as grubbing fingers free a tetrahedron the width of outspread hand. Its angles and heft suggest I've salvaged a chunk of cornice. I stop to swab off gunk with a handkerchief only after slogging back past the cordon of high-and-dry vessels.

Stubborn grains cling, but the wet sheen on bluestone helps me distinguish traces of carving. Over how many centuries have ocean currents smoothed bas-relief designs into tentative line drawings? On one face the letter S has been rotated in series to form a pinwheel, and alternating spirals and triskelions fill the loops of each letter.

The adjacent face startles me when I recognize it is, in fact, a face. Oversized eyes are round with pinpoint irises, as if in goggling trance. The nose has dwindled to a tiny bracket, like an upside-down upholstery staple, and the mouth is a somber hyphen. Sufficient hatch marks rise from crescent forehead to suggest bristly hair continuing beyond my fragment's broken edge.

No matter how I tilt and squint at these faint incisions in April sun, they won't resolve into a familiar style. I should have paid more attention in Art History class, not that it would have materially aided my two decades hawking real estate. I give up and drop my arm. Maybe ask at the hotel if similar rubble has ever cast ashore.

Quavery, singsong French spins me around. "Please, do not discard that! I know where it is from!" Despite my bilingual upbringing, lilting dialect takes some seconds to process.

Has black-clad codger been sitting on the nearest dory all along, practically a silhouette merging with dark hull? His thin jacket flaps in the nippy breeze. A patch of sun on one knee reveals pinstripes in woolen trousers. Hat with circular brim and round, shallow crown puts me in mind of country priest or ancient Roman peasant. I try to soft-pedal skepticism as I shout back, "How can you tell where it's from?"

He waves cavalierly at unburied treasure. "I would know that face anywhere!"

My skepticism lingers. The codger must be thirty feet away and would need sharpshooter vision to spot abraded features that fade into random scratches at arm's length.

But meanwhile, where are my manners, forcing a pensioner to strain vocal cords? I tread closer till his patronizing smile unsettles me. Gap teeth lend him the mordancy of a jack-o'-lantern. "Your little *objet trouvé*," he volunteers, "it is from Ys, of course!"

"From where?"

Now the pensioner gapes in disbelief. "You are here in Douarnenez and know nothing of Ys?"

"Should I?"

He feigns mild umbrage at my ignorance. Or is he feigning? "Ys was the most splendid city ever in Brittany, the richest, the oldest. It became great eons ago when the bay itself was young, not yet fully grown." He nods oceanward. "You could have stood here and seen dry land out to the horizon, and on that horizon were the shining bronze and silver roofs in the port of Ys. Douarnenez was among its beggarly suburbs."

He rattles off fairytale spiel like a tour guide. "But in later centuries, every king had to rebuild ramparts and dikes as the waves invaded and then surrounded their city, whose foundations came to be fathoms below the surface of the bay. Finally men could not prevail against God's will. Before the birth of Charlemagne, the pitiless sea destroyed the palaces, the counting houses, the temples, and plunged them into the deep. Some blame a spoiled and wicked princess for tampering with the sluice gates." He shrugs as if recommending I digest this one detail with a grain of salt.

Sounds like Atlantis envy to me, a Chamber of Commerce ploy to enliven dull boondocks with contrived lore. Saying so to earnest informant, though, would be cruel. Or will he slyly parlay his lecture into a plea for cash, as seems the case whenever characters accost me? I proceed on a sensibly even keel. "Shouldn't I surrender this artifact to the authorities? Isn't it considered state property?"

He sagely shakes his head. "The government does not believe in Ys."

"So keep it? Is it supposed to be lucky?"

His narrow gaze appraises my piece of legendry. "It is too big to go under your pillow. Still, you should dream of Ys if you put it under your bed. This I learned from my grandmother."

"Have you had such dreams? What was the city like?"

The codger purses bloodless lips. "Nobody believes the dreams of a penniless fisherman like me." A line, if ever I heard one, to tug at the heartstrings of a soft touch.

Let's save us both some time and shilly-shallying. "I appreciate this information and your generosity in giving me this relic. But it's more rightfully yours, and I'd rather not be an ugly American. What would you like for it?"

At first the codger regards me quizzically. What the deuce am I talking about? Then he gets it, and blows up at perceived insult. My apologies, my appeals for calm make no dent in the wall of bellowing indignation. I back away, prattling futile amends, reluctant to turn around lest he boil over and charge after me. Halfway up rocky path to the cliff-top hotel, I check on his position. He hasn't budged. Perhaps waiting for the tide to raise his vessel. Is that his laughter amidst the almost human cackle of gulls, or simply the gulls?

The vista from the hotel ranks among its less perishable assets. It occupies a headland, cloverleaf-shaped in aerial view, that probably won't erode away and deposit it next to Ys for another century or two. In that respect, the hotel's a sound investment.

The site presents another underutilized advantage. Research indicates tourism on the upswing in Brittany, and the Auberge des Falaises, at its slight remove from the village, should attract upscale guests averse to mixing with the hoi polloi.

However, that fails to factor in the current owner and his larval complexion, earth-tone wardrobe, and midlife dejection plainer than mine.

Architecturally this is a diamond in the dirt. Sheer façade, narrow multipaned windows, a row of pointy dormers in a steeply pitched roof cry out for allusions to "petit chateau" and "manor." Sadly, such grandiosity is moot behind tarnished green eaves and maroon walls mottled with white spackle patches. Blatant disrepair, dead rhododendrons out front, and a "For Sale" sign beside rusty-hinged door aren't helping. A less demoralized hotelier than Monsieur Kervigo might have summoned the wherewithal to cease operations, but here I am, with the staff and facilities all to myself.

E-mails in flawless French spelled out why I was coming. Yet on my arrival, reminding Kervigo I was the prospective buyer rated the blandest acknowledgment, as if I'd declared myself a pipefitter or a dentist. How depressed he must have been not to brighten at golden chance to unload his depressing business. And ever since, I've been left on my own, like any other lodger. No, I won't be soliciting his opinion about my fistful of enchanted debris.

My first afternoon on the premises, I begin to tally deficiencies inside and out. Obsolete furnace, leaky plumbing, rickety fixtures, threadbare carpets, mold in the vents top the list after cursory once-over. The kitchen's little more than a pantry and couldn't handle half-capacity in the dining room, even if can-openers do most of the prep work. None of the employees qualify as spring chickens, and they mope as if to one-up the boss's apathy. Not a curtain rod or banister but would flunk the white-glove test.

I'm too discouraged at the number of shortcomings in pocket notepad to put them in perspective by sorting the cosmetic from the profound. At suppertime I brave the dining room, where the staff and I at separate tables partake of ratatouille with no seasoning beyond the nagging tang of metal. Hard ciders, then snifters of calvados, help blunt my critical edge. They also break down resistance to nudging bluestone in among the dust bunnies and grit under creaky bed frame.

I hunker beneath multiple tatty blankets against April drafts and unsoberly challenge the bluestone, "Okay, what have you got for me?" Should I credit the power of alcohol, of suggestion, of an emergent wish to be elsewhere? After negligible gap in my awareness, the drab, fusty room switches to dreamland. I'm up and pacing along, still in the dark, yes, but moon and stars suffuse brothy sea mist around me with a wan glow.

My legs follow preset course, as I take stock as best the atmosphere allows. Faint in the befogged distance behind me is a monumental stone wall, high as an arena's, in which a stitchwork of iron plaques optimistically binds a crack together. Ahead of me is a gleaming zigzag boardwalk, less a street than a gulch between houses.

The houses, whether of quarried blocks or vertical planks, under clay tile or stoutly thatched roofs, bulk large as mansions. Their eaves, riding rugged beams well past gable ends, form dramatic overhangs. Stone piers and timber stilts elevate many of the foundations. The milky damp hides details of any ornament, yet accentuates the glitter of silver leaf on walls and on the boardwalk, which changes to flagstone pavement on a sudden upslope. I neither meet nor hear anybody. Where am I if not in Ys, a metropolis curiously devoid of nightlife? Or is the city deserted?

Toward the hilltop, houses and pavement peter out, and the incline merges with irregularly spaced stone buttresses against a precipitous white mortared wall. Like the iron plaques, they come across as *ad hoc* reinforcements against generations of floods or structural fatigue. The mist thickens with increasing altitude, concealing the scale of this edifice, though its eminence hints it's a citadel.

No gates or windows compromise the blank mortar corresponding to the first and second floors. Higher up till they're consumed in fog, a smattering of glassless narrow windows is scattered randomly, like slots in a punchcard. They affirm the city isn't abandoned because yellow light flickers in them all, and in one at the lowest level, a woman, to my chagrin, peers down at me.

The mist veils her like gauze, but as she brushes luxurious sable hair aside and leans out with supple confidence, I decide she's young and gorgeous. I can just distinguish dark criss-cross lacing down the center of ample bodice in translucent gown. She stretches a slim, bare arm into the night and beckons me with leisurely forefinger.

I'm not ready for such direct attention from a vision of loveliness. At the back of my mind hovers the knowledge I've been dreaming all along. I grab at that knowledge, to awaken with a jolt under motheaten blankets. The room now smells of stale kelp, instead of stealthy mildew.

My coastal excursion east to Carnac is theoretically multi-purpose, to flush cobwebs and fantasy from my brain, to better acquaint myself with the region, to preview the joys of tourism in which I might soon be immersed. This entire trip is also, by default, my closest approach to a vacation since Mom went into death-bound tailspin. At day's end, I exit Carnac with both food for thought and culture shock.

The sprawling Neolithic alignments occupy more village territory than its shops and homes, and are too incredibly much to absorb on one visit. About a dozen standing stones abreast, ranging in size from hassocks to upended Winnebagos, troop by their thousands for more than a mile, through scrubland, lawn, and glades, across a stream, and onward. Those glades allegedly contain the country's last wild-growing woad, the weed with which naked Celts stained themselves fetid blue before battle.

I rove the landscape overwhelmed, but only in part by the monuments. This is the off-season, though some Euro equivalent of Spring Break is pointedly underway. There must be three tourists for every menhir, climbing, bunny-hopping, or hammering for mementoes on these pillars of bygone sanctity, of superhuman devotional exercise. In French, German, English, Dutch, they jabber at companions to snap their photos, and collectively the loudmouths are like a polyglot flock of starlings. Do I really want a career catering to entitled Eurotrash?

By municipal parking lot where the alignments begin, a whitewashed cottage with slate roof and stubby chimneys serves as visitor center. I yearn to complain about the yahoos abusing cultural heritage, but the personnel are too busy selling them postcards, key rings, snow globes, and T-shirts—and anyway, what could they do?

Similarities of Carnac to other farflung archaic achievements like Stonehenge I dismiss as facile, coincidental. Not necessarily so, argues a flyspecked diorama in a neglected corner. Six millennia back, when megaliths were all the rage, a maritime Atlantic economy was already well-established, circulating goods and ideas between Portugal and the Hebrides. And peninsular Brittany was like a natural fulcrum, situated to tilt the balance of trade for the whole shebang.

Cruising west to the hotel along shoreline Route D781, I open my windows and endure chill winds to sniff salt water and pine groves. I try to picture this pastoral, sparsely settled geography as the center of a world, and wonder where its urbane elite could have dwelt, and speculate, Why not Ys? If Brittany was the hub of a coastal trading network, Ys, in a sheltering bay close to land's end, could have functioned as its lynchpin. If Ys existed, that is.

The name itself suggests profound antiquity, in common with others eroded by epochs of repetition into one brief syllable, like Aix or York or Ur. And why shouldn't oblivion have swallowed the reality of Ys along with most of its name? Volcanoes erased memories of Pompeii. Tremors drowned the glories of classical Alexandria and Jamaica's swashbuckling Port Royal. Venice and not Ys might be the esoteric footnote today, had "sea change" and engineering knowhow ordained differently.

What a fabulous realm I've rebuilt from one battered chunk of rock! Still, speaking intellectually, I believe no more in Ys than in any other useless dream. Vis-à-vis my dealings here, it's as irrelevant as anything under sludge at the bottom of a gulf. I've come too far to let Monsieur Kervigo delay negotiations further.

Tonight's supper of savory crêpes and mussels demands a level of freshness and skill evidently reserved for special occasions, a beloved saint's day or someone's anniversary. I fairly insist my host join me at table, and to offset impression I'm a pushy philistine, I attempt small talk about Carnac, about the stunning amount of prehistory there, and inquire after Neolithic remains in Douarnenez.

He blinks as if clearing film from his eyes and snaps, "Some things are older than dolmens." I'm both gratified and taken aback at prickly core beneath passive skin. Without expanding on cryptic remark, he excuses himself to preside at the employees' table. Any pretext for our celebration dinner goes unannounced.

I retire on the logy side, thanks to rich and heavy Breton butter cake and cheese platter and chalices of Bordeaux. Upstairs, misgivings that my piece of Ys would have vanished prove unfounded. The pillow's been fluffed and the blankets tucked in, but of course nobody's cleaned under the bed.

From her exquisite hand to my lips, she feeds me orange segments one by one, as if they're precious, exotic commodities. Yet they're scrawny and bitter, and despite the seductive touch of her fingertips, I almost say No thanks, I'm too full, as if I'm dreaming with the same midriff bulge I took to bed, as if it's minutes later in the same continuity. But no, mine is a dream self with appetite intact.

Roman affectation vies with less obvious provenience. My couch is firm like a futon and most resembles a prop from *Satyricon*. Silk cushion on shallow-angled headrest supports my neck while the lady lounges on a backless chair with its legs of crisscrossed ivory tusks. Blue glass bowl of oranges, grapes, and pomegranates rests on delicate checkerboard of a table. Terracotta lamp impersonates a gliding crow and hangs at the end of a chain bolted into massive ceiling beam. Between couch and narrow window, a beehive-like censer balances on a three-footed pole.

Aromatic haze from oil and incense can't obliterate every whiff of kelp, but obscures much of water-stained, flaking murals, excepting a naked archer with antlers, herons preening on the shoulders of bulls, a girl astride a dolphin. Thanks to the haze, I've also yet to see my affectionate hostess with pinpoint clarity. But she projects a grace, a glamour, a nobility radiant as the pure white of her sleeveless gown. How can she not be a princess?

Since I'm well aware this is a dream, I don't bother questioning why royalty would dote on me, or how I gained entry to this sanctum. The slipshod logic of REM state must also account for Dark Age lady's acceptance of my casual American attire and her impossible understanding of modern French when I look from my muddy loafers to her sky-blue eyes and ask, "Are you a princess? Is your kingdom older than the dolmens?"

She nods pensively, stacks leftover orange wedges on curly peelings, and slides another checkerboard table from under the platform of my couch. The straw upon marble floor bunches up around spindly table legs. She hunts among the clutter on the checkerboard for a petite soapstone figurine, which she presents as if it certifies eons of venerability.

Its workmanship is both painstaking and crude, and it's worn and polished like my bluestone. Quizzical, bald homunculus squats with knees up and wide apart, and arms snake under them to assert gender by tugging open hyperbolic vulva. Porn accessory or fertility fetish? As if they're mutually exclusive? A token of age immemorial, yes, but of an age sordid and debased. I quickly replace figurine on the table.

If my revulsion shows, the princess is too refined to acknowledge it. She's busy pouring blackish wine from a sleek bronze flagon, its spout a swan's long-necked head, its handle a leaping hound. Our cups are of burnished grey metal, each fashioned into three repoussé faces, side by side, beetle-browed, imperious.

I sit up as she passes me a cup and raises hers in wordless toast. I reciprocate and, before a trial sip, reflect warily on metallic bouquet that hearkens back to hotel ratatouille, and that I hope comes from cup and not beverage. But the princess smiles beatifically as if she's tasted nectar, prompting me to forgo caution. I'm instantly sorry. The consistency is syrupy and granular, the flavor at once sour and oversweet, as if honey could remedy spoilage.

To drink more is unthinkable. As is the prospect of offending my hostess. I plant feet on the floor, nod courteously, mosey past the censer, and pretend to swig again while gazing out the window. Maybe put my cup on the sill and forget about it? No, not yet anyway: she's already by my side.

"It's a wonder of the world, isn't it?" I gesture toward the city outside. She nestles into me, and full-body contact persists as if she couldn't share the view otherwise. Her point-blank scent blends sweat and musk. I'm not positive I like it, but it arouses me all the same. Still, even in a dream, to smooch her on raw impulse would be déclassé, so I focus on Ys from royal vantage.

The mist has condensed to a fine, lucid drizzle, in effect stripping the town's cosmetic veneer. Starker moonglow demotes the luster of silver leaf into moisture beading up on pitted surfaces or leaching out of cracks or glistening on streaks of luminous fungus. And ominously, a thin skin of water covers the boardwalks fanning out from the foot of citadel hill. Rising tide must seep in through chinks in towering barrier. How bleak to witness an Ys antediluvian in terms of more than showing its age.

Her probing gaze draws me like a flare in the dark. I haven't noticed until now she only comes up to my shoulders, as if regal presence made her seem taller. She reads and mirrors my melancholy, her gaze sidelong toward urban decay, and she murmurs, as best I can discern, "Nisudo ardanny groz." Is that Breton? Gaulish? Something more remote?

She takes another demure swallow from metal vessel, and her uplifted face may be seeking or dispensing sympathy, I can't tell which. To perch my unwanted cup on windowsill at this solemn juncture feels apropos, self-serving or not.

Her smile is bewitching, bidding me forget sorrow, live for the moment. With businesslike ease, she tugs at crisscross lacing to loosen her bodice well past functionality. One expert hand exposes right breast and cradles it, and as it nudges my shirtfront, resignation leavens her irresistible smile, as if she fulfills a sad duty.

Fierce itching distracts me. A titan among fleas is battening on my forearm. I slap it off and wake sitting up at bedside, in the middle of furiously transcribing noblewoman's lament, vandalizing the lacquer of wobbly nightstand with ballpoint pen.

Borderline erotic dreams of mythic city, as foretold by moody fisherman, I can handle in stride. To find a new guest at breakfast, however, strains credibility. He hunches frowning over a brie omelette no greasier than mine, and his head hangs too big for his torso, barrel-chested though he is. A furrow like that on a saddle spans his bald crown and competes for prominence with wicked black monobrow. I can't quite ID the cartoon character he resembles. Nobody memorable enough to click.

Newcomer petulantly shoves substandard meal around his plate, then hollers for the sluggish waitress. By the time his breakfast is inedibly cold and mine's a memory, she's fetched Kervigo, who leans inert against the nearest table through most of diatribe about abysmal cuisine. Just as well the coffee goes unsampled. Finally the customer, patently more riled the longer Kervigo listens unfazed, raves, "I have friends at the Departmental level who will hear of this!"

The owner then erupts from lethargy to laugh in the face of outrage. "If you have such important friends, what are you doing in this dump?" Kervigo's temper, in fact, brings to mind a happy dreamer's after rude awakening. He slouches off to leave cartoonish adversary sputtering.

What kind of twerp expects gourmet cuisine at a self-professed dump, anyway? The same kind, I reckon, who'd try enlisting me as sympathetic ear. I keep my head down, pretending to enjoy wretched coffee, and with pen I repeatedly scribble "Nisudo ardanny groz," as if it meant something, on green paper placemat. Just think, that hotelier with the shitty attitude could soon be me.

The placemat's almost out of space before I reconsider. In spite, or actually because, of this customer's ill-humor, I ought to engage him, as practice for the heroic forbearance I'll have to cultivate daily in Kervigo's shoes, an order of magnitude greater than realty sales required. Too late. Not only has the complainant decamped, but Kervigo has returned with a plastic basin to clear the dishes.

I'm nowise tempted to bring up my business with him. Annoyance still fuels his body language, and he might well spew vitriol at me for aspiring to buy his dump. Meanwhile, why am I loath to admit aloud my waning interest in the place? Then our sightlines lock, dammit, and someone has to say something. To my relief, he intones, "I am sorry to startle you." He arches an eyebrow. "You were dreaming, perhaps?"

At mere mention of dreaming I'm even more tongue-tied, for no conscious reason, than at outlook of buying the inn. I have to clutch at any change of topic. "Do you speak Breton?"

"No, not fluently," he concedes straightaway, as if I haven't jumped the conversational track.

"Nisudo ardanny groz?" Rising inflection conveys wishful thinking this is some of the meager Breton he knows.

Sallow brow crinkles as he shakes his head. I tear off a strip of placemat with several renditions of the phrase and thrust it at him on the off chance my accent is the problem.

He curtly glosses my scrawl and remarks, "An acquaintance of mine may be of assistance. You and I will meet later." He voices no interest in where or how I encountered this text, as one ordinarily might. Has a dream state begun to pervade my waking life here?

Hiking the couple of miles to Douarnenez proper for lunch might contribute to a new grip on normality, a reality check. Maybe I'll even hit upon a better hotel for sale. I make it as far as the cliff's edge where footpath descends to the beach. The tide is out, boats are marooned, and Kervigo is giving my scrap of placemat to the volatile fisherman, reseated on oblique dory.

I can't verbalize why I don't want them to see me. I just don't, as if they're in nefarious cahoots. I whip around and retreat to the inn—all the better, I tell myself, to intercept Kervigo with the fisherman's answer ASAP.

Another item for my list of demerits at Auberge des Falaises proves inescapable. Aside from eating, there's nothing to do here, nary a shuffleboard nor boules court nor library nor even stash of board games. Nothing helps the already quiescent staff while away breaks and downtime. Like a pinball down the drain, I meander into the dining hall, to partake of the same mushroom soup as the early birds among the crew. Nobody else acts bothered by a soupçon of mold, a smell akin to that from crusty heating grates.

Kervigo slinks in, and I welcome excuse to put spoon aside. He surveys my dubious fare askance. "You should have received bread. I will reprimand those at fault." He lays my green shred next to red luncheon placemat. "No easy job, but undoubtedly, this translates, 'We sink beneath the cross.'"

What? How does prayerful sentiment fit with soft-core scene I experienced? I'm slack-jawed with bewilderment.

"I am instructed to explain that Christians forbade trade with pagans. And that sea walls crumble without silver to uphold them." Kervigo as disinterested messenger gives me a second to absorb that. "You have spoken before with the person who provided this information, yes? Therefore, he felt sure you would understand."

That made one of us. Blindsided by this glut of revelation, I remember my manners only after a foundering silence. I thank Kervigo and request he thank our mutual acquaintance for me. Kervigo asks if he can be of further service.

Here's my golden ticket to a serious discussion about buying him out. Now or never, likely enough. In his blasé eyes I glean, rightly or not, that we're on the same page. Yet I'm not surprised, and neither is he, when instead I impose on him for a hard cider. He retrieves it and I drink alone, shunning even the company of wandering thoughts, as I fear they'd lead to grief about my mother.

The bottle's empty, my mind's an enduring blank, and I've pushed the soup into the position of stone-cold centerpiece when fiftyish waitress with frizzy blondish hair and sagging

waxen features lumbers over. She smacks a plastic basket of
quartered baguettes in front of me and departs, with the elo-
quent scowl of someone rousted at 3 A.M. for nothing.

The alternative to plain bread is no lunch at all. I finish it off
and decide a nap is in order. Or more to the point, I'm at a loss
for what else to do. Maybe I should leave that up to the
princess of Ys.

Her bodice is laced up again. We stand apart in separate con-
templations of the vista, as if we've retracted into shells. My
triple-faced cup still rests on the sill. I retain nothing of whatever's transpired between dreams.

Dank, stiff gusts skirl off the bay and through the window. I
shrink a little from the cold, but mostly from the fecal stink. No
mistaking raw, festering sewage. I'd sniffed well over my quota
while inspecting subprime properties. So where else during
Dark Ages would an island's waste go except straight into the
sea? And how could dysentery, cholera, et cetera not breed
rampant among the islanders, princesses included?

I covertly scrutinize her with new perspective, half pitying,
half squeamish. Undismayed by the odor, she gazes out tenderly, proudly, as if she always has and always will behold a
brilliant silver metropolis, stupendously rich, eternally true to
its legend.

She homes in on sneaking gaze and turns, stalwart with civic
pride, then adopting more playful mode. Big, wide-set, sky-
blue eyes fix upon me; she pouts coyly and sips her wine.
Subtle sexual charge gets under my skin. Without letting me
out of her sight, she sets her cup beside mine. She rakes lazy
fingers through abundant sable hair, and ignoring vagrant
streaks of grey is easy.

Behind more expansive smile her teeth peek out, and heav-
en help me, I have to shudder and fight to maintain deadpan
appearance. Enamel is stained dirty blue, the crowns are down
to a crooked serration, and inflamed, receding gums frame yellow snippets of roots. Should I really be shocked? The water
supply's a virtual Petri dish, and daily flagon of acidic wine is

the lesser evil, centuries from the invention of toothpaste. Her bid to cajole, to enmesh me, has miserably backfired. My God, her breath must be atrocious.

"Can we take a walk along the battlements, now that the fog's lifted?" I stammer. "To see your beautiful city?"

She nods brightly, glides over to the couch, sits and reaffixes coquettish look at me. She pats firm cushion right next to her. I can't move. All I've ever said to her was gibberish, wasn't it?

Epiphany arrives like a lead sinker in my stomach. No, she wouldn't be suspicious of a weird foreigner spouting nonsense and wearing flannel shirt and khakis. Nobody here can afford suspicions. Royal chambers have to double as brothels in this guttering pagan economy. And academic, I surmise, whether she's a princess duty-bound to prostitute herself or a palace courtesan leased out to every visitor.

This isolated outpost of a relict world, this pariah town on the edge of Christendom, is one tremor, one hurricane shy of final inundation. Please let it be now, to abort this excruciating situation! She bares rotten teeth again and, with faint sigh as if I couldn't be denser or more bashful, spreads her knees in unmindful imitation of profane soapstone fetish, hiking white gown with both hands above her hips.

At first I assume she's partial to Dark Age equivalent of fishnet hose. And then to flinch away is no longer an option, though I hate myself for gaping horrorstruck. From shoeless feet to naked loins, a scabrous disease like none I've ever seen mars profuse swaths of creamy skin. Overlapping ranks of brittle, black-tipped flakes recall the scales of water moccasin or salmon, as if she's undergoing piecemeal transformation into marine species.

Her womanhood *per se* isn't visibly afflicted, and she persists in smiling sweetly, as if intact womanhood is all that matters, and her fingers perform a salacious, kneading dance with bunches of her kilted gown. She's prepared to wait the whole night for me, isn't she?

Already, though, encouraging smile is tightening toward sardonic rigor, and in the blue pools of her eyes, wild insanity begins to surface. Whether staving it off or in submission to it, she croons a nigh inaudible tune, with the maudlin contours of an Irish lullaby.

I can't allow that singing to go on. I'm sorry she's trapped in such untenable straits, which doesn't imply I'm willing to be trapped with her. My panic rapidly escalates. She's a prostitute, right? She might desist if I pay her, yeah, but paper money won't exist for a thousand years. I trawl around left hip pocket for every coin and scoop out pennies, nickels, euros, dimes.

Now what? I don't dare venture closer, especially as stifled sobs intrude on whiny melody at ever briefer intervals. With shaky arm I aim a gentle underhand pitch at the upholstery beside her. Jangly cluster lands bursting at her feet instead, and roughly fourteen cents rebound against her midcalf scales. Her shriek could put a banshee to shame, and I've scarcely questioned how intercourse could occur amid such sensitivity when she springs at me, still shrilling away, and where the hell had she hidden that silver dagger in upraised fist?

Instinctively I raise protective arm and steel myself to feel defensive wound through flannel sleeve, and then that arm is straining against the bedsheet I've soaked in sweat, and I'm thankful to wake where no one cares if a guest is screaming for his mother at 2 P.M.

Am I packing to avoid overhauling derelict hotel and kowtowing evermore to obnoxious tourists, or to be shut of dismal Ys and grotesque princess whore? Moot point. Circumspect knocking extends the option of answering the door or not. "Come in!" I holler while stuffing dirty laundry into a plastic bag, and there's Kervigo. Who else?

He blinks at open suitcase on the bed. "You're leaving?" Must I dignify that with an answer? No. Without ado, he clears his throat. "About the defacement of your nightstand . . ." It's like I'd never brought up buying this shambles of a hotel. Thank God!

"Yes, I'm sorry," I jump in. "I'll pay to have it refinished. Right now, in cash. If you can estimate the cost." Fact is, I'll gladly pay extra to vamoose sooner.

He waves dismissively. No, no, I've understood nothing. "I must criticize how amateurishly you dream. Have any of us ever disturbed you? Whatever happens, our bodies sleep tranquilly and cause no damage or noise." He sighs regretfully, as if compelled to address my halitosis or armpits. "You would be well advised to improve your control."

My look must pose the question I'm too flummoxed to verbalize.

"Yes, we all dream of Ys here, with or without an artifact under the bed. What else could be of importance compared with that?"

With or without an artifact? My heart is racing with redoubled urge to hit the road. Is Auberge des Falaises a nest of lucid dreamers, adept beyond the need for talismans, for literal touchstones? Or maybe fungal spores taint the soup, the air, and elicit bedtime delirium, shaped by power of suggestion? What will staffers' brains and lungs be like in ten, twenty years? What of my own health after three days?

I nod deferentially. "I'll be down in a minute to settle up the bill."

He takes the hint, bows a token inch, and lurches out.

Kervigo has said his piece and shows himself no more. Reception is manned solely by gaunt clerk with droopy eyelids and the balky joints of early-onset rheumatism. Itemized bill does not refer to nightstand damage. At the door I turn for one last glance at forsaken investment opportunity, and the clerk watches my exit with mute indifference, probably because I'm the lobby's single moving object.

Anxious as I am to put miles between the hotel and me, I resolve to enjoy the scenery during headlong quest for saner lodgings. I must have a couple of hours till dusk, and the coast is crawling with accommodations.

Oh fuck. Penniless fisherman is sitting on the hood of my Renault. He flashes jack-o'-lantern grin. All is ostensibly forgiven? He hops off the car. Better and better. I won't have to deal with passive resistance before speedy getaway.

"Please do not presume to judge us," he greets me. Again, I won't approach too near his cavernous grin. "We who receive a portion of Ys build of it what we will. Yours was not a happy place?"

"No," I barely hear myself say.

He clucks in sympathy or disappointment, I can't decide which. "None of us would want to go on living if we could never enter the glorious city again." I suppress impulse to ask, Is that good?

His grin shines on, but his sentiments kindle overwhelming sadness in me. He adds nothing more, doesn't lift a finger to detain me as I clump past him into the car, ditch my suitcase on the passenger seat. He can readily see his words have found their mark.

Survivor's guilt rebounds as I follow the signs back toward Carnac. What had been wrong with me to envision Ys only at its bitter end, when others routinely navigate the millennia to its golden age? And how unjust of me and my dreary world to grind along when the magnificence of Ys is drowned and forgotten. I brood about Mom and the lifespan of insights and memories forever lost with her, with any person. For a city, a civilization to die, the loss is incomprehensible, unbearable.

I take a curve along rockbound shore a hair too fast and hear a soft thump as something in back tumbles off the seat. I park to investigate where the shoulder widens just enough to excuse signage about "scenic rest area." Paranoia whispers I have a stowaway as I exit the vehicle and swing rear door open.

I anticipate discovering foxy codger's parting gift of my discarded bluestone. It's much worse. Soapstone fetish with yawning vulva smiles coyly from the polyester carpet, looking not a day older after 1,600 years. Absurd to think he had a perfect replica of figment from my dream. In any case, the squalid thing must go. I pluck it up and take aim past guardrail at the breakers pounding boulders.

Spasm between thumb and forefinger locks my grip. Kervigo and crew always seemed to have one foot in dreamland, didn't they? Toward the horizon an island gleams brazen and silver, except where towering white citadel casts a shadow. Is it, and the figurine too, no more than spores in my brain? I lower my arm. Do I also blame spores for removing the guardrail, my car, the highway? And for sowing snaggly pine witchwood all around? I may never know what hit me if I premise otherwise, set off anywhere rather than wait for hallucination to fade. But suppose spores aren't the problem?

Singsong French draws my attention toward a shoreline yards beyond where it just was. The pensioner's dory is afloat at last, in a high tide of yesteryear. "Come, these waters are calm! Join us, or stand there till you starve."

"How do I know you're for real?" I shout back.

He laughs, and I laugh much more self-consciously. If there's a "real" guardrail ahead, I don't trip over it as I advance, whatever that means. Foxy codger, deliver me where the wine is drinkable and the women aren't deranged! Have I a better choice? In any event, I refuse to view death as positive outcome.

Willie the Protector

Lois H. Gresh

First the stench of whiskey, then the sourness in his mouth and his eyelashes clumped with dust, and he bolts up, alarmed by sounds he doesn't know. The Machine clanks as if every bolt and pipe is about to blow. Willie clutches his chest and scrabbles to his feet, *empty bottles clatter against steel,* and how much did he drink last night?

He trembles and his teeth chatter. Cold sweat on his back, he slicks hair out of his eyes, which focus through the darkness, *the room lit by a single oil lamp, the others died in the night,* and there it is, Willie's Machine gone mad. A behemoth of steel, brass, and iron held together by cables and bolts, lovingly anointed by Willie's gum sandarac and the fat of dead dogs, Willie's Machine strains to break free—bolts pop, cables snap, steel chains lash, *Medusa snakes against the walls.* The Machine heaves up, belches steam and grime, crashes back down, grinds into the cement, *writhes into it,* and Willie's mind flashes to what's behind the Machine, fourteen hundred and twenty-nine paces between where he sleeps and where *they* sleep.

He's not sure if he's screaming, and if he is, they won't hear him over the Machine, but he has to try. "Hattie! You okay, Hattie? Ebediah!"

Willie stumbles across the floor, *the cement cracks and snags his toes,* and he limps now, his left toes broken, and ducks beneath the steam pipes that snarl and beat each other like boxers in the ring. Even in the dark, he knows every inch of the Machine, the floor, the walls. He's the Protector who makes the city hum and run, and it's his job to know. He circles the snake pit, where valves clang open and shut, and the steam burns through the pipes and the liquid metal sparks, *lightning bugs.*

And Willie hears the screams of his baby, Ebediah, two weeks old and a premature birth. Hattie almost died, *still weak and she can hardly eat,* not that Willie provides enough to eat, and

something sizzles overhead

fire whips

stars crackle

and something's illuminated on the floor.

Willie trips over the softness, *small like a baby,* and squints to see a bloody bone. His hands quiver and pluck up the bone, *hard-as-steel bone now,* almost spherical with numbers and chiseled symbols, ω and σ and Δ. He wipes the blood on his pants, stashes the bone into a hole in the wall—the seventh bone Willie's found, the rest of them in a hole near where he sleeps.

"Willie, *help!*" It's Hattie, her voice dampened by the Machine. He's lost count of his paces, and how can he measure them with the floor rupturing and vomiting cement? He swerves, darts to his left, winces as his left foot comes down.

He tries screaming to his wife, but whiskey and dust clamp his throat. "I'm coming, hang on, Hattie, hold onto the baby, Hattie, I'm coming!"

The two-thousand-ton steam hydraulic pump clatters up and down, ceiling to floor, *morbid growth with hemorrhoid arms,* and its lesions and polyps burst in fireworks of pus. Willie slaps his head and shoulders where the molten drops burn and drags his foot over the last rip in the floor to reach his family.

In the hole in the floor behind Willie's Machine.

Hattie huddles down there on the blankets, the infant cradled in her arms, both faces red and drenched in tears.

Some Protector. He can't even feed his wife and child. How can he expect to protect an entire city? Deluding himself all these years. Weak, a failure, and Hattie is everything to him, and the baby unexpected, now the baby is everything, too.

"Hush," he says, "Daddy's here, Ebediah, daddy won't let anything happen to you. Hush, Hattie, come with me."

She whimpers and nods, so glad to see him, and such admiration and faith and love on her face. He helps them from the hole, the floor still splintering and Willie's Machine banging, and together they duck around the hydraulic pump. Hattie cries under a spray of liquid metal, snuggles Ebediah more tightly, and follows Willie past the hole where the eighth bone is, the one he just found.

He clasps her to him, arm around her waist. "We're almost there," he says. The baby twists toward Hattie's breast, seeking a nipple, and his tiny fingers slip into his mouth. Willie will find a quiet spot in an alley, where Hattie can nurse the baby. He'll steal plums and peaches, and maybe some wine and bread, from the market stalls tomorrow.

He needs more whiskey. Willie can't do without his whiskey.

Ignoring the pain from his broken toes, *not a big deal, he's suffered much worse injuries over the years from tending the Machine,* he leads Hattie and Ebediah around the snake pit and beneath the steam pipes. And there's his blanket on the shaking floor, and his gaze shifts up to where he's stashed the seven bones from all those other times. He wonders why the Machine erupted tonight, as this has never happened. Sure, the Machine hiccups every now and then, and sure, that's when Willie always finds the bones. But there's never been a time in all the years he's been Protector that the Machine went wild, never a time when bolts popped or cables snapped or steel lashed at him. *Never.*

He'll come back for the bones. But first, he must get Hattie and Ebediah out of here, and then he'll steer clear until the Machine calms down.

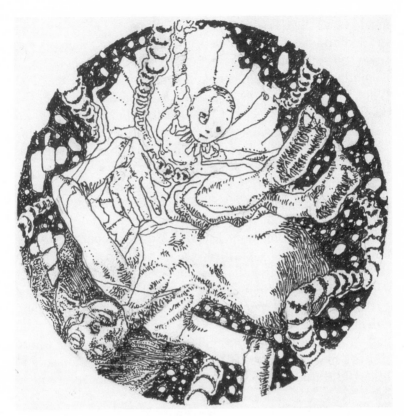

Willie unchains the vast overhead door, twists the handle, heaves his body against the steel, and lifts it so his family can escape. Hattie ducks under the door, and her legs and feet disappear into the evening gloom. From the distance, *must be Hotchingham Street,* the trolley lines buzz. Horse hooves clatter on cobblestone, *must be a buggy on Church Street.* Willie's Machine feeds the city. All the power comes from the Machine.

Willie turns slightly, and the Machine quivers, ever so slightly, tranquil and humming now as if asleep. Near the hole with seven bones, the oil lamp casts yellow stains across the floor.

The city is nothing more than a landfill where the rich toss their garbage. The buildings crouch low as if frightened, and the clouds, *clumps of mud,* slump over them. Willie and Hattie shuffle over the gravel, and in the murk strangers shift like shadows against the brownstones. When Willie and Hattie reach dumpster alley, they wedge themselves between piles of trash and sink onto newspapers, and a scrawny rat scoots past.

The last thing Willie smells is rotting meat, and the next thing he knows it's morning, and the sun weakly probes the soot hanging over the alley. His left toes burn with pain, *all swollen like little sausages,* and he can't put any weight on his foot. Already, the trolleys buzz down the roads, suspended from spiderweb wires that the Machine runs.

"My milk is thin," Hattie tells him. "I'm taking the baby to steal food on Market Street. The baby's so weak he can't cry, just look at him, will you?"

Willie rests a finger on Ebediah's cheek, coarse skin on angel silk. The baby gurgles, wakes slightly, and sucks on the dirty swaddling cloth. Ebediah is so small, Willie's never seen a person this small, not in his whole life. Such tiny grey eyes, and his nose, just a swollen bud really, opening and closing to filter in the air. Willie spits on his finger, then cleans the baby's nostrils and gently dabs his chin where Hattie's milk has dried. His wife and baby smell the same to him. Did Hattie always smell like this? Willie doesn't remember.

Willie's eyes ache, and his head pounds. Too much whiskey. Too *little* whiskey.

Hattie clenches his elbow and says, "Don't worry. I'll get what you need."

Willie needs whiskey and she knows it, *and he should be man enough to feed his own family, shouldn't he?* He's such a failure. Born into the Protectors, no escape from it, a son does what his father does in these parts. Paid nothing, but allowed to live in the Machine's building, this is the way of the Protector. Willie had no right to marry Hattie, who deserves better.

She struggles to her knees and wobbles to her feet. Willie remains beneath her.

"It'll be fine, Willie. Go wait by the Machine. If it's safe, go in, and if not, wait for me in the alley. I won't be long." A pause. "And you might go see Baron Fitzhugh."

She doesn't trust Willie to fix the Machine. She wants him to seek the advice of Baron Fitzhugh, who spends his time toiling over Master Jenkins's blueprints from three hundred years ago. Even Jenkins, who designed the Machine, didn't know how it worked. He died a week after drawing images of the Machine based on etchings he saw on the bones of a cadaver.

So ashamed, Willie can't even look at Hattie until her body is a reed squeezing between the dumpsters by the main road. He'll fix what he's done to Hattie if it's the last thing he does. He'll rise above his position, find a way to decipher the meaning of the eight bones. He'll figure out how the Machine works. He'll improve it. He'll move Hattie and Ebediah to a palace on Noble Avenue, where grandees like Baron Fitzhugh live. She'll wear silk and satin, and the baby will dine on puréed peaches and bananas. Ebediah will be a scholar. The chain of greasy mechanics will end with Willie Pyle VI, who broke the spell when he named his son Ebediah.

He scuffles to the main road, squints under a mahogany sky streaked with pine, the black clouds just straggling in from the east. He passes the derelicts strewn along the road, backs pressed against brownstone, shoulders drooping, chins resting on the lapels of torn jackets. Hands clutch at him, and he shakes them off. He holds his breath each time he nears a grate, where the steam belches and sewage burbles. He passes the meat grinder's rental. If only Willie had been born a meat grinder, his family could live in a one-room rental. It's not fair that a man has to be what his father was and nothing more, not ever. *It's not fair, is it?*

Willie stoops by the overhead door, presses the numbers on the lock in precise patterns passed through the generations. He doesn't understand the numbers, just knows what he has to do to get inside the building. And so, *300000 946 1012 197 207 82 79 5 8,* and the lock clicks, and Willie heaves open the door.

The Machine hums, gentle. The oil lamp still burns by his sleep area. His blanket is gone. Steel chains and cables dangle from the sides of the Machine, *limp like the derelicts on the street.* The pump slides up and down on gum sandarac and fat, the valves whisk open then ease shut, *and how is Willie's Machine running when it's so broken?*

He moves closer and sees that the joints are sealed and nothing leaks. He drags his bum foot by the snake pit, and steam burns through the pipes and liquid metal flickers. Twenty-eight rods connect the pistons to the crankshafts. The wheels turn, the gears mesh, the belts vibrate, the cylinders sweat. But the rear of the Machine has sprouted new limbs: hoses, cables, pipes, axles, belts, wheels, cylinders connected in steel formations that Willie has never seen, *and where did they come from?* The hole where Hattie and Ebediah huddled has caved in, *and where will they sleep?*

Panic grips him. His father never told him what to do if the Machine *grew.* At first, he tries to mangle some of the hoses back into their original configurations, but it's hopeless and he only manages to repair part of the mess. He swears there were only twenty rods on those pistons instead of twenty-eight. He removes eight rods, wonders if it's smart, then slips most of them back into place. Frustrated, he gives up and limps to the hole where he hid the bone last night, and he grabs it, then makes his way to the hole containing the other seven bones, and grabs them as well. He stuffs four of the bones in his right coat pocket, the other four in his left. The Machine grumbles.

And that's when Willie sees the gold. Chunks like gravel, but glimmering and lustrous, definitely gold.

His pockets bulging with bones and gold, he turns to leave.

Baron Fitzhugh stands near the door. What's he doing here? He wears a top hat and tailcoat all perfectly stitched in silk thread, with his face all shaving-cream smooth, his hair aligned more precisely than the pistons and rods Willie greases day after day in this airless room.

"What is it?" says Willie. The Baron's been harping on him for years, trying to get a piece of Willie's action, but Willie's been firm. Willie's the Protector, not Baron Fitzhugh. Only Willie will fix the Machine, and if anyone learns how the Machine works, it will be Willie. Fitzhugh should have better things to do, such as eating and carousing with his friends and, in his off-hours, getting what he wants from women, only to throw them in the trash later. *Isn't this what the rich do?*

The Baron stretches his neck as if his collar's too tight, extracts a cigar from his top left pocket, and twists it into a silver holder. He tips a match to Willie's lamp, lights the tobacco, sucks in the perfume, and exhales.

Willie straightens himself, too, wishing he had a fine cigar. "Can't you leave me alone? I have to adjust the Machine. I'm busy." He keeps both hands in his pockets so Baron Fitzhugh can't see the bones and gold.

"You ever wonder how this great Machine runs the trolleys and the buggies?" asks the Baron between puffs.

"They run on steel wires powered by the Machine."

"Willie, you know that's not what I mean."

Willie refuses to admit that he doesn't know how the Machine works. He wanders away from the light and takes his hands out of his pockets. "I'm busy. I have work to do, Baron." Willie rubs the Machine with salve, and he strokes the brass and steel pipes, cables, hinges, and bolts as the Baron might caress a mistress. Towering twists of metal buzz like nests of angry hornets.

"I found a bone, Willie. Just like the ones Master Jenkins said he found in that grave." The Baron flicks ashes at the Machine.

"Don't do that," Willie barks.

A slight bow, and the Baron inches toward Willie with a half smile. "You heard about the buggy accident yesterday?"

Willie knows nothing about a buggy accident. Must have happened when the Machine went wild.

"Authorities found this bone near the corpses. Five dead, Willie, four Gentleman and a Lady. Their crime? Off to a late supper."

Five rich are dead. Willie's head spins. He can't comprehend. The Machine malfunctioned and killed five people? As Protector, perhaps Willie's to blame. "I didn't do nothing!" Willie cries, hands back in his pockets, edging around Baron Fitzhugh and toward the door. He'll escape, run to Hattie and the baby, and then they'll all run away to some faraway land. But Willie's injured, and Hattie's weak from starvation, and the baby, premature and only newborn . . .

"No, *no,* my man, I'm not suggesting that this was your fault. The Machine requires study and adjustment by a learned scholar, a man of books and mathematics such as myself. The Machine is *off,* and even if the timing changes by a hair, people will die." Baron Fitzhugh's green eyes flicker over Willie face, *and it's as if the Baron's wondering if Willie has any value in this world at all.*

A nugget of gold falls from a hole in Willie's left pocket. Wildly, Willie snatches it up, but not before the Baron sees what's in his hand. "I also found gold by the five dead bodies," the Baron says.

Perhaps Willie's Machine is creating gold for the city. Perhaps it's paying Willie for three hundred years of service to it. Perhaps it's payback time, when the rich will no longer take everything from the poor. *Is it, and could it be so?*

"Come with me, Willie," and the Baron takes his arm and nudges him to the door. "Help me figure out what it means. I've been working on the math for years, and I do have some ideas."

But Willie has gold. Willie's rich now and doesn't need to follow the Baron anywhere. Willie no longer has to be Protector. Willie's free, and so are Hattie and Ebediah. "I don't know," Willie says as they leave the building.

"You're crippled, Willie, limping. I could knock you down with one swipe of my cane, and I could take your coat with all the gold in the pockets. So you might as well come with me."

The rich always get their way, and the poor always do as they're told, so Willie follows Baron Fitzhugh toward the market stalls that lie between the Machine and Noble Avenue. He tells the Baron that his wife is there, seeking food with his baby son. And the Baron suggests that the entire Pyle family stay with him and eat his food, "until we fix the Machine or until you feel it's necessary for you to leave."

Willie can almost taste the brandy and rum and whiskey. He can almost taste the plums and steaks, the chocolate puddings and strudel. How will it feel to bathe in hot water with perfumed soap and to shave with something other than a blunt-edged knife? Willie nods, *it's a good deal, yes it is, and Hattie will be so proud of him.*

"Where was the buggy accident?" Willie asks, and the Baron says it was near Noble Avenue, nowhere close to the market stalls.

Willie doesn't know what he'll do if something happens to Hattie or their son. His mind flits back to the rods he removed from the Machine and to the mess he made of the new components. In such a gigantic Machine, a few missing rods and hoses shouldn't matter.

They circle the corner to Market Street and slip under the trolley wires and buggy cables. Women paw through sardines and smelt, haggle over bread, *the loaves round and hard like the bones in Willie's pockets.* Hot tar bubbles on the pavement and sticks to Willie's shoes. His stomach growls, *and he's so hungry and spices lace the air here.* Baron Fitzhugh tosses two coins on Mistress Gorm's table, and she gives him two pastries. The Baron gives both to Willie and urges him to eat, *and the Baron isn't such a bad guy, after all, is he?*

Sweet custard on his lips, nectar filling his mouth, washing all the sourness down his throat. Willie licks vanilla from his lips, then he gobbles the first pastry as fast as he can and follows with the second.

His head whirls. He hasn't had sugar in over a year. It's good, and he wants more.

But now he sees Hattie and Ebediah over by the whiskey. "Baron, it's my wife and the baby. Come!" He tugs the Baron's elbow, and this time, carrying four more pastries, the Baron follows him past the seamstress with her flashing needles, past the wagon builder and his polisher, past the smells of leather and peaches and perfumes. Last stall on the right by Second Street, that's where the whiskey is—

She's buying him whiskey, Hattie holding Ebediah in one arm and giving the man a coin. She must have found the coin on the street.

As the coin drops into the man's palm, a trolley buzzes around the corner so fast that Willie barely sees the rails, the steps, or the faces. The overhead wires sizzle—

Five rich are dead

people screaming

fire cracking against the whiskey stall.

Willie stumbles forward, propped by the Baron, and they crouch by Hattie, Willie crying and the Baron consoling him. But there is no consolation, for Willie's soul dies and his eyes burn, and the pain in his chest is so deep it fills his entire being. And all Willie sees is blood, blood everywhere, and soft flesh— and the filthy swaddling cloth.

Hush, Ebediah, daddy won't let anything happen to you.

His wife lies in a pool of whiskey, marinating in fire. The Baron removes his coat and slaps the fire, but he can't put it out, and Hattie burns until Willie sees the last wisp of flesh curl into the smoke and she's nothing but bones. Ebediah rests atop the whiskey stall, his blood splashing to the gravel in big, round drops that seem to move slower than time. Willie crawls near and looks up, and in each drop he sees himself. He should have named his son Willie. Perhaps the Machine is angry because he named his son Ebediah and broke the spell. Willie should have taken his wife and baby far from this place. He should have protected them.

Hands claw Willie off the tiny body. They shield his eyes so he can no longer see his wife and baby. He's in a cart now. Horses trot in front of him. The spiderweb wires spark overhead.

Later in Baron Fitzhugh's parlor, he learns that nine more people died in the trolley crash. The Baron offers him brandy and rum, but Willie chokes down whiskey instead, *and the alcohol burns his throat just as it burned Hattie*. If only it would burn Willie to death, too, then he could switch off the images behind his eyes.

He sleeps on a duck-feather mattress under a blanket softer than Ebediah's cheeks. When he awakens, a maid washes him with hot water and pine-scented soap, then she shaves and dresses him in silk pants and a white shirt. She eases him back to the mattress and spoons eggs and bacon into his mouth. The meat smells good, *it isn't even rotten,* and the eggs taste like butter.

His stomach twists, *sour stomach filled with bile.*

He wants whiskey.

He pushes the maid away, falls into a stupor.

From time to time, he hears the Baron's voice, and he's not sure if he dreams their conversations.

"What's the combination to the lock, Willie?"

"300000 946 1012 197 207 82 79 5 8."

"Was there any sign of—excuse me, my man—any sign of death near the bones you found?"

"No dead bodies," Willie chokes out the words, "but always blood."

"And always gold?"

"Only the last time," and Willie no longer cares if the Baron takes his gold. Willie knows his place in life, and now he knows his place in the next life, too. *Don't need gold where Willie's going . . .*

"After it grew, you toyed with the Machine?"

Willie ignores the question and all that follow. He sinks into the place where dreams die.

The maid props him up, spoons beef hash and potatoes into his mouth. He spits out the food and shoves her away.

And now the stench of whiskey and a sourness in his mouth, and Willie bolts up. The bottle is on a night stand to his left. The Baron hunches over him on the mattress, green eyes boring into him in the glow of a lit match. The Baron sucks on his cigar and offers it to Willie, but Willie knows his place and grabs the bottle instead and sucks down the last drops.

"We must return to the Machine," the Baron tells him.

"All my fault."

"You can fix it, Willie, make it all right again."

But they're dead, and there's no fixing that, Baron.

"You're the Protector. The city needs you."

"I'm a failure, a nobody."

And Willie's done pretending to be a Protector of anyone or anything.

"I need you to come," says the Baron. "Only you know how to dismantle the Machine."

Dismantle it? Willie curses. "I'll rip the Machine to shreds with my bare hands!" He'll destroy the thing that killed his family. He'll get even, and then he'll leave and never return.

They wind their way from Noble Avenue to the gutters and sewage of Willie's turf, the Baron tall and stiff and Willie hunched and limping.

Early morning, and the sun is yellow piss. The buzz of a trolley, and Willie clamps his hand on the Baron's shoulder. "I can't—"

"Only you can, Willie."

"No, let me go . . ." Weak, Willie is so weak.

From a satchel, the Baron extracts a whiskey bottle and gives it to Willie. Then he pulls out Willie's eight bones and sets them on the gravel with two additional bones, "the one I found with the five dead, and a new one found with the remains of . . ." and he leaves the sentence unfinished.

Willie sucks down half the whiskey, *fire in his belly and it feels good.*

"Look at these symbols, man." The Baron gestures at the carvings on the bones. Willie has no clue what the Baron means—ω and σ and Δ mean nothing to Willie—and he drinks and adds more fire to his blood.

"Mathematics, Willie, differential calculus and derivatives. Integration. And geometry that—I think but don't know—may calculate distances in curved non-Euclidean space. You ever hear about Bernhard Riemann? Janos Bolyai or Nikolai Ivanovich Lobachevsky?"

The Baron scoops up the bones and keeps talking as he cranks the dials on the overhead door and enters the codes,

300000, "speed of light in kilometers per second,"

946 1012, "distance light travels in one year, 9.46 times ten to the twelve kilometers,"

197, "sum of protons and neutrons in gold,"

207, "sum of protons and neutrons in lead,"

82 79, "number of protons in lead and in gold, respectively,"

5 8, "and number of protons and neutrons in boron and oxygen, respectively."

"Say, what?" asks Willie.

"Numbers of the universe. When you changed the natural order of the Machine, you let them loose, those who live beyond our time and space. They've been slipping out. The Machine's old, and we don't know how to patch the openings. And so they come, they eat, they leave our bones. Their teeth imprint us with numbers of the universe." The lock clicks, and the Baron swings the door up.

"*Who* comes?" Willie doesn't understand.

"It's all in the math. Calculus, Willie. The *others* come. And I think in our world, they change lead into gold. They use boron or oxygen, or maybe both, and this is why we find the gold when they come and *only* when they come."

Willie doesn't understand math and calculus. He doesn't understand what boron and oxygen are and what they have to do with lead and gold. He only knows how to grease and anoint the Machine. Not wanting to admit that he knows so little, he keeps his mouth shut, and they enter the building, leaving the door open. Willie doesn't ask any more questions. He hates the Machine. He chugs the rest of the whiskey and hurls the bottle at the Machine. It fractures, *glass in a thousand pieces like bones crushed beneath a trolley.*

Willie wants to see the Machine bleed.

The Machine has grown again. Metal gears churn steam where Willie used to sleep, and pumps clang up and down where Willie walked fourteen hundred and twenty-nine paces to his family's hole. *Numbers.* Bolts vibrate and chains lash out, and one strikes the Baron's legs, and he falls. Willie tries to help him, but the Baron's legs are broken.

Steel bulges and splits into multiple beams. Pistons thrash against cables and wood, gears and wheels balloon and then hover over Willie like the black clouds of morning over the city. Willie grabs the Baron's collar and drags him toward the door. Bolts pop, metal multiplies, and the limbs of the Machine push against Willie's head and stomach, forcing him closer and yet closer to the open door. Oh, he wants out, that's just fine with Willie, and he rolls to his other side and shoves the Baron into the street. Willie crawls after him, sees the Baron's matches and takes them. But now claws dig into his shoulders and wrench him onto his back, and Willie can't breathe, the air is too thick with burning steam and molten metal.

The Machine, *it's on him*. Willie flails, tries to scream, but the Machine clamps him down, and tendrils of steam flare in the bowels of the building. The claws pierce his shoulder muscles, his chest, his neck. His clothes are soaked in blood, and hot metal cools and pastes his blood to his flesh. It burns him right down to the bone.

He twists his neck, watches the Baron roll into the gutter, where the sewage burbles. The Baron's arms are limp on the gravel, and blood and dirt streak his face. A bone pops from the Baron's left leg, the pants tattered and sopped.

Shivering now, and is this the end of Willie's life? Is this all there was, Protector and now *this?* And please let it be quick, let Willie join Hattie and the baby.

His teeth chatter. His body is cold. He needs whiskey. His bloody fingers clutch the matches, and his thumb breaks a match free.

Hot metal and shadows, the yellow piss of sun, the Baron in the gutter with the buildings crouched low as if frightened: this is Willie's city, spawned by Willie's Machine.

It's a blotch, this city, and if not for the Protectors, it wouldn't be this way, would it? Willie and his father, and before that, his grandfather and great-grandfather, they kept the Machine alive.

Willie was a good Protector. The problem was, he was a good Protector of the Machine.

Shadows slink from the Machine's vents. Liquid steel splits, fireworks over Willie, and the *others* come, they pour by the thousands from the crevices of the Machine. Shadows merge with liquid steel, and Willie sees claws and suckers and holes.

Willie strikes the match against cement and flicks it over his head right into the fireworks, and he sees the weird symbols and the numbers blazed into the bone of his right arm.

300000 946 1012 197 207 82 79 5 8

The last thing Willie sees is a metal sucker. And the last thing Willie smells is bloody meat.

Miranda's Tree

Hannes Bok

The old house on the hilltop, where the paved road ended on oiled dirt, had been remodelled so long ago that it had become old again—like a rejuvenated lady in need of another bit of plastic surgery. Above the newer, smaller homes, it loomed like a medieval castle over a small village, and was set apart from them by vacant lots, in one of which spread a gigantic oak.

The mistress of this house, Edna Thorpe, rocked restlessly on the battered porch swing, pulling on the pillows behind her, shifting uncomfortably about, her nose wrinkling disgustedly at her inability to achieve complete ease. She was a short, dumpy woman, dressed at present in a limp slack-suit which had been stretched beyond mere bagginess at the elbow, knees, and seat. Except for the assistance of eyebrow pencil, mascara, and lipstick, her features were as indefinite as though her face had been modelled of dough and then baked. Her frizzy sand-colored hair had been unimaginatively parted in the middle and then dragged back over her ears.

She squirmed toward the screen-door and shouted into the house, "Elaine!" There was no prompt reply, and she called again, this time with a note of menace, *"Elaine!"*

"What, mama?" The little girl's voice was a reluctant wail.

"Come out here when I call you; don't just stay in there and ask *what!*" her mother cried sharply. There was a silence, then several loud and hollow thumps as though someone within the dwelling were kicking the furniture about. Seven-year-old Elaine tiptoed out on the front porch, her round face too innocent to be credible. Hugged to the front of her soiled dress was a book. The screen-door slapped smartly shut behind her.

"All *right,*" the cold-eyed mother said. "Go into the house and come out again, and see that you *don't* slam the door this time!"

The child eyed her parent as if to gauge the extent to which disobedience might proceed unpunished, then turned, went into the house, emerged, and carefully closed the door.

"That's better," Edna conceded, relaxing. "The postman's coming up the hill. I want you to get our mail, if he has anything for us." She looked away as though expecting contempt in the child's eyes, writhed uneasily, and wrenched the corner of a pillow. "I'm too tired to get up," she added in explanation.

Elaine peered down the street. "He's stopping in at the Johnsons'," she said. "Mamie Johnson gets letters sometimes from her brother in the army. She does, because I saw one once!" She glanced at her mother as though awaiting a denial.

"What's that book you've got?" Edna Thorpe peered narrowly.

Elaine apprehensively scanned her book's red cover, and clutched it more closely. "It—it's just a book," she evaded weakly.

"I mean, what's the name of it?" Edna's eyes were hardening with suspicion.

Elaine's gaze was hunted. She affected to look at the title. "Why, it's just a book I got from the school library," she said at length.

Her mother put out a peremptory hand. "Bring it here."

Elaine hesitated; Edna's hand wavered ever so slightly, significantly, and the child hurried across the porch, laid the book on her mother's palm, and stepped back as though cowering from a blow, her eyes wide with anxiety, her mouth a circle of worry.

Edna read, "'Hans Andersen's Fairy Tales,'" and looked up at her daughter. "Well!" She inhaled deeply. "And what have I told you about reading fairy tales?"

"But Miss Davidson said I should read 'em—" Elaine murmured ineptly.

"I didn't ask you who said to read them. I asked, what did I tell you about reading fairy tales?"

"You said they're lies," the abashed child breathed.

"If you want to do any readin', you get something true to life, like 'Elsie Dinsmore,'" Edna Thorpe said. "No child of *mine's* going to fill her head with such asinine truck. I wasn't ever allowed to read such trash when I was a little girl like you." She thumped the book down beside her on the swing, and pushed back Elaine's worried and possessive hands. "You leave it lay *right there!* Here comes Mr. Markey. Go on now, and get the mail!"

The child's eyes clung to the book. Sighing, she turned away, but as she clattered down the porch steps, the tragedy was already forgotten.

"Elaine! Pick up your clumsy *feet!*" Edna scolded. She spread a practiced smile over her face, waving coyly to the mailman. "Hello, there, Mr. Markey! Have you something for me? Just give it to Elaine, will you? It'll save my walking down to the box."

The postman saluted her indifferently, offered some envelopes to Elaine, and trudged across the street to the opposite houses. The little girl scrambled up the porch steps, the wood resounding hollowly. She was curiously thumbing through the letters.

"Give those things to *me!*" Edna Thorpe snarled, snatching them away from the child and smacking the back of a hand on the girl's cheek. "How many times have I *told* you not to pry—"

She skimmed over the writing on the envelopes, important and speculative while her daughter stood with downcast eyes, pudgy fingers feeling the smarting cheek.

Elaine began to cry—not soft sobs, but the bawl of a siren.

"If you want to cry," Edna said, "go into the house and do it. I don't want the neighbors to see you making a spectacle of yourself, a *great big girl* like you!"

She pushed her daughter away. Elaine hesitated in the middle of a wail, deciding whether it would be more interesting to see what the letters contained, or to go into the house and cry. She preferred crying, and almost screamed her woe as she stamped sonorously into the house. Edna looked after her, a frown drifting across her forehead and away like a shadow as she tore open an envelope, smoothed out the folds of a paper by creasing it wrong-side out, and read, the paper so close to her face that she might have been smelling it.

There was a noise of furniture being tumbled about. Edna pictured her daughter, banging things around to transfer grief to them. "You cut that out!" she bellowed through the screen door, and calmly continued reading.

After a while, Elaine stepped out on the porch, her eyes reddened, but her cheeks rounded in a cherubic smile. "Who're the letters from, mama?" she asked sweetly, pushing the fairy tale book aside to sit next to her mother. She slipped an arm as far as it would go around her mother's waist, and leaned affectionately on Edna's flabby side.

"Here's one from your Aunt Miranda," Edna said, tapping the sheet with a forefinger. The name meant nothing to Elaine, who lifted her head and craned at delicate Spencerian handwriting, like a diagram for a will o' the wisp's dance. "I took you to see her a long time ago when you were just a baby, but you probably don't remember. She was living in Hanover, taking care of your grandma." She mused over the paper.

A scrawny boy of twelve had walked his bicycle up the hill; he wheeled it up the sloping grassy lawn and leaned it against the porch steps.

"*Jun*ior!" Edna glared at her son. "How often have I told you not to ride your bicycle over the grass?"

"I wasn't riding it, I was pushing it, and besides if I come up the steps, it'll bump, and that's bad for the tires."

"That's no excuse! Now take it back to the walk and come up the steps as you *should!*"

"Aw—" He pressed dirty fists on his hips, spreading wide his legs, his face a rebellious sneer.

"Jun*ior!*" Edna stirred as though about to arise, her head thrust forward like a snake's from its coils. The boy stepped back, nervously moistening his lips, dropping his hands at his sides. Mother and son stared eye to eye. Junior quailed. He lifted his wheel, bounced it down the steps and dragged it up again with unnecessary violence, as though desperately attempting to achieve a blowout—then he would raise pathetic eyes and cry, "*Now* see what you've gone and made me do!"

But the tires were unharmed. He rested the bicycle against the porch steps a second time, sheepish with frustration. "What're y' readin'?"

"A letter from your Aunt Miranda."

"Wha' does she say?"

Edna's eyes skimmed the letter for an item of possible interest. "She's lonely ever since Grandma died and left her in the big house all by herself."

Elaine pawed her mother's arm. "Is she pretty, mama? Is she pretty?"

Edna considered. "I suppose so. Your daddy almost married her instead of me!" She laughed a little at the preposterousness of it.

"But you got him first, didn't you, huh?" Elaine questioned hurriedly, with the sly look of a conspirator. Edna scowled at her, annoyed.

"Your father married me because he *loved* me," she said with dignity. "There wasn't any question about getting him first." She scrutinized the letter.

"If she's lonely," Junior said, "are you going to ask her to come and stay with us for a while?" He eased himself down on the top porch step and drew out a pocket knife, his finger-nail squeaking as he tried to pull out a blade.

Edna reflected. "I don't know. Maybe I'd better speak to your daddy first."

Elaine's plump fingers stole over the porch swing's cushions to her fairy book, lifted it secretly over the back of the swing, and laid it on the window ledge beyond. She turned back to her mother, her eyes round with purity of soul. "I'd better go in and see if my sick dollies are any better," she said. When she was tired of playing with her dolls, they were sick. She jumped from the swing to the floor, pushing with such vigor that the swing jerked wildly from side to side, Edna looking up angrily at the chains shrieking on the ceiling hooks.

Elaine closed the door very softly behind her, and catfooted through the disorder of the living room to the window overlooking the porch. Edna was opening another letter, and Junior was testing the blade of his knife by paring the edge of his shoe sole.

Elaine, her tongue protruding from the side of her mouth with effort, slowly slipped her hand through a tear in the screen, careful not to scratch it on the ragged wire. She lifted her fairy book inside, and pressed it to her chest again in triumph. She made a frightful face at her absorbed mother and carried the book upstairs to the dubious sanctity of her room.

In the glow of a floor lamp, Ralph Thorpe sat in his usual chair. Once he had been handsome and vital; now he was haggard and listless. He did not say anything critical as he searched for his unfinished serial story in one of the magazines which Edna had crammed, bending its corners, in the magazine rack. He read silently.

Edna was on the sofa, her work-basket overflowing beside her. She was sewing a lace collar on a dress, which she held up. "Oh, *damn!* It *still* isn't on straight! Well, I don't care. I'm going to leave it just like it is. *No*body'll notice, anyway."

Ralph turned a page of the magazine, and laid it down. Elaine had seen fit to cut paper dolls from the last page of the serial's installment. "What did the children mean about Miranda at the dinner table?" he asked.

Edna gazed at him. There was no trace of emotion in their eyes, no love nor hate. "A letter came from her today. She says she hasn't any money left from Mother's insurance, and doesn't know where to turn. Of course, she's hinting that she'd like to come here to stay with us—and there's really no reason why she shouldn't, is there?"

Ralph was silent, staring past her, his face softening with memories. Edna was perturbed. "Perhaps she's still got a crush on you!" she fleered. "I remember seeing your picture still up in her room the time I took Elaine to see her over in Hanover." She smiled amusedly, but her eyes were secretive and hard.

Her husband's lips tightened. "Besides," Edna said, plucking at the lace collar, "there's the children: I *can't* take care of them and still do all the housework. I'm not getting any younger, and it's about time that I had a little rest so's I can enjoy myself."

Ralph was disconcerted by her calculating gaze. He raised his magazine, peering at the print, hiding his face.

"I've always said that you ought to get a hired girl," he murmured mildly.

"Yes, I know. But I've been trying to save money by doing everything for myself. I thought you'd appreciate that." Her husband's fingers twitched on the magazine. "But now I realize that I can't go on, any more. So—well, I thought we could save money and still have help around the house if I told Miranda to come. She can use the attic room—it's just full of old junk now, anyway, and it'll keep her away from us if we want to do any entertaining."

"What's wrong with letting her have Elaine's room, and putting Elaine up in the attic?"

Edna raised her hands in horror. "Why, Ralph Thorpe, to think of doing such a thing to your own child!"

"Why do it to Miranda, then?"

Edna colored, and lowered her eyes to her sewing. "That's different. She's older—the heat won't bother her as much as it will Elaine. E*laine*'s delicate." She looked up defiantly. "Well— shall I tell Miranda to come?"

He shrugged, a trace of hurt in his eyes. "Do whatever you like."

Edna's triumphant smirk annoyed him. He arose and started out of the room, but at the door he paused. He turned. "You rather like the idea of having her here under your thumb, depending on us for her bread and butter, don't you?"

Edna stared at him, her face a mask of righteous indignation.

Ralph brought Miranda to the old house in a taxi, Junior accompanying him. As the car whirred up the hill, Elaine darted away from the little girls with whom she was playing, knocking over a tiny table and a chair in her hurry, sending tiny tin dishes clinking on the ground, disrupting a dolls' tea party.

She darted up the sidewalk, racing the taxi. "Daddy! *Yoo hoo,* Daddy!" Junior made a dreadful grimace at her from the car.

The taxi stopped with a jerk in front of the Thorpe house. Edna had been waiting on the porch, and now she came down to the boulevard-strip, her heavy steps jouncing the sagging folds of her chin. A door of the car flew open, and Junior tumbled out, banging a Gladstone bag on the grass. "Hello, Mama! We brought Aunt Miranda," he announced importantly and unnecessarily.

Ralph Thorpe stepped from the car, helping Miranda, who was clutching the handle of a newspaper-covered wicker basket. Her eyes were wide on the big house, and she clung to Ralph's fingers longer than Edna liked.

Elaine panted up to them, and leaned against her mother, her hands clutching her mother's dress, her eyes fascinated on the newcomer. She was noisily chewing candy, a rivulet of chocolate wending from her mouth down her chin.

"*Elaine!* Don't *touch* me! Just *look* at your hands!" Edna exclaimed, tearing her gaze from Ralph's hand still linked with Miranda's. Elaine snatched away her hands, hiding them behind her, backing away from her mother. Her interest swerved to Miranda, who stood as short as Edna, but was very thin and seemed much older. Her gentle eyes were grey, her hair streaked with white. She wore the dull clothing of a very old woman.

Elaine pointed a grubby finger. "Is *that* Aunt Miranda?"

"Yes. Aren't you going to say hello, and kiss her?"

The idea was obviously as displeasing to Miranda as to Elaine, but Edna's voice was a command. The aunt stooped, and the child pressed her sticky lips against a faded-tan velvet cheek, leaving a chocolate mark. She pointed ecstatically to it. "Look! I left some lipstick!"

"Carry your Aunt Miranda's bag up to the porch, Junior. Then you can go. Ralph, don't you see that Randy's holding a heavy basket?" But Miranda would not surrender its handle to Ralph. "*Well,* Randy!" The sisters kissed, and Edna stepped back, her eyes appraising her sister. "Well, you don't seem to have changed very much!" By jerking her shoulder toward the house, she achieved the effect of a pointing hand. "Let's go into the house, shall we?" They started up the front steps. "*Elaine!* Get away from under my feet, or I'll *step* on you!" Ralph remained behind to pay the cab driver.

Late sunlight lay among blue shadows like an unfinished gold-leaf project on slate. Miranda eyed the grass-choked flower-beds, roses badly in need of pruning, and the stripes of tall grass which Junior's hurrying lawn mower had missed. "You have a very pretty yard," she said. Her look strayed into the vacant lot and caressed the spreading oak. "What a beautiful tree!"

The oak was a ponderous giant which seemed to be crouching, ineffably sad, as though its friends had deserted it, leaving it to brood, huddled and forlorn. Its leaves were still; then they twinkled in the sunlight as a breeze pressed against the branches, dipping them down and flinging them upward like hands waving a welcome.

As Edna started into the house, Elaine surprised her by holding open the screen door. The party entered a dim hall cluttered with heaped tennis rackets, baseball paraphernalia, small wagons, dolls, and upset doll buggies, resembling a battlefield's wreckage.

Edna toyed with the brooch at her throat. "When Ralph told me what time your train was due, I knew it'd be no use waiting your dinner for you. But I have a nice snack ready for you in the kitchen. We can talk a little while you eat, and then afterward you can go and see what you think of your new home."

They stepped over the strewn toys, into the grimy-walled kitchen. Water dripped rhythmically into dishes piled high in the sink.

"I can't tell you how grateful I am—" Miranda murmured, near tears, sitting on the chair at which her sister pointed. Edna lifted a soiled tablecloth from a spread of dishes on the table, and dropped the cloth carelessly over the back of another chair. She jerked open the icebox door and slammed down a cream pitcher, a bowl of salad, a wax-paper twist containing minced ham.

"I'm worried about being an expense to you—" Miranda began.

Edna slammed the icebox door. "Expense!" She sniffed grandly, resembling a Pekingese. "Don't you worry about the money side of things!" She was striving to sound sisterly and reassuring, and was embarrassed, as she told Miranda to start eating, by forgetting to alter her tone.

"I was hoping you'd let me care for the children and help with the housework," Miranda offered. "I want to feel that I'm earning at least part of my keep—"

Edna poured tea. "Well, of course, I knew you'd want to help, so I planned it so you could." Ralph entered, Elaine behind him. "You sit there, Ralph."

"Mama—" Elaine hurtled against the table, laid dirty fingers on the cloth, her eyes round at the food. "Mama! Can I have something to eat, too?"

"No, Elaine," Edna said severely. "Run along now and don't bother us. We've got grown-up things to discuss."

Elaine's expression dulled. She whirled away resentfully from the table. Her eyes struck Miranda's wicker basket, on the floor in a corner. She squatted down beside it and lifted a corner of its newspaper covering. "What's in here? Did you bring a present for me?"

Miranda quickly lowered her teacup, left the table, and fluttered to the child. "Oh, do please be careful! They're the plants I brought along." She lowered her voice confidentially. "I held them on my lap all the while I was on the train, so that nothing would hurt them. See?" She kneeled, removing the newspaper as reverently as a madonna unveiling her child, disclosing half a dozen potted shrubs. She lifted her eyes to Ralph and Edna. "I gave away all the rest that I had, but I simply couldn't bear to part with these. Aren't they beautiful?" Her face was radiant with shy pride.

Elaine's finger jabbed a tender sprout. "What's this?"

Miranda's face lost its joy. "That's a slip from Mother's grave—an azalea, her favorite flower." She was almost whispering. Ralph was regarding her steadily, seeing her as she had been in the past, and her vision interlaced with his, sharing the memory. Edna watched them suspiciously.

Their attention was not on Elaine, who pushed her face down, touching the plants, sniffing at them. A shoot snapped off. She jerked up her face in dismay, but no one had noticed, so she pressed the end of the sprout into the dirt to hide the damage. She arose. "I guess I better be going. Good*bye!*"

Edna was guiding her sister up into the attic. "Here, now. Here we are. Take hold of my hand until I find the light switch. There! Now we go up these stairs. You have no idea of how really comfortable it's going to be—"

They blundered through a doorway. Edna pressed another light-button. The little room was semi-visible under a feeble light around which a moth gyrated.

"I'll get you another bulb. This one's in just temporarily. Elaine's been using this for a playroom, and there's no sense wasting light," Edna remarked, her eyes vigilant on Miranda's face for signs of opposition.

The pink roses of the wallpaper had faded to rusty grey, and Elaine had personalized portions of the wall with crayon scribbles.

"It's very pleasant, Edna," Miranda said. "Why, this bedspread! I remember helping Mother sew on it. She gave it to you—how long was it? About fifteen years ago, and you're still able to get some use from it."

"Maybe it's nothing wonderful," Edna assured, "but at least it's better than—well, I guess you'll find it's all right."

Miranda fingered the dusty window-sill. "Perhaps I could put up a little shelf here for my plants? I simply couldn't bear not having them near me—they're like old friends." She smiled gently, as if sharing a sweet secret. "What a lovely view there must be out through this window! I can look down and see that beautiful oak every morning when I awake." She turned and laid her thin hands on Edna's shoulders, "Oh, thank you, dear, for this room!"

Edna looked apprehensively at the hands, then shrugged carelessly to indicate that thanks were not expected and to shake away the sentiment of Miranda's fingers. She threw a last took around her, nodded with satisfaction, and ambled to the door.

"Of course it'll be better, later on," she said. "Ralph's going to do some more fixing on it. He hasn't had much time lately to make any improvements on the house."

She paused, her mouth lifting slightly. "*Fun*ny! As soon as Ralph heard that you were actually going to come, he became all entangled in his lodge work. You'd almost think that he was trying to avoid being home! I hope it's not because he dislikes you." She ran a tongue appreciatively over her lips. "I ought to warn you, Randy, he's a mighty peculiar fellow. Sometimes I wonder why on earth I ever married him!"

"Oh, but he was very sweet to me in the car!" Miranda exclaimed, and Edna's gloating oiliness vanished. "He seemed just as sympathetic and kind as he ever was!"

"Well—" Edna endeavored to radiate amiability, "I hope that you and he will manage to get along. You can find your way down to the bathroom if you need it, can't you?" She gave directions. "I've got to go now. I've some letters to dash off— they keep piling up on me so! I never have any time for myself at all, any more!"

She stopped at the door as though she had just remembered something. "Oh, say! Tomorrow I'm going over to the P. T. A. meeting at Junior's school. Would you kind of look after the place while I'm gone? You can answer the phone, and bring in the mail, and see that things-in-general are all right. There's a raft of dirty dishes in the sink, but I'll wash them tonight if I'm not too tired—"

"No! Let me!" Miranda's hands fluttered as she stretched them out in her eagerness.

"And I think you ought to put those plants of yours out on the back porch. You might spill water, carrying it up to sprinkle on them."

Miranda did not object, but her eyes were pained. Nevertheless she put out her hands timidly and lovingly to her sister. "Don't do the dishes, Edna. As soon as I've changed my dress, I'll be down to do them. I don't mind at all, really. I want to be of help."

"Well, if you really want to—" Edna said, barely concealing her relief. "Be careful when you come down. The stairs are steep."

As she clattered heavily down the steps, Miranda wandered about the room, smiling wryly at the threadbare coverlet on the scarred bed. She fingered the scratched bureau and touched the back of the rocking chair, which swayed creaking to and fro. Abruptly she shut off the light and pressed against the window.

The great oak lay below like a sleeping giant. Miranda rested her elbows on the window ledge, peering at the tree for many minutes.

In the night, Edna was unable to sleep. She lay on her bed, stirring restlessly, listening to Ralph's snores from the open doorway of his room. The wind dashed against the house with the sound of distant surf, making the walls creak, and outside, the old oak was threshing about, its fluttering leaves sighing dryly like the crumpling of endless quantities of tissue paper. The weighted cord of the window-shade, lifted by a draught, thudded erratic rhythms against the pane.

At last Edna reached to her bedside table, switched on the little frilly lamp, took a book from the table, and searched through it for the bent corner which marked her place. Light from a slit in the lampshade slanted over the page, so she revolved the shade with a poking forefinger until the slit was no longer a nuisance.

As she read, one hand dipped into the open candy box on the table, fumbled among the empty paper candy cups.

Encountering nothing, she lifted the box, peered into it, shook it experimentally, and set it down. Her eyes squinted. *"Damn Elaine!"* she said.

She returned to her reading, unconsciously dipped into the box again, and realized what she was doing. She moistened her lips and attempted to continue through the book, but her hunger was too strong. She laid the book down, considered, then slid her doughy legs over the edge of the bed and down into her slippers. Not bothering to wriggle into her bathrobe, she shuffled into the hall and downstairs.

At the kitchen door she stopped dead, her hand flying to her mouth in fright. Someone was moving about on the back porch! Whoever it was, he was opening the back door and coming in! She cowered back, limp with terror. Then the intruder passed before the blue rectangle of a window. It was Miranda.

Edna snapped on the light; both women blinked. "What on earth are you doing down *here?"* Edna asked sourly. "You nearly scared the living *day*lights out of me!"

"I was afraid that the wind was going to blow my plants off the porch rail," Miranda said.

"Those plants! The way you fuss about them, you'd think they were alive!"

"But they *are* alive," Miranda assured mildly.

"I didn't mean it like that," Edna said.

"No," Miranda replied, understandingly. "I know."

The two women stared at each other, Edna dubiously, Miranda shyly. Edna frowned to herself as she dragged her feet over to the icebox. She opened its door and bent over, peering in at the food, her lips spreading in a smile of greedy anticipation.

Dusk lay over the world like blue fog. Ralph, on the porch swing, was roused from lethargy by a light switched on in the living room, its yellow rays striking him through the window. He yawned and arose, caught sight of something pale and indistinct under the oak in the next lot, and squinted sharply. The dim thing moved. Curious, he sauntered down the porch steps, over the clipped grass.

Miranda was sitting under the oak, her back leaning against the jagged bark, her hands on snaky roots. Her head was tilted upward, as though she were looking at stars, but at the rustle of Ralph's footfalls on the grass, she lowered her face.

"Oh, it's you," he said. "I thought I saw someone here. Mind if I sit by you?"

"Ralph!" She was surprised. "Yes—yes, sit down if you like—"

He folded himself down carefully, grunting a laugh. "I'm a little stiff—not as young as I used to be. You neither, Randy."

She was silent. He felt, rather than discerned, that her gaze was on him. At last she said, "Yes."

"Are you happy, here, Randy?" His voice was wistful. "I think that Edna's loading you down with too much responsibility. I don't want you to be burdened all the time with work. You gave up everything so that you could take care of your mother—" He cleared his throat, and leaned toward Miranda. "Why did you have to go on taking care of her, when you knew I wanted you so?"

"Someone had to," Miranda murmured. "I knew that Edna was too giddy to do it."

"I didn't want to marry Edna, you know. I wanted you."

Silence curdled the air between them.

Miranda said, "But you married Edna."

"I was lonely. I would have married—anybody! But it was you whom I loved. Miranda—" He touched one of her hands; his fingers trembled. "I love you still—I never stopped—"

For once, she was stern. "Ralph—I love you too. But it's too late now. You've made your promise to Edna—you have the children—"

He drew his fingers from hers. "Yes," he said dully, "I know." He sighed. The darkness deepened. They could barely see each other. They were only two voices. "Miranda—I don't care! I love you still. I'll explain to Edna—"

Now it was her hand which touched his. "No! I'll deny it!"

"But having you near, reminding me of all that we used to feel for each other—"

Her voice was very faint. "I'll go away."

He was alarmed. 'No! Where could you go? You can't! You mustn't!"

"Then"—she was regretful—"we must never talk like this again."

She heard him arise. "Good night," he said dispiritedly. "I'm going into the house."

Her voice was the kiss that she dared not give him. "Good night, Ralph." His feet whispered over the lawn. She heard a door click shut. "Ralph," she murmured, unconsciously lifting her arms, her hands pleading. "Ralph, dearest!" Her arms fell. She stared with downcast eyes as though she actually saw something in all that darkness. She drew herself up on her feet, clinging to the tree. She patted the dry bark. "Oh, Tree!" she breathed, and again, "Oh, Tree!"

She slipped her arms around the trunk, hugging the oak as though it were a human being, capable of human response. She touched her mouth to the bark. "Ralph, dearest!"

A slight breeze slid across the yard, pattering the leaves soothingly overhead.

Miranda was tidying the kitchen, Edna sitting on a chair and watching without interest. Elaine wandered in. "Mama, will you help me make my dolly a dress?"

"Not now, dear. Mama's busy."

"Why? You aren't *doing* anything. You're just talking to Aunt Randy."

"I haven't time, dear. I've got to run upstairs and change my dress. Daddy and I are going to go visiting this evening."

"But I want you to help make my dolly a dress!"

"Now, listen, dear. There ought to be something nice on the radio—why don't you go in the front room and listen?"

"I don't *want* to listen to any ol' program!"

"Well, then, take your cloth and scissors and go somewhere and be quiet, just so you stop bothering me. Why don't you help Aunt Randy with the dishes?"

Miranda turned. "Yes, Elaine, dear," she seconded, pleasantly. "Wouldn't you like to help me?"

"I will if I can wear an apron like Mama does when there's company and she tries to look like she's been helping you."

"There's one over there on the hook behind the door." Miranda dried her hands to assist the child into it. "*There* we are!"

Edna groaned with luxurious discomfort as she struggled up from her chair and headed for the door, the dishes on the table rattling from her heavy tread. "Now you do what your Aunt Randy tells you!" She cocked a severe eye on Elaine, as she went out, the swinging door flapping back and forth after her with diminishing force, like a fan waved by a tiring hand.

Miranda returned to the dishpan. "Have you a towel?"

Elaine pulled a dish towel from a rack and wiped a handful of table silver, piling it all indiscriminately into the wrong compartment of the cabinet drawer. "Don't you think that I'm a real nice little girl for helping you, Aunt Randy?" Her eye was charmed by the sparkle of light on cut glass. "Oh, let me wipe the pretty bowl next!"

"No, I think you'd better let me do this one, dear. It's old cut glass, and very expensive. Your mother'd never forgive me if anything happened to it. But you can wipe these saucers—see the pretty roses on this one!"

"I don't *like* roses! I want the pretty bowl!" Elaine stamped her foot, then read the refusal in her aunt's eyes, and changed her tack. Her eyes swelled into reproachful moons. "Mama always lets me wipe that!"

"I'm sure that she doesn't. Come, now, dear—put the glasses away. Or don't you want to help me?" The child lunged forward, snatching at the bowl. "*Elaine!*" Miranda stepped in her way, gently pushing aside the eager hands. "If you won't do as I say, Elaine, you'll have to stop helping me. I've a lot of things to do, and your putting away the glasses will be just as kind as your drying that bowl. You might get me a fresh towel, if you'd like."

"I want the *bowl!*" Elaine insisted sullenly. Miranda shook her head and resumed her work, ignoring the child, who wailed, "All right for *you* then—*you'll* see!" She marched out of the kitchen. Presently she returned, sobbing poignantly, her mother behind her.

"Miranda Ford, what do you mean by striking my child?" As Miranda turned in surprise, Edna jerked her daughter protectively close. "Now don't deny it! And don't call my baby a liar! Whatever she did, I don't imagine it was bad enough to call for your hitting her." She stepped forward belligerently, tugging at Miranda's towel. "Here. *Give* me that! I'll finish your work. Goodness knows, you're as bad as a child yourself. You can't be left alone one teeny minute without getting yourself in trouble!"

Her eyes challenged her sister to speak, but Miranda merely relinquished the towel, took off her apron, hung it up, and went out on the back porch. Edna glared after her, then swung her gaze on her daughter. "*Stop* that bellowing, Elaine: Did you hear me? Else I'll give you something that'll *really* make you cry!"

After a time, Edna stepped out on the back porch. "Randy are you out there?" she called. "It's almost time for me and Ralph to go!" But there was no reply, so she hurried out, letting the door clatter shut, and searched the yard. She stopped, shocked, at the sight of Miranda embracing the oak.

"Why, M*iranda Ford!*" she gasped. "What on earth do you think you're *do*ing?" Miranda stepped back guiltily from the tree. Edna glanced sharply at the neighboring houses. "What do you suppose the *peo*ple will think?"

Miranda was rigid, pale, unable to speak in her fright.

"Why"—Edna muttered—"why, you were *kiss*ing that tree! Have you gone out of your mind?" She hurried to her sister, roughly took one of her hands and jerked her toward the house.

"N-no," Miranda stumbled. "I was feeling sad, and it was comforting to have something to put my arms around."

Edna scowled up at the leafy branches, like a mother damning her daughter's unworthy suitor. "You won't get much comfort out of a tree. You'll just get the people around here thinking you're insane, and reporting you to the authorities—that's all!"

"Yes, Edna," Miranda conceded humbly.

Miranda finished tucking Elaine into bed. She bent and kissed the little girl's forehead. "Good night, Elaine."

The child did not answer. Miranda said again, "Good night." As she snapped off the light and started through the doorway, Elaine sat up.

"When's my mama coming home?"

"I don't know just when, but she won't be gone very long. Don't worry. Just lie back and sleep."

"I want to sit up and wait for Mama to come home."

"No, darling. You ought to be very tired. I am—I'm going to bed myself in a few minutes." Miranda returned to the child's bed, pressed the child back on the pillow, and smoothed the covers. "Go to sleep now like a good little girl."

Elaine was silent, but the atmosphere quivered with the intensity of her resentment. Miranda stepped softly over the threshold and downstairs. Elaine sat up again, waited a moment, then dropped off her bed and tiptoed to the door. She hesitated, peering out into the hall, then slipped out, following her aunt.

From the kitchen door she watched Miranda open the icebox, pour out a glass of milk, close the refrigerator door, and walk out on the back porch. Elaine skulked after her.

She saw Miranda go across the grass to the oak and kneel before it. She heard the hiss of milk being poured on the ground, and Miranda's murmur, "Accept my sacrifice, O Tree—!"

At the breakfast table, Miranda was sober, her eyes flinching from Edna's. But Elaine was lively. Ralph had gone to work, and Junior had finished eating and been excused.

"Elaine, sit *still!*" Edna shouted. "Your wiggling around is enough to drive me *fran*tic! Randy, what's the matter with you? Still sulking about last night?"

Miranda raised troubled eyes, but could not rely.

"I know what's the matter," Elaine fairly sang. "Last night Aunt Randy was acting funny over by the big oak tree, so I smashed all her plants on the back porch, that's what's the matter!"

"You what?" Edna stared, stupefied, at her daughter. Then her right hand's knuckles whirred through the air and cracked over her daughter's mouth. Elaine was too stung by the pain to cry. Edna glared at her for an instant, then drove her attention to Miranda. "What were you doing by the oak tree?"

The kitchen clock clattered loudly, like the sound of a robot's running feet.

Elaine's upper lip was bruised, a drop of blood on it. She said, "She was kneeling in front of the tree like we do when we say our prayers at Sunday School, and she poured the milk and talked to the tree like it could hear that she was saying—"

Edna's eyes interrogated Miranda's. "Well?" Miranda nodded, abashed.

"Elaine, you can run along," Edna said bruskly. Elaine's eyes narrowed. Then she pushed back her chair and crept from the kitchen, peering back, frightened.

Edna's voice was without expression. "Why did you do it?"

Miranda put out her palm in a gesture equivalent to a shrug.

Edna asked coldly, "Were you worshipping the tree?"

Miranda considered, then nodded. Suddenly she brightened. "It understands me, Edna! I know it sounds peculiar, but it seems to understand—"

Edna sneered. "You're crazy!" The thought fascinated her.

Miranda leaned forward eagerly. "No! Listen! In the old days, there were the druids. I've read about them. They worshipped the trees, too. And in old France, all the women gave offerings to the trees! I *know* that my plants can feel. That's why I feel so bad. Elaine tried to kill then—to *murder* them!—but I can transplant them and save them—"

Edna's face was frozen in its derision. "You're—crazy—"

Miranda murmured urgently, "There are plants that catch flies and eat them! There are sensitive plants that jerk away if you touch them! After all, we're no more different from plants than we are from birds—our construction is different—but birds can understand us—"

Edna mocked, "But birds can move. Trees can't."

"How do we know they can't? Have you ever heard of anyone who has really tried to communicate with trees, studying them and proving that they can't respond?"

"All I know," Edna said, "is that my own sister has gone crazy. I'm going to tell Ralph about this. I think that maybe you ought to be sent away some place. You're a danger to the welfare of my children—"

Miranda was terrified. "Edna, please try to understand!"

"I *do* understand—that you've gone completely out of your mind!"

"Edna—if I promise never to go to the tree again—?"

Edna surveyed her, tingling with cold pleasure. "I'll think it over," she said slowly, and smiled. "Yes—I'll think it over."

Her chair scraped away from the table, as she arose, Miranda watching her, trembling with worry. At the threshold, Edna looked back disdainfully.

"Ralph probably saw this side in you, though I never suspected it. No *won*der he didn't marry you!" she gloated.

"He didn't marry me, because I had to take care of Mother!" Miranda's voice quavered. She blinked tears from her eyes. "I loved him too much to think of any other man. All I had was Mother and my flowers. Edna—don't be so un*kind*—"

She could not repress her sobs. She laid her arms on the table and hid her face on them, her shoulders shaking with grief. Edna scanned her indifferently, then walked out.

The sound of hammering drummed from the oak. Junior and two neighbor boys were up in it, building a penthouse. "Gi' *me* that board!"

"*Le'* go! It's *my* board! I *brought* it!"

Miranda straightened up from her basket of wet clothes. She ducked under a sagging line of wash and peered up at the tree.

"Gi' me some more nails!" Junior ordered one of his playmates.

Miranda glanced anxiously toward the house, then hurried under the tree. She shaded her eyes with a palm, peeping up. "Junior!"

He glanced down. "What?"

"Must you pound nails into that poor tree? Can't you make the boards hold just as well by using rope?"

"I haven't got no rope."

"I can find some for you."

Junior was almost tearful with fury. "I won't use it if you *do!* Can't I even build my *own house* without you poking your ugly old nose in?"

"But Junior, dear—" She extended an apologetic hand. He studied her for a moment, his eyes murderous. Then he dragged on a plank, balancing on a low limb, and reached down to steady it.

"Why don't you go away and mind your own business?" he fleered. "Nobody wants you around here, anyway!" His two companions had ceased their activities and sat, relishing the intercourse.

"Well, Junior, I merely thought—" She smiled foolishly, winking sudden tears.

"I don't care a damn what you think!" the boy furthered vehemently. "You had t' go and tell on me, that I was playin' hookey, and I didn't get my allowance for a *whole week!* I'm not a-scared 'f you! Why don't you go away and get yourself a husband or somethin'? Why don't y' leave *me* alone, anyhow? I never asked y' t' come an' snitch on me!"

Miranda's smile was fainter, her voice uncertain. "But Junior, dear, I *had* to tell your mother that you stayed away from school. You don't realize it now, but later on you'll be sorry that you didn't learn all that you could at school—"

"Aw, nuts!" He felt in his pocket for nails. "That's ol' woman stuff! That's what they *all* say! Tryin' to make y' go to school! You get the hell *out* 'f here—and tell my mother I told you that, too, why don't you?"

Miranda turned hurriedly, and started away. The boy hammered loudly, challengingly. There was a sharp crackling. The limb on which Junior was sitting bent down, broke clean. The boy screamed, his eyes wide as he fell, clawing the air. Miranda whirled and saw him strike the ground, rebounding from the fallen branch. He lay on his back, his hands clutching his middle, his mouth open, groaning.

From up in the tree, the faces of the other two boys stared, white and unbelieving.

Miranda sat in her room, the old rocking chair creaking under her, her hands folded on her lap. She stared with the intensity of a blind person. Edna stamped back and forth, her voice raised to a shriek.

"Well, it'll probably make you glad to hear that my poor boy will limp for the rest of his *life*—thanks to you! If you hadn't been *ar*guing with him, he'd have been paying more attention to what he was *do*ing, and this would never have happened. You'll either have to get out and take your chances at finding a job, Miranda, or live off charity, and that's *flat*! If nothing else, you can go into service as a domestic." She whirled upon her apathetic sister. "Did you hear me? *An*swer me! Did you *hear* me?"

But Miranda did not move. She might have been a waxen effigy.

Outside a gust of wind sighed through the oak. Edna stamped over to the window. "I wish *we* owned that lot! We'd have that tree chopped *down*! Every time I look at poor Junior, I think of you and that damned *pet tree* of yours—and him lame for the rest of his life!" She pounded to and fro, repeating her words, goading herself into hysteria. Miranda sat listening, wooden.

At last Edna was silent, spent. Her face averted from her sister's, she slipped from the room and downstairs.

Miranda still sat motionless. She seemed barely to breathe. The breeze stirred the tree outside, and as though a voice had called, she turned her head to the window. She stood, and walked over to the pane, pressed against it, looking out. The blown branches beckoned her . . .

In the morning, Edna climbed the attic steps with a breakfast tray. "Randy! Randy, darling! Are you awake yet?" She pushed open the door. "When you didn't come down, I thought—

Randy!" She laid the tray with a crash down on the battered bureau, and stared around, bewildered. The bed was neatly made. The closet door was open, and all its contents were missing. A note lay on the seat of the rocking chair, bright against dark. Edna snatched it up, read it.

Forgetting the tray, she raced from the room, thudding down the steps. "Ralph! Ralph!"

"What's the matter, Mama?" Elaine's head peeped from her mother's room, her cheeks frosty with powder.

Edna halted as suddenly as though she had collided with an invisible wall. "Has your daddy gone to work?"

"Yes, Mama." Then Elaine raised a hand to the powder on her cheeks; she pulled back her head discreetly.

But Edna was without interest in the child. She hurried down to the front hall, through the living room, the dining room, the kitchen. No, Miranda was not in any of them. Was she outside? Edna lifted a curtain and peeped through glass to the oak. What were those things underneath the tree? She frowned. They looked like suit cases—

She rushed outside. Yes, here was Miranda's Gladstone bag, and the pasteboard overnight luggage. She opened them: they had been packed.

And what were these lying beside them? Miranda's clothes— hat, dress, shoes, stockings, even underwear! As though Miranda had doffed then to go swimming—

Edna covertly eyed the neighboring houses. No one was watching. She gathered the garments into a bundle which she stuffed under an arm, then grasped the handles of the bags and carried them into the house.

She cried into the telephone, "Hello, *Ralph?* Randy's gone!" Elaine stood by, silent and wondering. "No, I mean that Randy's left us! I went up to her room this morning, and she wasn't there! She left us a note—it sounds pretty desperate. I'm afraid she may have done something awful to herself. Should I read it to you?"

She was excited by her sad importance. The note was the sort that unhappy people usually leave. Miranda had realized that she was a burden, and so she was going away. They would never be troubled by her again, and please, please forgive her.

"Oh, Ralph, where could she have *gone?* Suppose she never comes *back?* What will all of our friends say? My own dear sister running away from our house, when I loved and needed her so! She shouldn't have taken what I said so hard! I was just all wrought up by poor Junior's suffering and the doctor's bill. I hardly knew what I was *say*ing—"

Snow was falling, large slow flakes like milkweed seeds. Edna hugged herself for warmth as she waited on the front porch while Ralph searched the mail box.

"Nothing?" she asked. He shook his head, hurrying up the steps. Her eyes swung to the oak, naked and black against the snow.

"There's Miranda's tree. Every time I see it, I think of her. I wonder what's happened to her." She stared at the tree, not seeing it. "I sometimes think that she's dead."

Ralph slid an arm around her. "She's probably all right."

Edna was grateful for his kindness. "But why haven't we had any letters from her, or anything? Oh, I don't really *care* so much; if I were sure that she's dead, I wouldn't mind too much. I really believe she was crazy. It's the *not* knowing what happened to her that worries me. I keep on telling myself that I drove her out and that somewhere she's miserable and blaming me for it all—I only wish there was something that I could *do!*"

Summer had come again. The hot air was spicy with the scent of roses. Edna lay on the sofa in a sleeveless dress, her hair brushed loosely back from her perspiring forehead, her face glistening from heat. She held a book over her eyes, and one hand traveled continuously from a sack of chocolates to her mouth and back. The floor lamp's flare was unkind to her.

Ralph laid down his newspaper and stood up. "Where y' goin'?" Edna frankly discarded the book for the candy.

Her husband was gaunt, his eyes tortured. "Just out in the yard."

"Oh." She dismissed him from her consciousness.

Ralph went out to the front porch. The hot air was heavy with moisture. The chirring and creaking of insects quivered through the night like a goblin orchestra tuning up. The moon was a lightless red disk low in the west.

Houses and trees were velvet black cutouts against the grey-paper sky and the silver filings of stars. Ralph stepped down from the porch and kicked through the wet grass, lifting his head to follow the brief meteoric flight of a firefly.

A woman was bending over the roses! She was touching them as if they were responsive things, whispering plaintively to then as if wheedling favors from them. Her body was misty with a wan glow, and wherever her hands caressed the flowers, a trace of the luminosity lingered. Her voice was the faint sigh of a restless breeze, none of her words distinguishable.

She was like what Miranda had been many years before—a small, slim girl. She was stark naked, beautiful in her freshness and vigor of youth. Her long hair floated around her as though it were weightless, or as though she were under water and lazy currents were playing with it.

She turned her head, saw the man. For a moment her eyes explored his, utterly without recognition; they were larger than he remembered Miranda's, wistful, tender, and yet mocking— as emotionally enigmatic as the stars.

Something about Ralph perplexed her. She frowned, her radiance fading. As though against her will, her arms lifted yearningly toward him, and she smiled temptingly. He could neither move nor speak.

A breeze rustled the oak. The glorious woman cocked her head, as though heeding an urgent call. She sighed, regretfully shook her head at Ralph, and lowered her arms. Leaning forward, she floated past him on a strong, unseen tide, her light dimming until she had merged with the shadows.

Ralph was too amazed to turn and follow her, even with his eyes. He stared stupidly at the point where her face had been, then at last passed a hand over his brow and shook his head as though dashing away a loose blindfold.

As if freed from an enchantment, he squared his shoulders, breathed deeply, and jerked his eyes around through the murk as though they were searching hands. Then he shrugged, laughed shortly, as though at a poor joke, and returned into the house.

Edna was licking the last of the chocolates from her plump fingers. "They get all gooey when it's so hot," she complained. "Did you take a look at the roses? Aren't they just *won*derful? I do say that our yard keeps as green and nice as if we'd hired a gardener to take special care of it!"

She crumpled up the candy-bag. "Mrs. Cross told me that the man who owns the lot is going to chop down Miranda's tree one of these days."

"No!" Ralph's passion surprised him as much as Edna.

"Yes!" she said.

She lay awake. "Ralph!" she called softly. "Are you awake?" But he did not answer. She stirred uneasily, and snapped on the light, gazed at her bedroom. There was nothing to fear! She switched off the light and lay back. And there it was again—a whispering of leaves in the wind . . .

Someone was in the room! Edna dragged the covers up to her face, too frightened now to put on the light. It seemed to be a woman, a naked girl, her body faintly phosphorescent. A ghost! Edna hid her face under the bed clothes and sobbed.

Ralph was at work when the cutters arrived to fell the tree, but Edna and Elaine stood at the railing of the front porch, watching. The men had tied ropes to the thick limbs: they shouted to each other, stopped sawing on the trunk. They dragged on the ropes.

The air was stabbed by loud cracklings, like miniature explosions. The tree tottered, then toppled, crashing down, the ropes sagging. Elaine scrambled excitedly down the porch steps, over the grass toward the tree.

"E*laine!*" Edna reached after her anxiously. "Come *back* here: You'll get hurt!"

"No, Mama, I won't! I just want to get a branch and make me a switch!"

She tugged unsuccessfully on a broken limb, gave up and went around the fallen giant to admire the stump. Her eyes gaped; she slapped a palm over her mouth in dismay, then screeched and pointed. "There's blood on the tree! Mama, come an' look at all th' blood! Did somebody get *hurt?*"

Edna scurried off the porch to her; the cutters gathered around the stump. A slow rill of blood welled from the tree's split trunk. In the fissure was a woman's arm, bleeding badly. Edna's fingers clawed her hair, horrified, and she drew back, reaching down to haul Elaine with her.

The men worked feverishly to widen the split with crowbars and wedges. The news was shouted to passersby by Elaine and Edna, then relayed around the neighborhood. The scene became bounded by curious bystanders; newspaper photographers appeared to snap pictures, their flashlight bulbs weak lightning. When the woman was freed from the tree, policemen forced the pushing crowd backward, their shouted commands blurred by the babbling voices.

She was Miranda, her once aging body now firm and blooming, her thick hair glossy and glorious. She was unconscious, dying, and as she was carried into the house, her face was distorted by intense pain.

"She was *in* the tree!" Edna exclaimed again and again, her eyes vacant with shock. "But how could she get *into* it? She said once that there are plants that catch flies and move away if you touch them, but—" She shook her head, dazed. "When she wakes up, we must ask her—"

But when Miranda opened her eyes, just before she died, there was only one sound which she could utter—a whispering as of leaves, fluttering in the wind.

The Beautiful Fog Ascending

Simon Strantzas

Spiderwebs of branches, woven together in the brittle air. A sparrow's warble; the rustle of drying leaves. Manifold sat perched on the large rock, dressed in his finest suit, wringing his arthritic hands. He stared at the spot where the dirt path vanished into the undergrowth.

The sun had not risen. Instead, it had simply given up the fight and stayed asleep—much as Manifold wished he too had done. Light diffused through the grey sky in a uniform pale, illuminating everything, but nothing so much that Manifold could say it was lit.

He wondered why he had come, what he was searching for. What use was there in leaving the house when the outdoors held nothing for him but a reminder that the world continued? That he was but a small and insignificant cog in the great machine. No, not a cog, because without a cog the whole cannot function. There was nothing quite that special about him. He had lived his whole life to become unnecessary.

At least outdoors there was chatter, movement, unlike his unkempt house. Those four walls, once full of life, full of Sandra, had grown silent; forty years of life accumulated there with nothing to show for it. The house stood on, while Manifold slowly fell apart.

His pocket buzzed, the ring of the cell phone his son, Herbert, had bought him. Manifold did not answer it. No one telephoned him, not even Herbert, who was too busy with his wife and children to spend more than requisite holidays with Manifold; who since Sandra's death had barely seemed interested in doing even that. Sandra had been the bridge between the two men, and without her . . . Without her so much was gone. It was worse than he could have imagined. There were days when getting out of bed was impossible. Days when he could not bear to face the mundanities the world had in store for him. There were days when he wanted nothing more than to sleep so deeply he rose into the sky. He found himself praying for salvation, for some solution to his misery. He had searched every avenue of his life and come up empty. There was nothing.

The phone in his pocket buzzed again. He reached his aching fingers in and removed it, then set it down gingerly on the smooth rock beside him. Vibrations echoed through the flecked stone, deep reverberations subsumed by the greyish woods. Manifold stood up, his brittle knees complaining fiercely about the weight, and did not look at Herbert's gift, rattling. Instead, he abandoned it and walked toward that fading point where the path disappeared into the thickness of trees, that point where the woods converged, where everything else would be left behind him.

Each step he took sank into the soft earth, as though the ground itself were trying to stay him. He continued forward, persevering even as his wrought lungs revolted in excruciating pain. There was something beyond that vanishing point, something he sought that drew him onward.

Stones riddled the edges of the worn path, and they slowly rolled as he approached, revealing their once-hidden aspects. He stopped to witness the phenomenon and sensed beneath his feet the ever-shifting ground vibrate, detected in the air a low insectan drone. A peculiar noise distracted him, the sound of a bird like the laugh of a child, somewhere above in the trees. He looked up into the tangle of branches and saw only slate sky.

It had become colder than it should, even so late in the turning season, far colder than it had been earlier when he left his meager house. Had he closed the door before setting off into the woods? He could not recall—his memory in the weeks and months since Sandra's death more porous, his thoughts more clouded. He remembered, vaguely, cleaning the house one last time; he remembered laying out his wedding suit across the bed; he remembered washing his calloused feet and crooked toes. He remembered these things, and yet could not recall leaving the house, could not recall entering the woods, could not recall anything between that bath and sitting upon the smooth, flecked rock. A giggle in the air, a cold gust, the rattle of his phone in his pocket. He reached for it and realized it was only a ghost, vibrating against his skin.

A memory from the depths surfaced, unsummoned. Herbert's solitary visit after Sandra's death. How could Manifold have forgotten? He had arrived with wife and children in tow—no more familiar to Manifold than faceless strangers. Herbert's face was drawn down, as was his nameless wife's, yet both seemed insincere. The terrible children were honest at least, playful and indifferent. That perhaps was the most infuriating. Had none of them decency enough to respect Manifold's pain? Did they have to flaunt living before him so, when he had struggled and failed in his own search to go on?

And why did that memory manifest itself at that moment, while Manifold stood, breathless, in the midst of the autumnal woods? What was it about the trees' slender trunks, like Sandra's arms reaching for him from her deathbed, that made him recall all that had been sensibly buried?

He heard a suppressed cough. He turned, squinting in the cold to focus his eyes, but he saw nothing.

"Hello?" Manifold called, voice shaking. "Hello? Who is there?"

But there was no reply. Just the sound of butterflies, of squirrels.

Manifold looked down at the dirt path and wondered whose feet stood upon it; whose hands dangled at his side, wrinkled, emaciated, ancient. He wondered whose misshapen and bent body he inhabited. And, most importantly, he wondered what it was he searched for. What answer did he seek? It was difficult for him to remember, difficult to think things through. He winced, shook his head, tried to snap the loose wires back into place. At once the world shifted, focused, and in that brief moment of ultra-clarity he realized what he was being beckoned toward, but as swiftly as the thought formed it dissipated, narrowly escaping his tenuous grasp.

He was not used to walking, to any sort of exercise. He stopped repeatedly, panting for breath until his mouth tasted of rust. He looked behind him at where he had come from, and it was unfamiliar. Nothing was as it had been. Not the path taken, not his marriage, not his family or friends, nothing was the same, because everything was gone. His heart raced, his breathing rushed, and all he could smell was the sweat building beneath his clothes. He took off his wedding jacket and discarded it. He loosened his shirt, desperate for more air in his lungs.

He paid no attention to the vibrating phone in his pocket. If anyone needed him, they would have to wait.

When Manifold saw the large rock ahead, rolled to the edge of the path, he wondered if it was the same rock he had been sitting upon in his past. But this rock was covered almost entirely by black lichen and bore no evidence of human contact. There was certainly no cell phone left upon its stone tableau, though Manifold could still feel a residual ring echoing from below its surface.

His sweat had not abated since discarding his jacket, and his jaw chattered in such a way that he worried he might be suffering a stroke. His vision was blurred; his legs threatened to give way. He questioned not only his senses, but his slipping sanity. Nothing around him appeared real. Especially not the

advancing creatures resolving from the aether. They slithered through the underbrush, fallen leaves sluicing off their shadowy forms. Manifold managed to scramble onto the large rock as they passed underfoot, and he was panting as he watched them go, fading between the trees.

Manifold slowly climbed down, careful to avoid further scraping his feeble legs. When he stood, he realized his shirt had been stained black by lichen, a map of the rock's surface across his chest. It was ruined. One more cherished symbol of his love for Sandra destroyed.

Manifold unbuttoned his shirt with trembling fingers. He sensed Sandra there, shaking her head, not understanding, but paused when he felt another presence, appearing from nowhere in the wooded depths. He lifted his head to see a tall lean man watching him, standing where the trunks of the trees were their thickest; where, even leafless, the branches blotted out the sun. The dark-skinned stranger wore a thick fur coat that gave him a goatish appearance, and he smoked a long-stemmed wooden pipe. It was pungent and smelled of musky foreign tobacco. Manifold dropped his shirt and hobbled forward, stumbling over a root snaking from the ground. Cold prickled his naked back and arms.

"Excuse me," he said, straining to be heard over the birds chirping in the branches above. "I don't know where—I need help. I can't remember how I got here."

The man smiled and leaned against a tree. The wide trunk bent beneath his weight.

"Where do you think you are, old man?" The stranger placed the pipe upon his tongue as it puttered bluish grey fumes.

"For the life of me I don't know. I don't know how I got out here."

"Is out here not where you want to be?" An eyebrow raised.

"I don't know. I don't know where I want to be."

The man nodded sharply, then removed the pipe from his mouth and knocked the bowl against the flat of his heel. It made a hollow pop, and the birds in the branches above dispersed, scattered to the sky. The man put the pipe in his fur's pocket.

"Then come with me."

Manifold held his arms tightly, trying to shield himself from the chill. He half suspected the stranger had made off with his shirt and jacket, just biding the time until he could secure the rest, but Manifold did not yet know why. It had become difficult to piece things together. To think. Much easier, then, to follow.

They walked for aeons, the sky shifting colors as though floating on oil. Manifold's feet burned, and he looked down to discover his shoes were missing, his socks in tatters, his wrinkled yellowed toes exposed and bleeding. He could suddenly feel the mold and dirt and moss underfoot, squeezing between his digits. He looked to the stranger for some explanation, but the man had vanished, leaving Manifold alone. The buzz of insects had increased, and with it the rattling of branches as animals scurried.

It was then Manifold saw the tree.

Had there been ten of him, holding hands, their bodies pressed up against the deep-grooved bark, they could not have encircled its massive trunk. The giant tree was dark grey and old, and it reached up through the canopy woven by the woods' branches—up into the heavy blanket of grey clouds.

Ripples moved along the ridges of the trunk, and it took Manifold a moment to realize it wasn't his failing watering eyes but hundreds of thousands of insects of all sizes covering the tree. Flies buzzed around it, circled it, lighting for an instant before flying away. Ants scurried along the deep grooves, walking around and over the dull black beetles that remained still. And the branches, full of birds chirping and screeching discomforting songs. Everything in the woods was converging on that one place, at that one moment, and Manifold felt a chill trickle down his back. He was dreaming, yet could not wake.

He wanted to scream, the wave of emotions flooding over him, drowning him, but he could not make a sound. And yet the creatures had no trouble. The birds chirped, the insects buzzed, the woodland animals rustled and chittered and howled as they climbed over exposed roots or hung from hollowed-out tree knots.

Was this what the stranger had been leading him to? The giant tree, incongruous with what surrounded it? Was it what everything led to?

There was a sound beneath the buzzing and rustling and chirping. A sound like a voice, one he knew better than any he had ever heard. A sound he longed for so that it tore pieces from his heart. "Manny," it said, the voice from the distance, from somewhere up in the tree. "Manny."

It could not be Sandra's voice, but he knew it was. He gazed up into the thick tangle of gnarled branches and saw the amorphous swell of clouds, swirling among the canopy of twigs and branches. He strained, looking for movement in the mist, but ultimately found nothing. Only shadows of hopes.

He was naked, stripped of all ballast. His clothes, his family, his wife, his job—everything he had known, every place he had belonged to, everything he ever had—was gone. What remained was only this: the tree; the birds; the insects; the animals. All he had left was in front of him. The rest receded into darkness.

"What are you going to do?" the stranger said, and Manifold saw him leaning against the wide trunk of the tree, once again smoking his pipe, grey smoky tendrils twisting upward, up around the lowest of the branches.

Manifold paused in thought. He felt insects light on him, crawl over his flesh, buzz every few steps. Then he forgot they were there at all.

"I think—" he tried. "I think I'm going to—" He looked up again at the giant tree endlessly looming above. He looked behind him at the path he had traveled, his footsteps filling with dirt and moss. He looked ahead at the path that quickly faded away into nothing. A dead end. "I think I want to climb."

The man shook his head, blinked twice, then bared his teeth and laughed like some strange animal. His feet clopped like hooves on the rocky ground.

"You found it," the man said. "Allow me to give you a hand."

Mirthfully, he put his pipe in his mouth and held out his meshed, wrinkled hands. They looked familiar, but Manifold stepped into them anyway.

Hand over bloodied hand, foot over bloodied foot, Manifold climbed the tree, leaving everything behind him. He climbed upward, higher and higher, ascending into that beautiful grey fog.

Exit Through the Gift Shop

Nick Mamatas

What happened to the drivers so foolish as to stop for the phantom hitchhiker of Rehoboth? Nothing, really. He's just an intense red-haired man, eyes wild, musk dripping from his pores. When he vanishes, he leaves behind a cigarette, though it's been decades since anyone has lit up in another person's car without asking. And the laughter, the howling maniacal laughter?

What's so funny, anyway? Anyway, not *anyways*. That's hillbilly talk. A remnant of Middle English, preserved by the toothless and inbred lower classes of Scots-Irish extraction. You can always tell that a kid's some jumped-up bumpkin in town for his college edjumication if she says "anyways." This is New England. Anyway means one alternative way. Anyways means that there are so many possibilities out there, doesn't it?

But there aren't so many, are there?

Rehoboth is from the Bible. Surely the verse is on the tip of your tongue. "And he removed from thence, and digged another well; and for that they strove not: and he called the name of it Rehoboth; and he said, For now the LORD hath made room for us, and we shall be fruitful in the land." Genesis! Right near the beginning. Rehoboth is a place of enlargement and flourishing. Back in 1643, when the town was founded, people were familiar with the Bible. They knew what "rehoboth" meant way back when. Rehoboth was once much larger, but until recently it was a dinky little town of ten thousand—

Whoops, almost said "ten thousand souls." That would have been misleading. Ten thousand warm human bodies of various morphologies.

The joke is that in 1993, Rehoboth's local leading citizens got all dressed up in colonial garb and marched on Attleboro to reclaim their ancestral lands. That's the kind of town it is. Quirky. Nobody bothered to ask the local natives what they thought of all these shenanigans. Dinky.

Speaking of shenanigans: welcome to the attraction. With the decline of the mills and the recession and all that, the town fathers decided that tourism was the way to spark the local economy. There are hiking trails and a clambake, but this is New England. What about the stretch of time between Halloween and May Day, when it snows once a week, and the only way to stop a running nose is to wait for the snot to freeze?

Stretch of time, stretch of time you can imagine some old woman in a peach leisure suit saying, turning the phrase over in her head. Maybe she's at the one okay restaurant in town, her bubble haircut fresh from her weekly appointment, turning whisky over on her tongue as she concentrates. How can we get some money for the town during that stretch of time? Stretch, stretch, what a funny word that is. What else stretches? Roads! Aha!

And in that old woman's mind, *stretch of road* brings to mind the famous Rehoboth hitchhiker. It's just a local variation on the phantom hitchhiker that any chockful-of-snore town with more cemeteries than gas stations has. Lonely looking girl wants a ride. Lonely looking girl gets a ride. Lonely looking girl vanishes right outside the cemetery gates. Had things gone rather more poorly for the old woman back in her college days, she might have been the lonely looking girl, forever young and bored with her own tomb.

The Rehoboth hitcher variation is a darker one. A man, a red-head, not a conscientious passenger. He glares, he starts laughing, then shrieking. He'd kill you if he could, with an axe. He'd do much worse, if he could. It occurs to the old woman to check out the local newspaper's morgue, to have her secretary examine the death records. Rehoboth is a small town; if there are any red-haired men who died in their twenties, and on the side of the road, it would be in the town's records. The secretary turns up nothing. *It's not a phantom hitchhiker, after all,* the old woman decides. *It's the* demon *hitchhiker.*

Plans are put into motion. Letters are sent to particular individuals who have, in a fit of irony and pique, taken to living in Salem, sixty whole miles away. In-person inquiries are made in nearby Providence, because that's just a twenty-minute drive or so down the road. *Certainly we can help,* was the general response. Nobody had ever thought to have the witchy Salemites work with the fine upstanding Christians of Providence before, but the old woman believes in covering all the bases. In *enlarging* the possibilities. There is more than one alternative. Anyways, not just anyway. She's on the Cemetery Commission; her husband is on the Zoning Board of Appeals. Paperwork is signed, then shredded. Wheels are set into motion. She puts her shoulder to the task.

By Halloween it's done. The Haunted Stretch. No promises save one—you can drive as quickly as you want on the Haunted Stretch, and if you get into trouble, you can always make a hard right into one of the gravel-filled runaway car ramps.

Forty thousand dollars, for two miles. Your tags and insurance had better be up to date. Leave the Garmin in the glove box. GPS doesn't work on the Haunted Stretch, not anymore, and you won't need it anyway. It's a straight shot. The Commonwealth of Massachusetts knows nothing of it, nor does Bristol County. *It's our little secret* is the sort of thing the old woman would whisper in your ear, if she were here, and interested in whispering anything in your ear, which she is not.

You meet the crew in the parking lot of Uncle Ed's Front Porch, a small ice cream joint on Winthrop Street. It closes early, so nobody's there but the crew, and their flatbed. Two guys, both heavy-set and swarthy, eating ice cream. Your breath fogs before you.

"Isn't it a little chilly to eat ice cream?" you say. You regret it a moment later, then decide not to regret anything. *Forty thousand dollars.* You should be able to eat ice cream out of the high school quarterback's jockstrap for forty grand, not stand here in the frigid night making conversation with a pair of townies.

The one guy stabs his ice cream with his plastic spoon and says, "Naah." He's got a thick local accent. "Everyone here eats ice cream in the winter time."

"More ice cream is eaten per capita in the Boston metroplex than anywhere else in the United States," the other guy says. He's younger. No accent. They could be father and son. "It's the high fat content; keeps you warm."

"And in the summertime," the father guy says. "You'd better eat ice cream."

"Yeah, you'd better eat ice cream around here, come summertime."

"Why?" you say without thinking, and then they both smile and shout, "Or it'll melt!" and have a good laugh. The older guy gestures for your keys, and you hand them over. You glance at his work jeans—the ass is clean, at least. The son tilts the bed and invites you into the truck's warm cab.

You climb in, belt up, smile at the kid. He's probably a good kid, just working with his dad and trying to find a place in a small town that he's already a little too big for. He should be in school, in Boston, mackin' chicks or suckin' dicks depending on his preference. You'll tell him that afterwards, you decide. Maybe slip him a few bucks if he has any weed, to take the edge off the experience with the night.

"So, is this where you dose me with—" you don't get to say *the chloroform* before he hits you with the stun gun.

You wake up in your car, a cherry taste in your mouth. You feel very *good,* as if the jolt you took from the kid charged the juice in your spine. It was all in the watermarked, password-protected, DRMed, and self-destructing PDF you received when you sent your money in. Skeptics used to think that the enhancement drug was the core of the attraction—mild hallucinogens and the power of suggestion were enough to give most rubes the experience they deserve, if not exactly want.

The skeptics shut the fuck up after someone wearing Google Glass took a ride down the Haunted Stretch of Rehoboth. That's when you took out a loan, using your shitty Union City, New Jersey, condo as collateral, and got to filling out the proper forms.

You were never even all that much interested in ghosts, or religion, or the supernatural. You just wanted to experience something that most people won't ever be able to. Everything from cage fighting to summers among the Antarctic penguins is available for anyone with the money and spare time. But to keep out the losers, weirdoes, and journalists, the old woman added a wrinkle to her dark ride—the application came with a text box, and no instructions.

In it you wrote:

Honestly, whenever I think about my past, about stupid things I've said or done, I mutter aloud, "I just want to kill myself." Sometimes I actually sing it to myself, and add "doo-dah doo-dah" to the end. But I don't really want to kill myself. I just think about it for a few seconds every day, several times a day. Hopefully the experience will help me deal with whatever it is that I'm dealing with.

You were surprised at your own admission. Like how you drop a hot potato before you get burned, your fingers typed it in without you even having to think about it. Anyway, it worked. Either that, or they just have a lottery and you happened to win. *Anyways,* something happened and you're here now, behind the wheel of your car, your heart pumping liquid joy to your limbs. You don't want to kill yourself. You want to dig a hole in the asphalt and fuck the world till she comes. You want to drive so fast you'll zip past the patch of light made by your headlamps and into the swirling dark of Rehoboth's winter.

You move to turn the key in the ignition, and only then do you realize that the engine is already running. The lights are on, after all. It's warm in the cab, of course. You're so fucking stupid. But you don't think *I want to kill myself.* You smile; you lick your own teeth to taste more of the cherry gunk; you love being alive. Sing that!

I love being alive!

But you ease up on the accelerator. You've got two miles for something to happen, and that ain't a lot. Oh, how you want something to happen. You don't even care if it's just an actor, or a hallucination, or both. You don't even care if the redhead opens a mouth full of yellow tombstone teeth and bites your fucking nose off, like what happened to the guy on the other end of the Google Glass.

The car rolls forward, and you start to sweat ice water. Whatever the cherry stuff is, it's pretty crazy. Rehoboth should have just packaged the cherry stuff as an energy drink rather than going through all this trouble to balance the town's accounts. *Eh, it's probably extremely illegal,* you decide. Not like charging people forty thousand dollars to drive down a stretch of decommissioned town road.

Do I step out from behind a tree, thumb out? Should I materialize in the passenger seat and put my hand on your knee and wink and call you boyfriend? Or just rise up before the car, eyes and mouth wide, palm outstretched?

Fuck it, I take the roof. I don't feel a thing, but you sure do, when two-hundred-twenty pounds of mostly muscle slams into the slope of your PT Cruiser. I crack the windshield with my forehead, and scream and laugh and howl as you jerk the wheel hard to the left, then hard to the right.

I love.

The screech of the tires.

How they smell as they melt by millimeters.

Tree branches snapping against the windows.

Gravel like hail.

My fist through the window, spiderwebbing it.

Glass everywhere, like thousands of shattered teeth.

You're a toughie, man. A cookie what won't crumble easy. You actually throw a punch at me. Right at me. I feel it and everything.

I start laughing and laughing. Oh ho ho ho. That ain't blood pouring out my nose.

It's the cherry stuff.

Anyways.

No, as a matter of fact, I'm *not* from around here.

Hey, sailor? New in town?

Come here often?

I cut your legs out from under you and take a seat on your belly.

You fuck, you *fuck!*

What I am going to do, with my awesome magic powers, is remove your central nervous system, starting from this little slice at the bottom of your pinky toe.

Forty-five miles of string.

Don't worry. I work fast. I have all the time in the world. I'm well practiced. I can do three hundred yards with a tug. Leaves me all night to floss my teeth with the stuff, tie little knots where I want them, and to untie the ones you've tied yourself.

Fucking amateurs.

In the old days, I used to construct harps out of this shit, and human spines.

A phantom hitchhiker ain't nothin'. It's a fingerprint. A cosmic smudge on the night. Me, I'm the real deal, the genuine article. The thing what left the smudge. *Unleashed!* Thanks to the spirit of intermunicipal cooperation.

And you got me for forty grand! Not too shabby, Ace.

So what I am going to do now is tie one end of your nervous system to your brain stem and another to this bright little star I have in my pocket, and then I'm going to let go of it, see, and it's going fly up up up into the firmament, stretching the tissue till it licks the edge of space.

Move over.

Hahaha, I kid, I kid.

Forgive the nudge, I know you can't move over.

Let me just nestle down here and cuddle on up next to you.

The asphalt's nice and warm, thanks to the skidding. Good job with that.

Doesn't it look cool up there, my little star? It's like an awesome little kite, the string leading down to your nose.

You have a very distinguished-looking nose. The nose of kings, friend!

It's nice out here in Rehoboth. Not a lot of streetlamps, or tall buildings, so you can really see the stars.

One more nudge. See, look at that? Doesn't all the glass on the street look a lot like the stars? And the little snowflakes that are starting to fall? They look like the stars too, the teensy ones we can only see if we live out in the country and eat our carrots, like mama said.

That's some cool shit right there, Ace.

Okay. Now what you need to do, and I'll hold your hand and squeeze it until you do, is inhale.

That's right, suck it all back in.

We've got all night. Hell, we've got all night, every night. I hitchhike through space, not through time. I'm already all over this whole stretch of *time.*

Aw, do your fingers hurt? Well, inhale more, you dirty little *fuck!*

Like you're eating spaghetti with your nose. Slurp it all back in to your body.

And no, had you shown up wearing one of those streaming Internet glasses, I just would have ripped your face off. Fuck you apes, and your YouTube.

Keep it up. *Snort snort.* Oink for me, baby.

There is no alternative. Any way you slice it, and I can slice it any which way, you need to get all this stuff back into you, and I need my little star back.

It's a good luck charm.

You're doing real good. Real good. See, you can feel your face again. Yeah, it fucking hurts.

Don't cry.

I'll give you some more cherry stuff. Let me just—

There we go. Keep your head on my lap, just like a little baby, and drink all you like. I'm gonna let it pour right down my chin.

And keep snuffling your nerve tissues back into your body.

Let me tell you a bit more about the old woman. She picked me up once, even though women in those days didn't often drive on their own, and didn't ever stop for strangers.

She liked anonymous dick. There's nothing wrong with it. Lots of people do. *You do,* don't you?

People just don't like to think of civic-minded ladies as horny little nymphs wearing nothing but bush beneath their sundresses. She was a smart girl too. Went to Radcliffe, back when girls went to Radcliffe instead of Harvard proper. And when she picked me up, she sang:

> But if I should leave my husband dear,
> Likewise my little son also,
> What have you to maintain me withal,
> If I along with you should go?

She'd spotted me right off. James Harris, the Daemon Lover. I'm a goddamn English ballad, sport. But I had no ships upon the sea, no mariners to wait upon thee, anymore. They're all at the bottom of the Atlantic. Especially those fucking mariners. They got me here, to America, but they had to die.

So I have to hitchhike.

She picked me up. We had a wild time, a good one. I buried myself deep inside her. So deep she could never stop thinking of me, no matter how many husbands she burned through—and she's had four—nor how many other anonymous lovers she's had.

How many? Count the stars, son. How many can you see, on a clear night like this, through blurred and stinging eyes? And keep *sucking!*

She tried to forget me, but she couldn't.

She's watching right now.

Don't look around.

Anyway, this is how she likes it. It's how I like it too.

Anyways, there are so many things I like to do. And little old ladies are one of them. And my little old lady likes selling kitsch. There's a T-shirt in your goodie bag, back at the hotel.

I SURVIVED THE HAUNTED STRETCH OF REHOBOTH.

It says that, for real. It was blank before, but you're doing such a good job.

Tell your friends about us.

There. You're almost done. It's almost dawn.

Don't look around. Not at that hill on the right, that shines so clear to see. Not on the hill to the left, that looks so dark to thee. You look straight fucking ahead. Don't make me break your neck. Eyes ahead, you little shitsack. Anyway, any*ways,* you can.

Going to Ground

Darrell Schweitzer

So in the end he simply yielded to what had previously balanced somewhere between a wry observation and a morbid obsession. In the course of the many road trips he'd taken for his work, as he made his way up through northeastern Pennsylvania, through Scranton, Mt. Pocono, Jim Thorpe, and Chorazin, and into New York State by way of Binghamton and on to Rochester or Albany, he had begun to notice, particularly while driving alone late at night, how remarkably *empty* the landscape was of any trace of mankind at all, and how civilization, in the form of villages, farms, or rest stops, was only in the valleys. The ridges of the forested hills that stretched on for endless miles seemed absolutely primordial. He'd joked once to his wife that if an invading army of orcs ever followed those ridge lines and refrained from shooting off fireworks or playing their boomboxes too loud, they could make it nearly to the state capital in Harrisburg without being detected. Sometimes, at sunset, in the winter, when he could see the bare trees silhouetted by the glare of the sky, he fancied that he could glimpse mysterious shapes darting between the black trunks; and he imagined, too, that the light from beyond those hills was not entirely of this world.

Therefore, on this last night, in his great pain, he drove without knowing where he was going, like an animal mindlessly going to ground, and he pulled over in the middle of a particularly dark stretch of nowhere, without even the distant glimmer of a farmhouse in sight. He let the car roll into what might have been a natural clearing or the remains of some abandoned field. Then, because his nature must have been methodical somewhere else in his life, he put the gearshift in park, shut off the engine, pulled the parking brake, turned off the headlights, carefully removed the keys from the ignition, then got out and locked the car, placing the keys in his pocket.

His memory wasn't working. If he tried to think back more than a few minutes there was nothing. There was only the distress of inexplicable grief, which was giving way to a curious mental numbness. He did not know what he was fleeing from, only that he must *go.* It was like *letting go,* as if he had dangled from a railing over an abyss and released his grip, falling down forever. The impression was reinforced all the more by the fact that the ground dipped slightly as he began walking, and he stumbled into a ditch and lost his glasses before he regained his feet. But then he instinctively began to climb the rocky hillside, into the trees. Before long the darkness had closed around him entirely. He caught hold of the trees—thin, leafless—and hauled himself up.

It was like swimming in a dream, up, up away from a black void that threatened to swallow him, as if he were ascending into the sky.

Like a dream, it was silent. He heard only his own gasping breath, his heartbeat throbbing in his ears. Like a dream of drowning perhaps. The forest lacked all the usual night noises: crickets, birds, even the sound of branches creaking in the wind.

Instinctively, he struggled ever upward, perhaps for hours. Perhaps, as in a dream, there was no time, and this night would never end and he would go on climbing forever.

He wept softly, not entirely sure why. Something floated out of the darkness of his lost memory, like a painted white sign drifting up from the bottom of a murky pool, and it came to him that in the morning, if there was to be a morning, the sensational headline in the papers would say considerably more than MAN WALKS IN THE WOODS.

But what it would say, he somehow didn't want to find out. He refused to formulate that thought. He knew he mustn't. It was like when your mother tells you: *Don't pick at it.*

Don't.

Don't.

Don't.

Only after a very long time did he realize that he was not alone.

It wasn't so much that he heard anything, and he did not see anything but the darkness. Without his glasses, in any case, everything less than a few feet away would be a blur. When he looked up he saw nothing at all, either because the sky was overcast or because he could not make out the stars. (On a clear night, he knew, the stars out here could be brilliant, wonderful. This was not a clear night. Either that or, somehow, there no longer *were* any stars.)

No, he just *felt* a certain closeness, a proximity like when you are groping in a lightless tunnel and you reach out your hand, you are almost certain of the nearness of the wall, even if you can't quite touch it.

He continued for an endless time, certain that a great number of others were all around him, like a rising tide, sweeping him along; but that was when, catastrophically, either by malign accident or the perverse doings of Poe's Imp, which he often explicated in his professional lectures, he did not do the easy thing and just go with the tide, but *stopped.*

Something crashed into him, nearly knocking him over. He stumbled, staggering about noisily in the fallen leaves and underbrush, and he even called out, from stupid reflex, "Hey, watch where you're—"

Then he *did* hear motion all around him, like the rising susurrus of a tide, and—as the protective armor that encased his memory began to break—he recalled that he had a cigarette lighter in his coat pocket. His fingers, more than his mind, knew to how get that lighter out and flick it on.

The glare of the flame might have been a suddenly rising sun.

The faces revealed around him were all dead. He was sure of that. They were dead. No, their eyes did not glow. Some of them did not even have eyes, only dark pits. They were pale, so very pale, and he knew they were all corpses or ghosts, dead, walking up this hillside in the forest with him, yes, like a tide in their inevitability.

"Have you lost your way?" one of them said.

That was when he was certain, very certain, more fantastically certain than anything else in his life that this was wrong, so very, very wrong—and *why WOULD they say that he was mad?*— to paraphrase the line he used to use to punctuate his very popular Poe lecture up at the universities in Rochester or Albany.

"I don't belong here," he said. "I'm not one of you."

He tried to make his way back down the way he had come. He pushed his way through the crowd of the dead, shoving them aside, smelling the foulness of them, their butcher-shop odors of blood and spoiled flesh. Sometimes a hard, cold hand would grab hold of him, but he always managed to break free, and he was running now, running, almost flying, hurtling back down the hill, back toward—what?

And that was when he remembered everything. Maybe it was his perverse imp after all, or just malign something or other, picking, picking; and the armor that had shielded him thus far suddenly turned into glass and shattered into a million pieces. He sat down, weeping once more, as it all came back to him, everything he had forgotten, everything that had blasted his brain out into merciful, dark amnesia, now coming back, like a fire rekindled from smoldering ashes as he helplessly relived it all, the screaming argument, the obscenities, the struggle, the thunderclap moment in which his life, his existence, all his future *snapped* and was destroyed.

The gunshot.

The morning's headline, which would read something like COLLEGE PROFESSOR MURDERS FAMILY, FLEES.

Something like that.

He could only sit on the hillside now, with the dead passing all around him, drifting up that slope. He could only wait until the last of them approached him, and he, perversely, flicked the cigarette lighter one last time; the last of them walking up to him, his wife, Margaret, with the whole front of her blouse soaked in blood, and then his twelve-year-old daughter Ann, who wasn't supposed to have been there, who had come home too early from band practice and blundered in on something she wasn't supposed to see.

Half of her face was blown away, but she was the one who said, "Why, Daddy? Why?"

He had no answer. He could only protest that this was all wrong, that he didn't belong here, as cold hands took hold of him and led him up the wooded hillside after the others, up, up toward that mysterious ridge line where the black, naked trees stood silhouetted by pale fires burning beyond them, fires that, he was certain, no passing motorist, however observant or imaginative, ever saw from the highway.

Dark Equinox

Ann K. Schwader

There was a crack in the gallery's front window. In one of the small top panes, but still obvious, just as last fall's leaves on the porch were. Or the doorknob's accumulated grime, though the sign inside that door read OPEN.

Not for much longer, I'm guessing.

Jen frowned. Despite its website optimism, this place was on its last financial legs after the holidays—with any remotely valuable photographs long gone.

The door's anemic bell did nothing to boost her optimism as she entered. Beyond a desk cluttered with large-format books and brochures, there were only two narrow display rooms divided by a staircase. Their carpets, though good once, bore worn ghosts of patterns, and the walls held more faded rectangles than images for sale.

What she could see of those images didn't leave much hope. Still, Leonie Gerard was listed among the gallery's artists—and she was local to the Denver area.

Or had been.

Shifting her messenger bag across her back, Jen started her search. The first room held photographs of the modern West: no photomontages, nothing remotely experimental. She recognized few of the artists, though a spatter of tiny red stickers showed most were already sold.

The second room, though smaller, seemed more promising. One Uelsmann. A couple of Bonaths. One remarkably contorted Michel Pilon, and—

Not possible.

She stepped closer to the print. Against a carefully composed mosaic of images—mainly archaeological—three oval objects descended in series. They were almost, but not quite, eggs. No visible light source defined them, yet the closest bore faint scrawls of shadow.

Or perhaps harbored them within its shell. Waiting, and growing stronger, and testing for cracks—

She blinked. How had *that* thought come up?

Before her imagination could distract her any further, she checked the print's bottom border. Last year's date, in pencil . . . 3 / 7 . . . and a signature. Her signature.

Footsteps sounded on the stairs behind her, followed by a soft clank of bracelets as someone turned up the overhead light.

"You know Leonie's work?"

An elderly woman in Southwestern clothing stood in the doorway. She wore more silver than Jen had ever seen on one person before, and her long velvet skirts looked vintage. The gallery's owner, she guessed, hoping for one final sale this afternoon.

Jen nodded. "I did my thesis on her, two years ago."

Even at the time, she'd been dissatisfied with it—as had her thesis committee. To their minds, Leonie Gerard's photomontages were less a subject for contemporary art history than for science fiction, or possibly horror. Though Gerard limited herself to black and white, her juxtapositions of image-fragments from exotic locations had grown increasingly bizarre.

Jen suspected her thesis had only been approved out of loyalty to the local arts community. CU Boulder, got to love it.

Silver rang at her elbow. "And you followed her career . . . afterwards?"

"All the way."

In the silence that followed, Jen finally checked the print's information tag. *Vernal Ascension*. The date, again. Archival silver print. No red dot. And no mention of a price, not even NFS.

"So you'll know what this one is, then." The older woman's voice quavered. "Her last."

Three of seven, but only three had ever been printed. Jen hesitated.

"I've read about it, and seen a reproduction in an article. But I've never actually—"

"It feels different, doesn't it?"

When Jen nodded mutely, the other woman took the print down and turned it over, revealing the handwritten label. It gave her the same chill Van Gogh's *Wheat Field with Crows* did, though the image itself was oddly tranquil.

But was it for sale?

Before she could ask, the gallery owner replaced the image and stepped back, motioning for her to do likewise. Weak afternoon light from the front window picked out details: the shattered top of an obelisk, vine-smothered carved steps, the snarl of a jaguar god. Fragment upon fragment—until some critical mass of mind revealed the pattern beneath. A living landscape of antiquity and shadow.

"I don't think she ever made anything else quite like it."

Jen nodded again. While researching her thesis, she'd seen reproductions of most of Leonie Gerard's work—and experienced a few in person at museums. None of those skillfully assembled images worked the way this one did.

She couldn't say why, either. Something in the angles, perhaps, or the sites themselves. Where had the artist traveled? Though she recognized sacred sites in Belize and Turkey, and one T-shaped doorway from Chaco Canyon, most of the locations eluded her. She wondered how many were on the State Department's no-go list.

"I never got the chance to talk to her about it, either." The older woman's skirts swished as she walked back to the print. "Her brother brought this one in."

Now or never.

"Just for display?"

The gallery owner produced a tiny silver pen and a pack of business cards from her pocket. She jotted a number on one before extending it to Jen.

"Are you, um, sure about this?"

"For the right collector, yes." A shadow smile crossed the older woman's face. "And don't tell me you don't own anything else of Leonie's. It doesn't matter. You take her work, and her life, seriously."

Present tense. As if she already knew Jen's struggle for a Ph.D. Her failed applications, her need for more original work to get the attention of the right people, at the right schools.

Jen swallowed hard. "Thank you."

To her surprise, the gallery owner lifted *Vernal Ascension* down at once and headed for the front desk. Clearing herself work space, she began swathing it in bubble wrap.

"Don't you want to wait until your show's over?"

The shadow smile returned. "It's perfectly fine."

Minutes later, her card had been charged and Jen held the dreamed-of image. The gallery owner thanked her, but made no move to leave her desk.

"Is there anything else?"

Jen's fingers tightened on the bubble wrap. "You mentioned a brother." She hesitated. "Does he live around here? Would he be willing to talk with me about her work?"

The wrongness of the question hit her immediately. Mumbling an apology, she turned to leave.

"Just a moment, please."

Behind her, Jen heard a desk drawer open, then a rustling of papers.

"Sebastian Gerard," the other woman said, still digging. "I met him once. Interesting man, used to teach world mythology—Joseph Campbell stuff—at some community college. Now he owns rental cabins up in Estes Park, but it's the slow season. I suspect he'd have time."

She exhaled satisfaction as she shut the drawer again.

"Here's his card."

Jen took it and thanked her, then hurried out of the gallery with her purchase. No sense taking chances. This wasn't a bad part of town, but there weren't a lot of good parts this late in the day.

She was barely off the porch when she heard a noise behind her.

Glancing back, she saw that the gallery's door sign now read CLOSED. Only the building's upstairs windows were illuminated. When even these began falling dark, she tightened her grip on her prize and walked faster.

"I'm glad you called, Ms. Maxwell."

Sebastian Gerard's voice was older than she'd expected—and better informed. Jen frowned. How the hell did he know her name?

Insight hit a couple of seconds later. "I'm assuming the gallery told you—"

"—who bought Leonie's last piece? Yes. I'm afraid I asked them to."

Sunk deep in the folds of her beanbag chair, Jen still felt a chill. This was getting into stalker territory—aside from *him* waiting for *her* to call, of course. And it had taken her days to work up the courage to do that.

"I guess I can't blame you," she finally said. "It must hold a lot of memories."

"That's . . . putting it mildly."

Whatever was skewing his end of this conversation, it didn't sound like grief. Or even resentment.

More like anxiety?

Start over. "I'm so sorry for your loss, Mr. Gerard. Your sister's imagination was incredible. In those later images, it was as if she was assembling a whole new world."

"She was."

The chill she'd been blaming on her landlord's control of the thermostat deepened.

"I didn't realize she'd discussed her work with anyone. When I was researching my thesis, I didn't find many letters or notes. She didn't do a lot of interviews, either."

"No, she didn't." Gerard seemed to be gathering his own courage now. "Ms. Maxwell, I'd appreciate the chance to buy back *Vernal Ascension*. Every cent you paid—and some extra for your trouble."

He hesitated. "I never should have put it up for sale."

Jen's frown deepened. Hanging above her futon couch in pride of place—assuming pride even applied to this place—Leonie's last image pulsed with life.

The background ruins looked sharper than they had in the gallery, as if some jungle mist had started to lift. Their juxtaposed locations no longer felt jarring, but exuded an organic sense of rightness. The egg-objects were descending toward an earth womb prepared for them. Or perhaps there was only one object, plus two earlier reflections of the journey—

"Ms. Maxwell?"

Gerard's voice sputtered from a fold in the beanbag. Extracting her dropped phone, Jen started to apologize.

"You were looking at it just then, weren't you?"

Go with the weirdness. "Yes."

"I had the same experience with numbers one and two of that image, and I didn't know why at the time. Now I've at least got suspicions." Another silence. "Which is why I'd really like to buy back number three."

Jen glanced up again at *Vernal Ascension*.

The jaguar god's tongue lolled faintly red.

"I can't do that," she said quickly. "I'm working on my Ph.D. application. I'm not sure what that gallery told you, but—"

"—you need to start publishing. Which means original research."

He sounded tired. "Ms. Maxwell, I understand your fascination with my sister's work. And I'm deeply grateful for all the time and energy you've spent bringing it to the attention of academia. But this just can't—"

He took a ragged breath. "—it can't really be researched. And if you saw Leonie's studio, I think you'd understand why."

Jen froze. *Her studio?*

Almost a year ago, Leonie Gerard's career—and her life—had ended in a darkroom fire, which might or might not have been accidental. None of the references she'd found could tell her any more, and the rumors she'd chased in the arts community couldn't be confirmed.

All she knew for sure was that Leonie's studio had been in the Colorado mountains.

"Are you saying you could arrange it?"

"My sister lived up here in Estes when she wasn't traveling. I lent her one of my cabins, and we built her studio together." Gerard hesitated. "There's not much left of that. But the cabin's just as she left it."

Not *in* Estes Park, she knew, but somewhere outside it. At the end of an unpaved road knee-deep in snow. Or mud.

Owned by a guy she'd never met.

Way too far from help if he turned out to be dangerous.

Mentally sighing, Jen reached for a notepad. She'd need driving directions.

As it turned out, she had been wrong about the road. What twisted and plunged its way down to the Triple G Cabins office was more of a goat track, and almost a match for her aging Subaru.

Killing the engine at last, Jen drew a deep breath and rested her head on the steering wheel. What was she looking for here? In the handful of days since she'd spoken with Sebastian Gerard, she'd been unable to figure that out, despite her certainty that Leonie's studio—or its remains—held answers.

At least she and Gerard agreed on that much.

Moments later, the man himself tapped on her window. She lowered it halfway.

"You can't drive in to the studio. We'll have to walk from here."

Leonie's brother looked even older than he'd sounded, with a short grey ponytail and a lean, weary face. He barely waited for her to lock the car before heading toward a nearby stand of pines.

There was no real path through, but she'd worn boots and there wasn't all that much snow. Just discouraged grimy patches after a dry winter, with long-range forecasts not much better, and wildfire season looking worse. She'd always imagined it being beautiful up here, but this was—

"I don't suppose you brought your print with you?"

"Uh, no. " Her mind flittered back over their phone conversation. "Were you expecting me to?"

The weariness in Gerard's face deepened. "No, just hoping."

They walked on in silence through the trees. A lot of them looked unhealthy, with brittle needles and trunks clotted with resin. Not hard to imagine a fire up here, even without darkroom chemicals or amateur wiring.

Not hard to imagine it not being an accident at all.

Even so, Jen wasn't prepared for the view beyond the pines. Sticking up through the snow like a charred skeleton, the remains of Leonie Gerard's studio looked as if the tragedy had happened last week—not almost a year ago. Tattered blackout curtains flapped from window frames. Glass shards glinted on the ground. Even the ruined door still hung in place, barely.

Breathe. "Did you ever find out what happened?"

"She died."

No point in asking what volunteer fire brigade had tried and failed, what EMT had done likewise. What official conclusions came weeks later. The details of that March night were surely burned into Gerard's mind, but nothing she could say right now would bring them to the surface.

Apologizing, Jen moved closer to the doorway. "May I?"

Gerard nodded. The afternoon air felt suddenly colder, and very silent.

Pale sunlight through breaks in the roof revealed scorched trays, a shattered light table, sodden boxes of files and supplies. A wire drying line had survived, but held only curled strips of black in twisted clips. A much larger tangle of metal and half-burned paper blocked the path to the door.

She squinted. The metal looked like picture frames.

A sharp, improbable drama played through her mind: Leonie, distraught, piling up her work in the first convenient place. Igniting it. Realizing too late she'd blocked her exit—unless she'd never intended to leave in the first place. And all this inside her studio, destroying negatives and contact prints as well.

What had she wanted to burn so badly?

When she turned to ask Gerard, he was already standing beside her.

"She'd been preparing for a group show down in Taos, working nonstop. She was still recovering from her last trip . . . Sierra Leone, good God . . . but *Vernal Ascension* wouldn't wait. She said she needed to put the images together right away, while she could still see what they were trying to show her."

Jen started to ask the obvious question, but he went on.

"Meanwhile, the Taos gallery was getting antsy. Leonie printed the first three and shipped them off, but they kept calling. The night of March nineteenth, she locked herself in her studio to finish the other four—"

Jen held her breath, waiting.

"—at least, that's what she told me she planned to do."

Turning away from the ruins, Gerard began walking fast, heading even further into the trees. She scrambled to catch up.

"Ms. Maxwell, how much do you know about my sister's work methods?"

"She did digital photography for a long time, but switched back to film for the last couple of years—when she started doing photomontage exclusively."

Scraps of interviews she'd read came back to her. "She wanted the 'greater reality' of print over pixels. The tactile experience of fitting images into new wholes. Each image leads to the next, but it's like a jigsaw puzzle: you've got to have all the pieces to know where they fit."

Gerard swore under his breath.

"Each image leads to the next. You don't know how often I heard that from her, without understanding what it meant. Or even trying. She was chasing all over the world to get her precious images—South America, Africa, Mexico, places nobody sane goes these days—and all I did was argue with her."

His voice cracked. "I never asked the right questions."

When the stone-built chimney and plank walls of another building came into view minutes later, Jen knew without asking that this had been Leonie's cabin.

And that her brother, too late, had found his answers here.

Fishing a plastic-tagged key from his jacket pocket, he headed for the porch. "We had an agreement about this place. I own it, but I wasn't supposed to go inside—not even when she was traveling—unless there was an emergency."

He unlocked the front door and pushed it open for her.

"Depends on your definition."

The main room looked more like a crime scene investigation than an artist's living space, with cork boards mounted on the walls and propped against furniture. Black-and-white photos of various sizes had been pinned to the boards. Most were accompanied by handwritten notes, and each was linked to others with yarn. Red yarn.

As she moved closer, Jen recognized familiar images. A doorway from Chaco Canyon connected to a clump of megaliths swirled in Cornish fog. Which led on to the jaguar god—from Belize, its note explained—which connected to part of a Hindu temple, which led to the shattered obelisk.

By the time she'd traced a strand to the three egg-objects descending through their anonymous sky, sweat trickled inside her collar.

"Where did she take this one?"

"No idea." Gerard moved closer to the cork boards. "All I know is that she wasn't setting up shots in her studio. They could be anything." His brow furrowed. "Or *mean* anything. The shadows in the largest one don't help, because—"

"—they change."

Gerard stared at her. Jen swallowed hard. "Or at least the ones in mine do."

Without commenting, Gerard retraced the red yarn to its starting point.

"This is where it started," he said, indicating the Chaco doorway. "Her last series. The one that made her career." His voice dropped. "And ended it."

Jen nodded for him to go on.

"She had this ratty little travel trailer. Loved to stay at the campground down there. She said the night sky was phenomenal, so dark and clear she could just fall into it. Then one night she stayed up watching until dawn—"

He took a long breath. Jen held hers.

"—and she never stopped working after that. Traveling, shooting rolls and rolls of film, then back to her darkroom. No more digital. All old school. Fitting images together on her light table, doing enough prints to keep some gallery happy, then packing again and taking off."

He frowned.

"Sometimes she left me an itinerary, sometimes she didn't. Never when she was going somewhere risky—which was most of the time as the series went on. I never could figure out what she was after. Or why she couldn't stop."

Until she did. Jen shivered. While writing her thesis, she'd seen most of Leonie Gerard's last series, and it hung together in a way she couldn't explain. The diverse images created weirdly believable landscapes—not dreamscapes, as one reviewer had insisted, but real places a person might walk through.

Never willingly, though. Something about those landscapes—the angles, the light, the juxtapositions of objects—turned them alien.

As if an entirely different aesthetic was at work.

"*Vernal Ascension* was the worst. The traveling, I mean. She'd started off back at Chaco, and I hoped it would calm her down, but it did just the opposite. Something about that clear dark sky . . . She even set up a camera for long exposures, though she never used those images. Just blew them up—eight by ten, sometimes larger—and hung them around her darkroom."

He frowned. "She said they showed her how the pieces went together."

Moving away from the Chaco doorway shot, Gerard returned to the egg-objects—with their enigmatic sky much darker than Jen remembered from her print. And were those faint background flecks of white *stars?*

She was about to point them out when he directed her attention elsewhere.

A little above the descending eggs, a last small image had been pinned. No yarn linked it to any of the others, no note accompanied it, and it wasn't a ruin or a sacred site. Instead, an amazingly ugly little statuette stared back at her.

"I do know where this one came from," he said. "Sierra Leone. Somewhere in the south. The people there call them *nomoli,* but no one seems sure of much more than that. A few tribes even claim they were left behind by spiritual beings."

His expression hardened. "Whatever they are, Leonie took some awful risks to photograph them."

Jen looked closer. The statuette was carved from something like soapstone, which didn't allow for fine detail. Its exaggerated features and dwarfish body were partly obscured by a reptile (crocodile?) the little figure was grappling with. Or holding.

Or becoming?

She rubbed her eyes and checked again. Not two figures. Definitely one in the process of transforming, and the reptilian aspect was stronger, but vaguer: neither a crocodile nor anything else she recognized. Its scales flowed up the figure's arms to the shoulders, and—

Gerard pulled her away from the photograph, dragging her to the middle of the room before releasing his grip.

"It did that to me, too." He sounded more nervous than apologetic. "For a couple of hours, because I was alone and I'd had a few drinks. I was trying to figure out where Leonie fitted it into the picture."

"She didn't." *Why was she so certain?* "I've been over and over my print, and there's nothing like this in it."

Without asking for permission, she took out her phone and started photographing the whole sequence, taking closeups of the notes. It was time to quit freaking out. Sebastian Gerard had some seriously weird ideas about his sister's work, but she couldn't let them mess with her head, not more than they already had. She'd come up here to gather material for a couple of articles, at least. Maybe even a book. Real Ph.D. stuff.

By the time she finished, she'd nearly convinced herself.

Gerard sat silently in an armchair, watching her—or maybe watching nothing, staring into memory space. He had a big Ziploc bag on his lap. She didn't remember him leaving to get anything, but she hadn't exactly been good company these past few minutes.

"One more item for your research."

The bag held something flat and scorched. Jen took it gingerly.

"Leonie kept travel journals, always. Mostly work notes, but sometimes details about a location she'd visited, or a place she'd stayed. After the fire, I went looking for them. I don't know what I hoped to find. Maybe some explanation for all this—"

His voice faltered.

"—but it turned out she'd burned them, or tried to. The whole pile. In her darkroom, along with everything else. I only managed to recover part of her last one."

Jen slipped the ruined object out. It looked like a book cover plus a very few pages, much the worse for smoke and water. If there'd been any entries on those pages, they weren't—

Wait a minute.

On the final page, partially protected by the cover, was a list of five names. They'd all been written in ink, then crossed out in pencil.

"Make any sense to you?"

Jen read them through. One or two looked familiar from her thesis work.

"Other photographers, maybe. At least a couple of them are—but I'm not sure how Leonie would have known them. They're foreign."

Something else gnawed her memory. "And I think at least one of them is dead."

Tipping everything back into the bag, she zipped it with unsteady fingers and tried to hand it back to Gerard.

"Keep it. Maybe you'll figure out something I haven't been able to."

With a last glance at the boards with their red yarn and cryptic notes, he headed for the door. "And call me when you're ready to sell your print, OK?"

Jen hurried past him onto the porch.

Then away from Leonie's cabin, willing herself not to run.

Researching the names on that list hadn't been the hard part. There were only five, after all, and she'd had plenty of experience. Internet, academic databases, people who knew people: questions in, information out. Repeat. Compile.

And wish that compiled information made a little more real-world sense.

Or at least that it ruined less sleep.

Jen rubbed stinging eyes and reached for her coffee, carefully swiveling away from her laptop before taking a sip. She'd had some close calls lately—*gee, I wonder why*—and she couldn't afford to replace the thing. Not after clocking in late at work for the third time last week.

One more time, from the top.

Only three of the names on Leonie's list had been photographers. The other two were muralists whose fragmented styles resembled photomontage. All the photographers had used film rather than digital media. The muralists had worked directly on their walls. And all had traveled extensively to snap or sketch their images on-site.

The same images. On the same sites, minus the mysterious eggs.

It hadn't been quite that obvious: the sites had been visited at different times of year, captured with wildly varied approaches. One of the muralists had Picasso envy, and a couple of the photographers loved their filters. Fortunately, most of them had done more interviews than Leonie had—though not all were in English. She'd been able to piece together the rest from personal sites and gallery images. From what she could tell, they'd even visited each place in the same order Leonie had.

Glancing over the top of her mug at *Vernal Ascension,* she felt her stomach clench. Oh, yes, it was all one world.

And not her world.

Less so every day, though she tried to ignore the not-quite-green of formerly monochrome leaves. The mutating contours of those Cornish megaliths. The jaguar god's tongue reaching to the ground, starting to split into writhing, coiling—

Jen swiveled back to her desk and set the coffee mug down. Hard. *Way too much caffeine, girl.* Still, there was no arguing with that haunted landscape. The names of its ghosts now mocked from her laptop screen, annotated with the details of five disturbing deaths spaced one year apart: none of them natural, most of them violent.

All on the same date: tomorrow's date. Almost today's.

She wondered how Leonie (number six?) had found out about the others, though she suspected she wouldn't like the answer. Maybe those stars above Chaco Canyon had held more than a blueprint for the shared world she'd been creating. Maybe she'd seen herself there—the latest link in a chain it was too late to break.

Jen sighed. In the days and weeks since acquiring Leonie's last image, she'd almost gotten used to thoughts like that. Random acts of neurological chaos, she suspected, brought on by living with art she had no hope of understanding. There weren't going to be articles from this one, after all.

Some impulse made her stand and head back over to *Vernal Ascension.* Her rumpled futon couch—where she'd been collapsing most nights for the past week or so—creaked as she stepped onto it.

Descending through their deepening patch of twilight, the three egg-objects hadn't appeared in any of the others' images, yet they'd been the centerpiece of Leonie's. She'd given up trying to figure out why. Or where they'd come from. Nose to nose with the largest one, now, she watched shadows crawl across its surface like a storm seen from space.

Something new curled beneath that surface. Spectral, fetal, it clutched itself with curiously mottled limbs.

No, not mottled. Scaled—

Stumbling backwards off the futon, she landed hard and felt one ankle twist under her. *Sierra Leone.* The words throbbed in her mind as she dragged herself back to her desk chair. *Nomoli.* Leonie's last trip, her last shoot, her last big risk.

You've got to have all the pieces to know where they fit.

Each image leads to the next.

It cost breathless minutes to find the number on her phone, but Sebastian Gerard picked up right away. Or she thought he had. The connection hissed and popped and faded at random, garbling his words no matter how loudly he spoke them.

". . . hatching. It's what eggs do, right? World eggs . . . half the origin myths on the planet . . . ours just raw material for the next . . ."

This wasn't helping. Raking a hand through her hair, she tried again.

"Are your prints doing this, too? The crawling shadows? The—"

"—*Hundun* . . . Primordial chaos, in some translations . . . buried in the stars . . . worn-out worlds breaking apart, worlds remade from the shards . . . not ours any more . . ."

There was something familiar about the connection noise.

"Are you driving?" Jen sucked in breath as her ankle throbbed. "Where are you?"

After a long moment, their connection seemed to clear.

"Just got into town. Left Estes as soon as I realized . . . what I should have from the beginning. When I might have stopped her, if I'd been listening . . . Are you in your apartment, Ms. Maxwell? Is it still—"

Even from her desk chair, she could see the image. Couldn't stop seeing it. That solid knot of dark, just under the surface—

"Yes."

"Get out. Tear it up if you can, but get out."

She stood up cautiously, good foot first, testing the ankle. White pain stabbed through.

"Can't."

Gerard swore indistinctly. "I'm nearly there. Stay away from—"

"Are your prints doing this, too?"

"Not since I burned them."

Someone else's horn blared, followed by a screech of tires. He hung up abruptly. Still clutching her phone, Jen felt a cold wave of disbelief as she stared at *Vernal Ascension*. That spectral knot was still there, curled at the heart of the largest egg, but it hadn't changed since she'd fallen. There were no new changes at all. No cracks in that other world which was not her world.

Insomnia, she told herself firmly. Plus caffeine, plus academic desperation, plus this damned ankle she'd probably broken in a fit of stupidity. Maybe Gerard could drive her to a clinic when he got here.

Swiveling away from that strange patched landscape at last, she turned to her desk and the window beyond it. The street below was poorly lit, weeknight quiet, too iffy for pedestrians at this hour. There were only a few parked cars. Part of a moon.

Her world after all.

Gerard's old pickup showed up minutes later, nearly clipping a traffic sign on the last corner. It slid into a parking space across from her building, sputtering to a stop as the driver's door flew open and a coatless Gerard scrambled out. He stared up at her window. Then, without pausing to lock his vehicle, he started across the street at a run.

The massive van came out of nowhere, one headlight out and not even trying to stop. Somewhere beneath her screaming, Jen felt rather than heard the impact as Gerard's body flew. An answering crack of midnight sounded behind her, but it was only when the fire flowed up her arms—the gnaw of flesh transforming to reptilian scales—that her trance broke and she turned to face Leonie's final creation.

And beheld its occupant ascending at last, the world of its remaking streaming through.

A darkness more brilliant than light.

Et in Arcadia Ego

Brian Stableford

Great Pan was dead, and history was in gestation—
which is to say that the documents that were ultimately to provide the raw material of history were in production, but that their collation into a nascent narrative was yet
to begin. The two events were not unconnected, although the
connection was not of a kind that history could recognize.
Indeed, they were, in essence, the same event.

While history was still in gestation, however, and chronology
had not yet settled into a mathematical pattern, dead Pan's
reign of confusion had not yet reached its ultimate terminus.

It was almost noon when the poet found the dryad lying unconscious at the foot of her tree. He had seen nymphs in the flesh
before, but only fleetingly, and almost always after dark, when his
improvisations on the lyre achieved a fortunate combination.
Flesh was something such folk only put on rarely, for mysterious
purposes of an erotic nature. He had never heard mention of a
nymph appearing in broad daylight, even when in dire distress.

The dryad was small and delicate, dark-skinned and dark-
haired, but her skin was smooth, with none of the roughness
of bark, and her body hair, except for the pubic mass, was very

fine indeed. Her toenails and fingernails were neat, seemingly filed down. The poet put his fingers to her neck, feeling for a pulse; she did not flinch away from his touch, but a slight sound escaped her lips. She was alive.

Someone had hammered an iron spike into the dryad's tree. There was no reason why anyone would do such a thing, save for the purpose of killing the tree's resident spirit. How the would-be killer had known that the tree was enspirited was a mystery—perhaps it was a random act of hopeful cruelty—but the motive for the action was not. The spirit folk were being systematically hunted down and exterminated; their existence was held to be incompatible with the quest of civilization—or, at least, with the agriculture that civilization required as its mainstay. The extirpation was a matter of shame, however; it was not something people talked about, let alone recorded.

The poet, whose allegiance to the cause of civilization was as yet ambivalent, immediately put his bag and his lyre on the ground to one side and set about trying to withdraw the spike. He did not know whether that would save the dryad's life, but he felt obliged to try. He soon found that he could not hope to extract it without loosening it first, and that he could only do that by moving it from side to side—movements that brought little cries of agony from the stricken nymph.

The poet was so intent on his work that he never saw the faun creeping up on him, and was astonished, just as the spike finally came free, to find a hairy arm suddenly wrapped around his neck, attempting to strangle him. He tried to strike backwards with the spike—a blow that would surely have broken the faun's hold had it made contact with the creature's flesh, however fleetingly—but the faun had two arms and was ready for the ploy. His other hand gripped the poet's wrist and held it fast, twisting it to make the poet drop the weapon.

The faun was strong—considerably stronger than the poet, although he was shorter by a hand's width—and had had the advantage of being able to plan his attack in advance. The poet felt faint almost immediately, as the clenching arm prevented blood from reaching his brain, and he knew that he was in dire danger. He tried to throw the faun, using a wrestling move, and might have succeeded if the other had not been so powerful, but the maneuver failed.

Then, just as the poet had concluded he was doomed, someone grabbed the faun and dragged him off his victim, shouting for him to stop—not in Greek, of course, but in the coarse language of the Pelasgoi, which the poet had learned to speak in childhood, from the household slaves.

The poet had to overcome his dizziness and take several deep breaths before he was able to stand up straight again and look at his assailant and his savior. He had seen fauns in the gloom, just as he had seen nymphs, since learning to play his lyre, but he had never come into brutal contact with one before, and all those he had glimpsed had been true fauns—the young of their species—like the one who had attacked him.

The creature that had saved him was of the same kind, but very different in his individuality. The faun that had attacked the poet was only goat-like from the waist down, save for the shagginess of his head and his small horns, but the one that had saved him seemed at least four-fifths goat, and perhaps more than that, being human only in his upright stance and the bizarre configuration of his remarkable ugly face, which harbored human eyes and a human mouth within its masses of hair. The creature was leaning on a staff, in a manner that suggested that he might have had difficulty maintaining an upright stance on his oddly articulated and cloven-hoofed legs without that crutch, but the way he had thrown the faun aside suggested that he had strong arms as well as an authoritarian voice.

The "older" members of the satyr race, the poet knew—because he was, after all, a poet—were the sileni, and the oldest of all were the papposileni, whose antiquity was such that only a pleonastic name could represent them. The poet did not quite understand how the aging process worked in creatures that were supposedly immortal, but he was in no doubt at all that he was looking at a papposilenos, perhaps the oldest of the old.

Looking into that strange hybrid face, he felt slightly dizzy, as if he were somehow looking into another world, or another time. He could not meet the creature's stare and looked away, up the mountain slope at the distant cloud-shrouded peak. His gaze was immediately drawn back to the unconscious dryad, though. He had not felt lust when he first saw her, even though she was naked and by no means ugly, but the presence of the two satyrs seemed to have triggered a reaction in his own body that he had to fight to suppress.

"Imbecile," said the papposilenos to the faun, harshly. "He was trying to help her, not hurt her."

"But he *was* hurting her," the faun pointed out, not inaccurately. "Anyway, he's human. He's a city-dweller."

The papposilenos knelt down beside the dryad and touched her gently.

"Will she live?" the poet asked, in the language of the Pelasgoi. If the papposilenos was surprised to hear him speak in that fashion, his bizarre face gave no indication of it.

"Probably not," the papposilenos said. "She'll have a better death, though, if we can get her to the cave."

The faun reacted more angrily to that than he had to being deprived of his kill—and his expression was perfectly capable of blazing with anger. "He's a Greek," he repeated, "for all that he understands the true tongue!"

"Yes, he is," the papposilenos agreed—but his eyes were now fixed on the lyre that the poet had set down before trying to draw the fatal spike out of the tree. "Where did you get that, child?" he asked, his voice no longer quite as hoarse.

"I bought it in the marketplace in Athens," the poet said, refusing to take offense at being addressed as "child," in view of the fact that the satyr must be older than he could imagine. "The old woman who sold it to me told me that it was the lyre once played by Orpheus himself, with which he charmed the shades of the dead when he visited the realm of Hades—but market traders are unconscionable liars."

The papposilenos looked up at him, in a fashion that the poet interpreted to mean that he did not understand.

"The art of commerce is haggling," the poet attempting to explain. "It is more highly developed in Athens than anywhere else, because Athens is the only city in Greece, probably in the world, to obtain its food by trade rather than solely from its own surrounding fields. Its forges and its kilns produce goods made of vulgar metal and earthenware in vast quantities, whose sale brings precious metals, which are used to buy wheat with money. That process sustains a much larger population that any city reliant on its own produce, and the excess provides the scope for poetry and philosophy as well as . . ."

He did not finish, thinking it impolitic to mention the apparatus of war and genocide.

"Athens, then, is a city based on lies," the papposilenos observed mildly, obviously having understood more than the poet had imagined. The creature spoke distractedly, seemingly still wondering what to do about the injured dryad.

"And money," the poet reminded him. "If the science of calculation, which money has greatly encouraged, assists deception in trade, it also gives rise to accuracy in measurement; it is the source of a better honesty as well as the fuel of lies. That is why Athens is the guiding light of civilization. Where Athens leads, all cities will eventually follow, transforming the world. The future of humankind will rest upon the glory of Greece."

"This is not Greece," the faun opined sullenly. "This is Arcadia. You have no right here." The faun was keeping his distance from the dryad, as if afraid that his own touch might do her more harm than good, whereas that of the ancient papposilenos was safe.

"It *was* Arcadia," the poet stated, bluntly, "when the only humans here were the Pelasgoi—but it is Greece now. No cities have been built in this mountainous wilderness yet, but what was Arcadia is Greece nevertheless. Cities are the seeds of empire. Greece is the shape of things to come."

"Why are you here, child?" the papposilenos asked him mildly. "Your fellows come with packs of dogs, bows and arrows, spears and iron spikes. Having no war to fight between themselves, for the moment, they hunt, continuing the work of our extermination—but you have no weapons, no dogs, and no companions. My young friend would have killed you, had I not intervened. He is an imbecile—but what are you?"

"He would not have killed me had I seen him coming," the poet retorted, "and had I been able to reach my lyre."

"You really do think yourself the equal of Orpheus, then— able to charm the beasts and the spirit folk . . . and the shades of the dead?" The papposilenos had risen to his feet as he spoke and had taken a step closer to the poet. Although he had to look up to meet the human's eyes, he seemed somehow very massive and intimidating. Despite his caprine appearance, though, the aged satyr did not give off any discernible odor.

The poet did not step back; he held his ground. The experience was so unprecedented that it did not seem entirely real, and in dreams bravery sometimes comes easily. "His equal, no," the poet said, "but I'm learning—and how can I learn, unless I try my skill? But I am here because the news has spread through the cities that Pan is dead, and I wanted to know how that can be, since Pan is a god."

"And how do you hope to find out?" the papposilenos demanded, with a hint of mockery.

"By means of the lyre, of course. I know that it's capable of charming spirit folk . . . I have not yet had occasion to try it on the shades of the dead. Its magic seems to me to be increasing the closer I come to the heart of Ar—what was once Arcadia. I have not discovered all its secrets yet, but . . . here, I think, I stand a better chance than anywhere else. I have found you, after all, without even having to touch its strings—and you might be as old as time itself, perhaps older now than Pan, if the god really is dead."

"Kill him," advised the faun. "Even if he's no more than a fool, he'll bring the others after him."

As if what he said were an omen, the distant baying of dogs became audible—a hunting-pack perhaps forty or fifty strong, doubtless guided by a company of a dozen bloodthirsty humans. The dryad stirred in her coma, whimpering again; she was not yet immune to fear.

"Be still," the papposilenos told the faun, seemingly unworried by the proximity of the dogs. "You do not understand what is happening here." Then, to the poet, he said: "You will have to carry the dryad; I cannot, nor can the kid. If you wish to save her, you must bring her to the cave—but I warn you that, if you go in, you will likely never come out again."

Again, the faun seemed furious. "This is not right," he said.

The papposilenos turned to look his fellow satyr full in the face, and although the poet could not read his expression, it must have said something like: "Who are you to say what is right and what is not?"

The faun continued to strike a mutinous attitude, but obviously had no alternative but to comply with the older creature's instructions.

The creature with the staff looked back at the poet, who immediately picked up the injured dryad.

"Bring his bag," the papposilenos commanded the faun. "Give the lyre to me."

"Do you play?" the poet dared to ask the aged satyr, as the faun obeyed.

"You speak the true tongue fluently," the papposilenos observed, as he moved off, at a surprisingly rapid pace, heading up the slope toward the mountain peaks.

"I'm a poet," the poet said, as he followed, having no difficulty with the dryad's slight weight, "among other things. We have not yet educated all our Pelasgoi slaves in our own language. I never thought that I would have the chance to communicate with folk of your kind, but I was always intrigued by the Pelasgoi, and their tales . . . tales of Arcadia, and the god Pan. We have adopted him, you know, although he does not really fit our pantheon. Hephaestos and Ares as the gods of the future."

"And Aphrodite?"

The poet was momentarily surprised, as much by hearing the name of a Greek goddess on the lips of such a creature as by the fact that the question had been asked.

"Aphrodite too, alas," the poet agreed. "Had you an equivalent—if your friend there is not the equivalent in question—he or she would doubtless represent a purer lust, unrefined by social niceties." At least, that was what he tried to say. Fluent as his knowledge of the old tongue was, it had its limitations.

"Purity," the papposilenos observed, "is itself a social . . . nicety." The way he echoed the poet's word suggested that there was, indeed, an inherent inaccuracy therein.

I had not suspected that satyrs could play at philosophy, the poet thought. *This opportunity is even greater than I thought. I must not waste it.*

"The Pelasgoi who taught me their tongue," the poet said, "claimed that Pan is their only God—but I have overheard them, in the darkness, appealing to another. *Io Pan!* they cry, when they bemoan their fate and ask the god to strike their enemies with sacred panic—but they also cry: *Iä Shub-Niggurath!* When I asked who Shub-Niggurath was, however, they would only say: *the goat with a thousand young.*"

The faun, who was walking alongside the poet, listening to every word he said, seemed incensed once again by that remark—or, perhaps, by his suspicion that the papposilenos might explain—but all that the ancient satyr said was: "Great Pan is dead." His tone communicated no impression of mourning.

"Gods cannot die," the poet replied, insistently. "The Pelasgoi might well think he is dead, given that they have lost their lands and are disappearing themselves by death or assimilation, as are all his subjects . . . but we have adopted him. We have not lodged him in Olympus, with our other gods, and will leave him free to haunt the land that was once Arcadia, and other wilderness, but we shall keep him, and praise him, and fear him, and worship him—and thus, he cannot die."

"He is dead," the papposilenos repeated. "Nor can his shade be tempted by the lyre."

Again, the poet heard the baying of dogs, closer now than before.

"But there is something else I have heard the Pelasgoi say, when they believed no one was listening," the poet said, hurriedly. "*That is not dead which can eternal lie; and with strange eons, even death may die.* In which case, I beg leave to doubt that Pan is *truly* dead, incapable of resurrection."

"Imbecile," muttered the faun.

"I have strayed across some kind of boundary, have I not?" the poet asked suddenly. "I am no longer wholly in the world I was before, where the paradoxical folk can only be glimpsed in poor light, and then only when the orderly mind is slightly disturbed. I have somehow strayed into your reality, in which you wear flesh by day, existing to the full and not in flickers of distortion." Again, he was not at all sure that his final phrase could carry the meaning he intended to imply.

"I wish it were so," said the papposilenos, with a deep sigh, "but we are out of place, not you—and if we do not make haste, those dogs might bring us down."

"And if we do?" said the poet, obediently quickening his pace and drawing level with the ancient creature, who now seemed to be tiring of the uphill struggle. "If we reach the cave?"

The faun snorted, half in annoyance and half in derision.

"We might find a better death," the papposilenos said gently.

It seemed to the poet that his opportunity was going to waste after all, although it was hardly unexpected that the paradoxical folk should speak in paradoxes. "Why could the faun not carry the dryad?" he demanded bluntly. "He was strong enough to strangle me, and she's by no means heavy."

"You do not understand what we are," the papposilenos told him. "To put on flesh and to be able to bear burdens are different things."

"He's carrying my bag," the poet pointed out, "and you have my lyre."

"They are not burdensome," the other replied. "They have weight, but not . . ." He abandoned the sentence, evidently lacking a word other than *burdensome* to signify what he meant.

Fauns are personifications of lust, the poet thought, *while nymphs are, among other things, innate objects of lust. Perhaps fauns and nymphs can only interact in certain ways—whereas I, who worship Aphrodite, with all her complexities, can treat her as if she were merely a heavy object.*

He was not sure that the latter argument was entirely true, though. In the same way that the proximity of the satyrs had stirred something within him, contact with the nymph was imparting further sensations, teasing his emotions. It occurred to him that there might be dangers in his situation over and above—or perhaps under and below—the veiled threat relating to the cave.

But the faun is one thing, he added, following his train of thought, *and the papposilenos is another. If love is complex, so is lust. There is virile lust and absurd lust, lust that can be assuaged and lust that is futile. Nature is fecund, but also profligately, hectically wasteful. Age mocks and travesties the aged. He calls me child, but I am not a child as the faun is a kid . . .*

He stopped himself. *The more important thing,* he suddenly thought, *is the assurance that I have not crossed a boundary into their world, but that they have come into mine. Why?*

"Why are you here?" he asked the papposilenos, as the dogs gave voice again, so close this time that he could not doubt that the trail they were following was either his own or that of one of his companions.

The strange, inhuman face turned to look into his own again. "To die, of course," was his reply. "But better by far to reach the cave, if we can, than to face *them.*" He nodded in the direction of the hunting-pack.

"I can protect you," the poet was quick to say.

"With this?" the papposilenos said, raising the lyre. "From the dogs, perhaps—but from iron-tipped arrows and iron-tipped spears? Orpheus charmed the shades of the dead, but the dead are weak. The living tore him apart—not even hunters, but angry women. Whatever price you paid for the lyre, it was sold in desperation."

The papposilenos had quickened his pace again, and the poet was struggling to keep up, although the faun had now overtaken them and seemed impatient that they were lagging behind.

"Are you saying that it really is the lyre that Orpheus owned?" the poet asked.

"I've seen it before and heard it played," the aged satyr assured him. "But it cannot be owned and cannot be trusted."

The faun was practically dancing now, capering on his caprine legs, undoubtedly impatient because of the slowness of their progress.

He wants to run on ahead, the poet thought, *but dares not disobey the papposilenos.* The dryad was beginning to weigh more heavily in his arms now—and there was something other than weight that was troubling him in the contact of her flesh, the helplessness of her unconscious form. He felt an anger growing within him, at the dogs and the men that were following them. "I can protect you," he said again to his exotic companions.

"Not unless we can reach the cave," said the paradoxical creature that seemed possessed of the wisdom of age despite the slow eclipse of his human fraction—and the papposilenos increased his pace yet again, so that he was now half running and half hobbling.

The poet had to run too, in order to keep up with him, although the faun still seemed to be holding himself back, showing not the slightest sign of fatigue.

In other circumstances, the poet might have considered laying his burden down in order that he might run faster, but if that had ever been an option, it was an option no longer. He would have lain down his life rather than lay down the unconscious dryad, even though he had been told that she would very likely die whatever he did. The burden had taken hold of him; he was as much under a spell as the animals he had learned to charm with the strings of the lyre.

Was it the lyre, he wondered, that had brought him to this? No, he concluded. He was his own man. He had bought the lyre, at what the science of calculation told him was a fair price, and he had cultivated his own curiosity; he was still the master of his fate. If he could not put his burden down, it was not because he was a prisoner of lust or any other strange attraction. It was because he was a man and not a dog, a poet and not a hunter, a worshipper of Pan in the truest sense, who would not admit that the god could be truly dead while he still lived himself.

Pan, he knew, could have defended the Pelasgoi against the invaders who had stolen their homeland and enslaved them. Pan had the gift of spreading panic, the divine wind of terror that no human—not even a Greek—could resist. Pan could reach out now, if he were not dead, and blast the hunters who were tracking the two satyrs, with that particular horror and that particular dread. Instead, he had seemingly consented to play dead, allowing his followers, his companions, to become fully manifest in the human world, in bright daylight, where they might be hunted down and exterminated.

Why?

Io Pan! the poet screamed, silently. *Iä Shub-Niggurath!*

But there was no response.

The slope was steeper now and becoming even steeper. The poet's heart was pounding, and his legs were beginning to weaken. There was no sign yet of a cave ahead of them, although they were so high now that they had almost reached the cloud layer, and the gathering mist caressing the mountain-top sealed off his view no more than a hundred paces ahead.

Behind him, where the slope was still sunlit, the dogs had changed their tune—they had sighted their prey. But the dogs were tired too, and there was a certain breathlessness in the signals they were giving.

The poet risked a long glance behind. He could see the hounds, just as they could see him, but he could not see their human followers as yet, who must be even closer to exhaustion.

He wanted to ask more questions, but he would not have had the breath to spare, even if his head had not been buzzing with confusion.

I need music! he thought. *I need the music of the lyre, to calm my thoughts and soothe my heart and give me space to breathe.* But the papposilenos had the lyre, and whether the ancient creature could play or not, he was merely holding it in his free hand, dangling idly by his side: a trivial burden, but a burden nonetheless.

Io Pan! screamed the poet again, silently but with all the force of his anguish, no longer knowing what he was doing or why. *Iä Shub-Niggurath!*

And this time, perhaps, the prayer—if it was a prayer— seemed to find an answer.

Darkness fell, abruptly, although an instant earlier the sun had still been only halfway between its zenith and the western horizon. For a moment, the poet thought that he really had stepped into a hole and fallen into a grotto excavated in the mountain-side, but there were stars in the sky. They were the wrong stars, but they were certainly stars, and by their alien light he could still see the mountain slope up which he had run—and the chasing dogs.

He stopped dead.

The dogs were just as bewildered by the paradox as he was, and they faltered in their chase, uncertain what to do.

The papposilenos had also stopped. He reached out and touched the poet on the shoulder. "I can take her now," he said—and he raised his arm to offer the lyre in exchange. The faun was still dancing, but no longer drawing away. He still seemed angry, and was still protesting silently, but to no avail.

The poet placed the dryad carefully in the aged satyr's arms, took hold of the lyre, and then took half a dozen strides down-hill, toward the dogs.

When they saw him coming, they were able to make up their minds as to what they ought to do. They attacked. There were, as he had earlier estimated, at least forty of them.

He struck the strings of the lyre. It had never made such a note before. The dogs stopped dead—not soothed, but scared.

The poet began to play, reproducing a sequence he had com-posed and learned—but the melody that should have emerged, and presumably would have emerged in the light of the kindly sun, did not emerge here. Here, the air was differ-ent. He could feel that as he breathed it in, although it obvi-ously had whatever air needed in order to sustain life, and per-haps in abundance, for the atmosphere seemed intoxicating. Sound, however, was not the same here as it was in the air he knew. The melody, like the starry sky, was wrong.

Here, the sounds that should have soothed sowed distress. They sowed something akin to panic.

It was, however, a selective distress. The faun laughed, and the aged papposilenos emitted a cross between a chuckle and a gurgle. If there was anything of horror and terror in the emo-tion that flooded their being, they obtained a perverse enjoy-ment from it. It delighted them.

It did not delight the dogs. Nor did it delight the men who were following them: a dozen of them in all, some with arrows already fitted to their bows, others already lifting their javelins, ready to throw.

The dogs howled and turned tail. Whether it was panic or not that they were experiencing, they hated it and wanted to get away. As the papposilenos had suggested, however, in his own perverse fashion, the music that worked its magic on the dogs did not stop the men with murder in their hearts. If they were stricken with terror or horror or any other psychic devastation, it did not stop them. They came on, howling with rage.

Desperately, the poet played, but the little he had learned about the instrument's capacity was useless now; his fingers flew over the strings, but the music that emerged was all wrong, all dark.

This, he thought, is the cave. No mere covert in the mountain, but a world apart, where nature does not work as it does in my world. Great Pan is dead, indeed, and chaos is come again.

He was filling up with horror and dread himself, but somehow, it was displaced from him. He had carried the dryad, and although she had been burdensome, the burden she had left in his inner being was insulating him from the worst effects of his own deadly work. For the moment, he was only partly human; for the moment, there was something of the tree in him. It would not last, he knew, but the magic he was making could not hurt him.

It could hurt the hunters, but it could not strike them dead—and they were firing now and hurling their spears.

The first few missiles fell short, but the hunters were skilled men who knew their art. Even subject to dire distress as they were, the greater number of them knew their range and knew their aim. They had been tracking the satyrs, but they had another, more dangerous, enemy now, and it was at the poet that their projectiles were all aimed.

Within an instant, the poet knew, he would very likely be struck. He needed more than alien air. He might have called upon Apollo, then, or even Ares, but he knew better. They were the gods of the future, but for the moment he was not in the future but the unimaginably remote past, the cave of origins, of mythic time.

"Iä Shub-Niggurath!" he screamed, for the third time, with all the force of his troubled lungs.

And suddenly, he knew how to play the instrument he held. He was no longer part-tree but had something else within him that was far more alien. He was possessed by the goat with a thousand young: the parent not merely of the satyr-folk, but of Great Pan himself; something beyond a god, perhaps less powerful but infinitely more patient.

For a moment, the poet had all the time in the world. He not only played the instrument, but understood it. He played, and the world dissolved; the stars in the sky went out, and the cave closed in; substance itself disappeared, and there was nothing but potential existence, governed by mathematical rules. The poet saw the sense of those rules, but he also saw the essential paradoxes lurking within and behind their glamour. He saw the beauty of numbers, but he also saw the irrationality of numbers, the relationships that refused expression in numbers. He saw *everything,* and played the music that was far more fundamental than the music of the spheres: the music of the ultimate weaving of matter itself.

The blast struck all the hunters dead, instantaneously, and the satyrs too—but the satyrs, creatures of paradox themselves, died laughing, in a paroxysm of delight that was, in their own terms, eternal.

The poet was not a prisoner of the lyre; nor, even though he was possessed by Shub-Niggurath, the weaver of gods, the spawner of spawn, the shaper of matter, the goat with a thousand young, was he a slave to that ultimate impulse. He was free. He was able to choose.

But what choice, in all sanity, could he make?

He had to go home. In the grip of the ultimate horror, the horror of the cosmic cave, he had nowhere to flee but home— not to Arcadia but to the place that had once been Arcadia, where history, philosophy, mathematics, and science were in gestation, ready to be nascent, to begin the process of becoming.

He knew how to play that tune, and did so. Without ever losing his footing, without ever leaving the bare mountain-side, he wove the future that had always been incarnate within him, in his flesh, in his intellect, and in his nation. He wove the glory that would be Greece, and Rome, and every human reign thereafter.

He wove his own forgetfulness as he did so, because he knew that he would be unable to bear what he remembered, if he were able to remember, in his own world, that he had once been possessed by Shub-Niggurath—but while he wove that particular oblivion, for the space of three or four bars of the ultimate music, he could not help but know, not merely everything that had happened since the dawn of time, but everything that could be predicted of the unknown future.

There was less that was predictable than he might have imagined, but he not only saw the unfolding of the history of civilization, in all its awful, relentless logic, but the legacy of history, of science, of calculation, of understanding. And he saw that it was not only the particular hunters pursuing the satyrs that he had blasted with his curse, but billions of human hunters to come, in whom the seeds of knowledge would be the seeds of destruction. The human race, he saw, would not endure for more than ten thousand years from the moment it began to count years in earnest, and to create its own chronology; it would destroy itself, as befitted a culture that had made the choice to devote itself to civilization and commerce, whose entire life was founded on lies and calculation. As to what would come thereafter . . . well, it would not be Arcadia, but perhaps something akin to it.

It was not a prospect that pleased him in any way at all, and he was glad to forget it.

When the philosopher awoke on the mountain-side, there was a young woman lying beside him, entirely naked and entirely human. She was unconscious, but not badly hurt.

Further down the mountain slope there was a pack of dogs, wandering around the corpses of their former masters, who had been struck dead, as if by divine lightning.

The philosopher picked up the lyre that he had dropped and began to pluck the strings. As it sounded the familiar notes, he felt a strange sense of relief, although he could not imagine how it could possibly have produced different ones, because that would have been contrary to the principles of nature, which he understood very well, because he had discovered that there was a mathematical relationship between the various notes of the scale and the harmonic resonances between them, which he intended to work out more completely and teach his fellows.

He could only play the notes one by one, though. He could not play music—although some strange fragment of fugitive memory informed him, nostalgically, that there had once been a time . . .

The sounds he produced woke up the young woman. He found her some clothing in his bag, which lay on the ground a few paces way, although he could not remember having dropped it or how he had come to be so far up the mountain.

The dogs did not give him any trouble when he walked back down the mountain, with the young woman by his side. The philosopher felt oddly proud of her presence, as if he had saved her life by means of some heroic deed, although he could not remember having seen her before he woke up to find her lying beside him.

The name he gave her when she asked him who he was went unrecorded, as did the name she attributed to herself, but when history was born—because history abhors a vacuum infinitely more than it abhors a lie—its makers decided to call him Pythagoras, and hailed him as the father of mathematics and mysticism.

He would have been glad had he known, having forgotten that he had ever been a poet, or that he had ever wondered what it could possibly mean that great and paradoxical Pan was dead.

The Shadow of Heaven

Jason V Brock

There are more things in heaven and earth . . .
Than are dreamt of in your philosophy.

—William Shakespeare, Hamlet 1.5.166–67
(Hamlet to Horatio)

I.

"There—I think I see it, Commander."

Ensign Adams's breath disappeared overhead as he lowered his binoculars, pointing with a gloved hand at the unstable horizon through the ice-rimmed main windows of the ship. "Looks like something about ten kilometers out, sir." Backlit by the windows, he turned to face Commander Merritt, the senior officer aboard the destroyer USS *Higgins*. Cloaked in his winter overcoat, the ensign's brittle voice seemed distant in the cold dry air, his words nearly obliterated by the surging wind and unforgiving swells of the squall. Outside, colossal waves, some the size of buildings, slammed the *Higgins*— exploding across the ship's icebound hull in frosty white plumes, adding to the inches-deep transparent slick of frozen seawater on the deck as she plunged further into one of the most hostile environs on the planet: the Southern Ocean. Gales such as this arose suddenly and with terrifying ferocity this close to Antarctica, reducing visibility to a few feet, churning the barren seascape into a foamy lather as it thrust icebergs the size of city blocks into the path of interlopers to this foreboding, isolated part of the world. At times, mighty whitecaps pounded on the destroyer with such titanic fury that they caused the vessel to flinch backward, bobbing like an oversized cork in the roiling black depths.

Merritt, his drawn face numb from the chill, carefully considered the ensign's words, leaning against a deck rail to keep his balance as they rocked in the grip of the storm. Bringing his binoculars to his face, he scanned the dead grey interface between leaden sky and dark water beyond the icy windows Adams was motioning toward, noting the faint curtain of blue-green ripples from the southern lights, streaked by rose-colored lightning ribbons in the distance as freezing night collapsed around them. Even on the closed bridge, the saline-tinged atmosphere had gotten so frigid that the inside of his nose crystallized with each breath.

Our luck to be the closest in the vicinity of a distress call.

"Are you sure you saw a vessel? Maybe it was a 'berg," the Commanding Officer asked at last.

"It didn't look like an iceberg . . . " Adams was scrutinizing the horizon as he spoke: "One moment, sir."

As he worked against the storm's fury, the commander was troubled that, in their attempts to discover the exact whereabouts of the missing research ship *Terra Australis Incognita*, they might have gone astray. The weary leader and his crew of just over two hundred were stuck now, committed to the search even as they struggled with the dreadful conditions approximately 300 miles off the coast of West Antarctica—well off-course from their originally assigned bearing based on *Australis*'s last communique. Merritt was further aggravated that they had been pulled into this mess just as the *Higgins* was returning for shore leave after a long, tedious mission:

Subsonic underwater audio testing. The original search-and-rescue order had instructed them to triangulate the position of the troubled *Australis* once they were within its last known trajectory, but it concerned him that perhaps she had lost power after her final transmission to the Oceanographic Institute of San Diego, drifting farther than anyone had anticipated. That could mean she was gone—especially if these had been the circumstances for her and her crew in the two days it had taken the *Higgins* to re-route.

"Still not seeing it, Adams." Merritt grimaced in frustration.

"Sorry, sir. It was there just a minute ago . . . "

The haunting Mayday call that Warrant Officer McConnell had picked up as they were adjusting course, scratchy with static and crosstalk, had made it very difficult to decipher who it was, but the co-ordinates and the radar image supported the notion that it had come from *Australis*. Or at least from a crewmember that might be stranded on the so-called 'new islands' that *Australis* had been allowed to detour and inspect by the Institute.

Contemplative, Merritt lowered his binoculars, sighing in annoyance as he stroked his face. *Throw into the mix that the closer we get to the last known heading of Australis the worse the fucking weather gets . . . the more radio-electronic interference— faulty GPS signals, slow clocks, bad wireless connections. Adds up to a lot of irritating bullshit . . . Oh well—'Uneasy lies the head that wears a crown,' as they say . . .*

Higgins had endured several of these storms, as powerful as any Merritt had ever encountered in his twenty-plus years as a sailor, in their efforts to find the *Australis*. Then, as the mammoth destroyer heaved and fell like some vast rollercoaster— lights flickering, deck rolling in the strong seas—the senior officer thought he vaguely made out what the ensign had seen: A shadowy triangular central mass situated among a scattering of large icebergs looming along the periphery of his vision like some ethereal vanguard of the *Flying Dutchman*. He frowned while adjusting the focus ring, his brow wrinkled in annoyance as he squinted past the thickening fog and billowing sea spray. *Christ, it's like something wants to keep us away . . .*

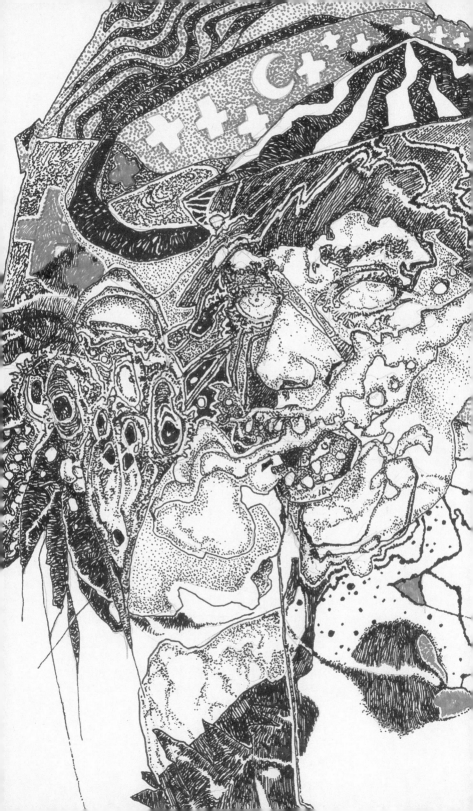

He glanced over at McConnell, his grey-haired scalp bristling. "You seeing this?"

McConnell worked to keep his footing as he peered through his binoculars. "Aye . . . *Some*thing. Appears man-made, sir, but hard to make out through the mist and—" A crackle from the headset around his neck interrupted him. Placing the speaker to his ear, he listened intently, then moved over to his station, his dark features pressed into a look of apprehension.

Merritt: "What's happening, McConnell?"

"Not—not sure, sir . . . There's a lot of static; I thought I heard . . . A *voice*. It was coming in on the same frequency as the last transmission—"

Continuing to monitor the gloom outside, Adams said, "*Definitely* something there, Commander. Looks to be a modest-sized vessel."

McConnell: "I've got something—putting up on speakers, sir. I have a radar reflection, too. One small shape and a few larger masses; the larger areas *could* be land, but hard to say in this climate . . . And I checked again—not on our maps."

A smoky haze of static filled the room, pushing back the sounds of the tempest for an instant: <<CH-CH-CH Gree! Mayday! [*blip, blip, blip*] Gree! CH-CH-ay! [*blip, blip, blip*]>>

More intense static. Then, garbled: "If you can hear my voice, please acknowledge! [*blip, blip, blip*] . . . is not— [*blip, blip, blip*] My name is Christopher Faust, over. [*blip, blip, blip*] . . . urgent mes— [*blip, blip, blip*] . . . communicate! Repeat: This is—"

Silence. The wind howled in the sunless tumult outside the *Higgins*, sending chucks of ice and snow to shatter against the windows of the darkened bridge. Lightning seared again: closer, redder, like an eruption of stroboscopic tendrils cracking the black-ice sky into pieces. Distant thunder bellowed.

"McConnell, stay on that frequency, but keep monitoring the others; Adams, your thoughts?"

The young ensign was staring into the starless night, struggling to keep his equilibrium in the storm. "I . . . I believe it's *Australis*, sir. Who else would be this far from McMurdo?

Granted, farther away than we expected her to be, but we heard the distress call . . . so we're obligated to check it out, Commander."

Merritt looked again, the stiff rubber eyecups of the Steiner chafing his eyelids: Illuminated by flashes of scarlet lightning, the triangular shape appeared to be a bow, with part of a mast attached as well; perhaps a half-submerged wreck, though it was too dim, too turbulent to make out anything definitive.

"Aye," the commander said. "Set a course for it."

II.

"Looks like we've found her, Commander. No one here, though." Ensign Adams released the button on his handheld as he stared into the blue-toned water, the white mast and bow of the sunken *Australis* thrusting up from the briny deep like the hand of a skeleton. The elements had relented since their post-midnight arrival; the ocean was almost peaceful.

At first light, Commander Merritt had deemed it safe enough to dispatch a small advance team of four men through the half-mile or so of chop between the moorage of the *Higgins* and the suspected wreck of the *Australis*. Though slightly overcast, the sun was evident, clear, though quite low on the horizon even now, at mid-day; it was urgent that they discern what was happening before night fell and the temperatures dropped.

"Roger that, Adams," McConnell replied. "Stand by."

As Adams and his crew of three awaited their next orders on the drifting rigid-hulled inflatable, he studied the *Australis*: It was spooky, surreal. The water here was so clear he could see far down into it, almost to the bridge of the research vessel. Straining, he swore he could see something . . . something large; a supple darkness—

"Adams, we have something near you, but not from the wreck, over."

Startled from his thoughts by McConnell's gruff drawl, Adams replied: "Roger that. What do you have?"

"Well . . . There's a signal coming from nearby. The co-ordinates are dodgy, as there seems to be some strange interference. Looks like it's coming from that mass I was explaining from the radar, though. Some seismic disturbances there. I got another signal a while ago like a voice, too. See anything? Over."

"Actually, yeah; over to my left there's a big fogbank. Looks like about 300 or so meters away. Could it be from there? Over."

"That's about the proximity of the radar image, over."

Adams brought his binoculars up. As he peered through them, he thought he saw something large move in the mist on the horizon: *What the hell* was that?

"Roger, McConnell. I see something; request permission to investigate, over."

There was a long pause.

"Roger, Adams; weather's returning. Merritt says you've got an hour, over."

III.

"Let us go then, you and I,
When the evening is spread out against the sky—"
Like the Indianapolis *at the bottom of the deep . . .*
Down to a dreamless sleep . . .
Drifting,
Spiraling:

IV.

Back onboard the Higgins, Adams was shaken, dazed as he reported what the search party had discovered: "So there *are* some islands, Commander," He looked from Merritt to McConnell as they stood in the infirmary, regarding the apparent sole survivor of the Australis: an unconscious man on a sickbay table. "The radar image was correct . . . We found *Australis*, and there was something else . . . something deeper in the water, looked like it was poking around in the wreckage—"

"What? Like a seal? A shark or something? Or did you see a body?" Merritt asked, his voice edged.

"I—I can't say; it was some weird . . . *black*-looking shape, but iridescent, too. Like oil on water. It seemed to be part of something else even larger . . . maybe it was just the water playing tricks on my eyes, or a part of the ship, but . . . Adams looked to the floor." "Anyway, after we went through the fog, we all noted that the temperature was rising; it was becoming quite humid, too. I had to lose a jacket I got so warm. Then, as we disembarked onto this beach we landed on, we were accosted by these *giant* . . . flying bats or something, but with feathers. They were shrieking and carrying on. Sounded very human at times. Like a cat in heat. Our compasses were flipping out, and that's when one of my guys saw a helicopter blade half-buried in the sand. We a search line and walked for a mile or so—"

Commander Merritt's hands clinched. "No one authorized that, Adams! You should have radioed—"

"We *tried*, sir. The radios went dead right after we landed, and once we found the pieces of the helicopter . . . Respectfully, we weren't trying to get into trouble; we just wanted to see if there was anyone hurt—"

McConnell: "He's right, sir. The radios were unresponsive after the first forty-five minutes or so, and they were DOA back onboard."

After a silence, Commander Merritt nodded: "Carry on, Adams. Then what happened?"

"Well, we thought we heard screams—human screams— coming from somewhere up the beach, though the place has strange acoustics; the surf, the wind make it pretty noisy, not to mention those flying things squealing overhead, so it could have been coming from the dense vegetation toward the center of the island. Anyway, after about ten more minutes of walking, we ascended a small dune, and that's where the rest of the helicopter was." Adams swallowed, staring at the C.O. in trancelike, unblinking remembrance. He motioned toward the man on the bed. "We found him like this . . . Completely nude, crumpled up next to a bunch of half-frozen papers and the debris of the 'copter with the walkie-talkie in his hand. Only a few scratches on him from what we could see, just knocked-out. I'm . . . *amazed* he's alive . . . ," Adams said. His voice was quivering. "How . . . how could he be alive? In those tempera-tures . . . *Naked*? I mean, it was warmer, but still plenty cold if you're exposed like that. And . . . and the helicopter was *demol-ished*, like there was an accident or something. The bloody clothing next to him had a tag: *Faust*. That's the guy from the transmissions, right McConnell?"

McConnell was gawking at the man in the infirmary bed, stunned, his hand covering his mouth. He shot a glance at Commander Merritt, whose red-eyed gaze was also fixed on the sleeping man, and nodded. "Tell him about the other thing you brought back, Adams."

Merritt broke away from his thoughts. "There was some-thing else? What?"

Adams swallowed, his face suddenly ashen, and looked to the floor. Merritt looked again at McConnell, who took a deep breath.

"What did Adams bring back, McConnell? Another survivor? Where—"

"No, sir," Adams interrupted. "Not a survivor. It's in another lab; one of the medics is investigating it."

"Well let's go see, Adams," the commander said. He looked at McConnell. "I want to know the *second* this guy comes to."

McConnell nodded again. "Yes, sir."

V.

"Commander, are you familiar with the term 'globster'?" Medic Aaron Randolph asked.

"Yes, I know it. Like sea monsters or something."

The medic smiled, thin blond hair falling over his forehead, freckled cheeks creasing at the corners of his eyes as he looked between the sullen Adams and his C.O. The ship was beginning to gently roll as night approached and a storm once more buf-feted the *Higgins*. "That's *sort* of it, sir. Globsters are . . . kind of mysterious relics that wash up periodically. They can be hard to identify, as they have features of several different animals, or it *seems* like they do. Almost like the chimeras from Greek mythology. Some people even claim they're 'cryptids'—previously unknown or undocumented creatures, possibly related by era or locale, like the Loch Ness Monster, or Bigfoot. I mean, maybe they are, but it's doubtful; apocryphal accounts of plane wing gremlins, Chupacabras, and moth men make no sense, as they're generally too divergent from one another." Randolph paused, then added: "Of course, there are exceptions. They didn't think Giant Squids, okapis, coelacanths, or Komodo Dragons were real once either. Usually, though, it's a *lot* less interesting than that—they're just pieces of some animal, like that huge blue eyeball that washed up a couple of years back that they now think belonged to a dead marlin, or the badly decayed carcass of a big shark or whale—"

Adams looked up sharply, eyes wide. "That's no whale, Randy. Look again!"

The medic raised his hand: "I hear you. It's weird alright! But stuff is starting to show up all over; things that were unknown before from the deep, or critters that normally never appear where they're found. Even mass strandings. Happened just recently in L.A.—one day a damn deep sea oarfish washed up, completely intact, then a few days later a barely-living Alaskan saber-toothed whale! They say it might be Global Warming or something, who knows? It's weird, though, and becoming more common. Not sure what this thing is; I checked it out under the 'scope, too. It's not like any other specimen we have onboard, that's for sure. The cryptozoologists would love it."

Merritt straightened up. "Can I see what you're talking about?"

"Absolutely, Commander. Right this way."

They walked to the rear of the room where the storage freezer and the other autopsy tools were stowed. The medic opened the locker door, pulled a covered tray from inside, and set it on the counter. The tray was about two feet long and over a foot wide; the white cloth covering the specimen barely concealed the bulging object underneath. The medic smiled at the C.O. and the ensign. "It's dense, heavy." He pulled the cloth away unceremoniously.

The thing on the tray was hard to comprehend; there was no visual context for it. It was a drab grey, mottled with blooms of light pink. On one end, it was severed all the way through, the raw wound displaying its musculature and a core of bone. This side was slender, smooth; toward the other end of its length, there were what appeared to be scales that became an almost chitinous, hard appendage of some type, resembling a fixed-open claw. Within this structure, there was a softer retracted piece with what looked to be a suckered tentacle covered in miniature hooks. This black flesh was pliant, and the appendage seemed to be gently moving within.

Merritt's eyes widened. "Is that thing—"

The medic nodded. "Yes: It's moving. It's been moving since I got it."

Adams spoke at last: "It was moving around next to Faust on the beach. Pretty vigorously."

"Jesus. What the hell *is* it?" Merritt asked, stepping back in revulsion. "And that smell! Is that—"

"Yes," Randolph confirmed. "As it warms up, it starts emanating that strange odor . . . Like plastic burning."

The intercom interrupted them: "Commander Merritt, this is McConnell. Faust is awake, sir. Not said anything yet, but he woke up a little while ago."

The senior officer looked from Adams to Medic Randolph to the slowly writhing thing on the countertop. "Keep me posted on this, Randolph; I want to know what you find out about the microscopic results. Christ—gives me the fucking *creeps*. Let's go, Adams."

Merritt thumbed the button on the wall speaker: "Roger that, McConnell. On the way."

VI.

Drifting,
Spiraling:
The breath of a sigh,
Or the blink of an eye
Is all that it takes;
And then the sleeper wakes—

VII.

"Faust. My name is Christopher Faust," the man on the bed replied. His voice was weak, strangled.

Commander Merritt: "Were you with the *Australis* crew?"

Faust nodded; his gaze was distant, fixed on something just beyond the officer. Ensign Adams watched Merritt as he continued to question the man. "Where are the other members of your crew? Did they go inland?"

Faust nodded again. "Yes. Three . . . of them went to the center of the island. We started with nine. I was . . . the aviator." Faust's voice was curiously flat and atonal. He never made eye contact, just kept them fixed straight ahead. "We . . . were attacked."

"Attacked?" Merritt shared a surprised look with Adams. "What do you mean? By whom?"

"Not whom—*what.*"

"Okay, then," Adams said. "What?"

Faust slowly, mechanically, turned his head toward the ensign, his eyes staring forward. "By . . . the things in the air. The things from the sea."

There was a tense silence.

"Okay, airman Faust," Merritt said at last, forcing a smile. "You've had a rough time. Let's reconvene this later, once you've been able to regain your strength."

Faust methodically turned to face Merritt again, features slack, rubbery, eyes unblinking.

"They're . . . alive on the *inside*, Commander. Three of them went to the center of the island."

Merritt nodded. "We'll see if we can—"

"And then," Faust interrupted, "the sleeper wakes."

Adams gasped, and the C.O.'s head snapped back in astonishment.

"What?" Merritt stammered, "What did you say, Faust?"

"The sleeper has *awakened*."

After a long and uncomfortable silence, Adams signaled Merritt to step out of the quarters.

"Let's go over and visit Randy again, sir," the ensign said as the two men moved away from the infirmary.

VIII.

"Wow. That's really *weird*," Medic Randolph said. "What does it mean? Is it from a book or something?"

Adams huffed. "Yeah, I'll say . . . it's from a weird dream *I've* been having—"

"And every time you nap or go to sleep," Merritt interjected, "this dream picks up at *exactly* the same place . . . Same strange feeling, same bizarre imagery, right?"

Adams stared at Merritt, his mouth hanging open. Finally: "Yes."

A cold sweat broke out on the C. O.'s body, yet he felt too warm. "I've been having it, too. Started around the time that we began looking for the *Australis*. Just shy of a week ago—"

"Oh shit, this is freaking me out, sir!" Adams exclaimed, plopping into a chair in Randolph's lab.

The medic stared at the two men who seemed suddenly unable to communicate. "Pretty strange. *Twilight Zone*-type stuff . . . Well, not to add *too* much more weird to it, sir, but I found something . . . *interesting* during the microscopic exam."

Merritt cleared his throat, rubbed his eyes, then turned his attention to Randolph. "Okay. What have you learned?"

"It's odd, I'll give you that, but just hear me out a minute . . . "

The medic sat down with the others, grabbed a pen and some paper and started writing and sketching. After a few moments, he began to explain his findings: "So this organism is . . . *unusual* physiologically. Perhaps you're familiar with the concept of the Hayflick Limit?"

Merritt shook his head.

"Well," the medic continued, "it's an observation in genetics. Basically, it's the idea that there are physical limits to the number of times a cell can divide . . . under certain conditions these limitations are able to be chemically or virally circumvented, avoiding the natural process of cellular suicide known as apoptosis. This thing not only looks to have solved this problem, but also has a 'workaround' for the shortening of telomeres as a creature ages. Conceptually, telomeres are the ends of genes that are worn down by cell division; imagine that they're like the little plastic caps on the tips of shoelaces that keep them from fraying. 'Younger' telomeres keep the genes viable. This is also the case with several cancers—that they can keep the telomeres 'young'—as a result, damage arises, in part, due to *unchecked* cellular division. Normally that's a good thing, as it would impact the length of the telomeres negatively, thus applying a kind of brake to out-of-control division—" Randolph drew some examples on the paper to assist the visualization; Merritt nodded for him to continue.

"Anyway, from what I can tell with this thing, there's very rapid, *controlled* cellular division, and an ability to deliberately allocate cell speciation. So in a way, these tissues have characteristics of a tumor, but without the need for a continuous—or in this instance any—blood supply, as they appear to take oxygen directly from the atmosphere; the integument acts as a porous gas exchange membrane, similar to the way insects breathe, but more complex. Sort of like an external lung." The medic glanced over to Adams who seemed to understand.

"So what does that mean?" Adams asked, leaning forward.

Medic Randolph tilted back in his chair and crossed his arms. "Not clear, but it looks like it makes these cells immortal. Not only that, but there's another strange element . . . " Randolph returned to the sketch paper. "See where I drew this? Here, and here?'

Adams and Merritt nodded their heads in understanding.

"It appears these cells are peculiar hybrids of some kind . . . They have aspects of genetic mosaicism, and are these little . . . *independent units* . . . they're like tiny mirrors of the larger organism—"

Merritt: "I'm not following."

Adams picked up the explanation: "What I think it means," he said as he glanced at Randolph, "is that *each* cell is a microcosm of the complete organism."

"Exactly: All of the material is there; each cell appears to have a pluripotent cellular reserve. It's not only immortal, like certain jellyfish, but *self-organizing*; completely contained within itself. And not only that," Randolph said, "but it seems that *every* cell is on some level . . . *conscious* for lack of a better word—"

"What are you saying Randolph?" Merritt asked, touching his temple as he struggled to understand.

"I'm saying, Commander, that the cells react not just as *cells*—meaning with respect to extreme heat, cold and some of the chemical agents I've applied to both the biopsy cultures and the entire appendage—but they cannot be 'killed' in the normal sense of the term; they regenerate, and relatively quickly. Not only that—they behave as though they have a type of 'collective awareness' and each can respond accordingly to the stimuli or circumstances as either A) a unified being, or B) as an autonomous *piece* of that organism, thus insuring survival at *all* costs. They even seem to be able to absorb and replicate other proteins, which gives them the ability to . . . *become* that protein."

Adams laughed without humor. "Oh my *God*. You mean like that fucking '80s movie?"

Randolph looked surprised. "Yeah, actually. Quite protean. Just like that, or *Invasion of the Body Snatchers*. There are other examples in nature microscopically, and so on. Besides, this isn't quite the same. I seriously *doubt* this is an alien; it's probably just an evolutionary strategy. Most likely a viral thing, or at least started that way. Hell, turns out a shitload of our so-

called 'junk DNA' is comprised of retroviruses that functional-
ly seem to have no purpose now. Might've had some uses at
one time, but those uses are genetically 'turned off', 'cause we
don't need them due to the way we've evolved. Proof of that is
the way our wounds heal; we have most of the same DNA as,
say, a salamander, but they can regenerate arms and legs, and
we can't. We just scar over."

Merritt's head was swimming. "So what did you do with
the—"

"With the specimen?" Adams finished.

Randolph nodded toward the storage freezer. "In there; won't
hurt it, but slows it down quite a bit. In fact, I noticed that the
severed part is re-growing. Looks like it's trying to re-create
the missing body."

"Shit! How do we rid of the fucking thing?" Merritt was genuinely alarmed.

Randolph assured him: "No worries, sir. It needs a *lot* of oxygen to facilitate this process. It's fairly immune to temperature
extremes, but it can't stay submerged—kills the tissue in a
matter of minutes based on my tests; of course, seems likely
that a completely . . . *integrated* organism might be able to overcome that problem. Could be multiple types of organisms, too:
They reported other strange creatures there, right?" He
paused, noting the concern on the C.O.'s features. "But with
respect to this thing, Commander, don't be too worried—it
takes a while to re-grow whole pieces. Probably a few days or
more depending on size, maybe longer. The absorption trick is
faster, but has similar limitations; I mean it's an 'organic
machine' in a way, so while the duplicated components are
nearly perfect, they occupy a state between being alive and
dead. Besides," Randolph said, shrugging, "this is the find of a
lifetime—we need to bring it back with us."

Before Merritt could mount a protest, the intercom sounded:
McConnell.

"Commander, something . . . *interesting* is happening. Could
you please report to the bridge?"

"What is it?" Merritt asked, pressing the switch.

"The ship near the island, the *Indianapolis* has—"

Adams gave a stunned look to Merritt: "Did you say *Indianapolis*, McConnell?" There was a pause.

"Sorry, sir. I'm tired, and I've been having this crazy dream . . . I mean the *Australis*—she's completely sunk now."

IX.

Equipped with sidearms, survival gear, and machetes, they returned to the island the next morning. Once on the beach, Faust stoically led Adams, Merritt, and three others into the forest at the center. McConnell had briefed them of increasing seismic activity during the past day, warning them to be mindful of possible tremors.

Overhead, huge bird creatures the size of small cars swooped and pirouetted in the overcast sky; as they were making their landing in the surf, Adams managed to photograph a bizarre, man-sized purple and red mega-crab exoskeleton that was drifting in a backwater near some crags. As was the previous case, compasses, radios, and GPS devices became unreliable.

Inside the canopy, the kaleidoscope of brilliantly-plumed flowers, lush plants, and fantastically odd-looking—even menacing—giant insects was overwhelming: The place was an explosion of noise, a jumble of odors, a riot of color. The weather had graced them with a fortunate reprieve.

"Christ, the biodiversity of this place is unbelievable. It's covered with all manner of independent ecosystems," Adams observed, slicing though the thorny undergrowth with his blade, face slicked with sweat. Merritt nodded in breathless agreement, but before he could speak, an awful shriek peeled through the tangled wilderness. It was human: female.

"Faust, you mentioned that *Australis* had a woman onboard?" Merritt asked, wiping sweat away with his sleeve. They paused, quietly trying to ascertain the direction that the scream had come from.

"Yes." Faust replied, staring at Merritt, his face waxen, his demeanor indifferent. After another moment, he pointed. "That way."

X.

The breath of a sigh,
Or the blink of an eye
Is all that it takes;
And then the sleeper wakes—
"What if Earth
Be but the shadow of Heaven, and things therein?"

XI.

The explorers had reached an opening in the mega-flora, the evident remnants of a collapsed volcano caldera: It was hot, humid; the otherworldly antithesis of Antarctica. Even more incredibly, inside the caldera were the apparent ruin of a vast city, with indications of a long dead, yet obviously advanced civilization. Merritt was in a state of mental shock as the team hacked a passage into the clearing: Caressing the intricate stone buildings, marveling at the complex etchings which scored the coarse rock edifices, some more than three stories tall, he was astonished that this place existed, and wondered about the people that had carved these stones. *How many places are like this on Earth, just waiting to be uncovered?* The commander took note of the sky: It was getting dark, and he observed that, strangely, there were no animals or insects to be found in this area. The heavy air was still, musky, preternaturally quiet.

"*Help . . . Help us!*" It was a hushed, breathy cry from somewhere in the twilight.

Merritt: "Adams! Did you hear that?"

The rest of the search crew paused to listen. Once more: "Help . . . "

Deep in the interior, the landing party found her: Julia Murphy—former crewmember of the *Terra Australis Incognita*.

What was left of her, at least.

XII.

As the Moon's shadow eclipses the Sun,
So Man stumbles; and thus ends his run—

XIII.

Murphy was lying in a supine position, naked on the ground near one of the buildings: The dim light from the sky overpowered the brilliant light originating from large, ornate green and blue fungi covering the lower part of her torso and obliterating her legs. As they watched, the men could see the carnivorous fungus creeping across her skin, dissolving it and fueling their grim, heatless glow.

"Help me . . . Please help . . . " Her face was sweaty, her breath shallow, her dry lips cracked.

Even though he was horrified, Merritt felt compelled to act, and rushed past the stunned group to get near the stricken woman. "I'm Commander Scott Merritt, of the USS *Higgins*." Leaning closer to her, he swallowed back a stab of bile, fighting a surge of nausea at the sickly sweet odor coming from her mouth. His mind was racing as he suddenly yearned to be home with his family. He felt for this poor girl; she reminded him not only of his wife, but also of all the things he most cherished, that he was compelled to do anything to protect. She smiled wanly, then unleashed a blood-freezing scream of agony. Merritt's chest thundered in pity and terror.

"It . . . it chased us in here . . . " Julia's bony arms were shriveled, drawn into a pugilistic formation, Merritt noticed; he distantly remembered that as a sign of neurological damage: The fungus was aggressive—moving from the exposed viscera of her guts and over her chest by fractions of inches in just a few minutes.

"It chased us . . . into the city . . . then . . . Captain Roland slipped. That . . . that was him." She motioned with her head to a blackened knot of dehydrated shapes; even the bones had been dissolved by the fungus; the only thing remotely humanoid was its general size and form, and possibly a lump that resembled the jawless head of a lamprey. The ground rocked slightly, followed by a low rumble, not unlike thunder in the distance; a very minor quake.

"Dr. Crowe tried to save him . . . but . . . it got him, too."

"There were three of you?" Merritt asked, face softly illuminated by the surreal glow of the predatory fruiting bodies, as eerie and distressing as a corpse candle. Merritt suddenly understood why there were no other animals here: The area was overrun by the creeping fungi—dimly glowing all around as the daylight extinguished. The other patches were smaller; less recently fed he suspected, and the whole place was littered with similar black masses to the erstwhile Capt. Roland.

Other animals! Jesus, it's like this whole island is alive.

"My *God* . . . " Adams had made the same mental connection just then: "We have to *leave*, sir! It's trying to lure us in!"

"No!" Julia screamed. "*Save me!*" At that instant, her mouth exploded outward with slimy black mold, the lower portion of her face collapsing like a deflated mask, the eyeballs falling into the pulsating, radiant mass of mushrooms and bloody tissue.

Merritt screamed: he jumped backward in abject horror and panic as the fungus consumed the girl.

Too late.

XIV.

Thus ends his run—
"I should have been a pair of ragged claws
Scuttling across the floors of silent seas."

XV.

On the *Higgins*, McConnell was frustrated.

He had not been able to raise anyone for hours, and now the party was stranded on the island for the night. Even though they had been lucky with the weather most of the day—no way that could hold much longer—the seismic readings had spiked recently. He felt a certain amount of dread that a major event was likely in the immediate future. Something about the whole scenario deeply disturbed him, but he was hard-pressed to articulate exactly what it was; the sooner they abandoned this godforsaken place, the better he would feel. It reminded him of when he was working on the blowout after the *Deepwater Horizon* disaster in the Gulf of Mexico, not far from his hometown of New Orleans. The name of the well prospect had been Macondo, just like the fictional town created by Gabriel García Márquez in his books. McConnell recalled that those had been nightmarish times, almost as surreal as the events in some of Márquez' work, as though the Earth was finally rebelling against the insult of humans overreaching their assumed dominion. BP, Transocean, and Halliburton covered up a lot, but there were things he had seen that still sickened him: trapped sea turtles burned alive; birds drowning because they were too heavy to fly away due to the thick crude slicking their bodies; massive, undocumented beachings as animals tried to escape the toxic sludge of oil, methane, and chemical dispersant. There had been other things; rumors of something else that had been discovered in the blowout, barely held in check by the final cap of the well. Some said it could never be capped permanently, and it was a matter of time before the fissures on the seafloor created by the disaster fractured to a point that whatever was there would become active again.

Adding to this anxiety, McConnell was exhausted; the strange dreams had been intensifying during the past two days the *Higgins* had been anchored near the uncharted atoll.

"Command Merritt, Ensign Adams, come in. Over." Static, a little radio interference. All freqs.

McConnell was homesick, too. They were scheduled for some leave after this last deployment researching low-frequency sonar, and he was glad to be done with it; the heartbreaking damage to the whales and their hearing was obvious when the dead ones floated to the surface. Who knew what else it did to the fragile marine environment, but they had documented some things, from devastating ecosystems to destabilizing underwater superstructures. *Where did it all end? Not with massive underwater blowouts, apparently, or man-made earthquakes in the Midwest caused by hydraulic fracking, or the murder of animals caused by human intervention in their environments . . .* He felt it was all so destructive, unnatural, evil.

"This is McConnell. Do you read, Adams? Over."

XVI.

Faust led the way out of the ruins; along with Commander Merritt, the horrific fungus had claimed two other men. Finally on the beach, as faintly bioluminescent waves lapped the windswept shore, hissing into the dark sand, Adams could see the lights of the *Higgins* off in the frigid distance. His walkie-talkie was useless; luckily their flashlights still worked for the time being. The ground shook again, adding to the tension on the beach.

"Great! We're trapped here on this insane fucking *rock* until morning . . . " Adams lamented, looking from the silent Faust to the other man, his breath trailing into the void. The man was a young enlisted that he vaguely recognized, but could not place by name. "And you are?"

"Seaman Recruit Anderson, sir." The man was visibly upset, but also seemed relieved to be on the strand, even in the extreme cold of the pre-dawn. "Never seen nothing like that back home in North Carolina, sir. Whatever had that girl . . . It was *bad*. Something *real bad*."

Adams nodded in a feeble attempt at reassurance, turning to face the *Higgins* out at sea, mentally struggling to figure out what to do next. "Yes, it sure—"

Abruptly, Faust tackled Adams from the rear, slamming him to the ground. The two thrashed on the damp earth while the stunned Anderson looked on, his light starkly flaring over the men writhing on the black sand. As they fought, Faust gained the upper hand, biting into Adams's cheek and savagely tearing a meaty chunk of flesh from the ensign's face, laying bare teeth, gums, bone. Adams was too panicked to think or feel—he reacted by unsheathing his machete and swinging wildly, yelling into the cold, dry night air . . .

The heavy blade found its mark, and cleanly separated Faust's arm from his body: He never screamed or made a sound, but in the cool LED illumination of Anderson's flashlight, a strange, acrid black smoke poured forcefully from both ends of the bloodless stump. Faust's mouth twisted in a silent mockery of pain; already the severed arm was crawling away in the surf, the end bulging with new growth, as the stump on his body began to display the withered approximation of a regenerated appendage, covered in mucus and red gore; overcome by the bizarre tableau, Anderson and Adams screamed in unified revulsion.

Faust, bloodied and determined, came at them, his half-formed arm quickly developing into a grisly, formidably hooked caricature of a human limb. Then his mouth opened, splitting past the natural hinge of his jaw as a great beaked face—its knobby flesh translucent all the way to an eyeless skull tufted by a delicate lattice of pinfeathers matted with opalescent slime—erupted from the gaping, bloody maw that had been Christopher Faust, but was no longer. The same vaporous black smoke spewed from his destroyed facial orifices, obscuring the flashlight beam.

As the creature closed the distance between the stunned sailors, the entire island unexpectedly shifted . . . half-sinking into the deep, flooding the beach and creating an enormous wave as the morning sun seeped redly above the horizon.

It was beginning.

XVII.

"I should have been a pair of ragged claws
Scuttling across the floors of silent seas."
A pause—
A revelation—
A comprehension—
"The other shape,
If shape it might be call'd that shape had none
Distinguishable in member, joint, or limb;
Or substance might be call'd that shadow seem'd,
For each seem'd either—black it stood as night,
Fierce as ten furies, terrible as hell,
And shook a dreadful dart. What seem'd his head
The likeness of a kingly crown had on."

XVIII.

"Shit!"

McConnell felt the shockwave on the *Higgins* just as he was about to drift off to sleep. It rolled past the ship, causing it to lurch sidewise in the water. Looking from his porthole, he could see the breaking dawn just clear the horizon, touching the clouds with fire. *Where are the islands?* Then he saw . . . *it*, and had to rub his bleary eyes in disbelief.

It started as a soft rolling on the water; then an object more than a mile across thrust up from the sea, perhaps a couple of hundred feet from the USS *Higgins*. The shape dwarfing the destroyer was vast; it seemed to sparkle from within as though some swallowed ancient-future galaxy shone through its ebon, sea-drenched skin. In another eternal instant, the great being—dripping with kelp and seawater, glimmering in the vivid dawn like some unearthly, newborn titan—reared up to its full, multistoried height.

McConnell's bladder voided unconsciously when he realized it was alive, and many thoughts crossed his mind: *Was this Satan? Or maybe an angel . . . Mother said that angels were fear-*

some creatures, not these little winged babies . . . Perhaps this was God itself?

Gripping the window opening, his knuckles taut, as he stared at the dreadful leviathan, McConnell's mind began to disengage. Somewhere, far away, it seemed, the sound of his ragged screams deafened him, as his overwhelmed consciousness tried to understand this being, to grasp the purpose of its hideous beauty. On the misty horizon, he noticed another giant rising up; this one was slightly different, but just as enormous . . . distantly, there was yet another on the skyline . . . and then another . . . They seemed to pull the very light from the firmament, gradually enrobed by wispy fringes of nightfall—as though their presence created a void in the fabric of life itself. As he watched, a great vortex began swirling in the ocean around the behemoth, slowly opening up and swallowing the destroyer . . . It was at that moment he realized something had changed in the world, and before the icy sting of Antarctic saltwater filled his nose and mouth, McConnell realized how lucky he was— indeed everyone aboard the doomed *Higgins* was—to be spared the horrors yet to come.

The great thing howled and his brain jellied, his ears bled, but the last thing McConnell saw before his consciousness was snuffed by the incomprehensible and his corneas stiffened from the freezing cold of the sea rushing in to fill him—to crush him, to wipe him from the memory of humankind—was the baleful sun blotted out by the extension of terrible, massive wings.

Flesh and Bones

Nancy Kilpatrick

"Please! We need to experience this! We have money to donate."

Joe thought that the old priest closing the door for the day must have heard the supplicant in Marielle's tone. Or noticed the obsessive flicker in her eyes. Or possibly it was simply religious compassion that compelled the man to open wide the huge wooden door and say something in Italian that neither Joe nor Marielle could decipher.

Marielle was closest, Joe right behind her, his body pressed lightly up against her too-warm flesh until they followed the priest in, trailed by a small group of five that had gathered, configurations of tourists who also demanded entrance to the Capuchin Church of the Immaculate Conception. Or, more specifically, to its bowels, the Capuchin Crypt.

The black-robed priest stepped aside and they entered, congregating just inside the door, waiting for him to move his hunched body to the table and sit so that he could collect a few euros from each visitor. Pamphlets were available on a rack for those who wanted them, and Joe snagged two, one in English for himself, one for Marielle in French, a euro each. Individually and in couples they all went down the half-dozen

stone steps and then started along the corridor that Joe estimated to be about sixty feet in length, with six 'rooms' on the
left side.

This was the most recent crypt on their itinerary, a tour that
had Joe and Marielle traveling from their home in Montréal to
various places around the world to investigate human remains
in the form of bones (her) and mummified flesh (him). Over
the last twenty years, since they'd met and married, they had
traveled as often as they could, every year on a four- to six-
week holiday, searching out exotic and macabre locations.
This year, Joe's tenure at McGill University allowed for an
eight-month sabbatical. Marielle had taken a very early retirement from her senior supervisory position with the Quebec
government two years before. "I won't live forever," she'd said.
"I want to devote my remaining time to my art."

And Joe understood that only too well. Her decision had
accelerated his own need. He was as dedicated to mummies as
she was to bones. And even after completing ninety-nine percent of this four-month trip through Europe and the United
Kingdom at tremendous expense, covering many dozens of
bone crypts and mummy museums, neither was ready to go
home, although, at the moment, Marielle's pet project called
more loudly to her than did Joe's to him.

Like all crypts, the lighting here was subdued, funereal, the
occasional small vent providing filtered natural light, creating
an ambiance that suited the dead. The scent of centuries of
dust and old mold permeated the cool air mixed with a tinge of
the traditional tallow from church candles. And while the others hurried through, surreptitiously snapping photos despite
the picture of a camera in a circle with a red slash through it,
Joe and Marie lingered. They took photos also, but with the
spy cameras each had acquired, two by two inches, Marielle's
on a key ring, Joe's disguised as a pen. Years ago they had realized that too many crypts, ossuaries, and museums did not per-
mit photographs. They needed photos, not merely as
reminders, or mental *souvenirs* as Marielle called them, and
not just to help with their personal projects, but more, to keep

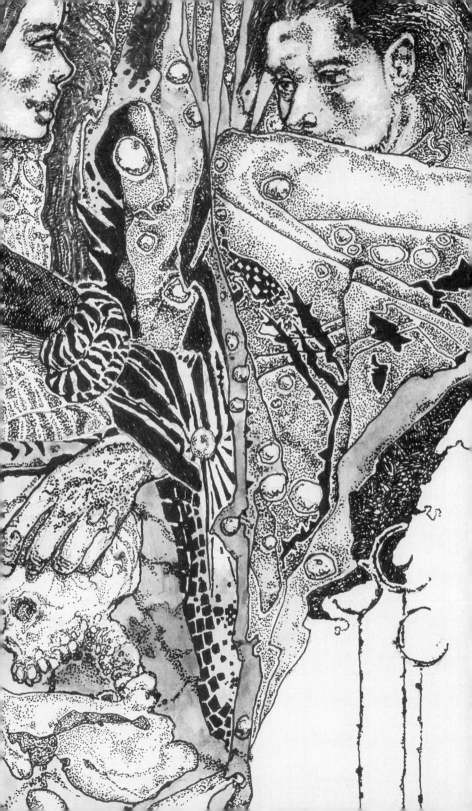

their spirits buoyed between trips when they could experience these wondrous remains in person and not just in books and on the Internet.

Joe reached the first room on the left. Inside stood a marble altar, a metal cross atop with the usual INRI inscribed over the crucified figure of Christ, and he felt a bit disappointed. Marielle was ahead of him, just passing beneath the corridor's first arched doorway that led to the rest of the rooms. She stopped dead, looked up, then turned to him with awe saturating her features and silently pointed above her head at the ceiling. He stepped aside to let the last of the other tourists pass who were ready to flee what they and most people likely deemed a place too morbid to enjoy. Joe joined Marielle and looked up.

Above their heads hung a large chandelier created from human bones, brown and smooth with age and sprinkled with crypt dust. "Mainly tibia and fibula," she mumbled softly, her voice reverent, "and the tarsals, of course," but Joe heard her.

"That looks like a clavicle at the center," he said, pointing, and she nodded.

Bones were what entranced her. She said now what she had said so often in so many ways, "They reduce us to our essence. It's the bottom line of the physical. After that, there is only *l'esprit, n'est pas?*"

He understood her fascination. He shared it, but not to the same extent. His focus was elsewhere.

He looked ahead, not even glancing toward the second room on the left, wanting to build the tension of his excitement because he knew what was coming. He often thought how this resembled sexual tension, allowing the erotic to expand and rise and finally release, like an orgasm. Yes, it was very much like an orgasm. And he could wait.

He continued along the corridor with Marielle. Unlike Les Catacombes de Paris, these bones were not simply piles of femurs and tibias and skulls artistically arranged; most if not all the bones of the body had been fashioned into shapes, objects. Several hearts lined the corridor wall, composed main-

ly of carpals and metacarpals, the small bones of the hand that
would allow for a rounded shape. The second arch they walked
beneath and those ahead were decorated in a kind of filigree
pattern with cervical and thoracic vertebrae making for a very
pretty and welcoming lace-like design to the entrances.

He still ignored the contents of the rooms for the moment,
teasing himself, and headed further up the short corridor until
he reached the back wall, admiring the artistry along the way.
This wall and the ceiling were crammed with images, and he
was, as always in places like this, astonished by the number of
skulls. A clock had been formed, the frame of cervical, thoracic, and lumbar vertebrae and ribs, the Roman numerals
employing metatarsals and phalanges of the feet but perhaps
also the metacarpals and phalanges of the hands—sometimes
these bones looked the same to him, but then, unlike Marielle,
he was no *ossa* expert.

Marielle whispered, "Look! *L'Horloge!*" The clock had only
one hand, he noticed. And as if reading his mind, as so frequently happened, she said, "Time has neither beginning nor
end."

There were flowers, vases, crosses of course, but the most
elaborate sculpture was a grim reaper, an entire skeleton,
dwarf-size, the skull large, gripping in its bony hands a bone
scythe on one side of its body, and a scale in balance on the
other.

"Oh!" Marielle cried when she saw it, deeply moved and
completely enthralled, and he smiled. He loved her passion for
bones. She could be profound in her insights, making connections that he struggled to get to, likely because she could really comprehend how all 206 bones in an adult human body fit
together and experienced the beauty of that completeness; this
helped him accept his own fixations, which, he believed,
required much more work to grasp.

Here and there a bone had fallen out of an image from the
wall or ceiling in the hallway, never to be replaced but crushed
underfoot, and when she noticed, she scanned the dirt floor,
finding two pieces of cervical vertebrae and what must be a

coccyx. Quickly and surreptitiously she pocketed these after a glance to make sure the priest was not watching. This was illegal, of course: they often mailed them home disguised in *objets d'art* they purchased, since getting human remains through airport security proved nearly impossible. But Marielle needed these for her work. She had bones from around the world, piecing them together carefully, a life's mission, to collect every adult bone and build a composite skeleton, an everyman, well, everywoman—the pelvis she had found was female. He admired her devotion to her craft. His own artwork required little in the way of props, just time and study.

Marielle was so taken with the artwork that she had yet to peer into the rooms built from the foundations of this church. They were alone now, and Joe valued the silence, the priest at the end of the corridor quietly, patiently reading.

He walked back up the corridor slowly, finally allowing himself a quick glance into each room, his heart pounding with excitement. These were three-walled, plus floor and ceiling, open at the front, built of the same dusty grey stone, and dimly lit.

Each room presented a kind of tableau created by bones, mostly skulls and crossed-bones—the only ones the early church believed were required for resurrection because, they determined, thinking and emotion were housed in the head, and one only needed the leg bones to stand for ascension.

Joe remembered re-reading on the Internet that morning that monks who had fled the French Revolution in the 1700s had come to join this church, built in 1642. Over the next century and a bit, four thousand of them had died here, their remains contributing to the ghastly decor. The Marquis de Sade had visited this crypt in 1775 and deemed it "an example of funerary art worthy of an English mind," created "by a German priest who lived in this house." But, in fact, the person or person who had arranged the contents of this crypt remained unknown, and that suited Joe. He wanted to keep this perfect blend of his and Marielle's interests anonymous.

There were altars, naturally, with crosses above, rounded or squared or rectangular tables and beds, all built from bones. But this is not what caused the adrenalin to rush through Joe's body. What set his heart quivering were those who sat or reclined in or stood near the bed-like niches along the side walls. These stone shelves were the final resting places for the remains of mummified monks, their dark, leathery skin with empty eye sockets and remaining yellowed teeth, the bones of hands and arms and feet extending from the sleeves and hems of the dusty brown robes with hoods they wore and tied at the waist with rough hemp belts. Each exposed face was unique, full of expression, so alive to Joe that he felt they were drawing him closer, wanting him near enough to converse with. He gasped in delight, then quickly looked down the corridor. The priest had looked up.

Joe turned away and took a few steps toward the front of the corridor, gazing at the ceiling, then stopped again, and out of the corner of his eye saw that the priest had returned to his reading.

He turned to the next room, his entrance again blocked by a waist-high fence and, spellbound, stared at the figures, willing them to move, although he knew they could not. He felt an intimacy with the formerly living, *home* for him in a deep sense, and could not tear his eyes from the garbed figures. He wandered back and forth before the rooms, lost in time and space, studying each monk, the supine, the standing, the sitting, their positioning and gestures, memorizing the browned flesh stretched over cheek and jaw and forehead until each face was imprinted in his memory, their hands and feet, their postures, back and forth, identifying every monk in his mind: The Silent One; The Reader; The Heavy One; The Sad Monk; The One Who Could Not Fully Submit . . . until the priest cleared his throat.

"We are nearly finished," Marielle called sweetly, first in English, then French, and if the priest knew either language, he did not let on.

This was Joe's signal to hurry and snap photos, and he removed the pen from his shirt pocket and a small book, pretending to jot notes while he took photos of these beautiful beings.

He exited the crypt with heavy sadness, as if leaving close friends or family whom he might never see again. Marielle, by contrast, was happy, talkative, discussing the artistic bone creations, and he found himself tuning her out. It was only later, after a late supper and to bed early because they were headed north to Ferentillo in the morning, that he lay in the quiet darkness apart from her too-warm body and wondered about why this was so, why this desiccated flesh appealed to him, excited him, made him want to be close, to touch, though he had not often been so close. But one time, in southern Peru, when they had been in the Camarones Valley, he had found part of the face of a Chinchorro mummy that must be five thousand years old. It was one of the few times he had been up close and personal with a mummy and had felt the parchment-like skin of this ancient being, caressing the millennia-old flesh that ultimately reached the most ancient part of himself, leaving behind the alienated being that took pride of place within him.

The Chinchorra were artificial mummies, the organs removed as with the Egyptian mummies that came two thousand years later. He preferred the naturally preserved and knew that the Capuchin monks whom he had seen here in Roma, as well as those in the enormous and overwhelming Catacombe dei Cappuccini in Palermo that housed about a thousand mummies dating from 1599, both religious and secular, were all 'natural' mummifications. It was the tufaceous rock, or porous limestone in the soil, which had done the work in nine months, *the time it takes to birth a baby,* he thought.

There were other natural mummies, of course, and he had seen almost all that had been discovered, including the 108 in the Museo de las Momias in Guanajuato, Mexico, exhumed from their graves in the adjacent cemetery; the bog people resurrected from the peat bogs of Northern Europe, preserved by the acidic water, low temperature, and lack of oxygen; the thirteenth-century Maronite villagers found in a low-humidity grotto in the Kadisha Valley, Lebanon, the soil free of decay-causing organisms; the thousand tombs housing mummies in the Astana graves at Xinijang, China, preserved by the arid air;

'Ötzi,' the 5,300-year-old Neolithic mummified man found in the ice-bound Italian Alps and housed at the south Tyrol Museum of Archeology, which they had visited just two weeks before . . .

When he thought about it, he became grim with the knowledge that he had now seen every known mummy that it was possible to see, even using his academic credentials to request study of those that were not available to the general public. Ferentillo was their last stop. And then . . . then what would he do? Go back to his regular life, crammed with students asking questions he had heard a million times, dealing with poorly thought-out papers, the obligatory wine and cheese *soirées,* the faculty meetings and politics that bored him to death, all of it miring life in mundanity, which he considered worse than death. How could he go back to his 'life'? He *needed* this connection. He could not survive without it.

The following morning they took a train and a bus, and then walked two miles through a sun-soaked valley to the sleepy village of Ferentillo and had to wait for the Chiesa di S. Stefano to reopen after lunch. They sat in the sun, watching two slow-moving cats wander up the steep path toward where they sat at the church's doorway.

"You seem pensive," Marielle said, petting one of the cats. "Do you regret going home?"

"Yes. Don't you?"

"Not so much this time. I have what I need."

Joe knew she was referring to the bones she found on this trip, enough to complete her project. He, though, did not share her sense of completion. For him, the mummies would always be elsewhere, never with him, where he needed and wanted them to be. And now that he was about to have seen them all, he felt at a loss.

Marielle reached over and placed her hand on his. "Today is a special day, *mon cher,*" she said. "You are finished, too, *non?*"

He said nothing. What was there to say? She was right; his quest, as much as hers, was over. He felt emptiness swell within him that until now he had been able to keep at bay.

Once the crypt beneath the church reopened and they were inside, Marielle immediately headed to a small back room and listened to the caretaker talk about how the mummies and particularly the shelves of skulls had been found. This crypt had only been partially excavated, and there was much more work to do, digging back into the rock to find what could be fifty times as many mummies, but there were no plans in the near future for that work.

Joe only half listened until the caretaker said, " . . . mushrooms in the soil preserved them . . ." This is what he already knew—what, here in Italy, seemed to have been responsible for most of the natural mummification.

He wandered the main crypt area, only a half-dozen tall glass and wood cases, one or more mummies within each, dressed, undressed, the sheets of glass keeping them temperature-controlled, keeping him from them.

He studied a mummy family, man, woman, infant. Then what might have been a field worker, shreds of a shirt and cap still adhering to the body. A young couple was preserved side by side, the woman's long braided hair hanging over one shoulder the way Marielle sometimes fixed hers. These mummies were pale in comparison to those in Roma, their features closer to what they would have looked like alive, and he presumed that the soil that had created the conditions for preservation were responsible for this.

Since arriving in Italy and discovering that the soil combined with various fungi had been the source of drying out a human body in as short a time as four months, his ideas for his own project had shifted 180 degrees. He wanted to explore the possibilities of this fungal soil and consequently touted his academic credentials to allow for the collection of samples he could send home from various locations, where permitted. Unlike the Capuchins in Roma and Palermo, here he received permission to collect soil samples for study, which is what he now did. He opened his metallic samples case and filled two dozen large wide-mouthed Teflon-coated glass containers with the dirt by the stone wall at the back of this crypt, which would be less contaminated by human presence, although not many visitors made it to this hard-to-reach town. In Palermo, he had taken soil samples from inside a well near the crypt. The oldest mummy, an early Capuchin monk, had died in a well. His disinterred remains had mummified and Joe had been privileged to view Brother Silvestro.

When he and Marielle were finished with the crypt, they headed back to Roma for their flight home the following day. Joe thought about all the places he had been, the mummies he had seen, and the scope and breadth of memory filled the emptiness within, at least temporarily. If only he could hold onto that feeling! If only his life could brim with mummies and the connection he felt to these beings, so real to him, alive to his senses, his way of thinking, connected to his soul . . . If only . . .

Montréal winter met their arrival home. Joe thought that this frigid cold must be similar to what had preserved Ötzi in the Alps for millennia.

But their apartment was comforting, overflowing with sculptures Marielle had constructed, early ones created from animal bones. Since her retirement, the artwork was formed exclusively from human bones she had rescued from everywhere they had traveled. The Sedlec Ossuary in Kutná Hora near Prague had supplied a few. Many were from odd cemeteries, like Cimetière Notre-Dame-de-Belmont in Québéc City, which has a junkyard adjacent where workers tossed old gravestones, coffin pieces, and human remains from abandoned graves so the plots could be reused. Once Marielle had crawled into a dumpster against the fence of the Lafayette Cemetery in New Orleans and managed to smuggle home inside voodoo dolls the bones she found there. "So much for perpetual care!" she'd said, but these were all terrific finds that bumped up her work several notches.

Joe had no material from a mummy other than the four-inch square of skin he had smuggled out of Peru. But he did have soil, collected everywhere, searching always for that elusive combination of ingredients that caused natural mummification.

He experimented on dead birds he found in parks, mainly pigeons, and occasionally a larger animal, like a cat. Once he'd come across a dog that had been hit by a car. The soil from Italy showed more promise and, over the months of the cold weather, in his climate-controlled lab at the back of the apartment, he had managed to mummify a dead mouse.

During those same frozen months, Marielle finished her sculpture, the 206 bones threaded with forty-gauge wire, thin enough to appear invisible, creating a strangely disjointed figure but lovely in its own right, perpetually in motion, and Marielle was ecstatic. Weeping, she admitted, "I have not the words in any language, *mon amour*. I feel my life is now complete."

Joe debated what to do to move his own project along. He knew what he *wanted* to do, but the climate outside his special room did not inspire this, at least not yet. And like the weather, preservation could not be hurried.

On a day after winter had given way to spring and summer felt within reach, Marielle's spirit seemed to wither before his eyes. She was even more of an introvert than he, and spent hours alone with *La Femme,* as she called the skeleton she had constructed, whispering to her creation.

Her depression deepened until physical symptoms appeared. "Should you see someone?" he asked, but she did not trust doctors and he knew what her answer would be.

"I will drink my *tisane*."

He made her pots of tea throughout the day, the herbs she had drunk all her life, declaring that they would cure anything. But this time, they did not.

"Do not worry, Joseph. Life ends for us all, and I know my time is near. I wish to die as I have lived. You know that, you know me, and you will respect my wishes?"

"Yes, of course," he assured her, and did not argue about it; they had discussed their plans so many times. Joe believed that they had been fortunate to find each other; their passions dovetailed. And while he felt closer to Marielle than to any other living being, still, he felt closer to the preserved dead. He caressed her face, a face he had known and loved for twenty years. Her skin was sallow and dry, the fat and muscle beneath shrunken, and he did not mind this at all; it reminded him of the mummies, and he wished he did not but he preferred her this way.

At the end, Marielle suffered to some extent, but there were drugs for pain relief that he had gotten from his doctor ostensibly for himself, but really for her, and without asking, he crushed the precious blue pills into the tea she drank religiously but eventually could barely swallow.

Joe sat with her, her skin parchment, her eyes, when they opened, glitteringly bright, though sunk into the hollows of her eye sockets. "Remember your promise," she whispered.

She stared at him until he nodded, gently squeezing her arid hand, then her eyes closed, her lips parted, and a sigh like a spirit left her body.

That night, Joe drove to the Cimetière Notre-Dame-des-Neiges, to the isolated crypt they had built together a dozen years ago, a small affair, nothing like the elaborate houses of the dead that had been constructed amidst the common graves a century or more ago, or the modern monoliths lacking grace and beauty. Theirs was only wide enough to house two coffins, side by side, with a narrow passage between and a door not four feet from the foot end.

Joe carried her in, her body paper light, naked, washed at home, brought here to her final resting place, and lay her in the open coffin devoid of silks and satins and fancy pillows for the dead. These two caskets were plain affairs, built by Joe of local hardwood, made to measure in length and width, only deep enough so the lids could close if need be.

Rigor mortis had claimed her, and while it would pass in a few hours, he wanted to position her right away and struggled with the locked muscles until he was satisfied. Then he sat on the edge of the other coffin, the one measured for his body, touching her now-cool skin.

"Forgive me, Marielle. I know this is not everything you requested. You wanted to be interred here without embalming, and I've done that for you. You wanted your body to decompose over time until only your bones are left." He paused. "I'm sorry."

He had placed her on soil he'd collected from around the world and now emptied buckets of tufaceous fungal dirt on top of her, submerging her limbs, her torso, surrounding her head, leaving only one hand and her moon-face exposed, reminding him of the hooded Capuchin mummies.

Finally, he left her to do the things he needed to do to finish up a life. Joe had a sister out west with whom he hadn't had contact in over a decade. Unlike him, Marielle had no living relatives and, being a hermit by nature, no close friends. Her pension, as with his salary, was a direct deposit into their bank account, bills paid automatically. The condo ran on its own steam and the neighbors, well, they hardly saw them and rarely spoke.

As he returned the rental car, he thought that with some luck, no one would think to check the crypt.

Two months! he mused, taking the bus in the middle of the night, climbing the cemetery's fence, moving in his dark clothing through these moonless grounds toward the crypt backed up against the forest, which he unlocked, entered, and relocked from inside. *Not much time for preservation.* He had brought a single candle, which he lit and glued with candle wax to the top of the skull of *La Femme,* which now stood undulating in the corner as if guarding her creator.

He so wanted to move the soil away and examine Marielle's body, but that made no sense. A little more than a week wasn't enough time for the drying process to get underway. It would take the full two months of a sweltering summer, and he just hoped there would be an Indian summer this year, extended heat. All the elements were right—the heat, the soil, the fungus—but the time was so short! Well, there was nothing much he could do about that.

Her face looked excruciatingly sweet to him, even more shrunken, skin stretching tight across facial bones already. There was a noxious odor of the gases and other excretions of death, but he didn't mind because it would eventually evaporate and the end result was what mattered.

He covered her face with half of the remaining fungus-embedded soil he had brought here when he'd had the car and had also created the bed of soil in both coffins. Then he undressed and lay in his casket, strapping down his ankles, thighs, stomach, and one wrist.

It was cooler in the crypt, but still hot from the day's blazing sun and humidity. Thirty or more Celsius in the day, twenty-eight at night. Not the dry heat of Italy, but maybe it would be all right. He swallowed most of the water in the large water bottle he'd brought along, then took her marble-like hand in his and thought about the process.

Over the last days of Marielle's life he had fed her tea that contained half a cap of *Amanita bisporigera*—Destroying Angel—a poisonous mushroom that grew abundantly in the forest behind their crypt. This small amount had caused pain but did its work quickly on an immune system defeated by depression; a body with his constitution would suffer much longer and the effects would be more extreme. That's why he had eaten a cap and also dosed his water with two caps, chopped fine in the blender until they were miniscule grains containing the ama-toxins. He could already feel the poisonous effects.

"I'm sorry," he said to her again, "but I need you . . . this way."

Before he lost the ability to act, he needed to spread the remaining fungal soil from Ferentillo over his body and face. He reached down between the coffins for the container, and accidently knocked it over!

Powerful stomach cramps hit, and he knew vomiting and diarrhea would follow quickly; delirium was creeping through his mind. Horrified, he no longer possessed the strength and coordination to free himself and re-collect the soil. All he could manage was to tighten the strap holding his neck in place, sensing the convulsions about to begin. He again reached for her hand, caressing the cool, dry skin, intertwining their fingers, struggling for consciousness amidst the sharp agony racking his body, suddenly shocked by the clear thought: this would not, *could* not work!

"Flesh and bones!" he cried. *She* would be the flesh, but *he* would become bones!

Tears streamed from his eyes that he did not understand. But one thing he was certain of: he had never felt so close to her.

The Sculptures in the House

John D. Haefele

I was a Pinckney too, but my uncle Edward could boast of his straight descent from those famous Federalist-Pinckneys who fought in the Revolutionary War and then later shaped the Constitution. But when Edward Pinckney became a recluse, his claim, though undeniably true, lost much of its luster, and by the time the old man disappeared we all thought he had proved it was nothing at all to brag about.

I suppose that helps explain why strange disappearances enthrall me today, though not Uncle Ed's mystery by itself— oh, God, no! After all, he was in his nineties. But I don't mean abductions either, nothing related to UFOs. Those, even if they harbor some truth, mean little to one who cares nothing for the sky, who they say earth-gazes while he walks, keeping his eyes to the ground, but who I admit always *hears* more than he sees on the occasions he goes out. Indeed, I am always listening; I listen into the Earth.

These are mannerisms I acquired suddenly, after paying a visit last year to Ed's rented house in Sac Prairie. One result of that nightmare is that the disappearance of Edward Pinckney was duly recorded. (Village police at first demurred,

having themselves no suspicion of foul play, and because he
was a non-resident.) All other results, I realize now, were
buried.

And buried they stayed until, following a chance discovery
made a few weeks ago while probing a blocked lateral, the
Sac Prairie Department of Public Works unearthed the
5,000-lb. mass of fused metal, rubber, vinyl, and plastic not
much bigger than a large picnic cooler, with its crest-like
coat-of-arms pressed to several times its former size, still
unmistakable, though now paper-thin. Here in Boston, a
thousand miles away, I had been tracking every bit of Sac
Prairie news, as I always did (electronically, quietly, so as
never to interrupt radio-wave transmissions), and saw online
the perplexed workers when they hit and the backhoe scoop
broke. Within days the village served the property owner, so
that engineers could dig deeper, and from two sides dig in,
and then, with heavy chains, keel-haul out what they thought
might be a lost relic from below the house. In the end they
left the thing they'd found sitting out in the open, atop the
east driveway.

It took a full week before they realized what it was they dug
out, but I knew right away. It took a full month before they
were done prying it apart.

Unfortunately, no human remains were recovered.

Looking back, I remember everything the day of that visit—
every action, every emotion—yes, every fugitive thought. It
was early June when I arrived, dropped off by a friend near the
bridge on Water Street in front of the Sac Prairie Post Office.
From there I walked north on the main drag, beneath old-fashioned hanging street lamps, past crows gathering on rooftops
(including the town's noisiest tavern), finally to meet the local
police where they held the keys I would need, their small
department cradled in the City Hall. They would have driven
me the rest of the way, but I chose to walk, even as rain threatened—one block north, go west on Polk Street, another block
north, go west again, to the end of Bates Street.

The little house Ed rented had the atmosphere of an earlier century about it, as did all of Sac Prairie. It leaned out from its rectangular lot facing the street, one among numerous quaint structures in that old section of the village. It was separated from its neighbors on two sides by sighing green hedges, and on the third by a lane used to park cars. Black earth and loose gravel formed a driveway that ran between Ed's porch and the neighbor's heavy fence, which was a bulwark of unpainted and uneven timbers too tall to see over. Loose boards creaked in the rising wind; it was an uneasy sound I would hear most of that night, even over fence owner's dog's frequent barrages of barking. I could not see the animal in its yard behind the fence, but did sense its alarm: not over me, I realized, but over what I could not hazard a guess.

The house itself, I remember, was glossy white, covered with thick old coats of oil-based paint and framed with green trim. There was no basement, only the one level set above ground on a rough cement foundation. There were two featureless doors, one facing the street, and the other the drive where it opened onto a pier-like stoop set against the gravel. The blinds behind deep-set windows appeared to be closed. Notwithstanding lilacs, lilies, and tulips, and despite many ferns, roses, and blood-red poppies, it was the crushed stone surface of the driveway that caught my fancy and arrested my attention as I approached, a shimmering sheen of wetness (though it hadn't yet rained) dancing misty and mirage-like for a long moment above it.

Unlike most houses on the block, there was no garage at the end of this drive, only a line of rusty barrels emerging from the loose stone like a few bad teeth. With shining gravel inside, too, they appeared still to be sinking, which brought to mind the proverbial sailors who because of the Philadelphia Experiment were fused into the bulkheads of their ship.

I went in the front door and found the house clean and neat, well maintained, the clock giving the correct time, the refrigerator running. Pulling one lever returned hot water, pushing another flushed the toilet. And all about I could plainly see what had occupied Ed last—it was everywhere, as if he had been forced to drop everything and just leave. On a great table in the kitchen were his memorabilia of Mr. Jason Wecter (a figure of my childhood, though not one I've thought about in years), a man who decades earlier had been Ed's closest friend, before he too disappeared under the shadow of a sullied reputation. In the late 1930s, Wecter had been the music and art critic here at home for the old Boston *Dial,* a critic whose sharp reviews wounded many reputations. Somehow Ed fell into Wecter's circle of close associates, though at the time he was himself only a college sophomore.

Thus I began studying more carefully the materials set out. Careful not to mix things up, I noted how Ed arranged chronologically some of Wecter's reviews on the table and across countertops, copies that he must have culled from the archives in Boston. There were pencil markings in the margins and related items strategically positioned nearby, but most of Ed's notes were gathered in one large marbled-covered theme book.

More thought-provoking than these by far were the dozen or so stone sculptures of various weights and heights (though none over a foot) that occupied the kitchen table. Two of these had name-tags affixed with a loop of string: one was called "Elder God" and the other "Tsathoggua," which I remember I practiced saying aloud.

"Elder God" was the more interesting of the two, a bust of sorts, carved from mottled bluish talc, equine-faced, but with tentacle-like appendages emerging from the chin. The other was a squatting creature carved from black stone, heavily muscled with mammalian limbs, but having overall slouching, toad-like contours. The larger was the centerpiece of the arrangement, but it was the "Tsathoggua" figure I found disquieting to contemplate, even difficult to look at. Surely, I thought, references to these figurines in the notes must yield a clue to Ed's whereabouts. But first I wanted to get organized.

A shelf on the inside wall parallel to the drive, running from kitchen to side-door, is where I emptied my knapsack. I used it to stage my phone and the two-way radio Taylor asked me to

bring, probably because her father had insisted. It was a powerful unit, to which Henry held a soon-to-expire license, which
for the time being allowed us to broadcast. I longed for Taylor's
company, but knew she wouldn't arrive until well after dark.
Driving straight from home, she'd pull in with her father's
long-in-the-tooth DeVille, blazoned with its distinctive emblem;
Henry always believed she traveled safest that way.

I opened two windows for fresh air, but only inches so as not
to disturb Ed's materials. I set out a foil packet of coffee I
brought, hoping to brew it with equipment on hand, but the
element was dead below a boil-marked carafe. Apparently Ed
left with the coffeemaker on. My consolation was a wrapped
bottle of wine I had stowed, which I wanted to open but would-
n't, not until Taylor arrived.

There was little in the house left to explore, only a bedroom
with two small windows, one facing the street, the other looking west. The westward prairie view had long been blocked,
first by houses similar to the one I occupied, and then by the
cloistering hedges. The closet held the meager assortment of
Ed's clothes, including socks and underwear stacked loosely
on a shelf. I couldn't help noticing how deep and comfortable
the bed looked, and I found myself thinking of sex with Taylor,
wondering if she'd put up with the floor. I was oblivious to the
fact this would be my last carefree thought. That's when the
phone rang.

I ran to that familiar ring-tone on my cell, on the shelf where
I left it. I remember glancing through the side-door window,
down at the bed of gravel still glimmering in twilight, a rectangular reflection of heavens above, I guessed; a door, I imagined—fancifully, ironically—a door opening to magical places
far beyond the familiar fields we know. That such a display
would be impossible because of the overcast sky did not cross
my mind.

Taylor's voice cheered me up— shut out, too, the sometimes
barking dog, the straining fence, the whirl of the wind in the
trees and along the eaves.

"Hi, hon!" she said. "What time do you have?"

I still see that clock-face today, how it had been already half-past.

"8:30, right on the button," I answered.

"Together at midnight," Taylor replied. Then she laughed, which to me augured well.

"What will you need to find me?" I was ready to dole out directions, knowing the Caddy lacked GPS.

"Nothing," she returned. "Got my map already, your town's only a few blocks wide."

"So in my arms at twelve," I insisted.

"Uh-huh!"

And in my bed at 12:01, I tacked silently on, thinking myself so clever that I winked at "Elder God." Later I moved that stone fellow onto the counter to watch out the door.

Now . . . let me repeat myself: I've had all year to mull over everything that happened that night, though nothing did immediately. I waited for Taylor so that together we could parse Ed's notes and Wecter's reviews. Besides, I was strangely reluctant to rummage through Ed's papers, because being in his home and seeing their careful arrangement made it easy to fear his impending return, how he might step suddenly through one of the two doors and demand my explanation. I was restless, too—painfully aware I couldn't link the disparate facts of a little house bordering the Wisconsin prairie, a missing old man, and a collection of odd carvings—in fact, restlessness seemed already to be in everything that night. But the alternative was to do nothing at all while suffering the hours. And so I began.

I discovered how Ed was marshaling every detail he could discover about the stone figures into the theme book. It is true that they, not Wecter, had become the primary focus of his studies. And indeed those monster-figurines were unusual; even then, from the table where they silently stood, the carvings conveyed substance and weight far exceeding their diminutive size.

It was easy to see why they fascinated Ed. The artist, according to a biographical note, was Clark Ashton Smith, whom Ed and Wecter knew personally, but who I knew only as a formative science fiction writer. Ed's entry explained how Smith discovered in California's abandoned copper mines the minerals used, materials that were soft enough for a knife to carve, before baking them hard in a kitchen oven.

According to Ed, "Tsathoggua" and "Elder God" had belonged to Wecter, prized in his collection when Ed knew him, but had been returned to Smith in the months following Wecter's disappearance. Smith later sold these and newer carvings to the publisher of his fiction books, living right here in Sac Prairie. Unfortunately, nothing in those notes suggested any specific reason why after so many decades Ed got interested in these again; but the sequence of events made sense: With Smith's publisher now deceased, Ed necessarily completed his work here, in the town where the collection resided, using pieces still owned by the publisher's children.

With that, I moved to sit in the front room, because it had the only soft chair near a window, and because I could look out between the elms as far as the street. There I tallied what little I once knew of Ed's history: When the Great War threatened, Edward Pinckey already lived near Jason Wecter in Boston's tiny Bohemian district, which was close to being overwhelmed by unemployed, avant-garde students waiting to be called into service. Perhaps trading on his name, Ed infiltrated Wecter's small circle of associates and before long became his closest friend and confidant.

Wecter's reputation in those years grew so that it soon overshadowed famous contemporaries based in New York City. But then something unexpected happened. Wecter's disposition changed radically, his reviews became gloomy and pessimistic and hurtful, often wandering far afield from their reputed subjects. So caustic did Wecter become that others warned he should fear retaliation. It was big news when Wecter disappeared off the face of the earth in 1942. Believe me if I say that cliché is most *apropos:* Wecter's fate to this day is a mystery.

But I did find in Ed's jottings a coda to the story involving his hobby. Apparently it is true that Wecter lost his mind, though it was kept a well-hidden secret from everyone except his closest friend. Ed's biographical entry records plainly how Wecter during that period began suddenly speaking with authority about "border dimensions" and "planes of existence," as if sure those concepts were real. He claimed to know where the points of contact lay between these and our world: there are doorways, he said, that would open and shut. Then, just before he disappeared, Wecter began to fear a wooden carving he had in his art—artifact collection, claiming he could perceive it existing on two planes at the same time, here physically as the merely three-dimensional if monstrous carving, but also multi-dimensioned, a miles-high *thing* interweaving the mundane world.

Ed shared these delusions with Smith, the writer-artist; only Smith seemed to play along. Perhaps he was mad too, for I found stapled to the catalog a clipping with a transcription of an interview he gave (in affected English but otherwise straight-faced) about the "Tsathoggua" carving: "Most certainly this palaeogean eidolon dates from a past anterior to the existence of any life-principle native to this earth or to our three known dimensions; & it carries in every line & angle the spirit and mysteries of its extra-cosmick artificer." In fact, one listener pointed out how it *was* a mystery Smith carved so ably, without model or previous knowledge, the Great Old One of a primitive cult. Based on post-interview written comments, that same coincidence bothered the interviewer: "How came it that the modern sculptures of Clark Ashton Smith bore such a resemblance to it?—and was it not more than a coincidence that Smith's figures created out of the stuff of his weird fiction and poetry should parallel the art of someone removed many hundreds of years in time and leagues in space from him?"

I, of course, had been a young child those years and had no interest in anything involving Ed; but I did recall how on occasion he would defend Wecter in front of the family, often following some catty remark.

In the end, time passed quickly, because I fell asleep. And for a while, perhaps for hours, I slept peaceably, until the frantic sounds of a barking dog began to invade the margins of my awareness, remote at first, but drawing closer, and then suddenly becoming much louder. I knew the animal must be the neighbor's dog, but it seemed then a definite part of a dream, a tenebrous connection with another world, more real than the house I awoke into. As I did so I drew myself up, cognizant of foulness in the wind against my body that came forcibly through the partially opened windows. Words don't suffice, but I sensed everywhere mounting oppression, crushing despair, unwholesomeness settling about the house; it was a cloying, infiltrating loathsomeness that was nearly tangible.

Then suddenly the real dog was slavering at the window, threatening to hoist itself into the opening. It was the neighbor's, a basset. And either by breaking through or by flanking, it had found its way past the fence into Ed's front yard while I slept. Nearly beside itself, the dog alternately nosed the window or fell back in a fit of whining and growling.

But the savage display was not meant for me; the animal's hostility was leveled toward the back yard east of the house. I could at these intervals plainly see the dog's imploring eyes through the small opening. Between us was manifesting a curious, almost palpable, empathy.

With apprehension—not because of the dog, but against whatever was unhinging the animal—I hoped fervently it could sense my intention to open the side-door and come into the kitchen. Don't ask me to explain, but for no good reason I feared *for* its life.

I looked back. The dog did not move, but stood there whining through bared teeth. As I moved further toward the kitchen, passing the side-door, I again saw dirt and gravel outside gleaming hellishly. I glanced all the way back, in time to see the dog disappear below the sill, telling me she chose that instant to make her move; she'd be rounding the corner, so I swung the door to receive her.

I heard one of those prehistoric animal-screams (the kind you'd expect to hear close by, at midnight, if you camped in the Amazon); this was punctuated by a bone-shattering crack, but it was too dark near the house to see any more than that something had loomed up tall before quickly sinking away. Then burst forth a hot gust of wind, which with unintended finality slammed the door closed.

Of course I realized I should go out, but providentially the blessed phone rang. I never saw or heard the dog again.

"Wake up!" Taylor sounded excited. "I'm almost there." Then she too was gone.

Twin circles of warm lamplight provided the only contrast against the terror and loathing caused by the evil I could sense invading the prairie house, pouring up the walls like invisible fog. I backed away from the door, into the hallway—it was the same out there; further then, into the bedroom—nothing was different. Inside everywhere, but along the east wall especially, there brooded this malign and terrible evil.

I returned to the kitchen, grabbed my cell. Face to face again with "Elder God" I hesitated, shaking. Did I see in those stone eyes a hint of alien life? Or was it headlights outside? I dialed.

Taylor answered, but set down her phone saying, "Hon, wait just a sec."

I heard the engine. I knew she was just about to tease the big Cadillac onto the small driveway.

"Pull far to the right!" I screamed into the cell, loud enough for her to hear no matter what. "And go out the passenger door, straight onto the grass, touch only the grass. Do you understand? Grass . . . *only!*"

Twin beams passed the window, smoothly, lighting up the sill. Then they jolted around.

They pointed straight up. Into the sky.

They swung wildly toward the fence. Illuminated all the leaves straining straight up.

They winked out.

I snapped on the porch light, wondered why the hell I hadn't done that already.

Taylor—the Caddy—both were gone.

I looked at the cell, the connection broken. I noticed the jeweled plane of the driveway's surface, rippling.

It didn't add up—mind must be shorting—I knew the car was too damn big to be anywhere but right out that window, shining or no shining.

Safe in the Caddy, I calculated. She didn't back out, no time, she didn't drive over barrels, I could see . . .

Next to "Elder God," a little green strobe on the two-way radio flashed. I tried to comprehend. Eternity passed. Then I remembered; I selected the zone and flipped through the channels, and through static heard Taylor scream.

"Help me! Alex, Help me! I'm sinking! It's taking me!"

She was sobbing then. It was the first time I ever heard Taylor sobbing.

There was one channel on the radio, used to receive or to transmit, not both. I pushed the button and cut her off.

"Sinking?" I repeated foolishly, rooted to the floor, logic failing me.

Sinking made no sense, the river a mile away and Taylor just here. I choked, couldn't find my voice, had nothing to ask, nothing to say.

"Stay inside!" I decided finally, then hit the button again, hoping for another green light . . .

"I . . . out . . . *your* house," Taylor croaked from wherever she was. This house? I ran window to window again, radio in hand.

"Below . . . it's the *bottom* I see," she yelled. "I'm looking up at it!"

I cut her off.

"What do you *mean?*" I yelled in return, viciously. She was nowhere near the house.

Green light!

Taylor's voice, then dreamy and awestruck . . . pretty soon she would begin wordless screaming.

Looking *up,* she said, at the foundation, she thought; I realized she was seeing the foundation slipping by.

Only she couldn't be underground is what I thought, because I didn't see a sinkhole, and then because of what she said was behind it all, superimposed . . .

Stars glimmering. Suns and planets.

I swung the back door open again, but didn't look down; instead I looked up, studied the sky over Sac Prairie: It was starless, empty, dirty grey—there was rain pattering down . . .

Taylor choked out more words.

"Between stars, moving . . . gigantic . . . shapes," she managed.

A pause, then—

"The Great Old Ones are close. Do you hear?"

I did hear, over the static, through the two-way, and in my bones; it was barely audible noise in the room, but in my head it became wave after wave of enigmatical sense-impacts, indescribable, uninscribable; and only one word of it did I recognize—the word most frequently repeated—"Tsathoggua."

"Oh, please, *please!*" Taylor shouted out. "*Iä!*—the sunken red world—*Iä!*"

Forcing myself, I tried *moving* again. To do what, I didn't know. I swung open the front door and stared long and hard in every direction, flashed lights for anybody to see, hoped for lights I would see. I saw nothing up or down the street. I hurried again from window to window. I saw nothing but the bright stones. Was I the one who was mad?

"Down," Taylor stated, resolute, overcome. "Oh . . . black nest, the basalt nest is open—no more time, timeless—Tsathoggua rises."

I tried looking where the car had been, where the dog had run, at a driveway almost normal now, at a gate almost closed.

I was helpless to do anything. The assault in my head continued. Taylor's frightened rant continued, but with fewer words.

"Here . . . now, here *now*—can't be—huge, huge . . . *huge!*"

Then came her last rational utterance. She began, "We're so small compared to it . . ."

In fact, it was her voice that seemed very small and it sounded very far away.

"Small as a seed compared to the pumpkin," my dear Taylor whimpered, "Seed . . . pumpkin," she repeated.

Then she screamed and she screamed and she screamed.

A terrible din came next—loud enough finally to wake the town and bring the police—clamor proclaiming somewhere the twisting, screaming, and collapsing of metal. It ended just as abruptly with one final report, one to set all the dogs in Sac Prairie barking; I thought the mythic iron gate of a Titan had slammed shut. The sense-impressions stopped that instant. The radio was silent.

I dove out the front door onto the lawn. Hedges were hissing in the wind. But everything else lay undisturbed; the black drive seemed completely normal then, half-hidden in darkness. High above deceiving lilacs and lilies, dark stars were also still hidden, though the rain had stopped. Nothing at all suggested Taylor had ever been.

With two-way in hand, its range good for ten miles at least, I spent the rest of that night circling Sac Prairie before going home. Back here in Boston I reported Taylor missing, saying only that she had promised to meet me, but never did. And here, thinking I must be guilty of something that will someday be discovered, old Henry refuses to speak to me about the girl we both love.

Eventually they found the wallet, the phone, and a set of Ed's clothes (but not him) next to the stoop, about eight feet down, with miscellany that included animal collars, an amulet, and five coded soapstones. But there was no reason that made sense for the village to dig up the adjacent gravel drive, so they didn't.

Only the disturbing lack of any explanation to fit the facts for a while was sufficient to resurrect in the news the famous Pinckney name and lineage, probably for the very last time. Even rounding me up was without reason. The only fact I know is how pure physics rules out everything that happened there.

I suspect that behind everything lay those idols Wecter unearthed for his collection, and those creatures Smith unwittingly sculpted. Primitive religions, black magic, what have you, I know now how real it is, just as I know that Tsathoggua exists inside of the earth; and so I "listen" and now ask you, how many disappearances might *that* fact explain?

God knows how intuitions happen, those vague notions that come out of nowhere to stretch the mind. They came when I tore open the packaging that night to yank out a set of fresh batteries. It came first when I let the debris fall to the floor. Suddenly I was fearing for what had been similarly discarded somewhere below that house. And seeing again the old Caddy's crest was the bellwether, I think.

But mainly it was intuition that imparted the importance of the batteries themselves. My apartment (which I only leave these days to buy supplies) is littered not only with packaging and receipts, but with batteries. Not everything plugs in, you know, and electric power is known to fail. Lining the room, decorating the shelves and tables, you'll find all kinds and brands of battery-operated two-way radios, though none of them do what I want, none except the one with the green-lit display. I've kept it going for a full year now, but never so loud that it disturbs anyone, hoping one day to discover any clue as I listen tearless to Taylor's never-ending screaming, pleading, and nonsense, wherever she is.

Ice Fishing

Donald Tyson

The big red ball of the sun spread itself across the western ridge, its light spilling between the leafless maple trees and around the brooding dark spruce to lie over the ice on the lake like a pink carpet. There was no trace of wind, but the air was cold enough that every noise had a ring to it, like struck brass about to break. The doors of the old Ford pickup creaked and clunked, brittle enough to drop off their hinges.

Two men waddled their way from the still-steaming truck down the snow-covered slope to the ice, a big red-and-white plastic cooler hung between them on their mitten-covered hands. One was fat and the other thin, but they were both about the same height. Each carried a bulging plastic grocery bag in his free mitt. Puffs of effort hung white around their heads, which were covered in knitted wool caps with ear flaps and wrapped in wool scarves to the eyeballs.

They did the Canadian duck walk across the lake. Every Canadian learns it about the time they learn to walk. You keep your ass clenched and the muscles down the insides of your thighs tight to prevent your feet slipping out sideways, and you shuffle along with your shoulders hunched so that if you slip and go bass ackwards on the ice, you hit with your back and don't bang your brains out.

Their destination was a little wooden structure that was nothing more than four plywood walls and a sloping sheet of plywood for a roof. It was unpainted. It had a door but no window. More than anything else, it resembled an old-fashioned outhouse.

"I don't know why you had to put the shack so far out," the thin one grumbled.

His corner of the cooler brushed the ice at each short step.

"Gotta put her where the fish are, Mickey D.," the fat man said between puffs. "Lift her up, will ya?"

The shack was about a hundred yards from the shore. Halfway there they set down the cooler and straightened their backs with grateful little groans.

"Did you hear about Billy Bignose?" Mickey D. Mackintosh said as he squinted into what remained of the sun.

"Never heard nothing. What happened to him?"

"I'm telling ya, Gump, so let me tell ya."

Gump Cameron unwound the scarf from his face, revealing a bristling grey moustache and cherry-red cheeks. He turned his head, snorted snot from the back of his nose into his mouth, and spat it across the ice. It was a good one—ten feet or better.

"So tell me."

"Way I heard," Mickey D. continued, "he went to his shack one night and never come home."

Gump Cameron squinted through hairy iron-grey eyebrows at the last redness of the sun as it winked out, leaving the breathless world in twilight.

"Where'd he have his shack?"

Mickey D. pointed east across the ice.

"Down by the narrows with them others."

Gump turned and peered into the distance. Where Crooked Cove narrowed he saw three other fishing shacks on the ice. Smoke spiralled from the stovepipe chimney of one of them.

"When was this again?"

"Two weeks, there abouts. Just went to his shack, and never come home. Now what do you think of that?"

Gump shrugged and wrapped his face in his scarf, then bent to pick up the cooler. He waited with his back bent until Mickey D. got his end, and the two men completed their waddle to the shack.

The old shed door they'd salvaged was frozen shut. Gump kicked its boards to break the ice around its edge and pulled it open. An odor of stale grease and fish came out. Neither man showed signs of minding it. They lugged the cooler and their plastic bags into the darkness. The bags were so cold they rustled like dry paper.

"Get the lantern," Gump said as he tugged the cooler into the corner.

When the glow from the Coleman kerosene lantern lit the shed, the fat man pulled the door shut.

"Colder than a witch's tit out there," he said.

"Good thing there's no wind," Mickey D. agreed, surveying the contents of the shack with satisfaction as he hung the lantern on its wall hook.

Nothing was missing. The shack was never locked, but it was an unwritten rule on Cape Breton Island that you didn't steal from a fishing shack. There were a couple of folding chairs, an old wooden card table, a bench that supported a little green Coleman stove that ran on white gas. In the corner stood a long metal screw with a wide T handle. The shack had no floor, but straw was scattered over the ice to keep it from melting and becoming slippery from the heat of the stove.

Gump opened the lid of the cooler. Four six-packs of Keith's India Pale Ale lined the bottom. On top of them rested a one-pound package of Maple Leaf smoked bacon and a loaf of Ben's sandwich bread. He took out two of the brown bottles and set them on the table.

Mickey D. unwound his scarf and pulled off his mittens with his teeth, then lifted his grocery bag to the card table and carefully removed a flat of eggs and a foil-covered brick of butter. They had been transported in the cab of the truck and were not frozen, although the trip between the truck and the shack had chilled them down.

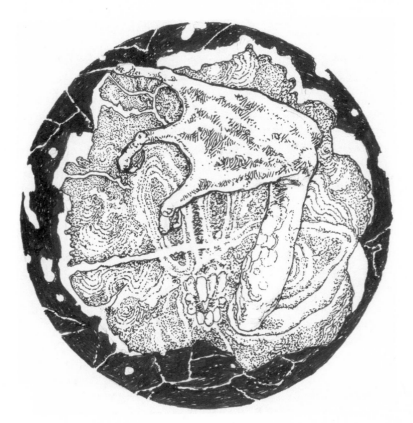

"I hope we brought enough food this time."

He went over to the Coleman stove and took the iron skillet from its top. He tilted it to look into it with a doubtful expression on his lined and freckle-covered face. Both men were fifty-seven, but the lines in his cheeks and his snow-white hair made Mickey D. look ten years older. Anyone looking at them would never guess they had gone to the same elementary school in New Waterford, half a century ago.

"One of these days we should clean out this fry pan."

Gump shook his head. "That would ruin it. Light the stove, will you?"

After a while, with the lantern and the stove burning, it was warm enough to take off their wool caps. Their breath no longer formed puffs of cotton in front of their faces.

Mickey D. peered down into the fishing hole in the center of the floor.

"She froze up much?" Gump asked.

"In this cold? What do you think?"

Grunting, Gump got the auger and fitted it into the hole, and they began to turn it. After a while it broke through the ice to the water beneath. They pulled it out with care to avoid splashing water all over their floor. Mickey D. found a little dipper with a long handle and ladled out the slush into a bucket. When it was full, he opened the door of the shack and threw its contents across the ice. Already it was dark, but the quarter moon that rode high among the stars cast down a little silver.

They opened their beers and settled in to the serious task of fishing. Not many words were exchanged. They had been friends since early childhood and each had stood at the other's wedding. They had ice-fished the brackish water of the Bras D'Or Lake every winter for three decades. There was one difference, however. This was the first year they had set their shack on Crooked Cove. The old cove closer to Sydney had got too crowded. There were so many shacks it was like a little town. Both men liked the quiet, so by common consent they moved the shack here.

"Funny there aren't more Mi'kmaq fishing this ice," Mickey D. said around the stem of his pipe. He had given up smoking cigarettes but still used the pipe in the shack.

"Why is it funny?" Gump asked as he fiddled with the lines that dangled into the hole.

"Just seems funny, with the reservation so close, and the fishing so good. Not like the Indians to pass up good fishing."

"You want more people out here?"

"I didn't say that, Gump," the freckled man protested. "Don't go putting words into my mouth."

The empties began to multiply on the card table. They pulled up three good fryers, and then there was a lull as the fish seemed to lose interest in the bait. Gump cleaned the fish outside on the bare ice with his folding knife and left the heads, tails, and guts for the ravens to find in the morning. He brought the fillets back in and threw them into the already heated iron pan. They sizzled when they hit. He used his bloodstained knife to cut off a corner from the block of butter and dropped it into the pan with the fillets. The rich smell of frying fish filled the shack. The smoke rose up and hung in the air over their heads, but there was enough of a vent in the high edge of the roof to let it out before it became too much of a nuisance.

"Now that I think on it, this cove's never been very popular," Gump said in a meditative tone. "Billy Bignose used to brag about her, but he was about the only one."

"The Mi'kmaq got some legend about this cove," Mickey D. murmured. His tongue was fuzzy with beer.

"What legend?"

"I never heard it. I just heard a couple of them talking about it once at a gas station. Forgot all about it until just now."

"What's the legend about?" Gump asked with deliberate emphasis.

Mickey D. tilted his head back and looked up at the smoke gathered near the roof of the shed.

"Something about fishers of the cove . . . or maybe it was fishers on the cove."

"What the hell does that mean?"

"They fish at night," Mickey D. went on. "They fish through the ice."

"Those Indians must have been talking about ice fishing," Gump said.

"Maybe so," Mickey D. agreed, taking a pull on his current bottle of beer. "Only thing is about that . . ."

He stopped talking. After a while he realized that Gump had stopped fiddling with the fish and was staring at him, waiting.

"They looked scared, that's all," he said with a shrug.

A loud crack made them both jump. They stared at each other.

"Ice must be moving," Gump said.

"Shouldn't be moving tonight," Mickey D. said. "There's no wind."

"That's true enough."

They stood listening for half a minute before they relaxed.

"Fish is done," Gump said.

"I'll get the hooks up so we can eat."

Mickey D. bent over the hole in the ice and carefully began to draw up their fishing lines. He cursed.

"Did you see that?" he said.

"See what? I've got fish in my hands."

His friend's silence made him turn and look. Mickey D. was on his knees, staring down into the hole.

"Something flashed down there. She looked like metal."

"What do you mean?"

"Something flashed in the lamplight."

Gump deposited the fish fillets onto two mismatched plates and added the fried eggs and bacon beside them.

"Maybe it was a piece of cigarette paper caught in the current. Or maybe a fish."

"She wasn't no fish," Mickey D. told him. "Cigarette foil, maybe."

He peered closer.

"There it is again," he said.

He pushed himself to his feet and took up a long metal rod with a crook on its end.

"What are you doing?"

"I'm going to see if I can hook it."

Down on his knees, he reached the long rod into the water and began to jig it up and down. After a time, he cursed softly to himself and took off his bulky winter coat. He unbuttoned the cuff on his red-and-black check flannel shirt and pushed the loose sleeve up above his elbow. He noticed Gump watching him.

"I need to go deeper. Maybe if I stick my arm down into the water—"

"For Chrissake, Mickey, the fish are getting cold. Eat your fish."

Mickey D. got up and accepted his plate without argument. He rummaged into the plastic tray that held silverware until he found a fork. Gump pulled his chair around to the other side of the card table and cleared a space between the beer bottles. They ate their fish.

When they were done, they used a drift of snow to clean the plates and silverware outside the shack. Intense cold made the snow as dry and hard as sand. The light from the open door cast a pale golden rectangle across the ice that contrasted with the chill silver of the moon. Not a sound came from anywhere, not even from the ice shacks further down the cove. Smoke no longer curled from the pipe in the roof of one of them, as it had earlier. The shacks looked deserted.

Gump handed his scoured plate to Mickey D.

"I need to take a dump. Be right back."

By common consent, when they needed to do the old number two, they did it in the woods on the shore, not far from where they parked the pickup. Gump headed back into the shack for toilet paper.

"Put on your hat and mitts. It's brutal out here," Mickey D. said.

"What are you, my mother?"

In spite of his retort, Gump dutifully pulled on his wool cap and mitts, then made his waddling way across the ice toward the dark line of trees. He was jumpier than usual. Truth be told, he did not want to leave the light and warmth of the shack, but when Nature called, you had to answer.

It came into his mind to wonder how many animals had been killed by predators while in the very act of taking a dump. Probably a whole lot of them, he thought. That was why a dog could do his business so quickly. Survival mechanism, they called it. The less time you were vulnerable with shit hanging out your ass, the better, if you were a wild creature in the woods. Especially at night, when everything was so goddamned black.

At the edge of the ice, he turned and glanced back at the shack, then stopped still. Just for an instant, he thought he saw movement. He waited, but nothing stirred except the smoke that worked its way through the roof vent and rose in an irregular white plume. Maybe Mickey D. had walked around the outside for some reason, before going back inside.

His lower belly gave a twinge. Grunting to himself, he continued up the bank and into the trees to the usual place. The moon showed where he had squatted since the last snowfall, but there was no stink. Everything the men had deposited there on previous nights was frozen as hard as iron bolts. He unhitched himself, lowered his pants to half-mast, and squatted, taking care not to let any of the clothes dangle under his ass.

A drawn-out cry sounded across the still, crystal air.

"Jesus," Gump said and stood up, then said, "Oh fucking Jesus Christ."

He spent several minutes using the roll of toilet paper to wipe the shit off his pants and belt, then finished his business and cleaned his ass. He hitched his pants back into position and cursed again softly under his breath. They were still sticky.

The cry had sounded like some animal in pain. Maybe a moose. He stood amid the young spruce, staring around at the shadows of the forest as he listened. He was not sure if the cry had come across the lake or from the woods behind him. Maybe coyotes had brought down a stray dog in the trees. If so, why weren't they barking in celebration?

When he started back toward the lake, he found it an effort not to run. The woods made him nervous. All the way across the naked expanse of ice, he kept looking over his shoulder. When you expected to see something, it was easy to mistake the black shadow of a spruce for a crouching figure. None of the shadows he stared at moved. By the time he reached the shack his heart pounded in his chest.

The door was shut to hold in the heat, as expected. He opened it and went inside. The shack was empty.

He came out again and walked all around it once, then stood looking across the ice at the pickup truck. Maybe Mickey D. had gone to the truck to get something. There was no movement on the snow-covered bank and the cab of the truck looked empty. Gump walked toward the truck.

"Mickey D.?" he called in his gruff voice. "Where'd you go?"

The truck was deserted. Gump stood beside it, looking back across the ice at the shack, which the moonlight lit with pale silver and grey. If Mickey D. had gone to the woods to relieve himself, they would have met each other coming and going.

For an instant he felt the intense urge to dig out his key, climb into the truck, and drive away. He fought it down. He could not leave Mickey D. alone at the cove. He had to be here somewhere.

Suddenly the answer came to him. The bastard was playing a practical joke.

"That's all right, Mickey D., you stay in the woods," he said loudly so that his voice carried. "I'm going back to the shack to fish."

On the way back he looked for footprints in the thin drifts of snow that partially covered the ice, but saw only the lines of tracks he and Mickey D. had made earlier. The sneaky bastard must have walked backwards in his own footprints to the truck, then hidden in the trees. It was probably he that had made that weird cry.

Back inside the shack, when he took up a fishing line to set its hook into the water he noticed drops of blood on the straw around the hole. It didn't look like fish blood. It was too dark. He wondered if Mickey D. had cut himself and had wandered out on the ice in pain and maybe collapsed unconscious.

Gump put the lines aside and went outside. He did a slow walk around the shack, peering across the ice for any shadow or lump that shouldn't be there. The expanse of ice was as flat and empty as a silver tablecloth. There was nowhere to hide.

Could he have fallen through the ice? No, it was at least a foot thick, probably thicker. He could have driven his pickup out to the shack had he wished—except that he never took the truck on the ice, just from general principle. Ice was treacherous and let you down when you least expected it to fail. He knew too many people who had lost trucks or snowmobiles through the ice.

"Mickey D.! . . . Mickey D.!"

His voice rolled across the lake through the frozen air. They must be able to hear it in the other shacks, if there was any-body left in them. He looked eastward at the tiny rectangles.

Could Mickey D. have walked over to them while he squatted in the trees? No, they were more than half a mile away. There would not have been time to reach them before he returned to the lake.

He squinted in the silvery light. Something moved between the distant fishing shacks. They were not deserted. He saw several outlines of shadow sway beside the shacks. Cupping his mitts to his face, he shouted with all his force and then waved his arms. The tiny shadow-figures near the shacks stopped moving and stood still. They must be looking this way, he thought, and waved his arms again. Instead of returning his wave, they slowly slipped behind the shacks and disappeared from his sight.

"Mickey D., I swear to God if you don't come out of them trees, I will kick your skinny ass six ways to Sunday."

From the corner of his eye he saw something move between the trees, but when he turned to look at it, whatever it was had hidden itself. An animal, maybe, he thought. Or that son of a bitch he was going to kill.

Uttering a curse, he returned to the shack. There was nothing in the world he hated more than a practical joke. Mickey D. knew this and pulled them on him regularly. He's been doing it since elementary school. This time, he vowed to himself, he would not give the little bastard the satisfaction of reacting. Let him stay outside in the cold. Then the joke would be on him, when he finally came back to the shack, frozen to the bone. He had the only set of keys to the truck, so Mickey D. was not going anywhere.

It was their habit, when they came to the shack, to fish for their dinner, eat, and then fish to take something home to their wives. Gump had no intention of letting his friend's warped sense of humor change that. He baited the hooks and dropped the lines through the hole. The burner on the Coleman stove was set on a low blue flame, and the iron fry pan on top of it cast enough heat to keep the hole from freezing over, once it was opened. He sat in his chair facing the closed door and nursed on a beer bottle.

After ten minutes or so, a tapping came on the wall of the shack. It started on the right side and moved slowly around the structure. It would tap three or four times, stop, and then do the same thing a few feet over. Gump sat listening to the tapping with a scowl on his face that drew his bushy eyebrows together and pushed his red lips out beyond his moustache. The tapping slowly crept down the right wall, across the back of the shack behind him, and up the left wall, moving toward the door. *Tap-tap-tap,* pause, *tap-tap-tap-tap.*

Gump slowly stood up and moved toward the door. He put his hand on the frosty metal latch and waited. When the tapping reached the front corner of the shack, he threw the door wide and jumped out.

"You son of a bitch—"

He stood with his head around the edge of the shack, the words dying on his lips. The ice stretched away, smooth and empty.

A kind of shiver ran along his spine. Moving as silently as he could on the ice, he ran to the rear of the shack and looked around it. The moon peered down at him impassively. He listened. Silence. He continued across the back wall and up toward the front on the far side.

From inside there came a scrape, as might be made by a chair pushed back out of the way, and a splash of water. Gump grinned.

"I've got you now, you bastard."

He rounded the corner and stepped in through the open door. The shack was empty. His chair lay on its side. He stared at it, and for the life of him could not remember if he had tipped it over when he stood up from it.

"Mickey D., I don't know how you're doing this, but you are starting to seriously creep me the fuck out," he said in a raised voice.

Just to prove to himself that he could do it, he went back out into the darkness and walked slowly once around the shack. There was nothing in any direction. He stood looking across the ice at his truck for a few seconds. The moonlight was bright enough to show that the cab was empty. Reluctantly, he went back into the shack and shut the door.

The lines were twisted and out of place in the hole. He straightened them with numb fingers and put his mitts back on, then set his chair upright and sat in it.

A long, drawn out howl came from outside and far away over the lake.

"Jesus Christ!"

He held his breath and listened, but it was not repeated. After a while he relaxed and went back to his beer.

What was that? Gump cocked his head to the side. His right ear wasn't a hundred percent anymore, but his left was still pretty good. It sounded like tapping. He leaned forward with a frown of concentration. It didn't sound as if it were coming from the side of the shed. His eyes slowly widened, and he stood up and bent over at the waist. It was coming from the ice—from under the ice. The sound was almost metallic, like a sharp little pick hitting the bottom of the ice with a rhythmic *tap-tap-tap*.

Something flashed silver deep in the fishing hole. He looked down. There it was again, a quick gleam, like light reflected from a shiny bit of metal. He leaned closer. There was something else down there, deep enough in the murky water of the cove that the brightness of the Coleman lantern did not quite reach it. He lifted the lantern off its wall hook and held it closer over the hole. It was a kind of yellow disk with a black slit down the center of it. No, wait, there were two of them, and between them a sort of ridge.

"Sweet Jesus mother of God."

The words came forth spontaneously from some dusty place where they had slumbered since his Catholic adolescence, when going to church was a weekly ritual.

Gump realized that he had fallen backwards over his chair and that the lantern had gone out when it hit the straw on the ice. By some wonder it had not caused a fire. He blinked to clear his head. The blue flame from the burner on the Coleman stove cast an eerie glow.

I've got to get out of this place, he thought to himself. I've got to get off this fucking ice.

He pulled himself up on the card table and went out the door without bothering to look behind him, but stopped. Some forty yards away were three shapes on the ice. They looked like the shadows of spruce trees, but as he looked at them they swayed from side to side and moved. They moved toward him.

He felt the corner of the shack against his shoulders and slid his way around it. There were two more of them between him and the pickup. He edged his way to the other side. Three of them, near enough that he could almost make out their faces. He did not want to see their faces. They had him blocked on all sides. There was nothing else to do but slide backward into the shack and shut the door.

His mind wasn't working very well. He did things without thinking about them, without realizing what he was doing until after he had done it. He turned up the burner on the Coleman stove and by its light found the lantern on its side on the straw. He was able to relight the lantern and set it down on the card table. He found himself holding the long steel hook, but didn't realize what he was going to do with it until after he had slid it diagonally into the latch of the door, jamming it shut. Now the door could not be opened from the outside.

It was only then, when he had time to think, that he wondered if he should have tried to run between the lurching shadows to reach the truck. But it was too late for second thoughts.

The door rattled in its frame. Something slammed against the side of the shack and began to hammer on the plywood. The banging came all around him, from every side. Between the thumps he heard something that might have been voices, but they were low-pitched—too low for a human throat. They were deep, gargling animal noises, but they almost sounded like words in some gulping language.

Something clutched his ankle and nearly threw him over backward. It was an arm, extended up through the hole in the ice. Its skin was blue-black in color and glistened with water, like the skin of an eel. It was impossibly long and seemed to bend and flex as he pulled his leg against it. He saw that the fingers on his boot were webbed, and grabbed up the hot fry pan from the stove. He hammered at the arm near its wrist with the edge of the heavy iron pan, while around him the walls of the shack flexed inward and thundered under the blows of the things outside in the darkness.

The creature beneath the ice did not release his leg. Instead of retreating, it forced its sloped head into the ice hole beside its elongated arm. Gump stared down at its bulging, malevolent yellow eyes, which were like the eyes of a frog, and shook his head in disbelief. The fucking hole was only nine inches across. The blue-black head of the thing squeezed together like a rubber ball and popped up through the hole.

Gump started to whimper. He hit the wrist of the arm over and over with the sharp edge of the fry pan. Suddenly, he was free. The severed stump of the wrist waved in the air, spraying a kind of dark, thick liquid that might have been blood.

He realized that the hand still grasped his ankle. Backing away from the hole, he pried each long, clawed finger off and kicked the hand away. It continued to clutch the air where it lay in the straw under the table near one of the table legs. Attached to a finger on a short chain was a silver spiral of metal, like a kind of jewelry. It glittered in the lantern light and made a tinkling noise against the wooden table leg as the hand contracted and relaxed in spasms.

The head and neck of the thing was out of the hole. It did not appear to notice that it was missing a hand. It struggled to get its other shoulder out, while its mouth worked open and shut with the effort. Gump saw that its mouth was lined all the way around with multiple rows of small white teeth in the shape of hooks.

The entire shack rocked back and forth. One wall lifted up from the ice, letting in a rush of frozen air before falling back to the ice with a crash. In that moment he saw the dark, glistening legs and webbed feet of the things that pushed it. There were so many of them. Too many.

Police found the shattered ruin of the fishing shack the next morning, after the wives of the two men contacted them to express their worry. The investigators puzzled over it for a long while, then concluded that the shack must have been shattered by an enraged bear that had awoken prematurely from hibernation. That explained the long scratches in the plywood, which resembled claw marks. The strange animal footprints in the drifts of snow on the lake lent support to this theory, although they did not look exactly like any bear tracks the police had ever seen before.

In the spring after the ice melted, the inlet of Crooked Cove where the shack had stood was dragged. No bodies were found. The story got around that Gump and Mickey D. had grown tired of their wives and had lit out for Ontario in a rented car to cover their traces, leaving Gump's truck behind at the lake. At least it was some kind of explanation, and the human mind always needs an explanation for the uncanny. Neither of their wives ever believed it. They still visit Crooked Cove and lay wreaths of flowers on the shore, across from where the fishing shack stood. The Mi'kmaq have their own story about what happened to Gump and Mickey D., but they don't share it with white men.

Notes on Contributors

The Editor:

S. T. Joshi is the author of *The Weird Tale* (1990), *H. P. Lovecraft: The Decline of the West* (1990), and *Unutterable Horror: A History of Supernatural Fiction* (2012). He has prepared corrected editions of H. P. Lovecraft's work for Arkham House and annotated editions of Lovecraft's stories for Penguin Classics. His exhaustive biography, *H. P. Lovecraft: A Life* (1996), was expanded as *I Am Providence: The Life and Times of H. P. Lovecraft* (2010). He has edited the anthologies *American Supernatural Tales* (Penguin, 2007), *A Mountain Walked: Great Tales of the Cthulhu Mythos* (Centipede Press, 2013), *The Madness of Cthulhu* (Titan Books, 2014), and the ongoing *Black Wings* series (PS Publishing, 2010f.). Joshi has won the World Fantasy Award, the British Fantasy Award, the Bram Stoker Award, and the International Horror Guild Award.

The Contributors:

Michael Aronovitz's debut collection *Seven Deadly Pleasures* was published by Hippocampus Press in 2009, and his first novel, *Alice Walks,* was released by Centipede Press in 2013. Hippocampus recently committed to Aronovitz's novel *The Witch of the Wood* (release date in early 2014). Aronovitz's short ghost story "How Bria Died" was featured in Paula Guran's *The Year's Best Dark Fantasy and Horror, 2011,* and he has published short fiction in *Weird Tales, The Weird Fiction Review, Bosley Gravel's Cavalcade of Terror, Polluto, Kaleidotrope, Black Petals, Studies in the Fantastic, Philly Fiction, Demon Minds, Metal Scratches, Death Head Grin, Schlock Webzine, Lost Souls, The Turks Head Review, Fiction on the Web,* and many others. Michael Aronovitz is a Professor of English and lives with his wife, Kim, and their son, Max, in Wynnewood, Pennsylvania.

Hannes Bok (1914—1964) was best known as one of the premier artists in fantasy, horror, and science fiction during his lifetime, but he also wrote a substantial amount of weird fiction, including *The Sorcerer's Ship* (1942/1969), "The Blue Flamingo" (1948; expanded as *Beyond the Golden Stair,* 1970), and two collaborations with A. Merritt, *The Fox Woman and The Blue Pagoda* (1946) and *The Black Wheel* (1947). His artwork was gathered in such volumes as *Beauty and the Beasts: The Art of Hannes Bok* (1978), *A Hannes Bok Treasury* (1993), and *A Hannes Bok Showcase* (1995).

Jason V Brock has been widely published in magazines, comics, and anthologies such as *Butcher Knives & Body Counts, Weird Fiction Review,* S. T. Joshi's *Black Wings* series, *Like Water for Quarks, Fangoria,* and other venues. He has published the short story collection *Simulacrum and Other Possible Realities* (Hippocampus Press, 2013) and the novella *Milton's Children* (Bad Moon Books, 2013), and is the editor-in-chief of a digest called *[NameL3ss].* Brock served as coeditor/contributor (with William F. Nolan) to the award-winning Cycatrix Press anthologies *The Bleeding Edge* (2009) and *The Devil's Coattails* (2011). His films include the documentaries *Charles Beaumont: The Short Life of Twilight Zone's Magic Man, The AckerMonster Chronicles!,* and the forthcoming *Image, Reflection, Shadow: Artists of the Fantastic*. A health nut and gadget freak, he lives in the Vancouver, WA area, and loves his wife, Sunni, their family of herptiles, and practicing vegan/vegetarianism.

Ramsey Campbell has been described by the *Oxford Companion to English Literature* as "Britain's most respected living horror writer." He has received more awards than any other writer in the field, including the Grand Master Award of the World Horror Convention, the Lifetime Achievement Award of the Horror Writers Association, and the Living Legend Award of the International Horror Guild. Among his novels are *The Face That Must Die* (1979/1983), *Incarnate* (1983), *Midnight Sun* (1990), *The Count of Eleven* (1991), *The Darkest Part of the Woods* (2002), *The Overnight* (2004), *The Grin of the Dark* (2007), *The Seven Days of Cain* (2010), *Ghosts Know* (2011), *The Kind Folk* (2012), and *The Last Revelation of Gla'aki* (2013). His collections include *Waking Nightmares* (1991), *Alone with the Horrors* (1993), *Told by the Dead* (2003), *Just Behind You* (2009), and *Holes for Faces* (2013) and his nonfiction is collected as *Ramsey Campbell, Probably* (2002). His novels *The Nameless* and *Pact of the Fathers* have been filmed in Spain. He is the President of the Society of Fantastic Films.

Gary Fry lives in Dracula's Whitby, literally around the corner from where Stoker was staying while thinking about that character. Gary has a Ph.D. in psychology, but his first love is literature. He is the author of thirteen books, including the first in PS Publishing's Showcase range (*Sanity and Other Delusions,* 2007), as well as several novels, novellas, and short story collections. His latest books are *Emergence,*

Conjure House, Lurker (all from DarkFuse, 2013), and *Shades of Nothingness* (PS Publishing, 2013).

Richard Gavin is often cited as a master of visionary horror fiction in the tradition of Poe, Blackwood, and Lovecraft. His books include *Charnel Wine* (Rainfall Books, 2004), *Omens* (Mythos Books, 2007), *The Darkly Splendid Realm* (Dark Regions Press, 2009), and *At Fear's Altar* (Hippocampus Press, 2012). Richard has also published meditations on the horror genre and essays of arcana. He lives in Ontario, Canada.

Lois H. Gresh is a *New York Times* bestselling author (6 times), *Publishers Weekly* bestselling paperback children's author, and *USA Today* bestseller of twenty-seven books and fifty-five stories. Her books have appeared in twenty-two languages. Titles include *Eldritch Evolutions* (Chaosium, 2011), *Dark Fusions* (PS Publishing, 2013), and *The Mortal Instruments Companion* (St. Martin's Press, 2013). Current stories are in *Mark of the Beast, Eldritch Chrome, A Mountain Walked, Black Wings III, The Madness of Cthulhu, That Is Not Dead, Expiration Date, The Darke Phantastique,* and others. Lois has received Bram Stoker, Nebula, Theodore Sturgeon, and International Horror Guild Award nominations.

John D. Haefele is well known in Lovecraft and Derleth literary communities, having written for the *Cimmerian, Lovecraft Studies, Nameless, Weird Fiction Review,* and other publications. In 2009, H. Harksen Productions issued his monograph *August Derleth Redux: The Weird Tale 1930—1971,* and in 2012, *A Look Behind the Derleth Mythos: Origins of the Cthulhu Mythos.* Scheduled for 2014 is *Derleth Demythologized: H. P. Lovecraft, August Derleth and Arkham House Publishing.* The first tale of haunted Sac Prairie appears in *Dark Fusions,* edited by Lois Gresh (PS Publishing, 2013).

Caitlín R. Kiernan is the author of several novels, including *The Red Tree* (Roc, 2010; nominated for the Shirley Jackson and World Fantasy Awards) and *The Drowning Girl: A Memoir* (Roc, 2012; nominated for the Shirley Jackson, Nebula, Mythopoeic, Locus, and Bram Stoker Awards, and winner of the James Tiptree, Jr. Award). Her short fiction has been collected in several volumes, including *Tales of Pain and Wonder* (2001, 2008), *To Charles Fort, with Love* (2005), *A Is for Alien* (2009), *The Ammonite Violin & Others* (2010), *Two Worlds and In Between: The Best of Caitlín R. Kiernan, Volume 1* (2011; Volume 2 to be released in 2014), *Confessions of a Five-Chambered Heart* (2012), and the forthcoming *The Ape's Wife and Other Stories,* all from Subterranean Press. She is currently scripting a critically acclaimed series for Dark Horse, *Alabaster,* based on her Darcy Flammarion character, and working on her next novel. She was recently hailed by the *New York Times* as "one of our essential writers of dark fiction." Born in Ireland and raised in the American Deep South, she now lives in Providence, R.I., with her partner, Kathryn.

Nancy Kilpatrick has published eighteen novels, more than 200 short stories, and a few collections of stories, the most recent being *Vampyric Variations* (Edge Science Fiction and Fantasy Publishing, 2012). In addition, she is the author of the nonfiction book *The goth Bible: A Compendium for the Darkly Inclined* (St. Martin's Press, 2004). She is also an anthologist of thirteen volumes, the most recent being *Danse Macabre: Close Encounters with the Reaper* (Edge Science Fiction and Fantasy Publishing, 2012), which won the 2012 Paris Book Festival award for best anthology. She lives in Montreal but travels frequently.

Nick Mamatas is the author of several novels, including *Bullettime* (CZP, 2012) and *Love Is the Law* (Dark Horse, 2013), and more than ninety works of short fiction. His stories have appeared in *Asimov's Science Fiction, Weird Tales,* and *Best American Mystery Stories.* As an anthologist, he won a Bram

Stoker Award for *Haunted Legends* (Tor, 2010; with Ellen Datlow), and also edited the acclaimed *The Future Is Japanese* (Haikasoru, 2012; with Masumi Washington).

W. H. Pugmire created Sesqua Valley in the early 1970s, after returning from his duties as a Mormon missionary and feeling that new religious fervor: obsessed H. P. Lovecraft fanboy. He is devoted to a career of writing book after book of Lovecraftian weird fiction. Some recent titles include *The Tangled Muse* (Centipede Press, 2011), *Some Unknown Gulf of Night* (Arcane Wisdom, 2011), *Gathered Dust and Others* (Dark Regions Press, 2011), *Uncommon Places* (Hippocampus Press, 2012), *The Strange Dark One: Tales of Nyarlathotep* (Miskatonic River Press, 2012), *Encounters with Enoch Coffin* (Dark Regions Press, 2013), and *Bohemians of Sesqua Valley* (Arcane Wisdom, 2013). Pugmire dreams in Seattle.

Ann K. Schwader's poetry and fiction have appeared in *A Season in Carcosa* (Miskatonic River Press, 2012), *The Book of Cthulhu* and *The Book of Cthulhu II* (Night Shade Books, 2011 and 2012), *Fungi* (Innsmouth Free Press, 2012), and elsewhere. Her most recent poetry collection is *Twisted in Dream* (Hippocampus Press, 2011). She is an active member of both HWA and SFWA, and a 2010 Bram Stoker Award finalist. Schwader lives and writes in Colorado.

Darell Schweitzer is the author of three novels, *The Shattered Goddess* (Donning, 1982), *The White Isle* (Weird Tales Library, 1990), and *The Mask of the Sorcerer* (New English library, 1995), and about 300 stories, which have appeared in a wide variety of magazines and anthologies since the early 1970s. He is a four-time World Fantasy Award nominee and one-time winner. His novella *Living with the Dead* (PS Publishing, 2008) was a Shirley Jackson Award finalist. His most recent story collections are *Echoes of the Goddess* and *The Emperor of the Ancient Word* (both Borgo Press, 2013). He was co-editor of *Weird Tales* for nineteen years and has since edited anthologies.

John Shirley is a novelist, screenwriter, television writer, songwriter, and author of numerous story collections. He is a past Guest of Honor at the World Horror Convention and won the Bram Stoker Award for his story collection *Black Butterflies* (Ziesing, 1998). His screenplays include *The Crow.* He has written teleplays for *Poltergeist: The Legacy, Deep Space Nine,* and other shows. His novels include *Demons* (Del Rey, 2002), the *A Song Called Youth* trilogy (1985—90), *Wetbones* (Ziesing, 1992), *Bleak History* (Simon & Schuster, 2009), and *Everything Is Broken* (Prime Books, 2012). His newest books are *New Taboos* (PM Press, 2013) and *Doyle After Death* (HarperCollins, 2013). His latest story collection is *In Extremis: The Most Extreme Stories of John Shirley* (Underland Press, 2012).

Brian Stableford's recent fiction includes a series of novellas and novels featuring Edgar Allan Poe's detective Auguste Dupin, some of which—including the title story of the collection *The Legacy of Erich Zann and Other Stories* (Borgo Press, 2012) and *The Cthulhu Encryption* (Borgo Press, 2011)—confront him with aspects of the Cthulhu Mythos. The latest in the series is *Yesterday Never Dies* (Borgo Press, 2013). He is currently translating a good deal of early French *roman scientifique* for Black Coat Press, with a view of writing a history of the genre that will form a companion piece to another work in progress, a four-volume *History of Scientific Romance.*

Simon Strantzas is the author of the critically acclaimed short story collections *Beneath the Surface* (2008), *Cold to the Touch* (2009), and *Nightgale Songs* (2011), all published by Dark Regions Press. He is also the editor of *Shadows Edge* (Grey Friar Press, 2013). His writing has appeared in *The Mammoth Book of Best New Horror* and *The Year's Best Dark Fantasy and Horror,* and has been nominated for the British Fantasy Award. He lives in Toronto with his wife and an unyielding hunger for the flesh of the living.

Melanie Tem's work has received the Bram Stoker, International Horror Guild, British Fantasy, and World Fantasy Awards and a nomination for the Shirley Jackson Award. She has published numerous short stories, eleven solo novels, two collaborative novels with Nancy Holder, and two with her husband, Steve Rasnic Tem. She is also a published poet, an oral storyteller, and a playwright. Her stories have recently appeared in *Asimov's Science Fiction Magazine, Interzone, Crimewave,* and *HorrorZine,* and the anthologies *Supernatural Noir, Shivers VI, Portents, Blood and Other Cravings, Werewolves and Shapeshifters,* and *The Madness of Cthulhu.* The Tems live in Denver. They have four children and four granddaughters.

Steve Rasnic Tem published three story collections in 2013: *Onion Songs* (Chomu Press), *Celestial Inventories* (ChiZine Press), and *Twember (Science Fiction Stories)* (NewCon Press). In 2014 these will be followed by a standalone novella for PS Publishing, *In the Lovecraft Museum,* and his new novel from Solaris Books, *Blood Kin.*

Jonathan Thomas was born in Providence, R.I., and has been married since 1991 to artist and country singer Angel Dean. Books include *Stories from the Big Black House* (Radio Void, 1992), *The Color over Occam* (Arcane Wisdom, 2012), and from Hippocampus Press, *Midnight Call* (2008), *Tempting Providence* (2010), and *13 Conjurations* (2013). Since 2010, his short fiction has appeared in *Black Wings I-III* (PS Publishing and Titan), *A Mountain Walked* (Centipede Press), *The Madness of Cthulhu* (Titan), *Nameless,* and *Weird Fiction Review.*

Donald Tyson is a Canadian writer of fiction and nonfiction dealing with all aspects of the Western esoteric tradition. He is the author of *Necronomicon: The Wanderings of Alhazred* (2004), *Grimoire of the Necronomicon* (2008), *The Necronomicon Tarot* (2007), and *The 13 Gates of the Necronomicon* (2010), as well as a biography of Lovecraft titled *The Dreamworld of H. P. Lovecraft* (2010) and the novel *Alhazred* (2006), all of which were published by Llewellyn Publications.

Searchers After Horror

First Edition
2014
Searchers After Horror was edited by S. T. Joshi
and published by Fedogan & Bremer,
3918 Chicago St, Nampa, Idaho, 83686.
Fifteen hundred copies of the trade edition and
one hundred copies of the limited edition have
been printed from Century Old Style
by the Thomson-Shore Company.